Paradise City

ELIZABETH DAY

BLOOMSBURY CIRCUS

LONDON · NEW DELHI · NEW YORK · SYDNEY

FPbk

Bloomsbury Circus
An imprint of Bloomsbury Publishing Plc

50 Bedford Square   1385 Broadway
London   New York
WC1B 3DP   NY 10018
UK   USA

www.bloomsbury.com

BLOOMSBURY and the Diana logo are trademarks of Bloomsbury Publishing Plc

First published in Great Britain 2015

British Library Cataloguing-in-Publication Data
A catalogue record for this book is available from the British Library.

ISBN: HB: 978-1-4088-5499-0
         TPB: 978-1-4088-5500-3
         ePub: 978-1-4088-5501-0

2 4 6 8 10 9 7 5 3 1

Typeset by Hewer Text UK Ltd, Edinburgh
Printed and bound in Great Britain by CPI Group (UK) Ltd, Croydon CR0 4YY

To find out more about our authors and books visit www.bloomsbury.com.
Here you will find extracts, author interviews, details of forthcoming events
and the option to sign up for our newsletters.

To Emma – here's one for the rogue

HOWARD

*H*E LOVED HOTELS. THE warm swish of the automatic doors. The careful neutrality of the carpets, swept with the indentations of that morning's vacuuming. The bright smile of the receptionist, the way her make-up acted both as deterrent and encouragement. He loved the apples in glass bowls, although he had eaten one once and been disappointed by its mustiness, the slight furry staleness that he can taste – even now – on the back of his tongue. He loved the furtive glances across lobby armchairs, the reassurance of anonymity, the cocoon of safety offered by the standardised semi-luxury of faux leather and freshly spritzed white orchids in pots.

He loved the illicit meetings: the flirtations between adulterous couples, the City insider imparting information, the journalist who is talking to a grey man of indistinct appearance, jotting down notes. He loved the hushed business, the suggestive smiles, the fountain pens proffered when he has to tick a box for a morning newspaper or sign for 'any additional expenses, if you wouldn't mind, sir'. He loved it all.

And today, now, on this particular morning, he can feel a benign calm wash over him with the first step he takes inside the Mayfair Rotunda; with the first slight pressure of the tip of his leather-soled bespoke Church's shoes on the marbled floor, he senses it. He breathes in an air-conditioned lungful, allows his

Italian leather overnight bag to be taken from him by gloved hands, and strides across the floor.

'Nice to see you again, Sir Howard,' says the receptionist. He squints at her name-badge. 'Tanya', it reads, in sans serif font above two miniature flags – one of them is Spanish; the other he can't make out. Eastern European, he shouldn't wonder. Probably one of the former Soviet states. They were getting everywhere these thin, ambitious girls with their black hair and sharp little faces. He wasn't sure it was a good thing. The last time he'd rung Le Caprice for a reservation, the girl at the end of the line had asked in a thick, guttural accent how to spell his name. He'd been going there for years.

Nevertheless, he is not one to pre-judge. He admires chutzpah, in the right place. He's fond, too, of romanticising the immigrant experience, of reminding himself that, if it weren't for the British, his forebears would have been gassed by the Nazis. The Finks, as they were then, would have been rounded up by jack-booted monsters if they hadn't managed to get to England in 1933. And now look at them, he wants to say. And now . . .

He has never been to the death camps – can't face the idea of them, let alone the reality – but his personal history remains a matter of considerable pride. On the one and only occasion he had been asked by the BBC to take part in a current affairs discussion programme, he had supported the relaxing of border controls and received one of the biggest cheers of the night. Looking back, he wasn't even sure why he'd said it. He voted Tory, for God's sake.

He smiles at Tanya, dazzling her with his expensive teeth (veneers and whitening done by a dentist recommended to him by a minor Royal. He isn't one to name names).

'Thank you.'

'You're in your normal suite, Sir Howard.'

For a brief moment, he wants to weep with gratitude at this kindness, this foresight, this human generosity shown to him by a global corporation. He's always been sentimental: easily moved to tears by charity television adverts with soulful-eyed children in hospital beds. But Tanya remembering his name has demonstrated – in a small, but significant gesture – that he is who he thinks he is; that his importance as a businessman is an acknowledged fact. He is reminded, by Tanya giving him his normal suite, by intuiting his needs, that he has made his way, that he has his own part to play in it all: in the oiling of cogs, in the handshakes that lead to the lunches that lead to the buying and selling that lead to the acquisition of influence, to the stake in governance that results in the eventual spinning of the world on its axis. He can make things *work*. At this, he is undoubtedly a success.

Here he is, then, Howard Pink (formerly Fink), a man with complete awareness of his status in life, confident in his opinions, blessedly certain of the rightness of his decisions. A man of fortune, yes, but also of distinction.

The financial press will insist on putting 'self-made millionaire' after the comma. Howard used to wear this as a badge of pride. These days, however, he can't help but feel there is something patronising in the phrase, a sense among the blue-shirted City bigwigs that he is not quite of their sort. He has always found it magnificently ironic that men (and it is, by and large, still men) who revere money for the power it gives them dismiss the ownership of it unless it has been inherited.

Because, Howard thinks, as he turns towards the lift, isn't it more impressive to have generated £150 million from nothing than to have been handed it on a plate by a doddery great-uncle with a baronetcy and a mouldy pile of National Trust stones? Isn't it better, somehow, to have made one's own way by selling clothes on an East London market stall, clothes sewn by his mother, God rest her soul, bent double over her Singer machine with pins in her mouth (he was for ever telling her not to put pins in her mouth. Did she listen? Did she bollocks), clothes that he took and marked up and pushed onto the unsuspecting hordes of Petticoat Lane Market? Wasn't that more admirable? To have made a profit, to have ploughed it back into better stock, to have

5

sold more, of better quality and at a higher price, and to have done this over and over again, with one canny eye always on the bottom line, until he owned Fash Attack, the fastest-growing chain of clothing shops on the British high street?

Wasn't that worthy of some respect?

Because, after all, you only sold product by knowing first how to sell yourself.

As a young boy, Howard had once seen the Petticoat Lane crockery-seller assemble an entire place-setting, one plate on top of the other, and then throw the whole lot into the air. The trader had caught it on the way down with a giant clatter of noise and not one single plate had shattered. The housewives couldn't open their purses quick enough after that.

That was how you shifted stuff. It was a question of performance. It was a matter of confidence.

He feels a moistness under the armpits. The collar on his shirt is too tight, even though he has spent an arm and a leg on it – forgive the pun. The shirt is made by a company called Eton. They normally sold shirts for tall, thin men but he'd insisted they custom-make them to accommodate his ever so slightly more corpulent form. Initially the name amused him – the conjunction of the country's most famous public school with the rag-trade he knew like the back of his hand – but the joke didn't last for long. Now, in the mornings, it depresses him to catch sight of the label.

He presses the button for the lift. Behind him, there is a squall of high-pitched laughter. He winces, then glances across. There are four people sitting in high-backed armchairs to one side of the lobby, being served silver trays of miniature scones, sandwiches and cupcakes. Two of them are older, their features bled of colour, their eyes faintly wrinkled. They look as though they are trying to enjoy themselves but would rather be at home, listening to *Gardeners' Question Time*.

He guesses they are parents who have come into the city at the behest of their children to celebrate some family anniversary.

6

Their offspring sit opposite them now – two young women, shrieking with hilarity, wearing skinny jeans and dark-coloured jackets, their hair slicked with the shine of urbanity, their lips stretched with the complacency of youth. A mobile phone, encased in pink diamanté, lies on the table in front of them. One of the girls sees him looking and stops laughing abruptly.

He thinks of her, then, as he had known he would. He thinks of the person he tries daily to forget without actually wanting to do so. He allows himself one brief flash of recall: her hair in bunches, a gap where her front tooth should have been. She is wearing a tartan dress and crushing rose petals in a mixing bowl to make what she calls perfume.

His daughter. Ada. Named after his mum.

The lift pings. He walks in, forces himself to smile at the reflection in the mirror. On the fourth floor, the doors part and he turns left down the corridor, glancing at the cardboard key holder to remind himself of the number. Room 423. A corner room.

He slips the plastic key into the slot. The door handle light winks green. He enters. His luggage is already there, on the rack by the television. The inner curtains are half-drawn, the white net giving the room a drowsy, shadowed feel. The flat-screen television is set to a personalised welcome message. Two glass bottles of mineral water stand on the capacious desk. The mirrors are all discreetly tilted and lit in a way that makes him look at least ten pounds lighter. He knows, without having to open it, that the minibar will contain a half-bottle of fine Chablis and a bar of Toblerone.

Safety, he thinks, inhaling the familiarity of the surroundings. There is a particular security, for Howard, derived only from an ease that has been painstakingly thought out by other people for his benefit. He admires the competence and does not mind paying over the odds for it. It allows him, for a few hours, to be entirely outside himself.

He removes his jacket, places it on the back of a chair, slips his BlackBerry out of the inner pocket and turns it off. He unlaces

7

his shoes. And then, in spite of the fact that it is three in the afternoon, in spite of the fact that Tanya the receptionist would be surprised at what he is about to do, in spite of the fact that Sir Howard Pink has appointments to make, places to be, people to meet, companies to manage, emails to answer and balance sheets to read, he pads into the bathroom, turns on the tap and runs himself a deep, deep bath.

This is what he does on the first Monday of each month. A ritual, if you like.

Afterwards, smelling of generic spiced shower gel, he puts on his robe. Howard notes with displeasure that the edge of one cuff is bobbled. He can't abide untidiness in clothes. He has been known to throw away a pair of trousers after finding a badly stitched seam or an unravelling thread. Fastidious, that's what Claudia calls him. It was one of her words, deployed in conversation to confuse those who imagined she was little more than a silicone-enhanced trophy wife. He found her reading the dictionary sometimes in bed.

'What are you doing that for?' he'd ask.

'I'm improving myself, Howie. You should do the same.' And then she'd read out one of the definitions and get him to guess what word it belonged to.

'"Pertaining to a gulf; full of gulfs; hence, devouring."'

'I dunno.'

'"Voraginous."'

He'd never get the right word. But that, of course, was part of Claudia's cunning. She wasn't clever but she knew how to jab him in the ribs, how to bring him down a peg or two when necessary. Everyone knew he'd left school at fifteen without qualifications: it was part of the Howard Pink myth. In the interviews he'd done way back when he'd opened his first flagship store in Regent Street, he'd been delighted when the journalists brought it up, had revelled in the image being created for him of a hard-working lad with gumption and guile who didn't suffer fools gladly. He can admit now he'd been flattered by the

8

attention, by the notion that these Oxbridge graduates from *The Times* and the *Telegraph* with their economics degrees and their flashy dictaphones were wanting to talk to him – to Howie Pink of Pink's Garments on Petticoat Lane – and record his answers for posterity.

One of the headlines had read: 'Howard Pink: the self-made tycoon who's got it tailor-made.' The accompanying photograph showed him mid-laughter, his stomach billowing out like a sail in full wind, his face scrunched up, his tongue lolling grotesquely to one side. He'd liked the idea of being a tycoon.

The picture did him no favours. Still, he thought he could live with it.

But through the years, that photo had been used again and again. Even though it was now twenty years out of date and he'd stopped giving interviews after what happened, they still used it like a taunt, a reminder of his perceived clownishness. For a while, for obvious reasons, he'd become 'Tragic self-made millionaire Howard Pink' and the photograph had disappeared, but now there had been a sudden resurgence.

It had popped up again last month in an in-flight magazine. He'd been flying back first-class from Munich and there it was, in full Technicolor glory, when he leafed through *Airwaves*: a gurning facsimile of Howard Pinkishness, used to illustrate a four-page feature on British businesses. He'd been fatter back then and had indulged in a misguided attempt to grow some facial hair. It was before he'd had his teeth done too. Suffice to say, it wasn't his best angle.

After the in-flight magazine, he'd called Rupert, his PR man.

'Anything you can do to stop them using that fucking thing?' he'd asked.

'Legally, you mean?'

'Legally, illegally, I'm not fussy.'

There had been a quick intake of breath on the other end of the line. Rupert could never tell whether his boss was joking or not.

'Er, well, Howard, we want to keep the media on-side, for obvious reasons, so I'd caution against doing anything too draconian—'

'Draconian'. Another of Claudia's words.

'But why don't I do a quick call-round of the newspaper editors and ask them to refrain from using it? They'll be only too willing to play ball if it means they get more access.'

'I don't want to give more access, Rupe.'

Rupert tittered 'Yes, but they don't need to know that, do they? Leave it with me, Howard.'

Rupert had done his ring-round and, for a few weeks, the photograph had retreated from view like an unsightly child. But then, yesterday, there it was again: slap bang in the middle of a page in the *Sunday Tribune*, accompanying an article based on the wafer-thin scientific premise that life is kinder to optimists. The caption read: 'Despite personal unhappiness, the self-made millionaire Sir Howard Pink has always looked on the brighter side.'

He's sick of everyone assuming they know him. He's sick of the caricature. He fears he'll never be taken seriously. The BBC had never asked him back, had they? Instead, any time they needed a talking head, they got that preening old buffer with the luxuriant white hair who ran the Association of British Retail and who wouldn't know what good sense was if it painted itself purple and jumped on his nose. Wanker.

'They can't disassociate you now from what happened with Ada,' Rupert had told him once, choosing his words carefully. 'They see the tragic backstory, not the business acumen.'

'The tragic backstory'. Those had been his exact words.

Howard feels anger rising in his gut. He goes to the window, draws back the curtain and peers out at London's grubby week-day glamour, looking for something to soothe his nascent agitation. A black trickle of taxicabs is beetling its way to the hotel entrance like a spreading trail of petrol. From his vantage point, Howard can make out the shiny hardness of their bonnets, the lucent yellow of each 'For Hire' sign reflected in the dark pool of the paintwork. Shifting his gaze along the road, he sees a young woman in high heels and a flapping mackintosh, belt knotted at the back, a copy of the *Evening Standard* peeking out of her handbag. She is holding a lit cigarette between two fingers and a café-chain cardboard cup of coffee in the other hand and she is walking so quickly that the coffee keeps spilling over the aperture in the plastic lid and splashing onto the checked lining of her coat. He wonders if she'll notice soon, or if it will only be later, when she takes off her coat and is assailed by the musty smell of stale, too-sweet coffee, that she will realise. He wishes he could follow her to find out. He likes to know how a story ends.

The woman carries on walking: a brisk tick-tacking on the paving stones that echoes then fades. Up above her, a metal criss-cross of scaffolding has been erected to cover the façade of the mansion block opposite, each slotted-in pole the precise pigeon-grey of the sky beyond, each brick the damp russet colour that Howard has come to associate uniquely with his city. A builder in a hard hat and a reflective vest sends a formless shout into the street below.

Howard wishes they'd stop tampering with everything. There was so much building going on in London these days. Lumbering mechanical cranes pierced the skyline at regular intervals. Hoardings patterned with the meaningless insignia of redevelopment had cropped up everywhere. Streets were shut down, traffic diverted, bridges closed, all in the name of a frantic progress, an endless quest for more things that were shiny and new and glittering, when increasingly all Howard lusts after is the past, packaged up, preserved and honoured. Nice, historical buildings that didn't demand attention, designed to a manageable scale so that everyone knew what they were getting.

He lets the curtain fall and then reminds himself he is not here to get annoyed by modern architecture. These monthly nights in this Mayfair hotel are meant to be his meditation space, a few hours' holiday from himself and his memories. Only Rupert, Claudia and Tracy, his PA, know about them. Everyone else is told he's away on business. He tells himself he must make the most of it before going back to normality tomorrow morning.

He takes slower breaths. He pushes back his shoulder blades and stretches his arms. He tries counting to ten but only gets to three before he remembers the Chablis.

Howard takes the bottle out of the minibar, unscrews the top and pours himself a healthy measure. The glass frosts up satisfyingly. Perfect temperature. A viticulturist (there are such things) once told him he shouldn't over-refrigerate white wines. Howard repeated this to anyone he thought might be impressed and sometimes sent back cold wine at restaurants just to show he couldn't be made a fool of. In the privacy of these four walls, however, he felt at liberty to indulge his own secret taste.

Or lack of it, as the case may be.

There is a knock on the door.

'Housekeeping,' comes a disembodied voice from the other side of the lustrous wood laminate.

Howard looks at the bedside clock. He is shocked to see it is already 6 p.m. and the maid is coming to do the pre-dinner turndown. He opens the door. A black face smiles at him broadly.

'I can come back later if you like,' the woman says, her voice lightly accented. Howard takes in the smoothness of her skin, taught over high cheekbones, and the compactness of her diminutive frame, clad in a fitted black blouse and black trousers. She is carrying a moulded plastic basket, filled with cleaning products and mini-packets of shortbread.

'No, no,' he replies, loosening the belt of his robe ever so slightly. 'Come on in.' He holds the door with his arm so that the maid has to bend under to walk through. She giggles as she does so. Howard is encouraged.

The maid checks the tea tray and replaces a sachet of hot chocolate, then goes into the bedroom with a quick economy of movement. When Howard follows, he sees she is piling the purple and brown cushions neatly at the foot of the bed. She glances over her shoulder, catches his eye and giggles again. He laughs

12

lightly, then takes two steps towards her. She is bending over the bed and her backside is pressing against the fabric of her trousers. Howard, who knows how these things are done, who has successfully initiated a handful of similar transactions in high-end hotels across the globe, comes up close behind her, puts his hands on either side of her waist and nudges the knot of his robe belt against the maid's haunches.

For a second, she tenses and does not move. Then, without looking at him, the maid straightens up, letting the pillow she is holding in one hand drop onto the Egyptian cotton, 450-thread count sheets.

'Sir . . . I . . .'

'Shhh,' Howard says, nuzzling her neck, smelling the sweetness of cocoa butter. He does not like to talk in these situations. Talking would make it more real.

With the maid still turned towards the bed, he unbuttons her shirt with the quick fingers bequeathed him by generations of Finks. He slips his thumb underneath the wiring of her bra, easing in his hand until it cups the maid's right breast. He groans, in spite of himself. With his free hand, he undoes his belt, lets the robe fall open, and grips his erection. He starts slowly, rhythmically, moving up and down the shaft, all the while holding the maid's breast, feeling the nipple turn hard underneath his touch. She is breathing more quickly now. He cannot see her face but he knows, without needing to have it confirmed, that she is smiling, that she is enjoying this, that she is loving the attention, that she is gagging for it, that she needs him to thrust against her and take her and spill his white seed across her skin . . . He comes with a half-suppressed sigh and a feeling of disgust. It is all over in a matter of seconds.

He is aware, even in the midst of his supposed abandon, of the need not to stain the maid's dark trousers.

Once a tailor, always a tailor, as his mum might say. God rest her soul.

ESME

*E*SME HAS STARTED WALKING to the office as part of a springtime health kick. She lives in Shepherd's Bush and works on High Street Kensington, so admittedly, it's not the most arduous walk and, according to those miserable cut-out-and-keep fitness guides in various women's magazines, it will hardly burn any calories at all (something called spinning does that, she has discovered, and she imagines a stuffy room filled with Victorian peasants frantically producing exercise leotards from their super-fast spinning wheels). Anyway, apparently spinning gets rid of 450 calories an hour. A Mars bar contains 280. So the chances are that her forty-five-minute walk will allow her to eat approximately half a molecule more chocolate than she would do otherwise.

But the walk makes her feel better, mentally. It makes her feel she's doing something, at least, instead of sitting on her arse all day, either at her desk or in the train on the way to another futile doorstep on editor's orders. Esme doesn't need to lose weight. She possesses the natural slenderness of the terminally neurotic. But, being a woman, she feels guilty about not exercising. And her colleague Sanjay once told her that your metabolism slowed down to a crawling pace when you hit thirty. She'd been eating a baked potato at the time.

'You won't be able to do carbs any more,' he'd said, flicking an elegant wrist in her direction. 'You'll want to be eating seeds and grains.'

'Seeds and grains?' She pushed the baked potato to one side, regretfully. 'What, like birds?'

Sanjay nodded knowledgeably. He was the health editor and abreast of such things.

'Keen-wah,' he said. 'That's what you'll need.'

'Bless you.'

'Ha-de-bloody-ha. I'm only telling you this for your own good, missy. This' – he flapped a hand in front of her torso – 'doesn't come for free.'

When she'd turned thirty last December, Sanjay's words had jangled in her head like a drawerful of mismatched cutlery. She was terrified that she'd pile on unwanted pounds purely by eating the same as she'd always done. For about a week, Esme had stuck faithfully to the recipes provided by a 'Low-GI' website but, by the end of seven days, she was heartily sick of egg-white omelettes and slow-release oats. Then it was Christmas anyhow so there was no point in thinking about calorie control, and after a few months she realised nothing had changed. She still hovered around nine stone and ideally wanted to be eight, like Liz Hurley, but there were some things you just had to live with.

If only she were more like Robbie. Her brother had an innate capacity for getting on with life. He never worried too much about anything and, as a result, he seemed to love exercise purely for the uncomplicated physical motion, as if the pump and pound of each straining muscle could push out extraneous thought. He'd done the London Marathon last year in under five hours without even trying. She'd been there to cheer him on past the finish line and he'd given her a huge, sweaty hug from underneath a crinkly silver blanket that was meant to help his muscles relax.

She hates running. The walking though . . . the walking was a good thing. Esme liked the routine of it. She liked putting on her trainers (last worn when she tried out – unsuccessfully – for the university hockey team) and packing her smart shoes in a bag to change into later because it prolonged the morning, delaying the inevitability of work just that little bit longer.

The trainers make her feel she is bouncing along the pavement. Today, the bounce is accentuated by her good mood. She'd had a page lead-in on Sunday about the power of optimism that was followed up by most of the dailies including the *Mail*, which carried a substantial op-ed piece by a 'self-confessed Victor Meldrew' headlined: 'Optimism? Bah humbug!' For the *Mail* to follow you up was a considerable feather in your cap. Dave, the news editor, would be pleased.

She reaches a stretch of Holland Park Road lined by upmarket shops. There is a butcher's here that is rumoured to be patronised by the Queen. Esme once bought a chicken from them in an emergency (she'd forgotten the main part of a roast she was meant to be cooking) and was charged £16 because it had been 'corn-fed'. At £16, she would have preferred it to have been fed the sacrificial entrails of small human babies, but she didn't complain out loud. Most of her fury was internal. She was that kind of person.

She crosses the road at the traffic lights, upping her pace to fit in with the rhythm of a new boy-band hit that is storming the charts. It is a saccharine number about finding teen love and although Esme knows she should hate it, knows that any journalist worth their salt would pour cynical bile over the lyrics and the sentiment, secretly she loves it. At work, Esme tries to keep her naïve idealism under wraps, but it's not easy. When they'd covered the Royal Wedding last year, she'd cried a little watching the service on the big screens in the office – just at the bit where William saw Kate in that amazing dress for the first time – and Dave had caught her.

'Time of the month?' he said, patting her on the shoulder. And then, condescendingly, 'Don't worry, Es. Harry's still on the market.'

Her prolonged single status was a source of much office merriment. Well, she thinks, as she powers on up towards Notting Hill, she'd rather be on her own than in a marriage like Dave's.

He'd been with his wife since time began but was known as a shagger – it was all those long office hours and willing student journalists, desperate for a job on a national straight out of the City postgrad course. Shame, really, as his wife was lovely and normal: she'd been to a couple of the office Christmas parties and was a petite, surprisingly pretty blonde woman who worked as a supply teacher and – shockingly – didn't drink much. They had four photogenic children at various schools and universities which meant Dave had no hope of quitting any time soon, unless an exceptionally generous voluntary redundancy package came his way.

'You want my advice?' he'd said to Esme at a recent leaving party, slurring his words and bending his head in too close to hers so that she could smell the brackishness of hours-old white wine on his breath. 'Get out while you can. Go and make some money. Wish I'd done that. Wish I'd gone into fucking PR like my mate Rupert . . .'

She didn't like it when Dave got drunk. It demeaned him, she thought, made him like all the others. Sober, he was a brilliant news editor: dogged but instinctive and blessed with a peculiar ability to inspire loyalty despite his personal failings. You genuinely wanted Dave to say something you did was good. In his day, he'd been a solid but unexceptional reporter on the *Express* and covered the first Iraq War. But it was editing that brought the best out of him, that played to his sense of mischief and his mistrust of authority.

Esme sighs. She has a bit of a crush on Dave, actually, which is odd considering he isn't what you might describe as a looker. He is half an inch shorter than her for a start, with boxer's shoulders and a chunky, muscular frame: not the type she'd normally go for at all. But there's something about him. She's always been a sucker for men in power, for a start, and he's funny too, in a quiet, lethal way. She catches him sometimes, just after he's issued one of his sarcastic put-downs to an unsuspecting reporter, and his face looks like a small boy's: cheeky eyes and a lopsided grin that almost makes you forget the bad teeth and the irritating habit he has of practising his golf swings when you're trying to talk to him.

She's not stupid though. Esme won't let anything happen. It's hard enough being a woman in a newsroom without the whispers behind your back that you're only getting the good jobs because you're sleeping with the boss. Besides, she flatters herself that he respects her too much to try it on.

She turns right down Kensington Church Street, looking in the windows of all the lovely antique shops as she passes, filled with beautiful trinkets she would never be able to buy. The blossom is out on the trees: big pink clouds that she wants to squeeze, like a baby's legs. Esme feels a surge of happiness that spring is here. The evenings are lighter and longer, sunlit by the yellow-green London glow. Ever since she moved here from her family home in Herefordshire, the excitement of the city has pulsated through her veins: a buzzing, booming sensation of being at the centre of things, of believing anything could happen.

Her pleasant mood is accompanied by a feel-good soul number, courtesy of Radio 1, so that, for a few moments, she feels as though she is the star of a beautifully shot indie film with an interesting soundtrack.

Then she remembers that morning conference is less than an hour away and a panic rises in her gullet. Stories, she thinks. I need stories.

The *Sunday Tribune* was one of the only nationals that still insisted its reporters must gather at 10.30 a.m. on a Tuesday morning in the offices of the overall editor and pitch two news stories for the weekend's edition. When Esme first started there a little over eighteen months ago, fresh out of the Hunter Media trainee programme (flagship publication: *Trucking Today*), she had been desperate to impress. She'd brought in a bona fide scoop in her second week, involving the discovery of a protected bird species on land that had been earmarked for a controversial detention centre for asylum seekers. It ran on page five (right-hand pages were always the best) alongside a picture of an owl and some sad-looking Africans. The RSPB had called her story 'game-changing'. The detention centre had to be shelved. A local MP had written to Esme to thank her in person. Dave hadn't publicly acknowledged her success, but she had detected a slight thawing in his attitude towards her. She'd been thrilled.

But now, after a year and a half of Freedom of Information requests on how many chocolate HobNobs Cabinet ministers bought for hospitality purposes and Googling consumer-friendly research studies from American universities, Esme was starting to tire of it all. She had one half-baked notion for this morning's conference about the rise in popularity of semi-naked charity calendars. They were everywhere, she'd noticed of late: middle-aged women with their baps out hiding their private parts behind a giant milk urn to raise money for some worthy cause. Esme had a hunch that the National Association of Nudists, a humourless organisation she'd dealt with in the past, would be unhappy about this. They'd probably think it wasn't taking nudism seriously enough. She was sure she could whip them up into some kind of newsworthy frenzy.

Other than that, the story cupboard is bare and she's almost at work. She alights onto High Street Kensington and looks up at the art deco Barker's department store building, squinting as she always does to see if she can find her desk through the narrow, slatted windows. She waves at the security guard because she never remembers his name, then swipes her pass over the electronic entry gates and takes the escalator to the first floor.

Looking down, she realises she's forgotten to take her trainers off.

'Shit.' Esme hates the thought of anyone seeing her like this: half-formed and unprofessional, like a mismatched extra out of *Working Girl* (perhaps her favourite 1980s film, in a closely fought contest with Ferris Bueller's *Day Off*). She struggles to get her heels from her canvas bag before the final step of the escalator. At the top, she changes shoes quickly, slipping her stockinged feet into a pair of mildly uncomfortable patent-leather courts from Marks & Spencer and putting her dirty white trainers back into her bag. She hopes no one notices. But then, glancing up at the mezzanine balcony where everyone goes for their fag breaks, she sees someone staring at her. It's Dave, shaking his head at her through a fug of cigarette smoke. The management had tried to move the smokers outside after the ban but no one had taken any notice and, in the end, they'd admitted defeat and built partitions on the balcony to pen everyone in. You could always tell what time of day it was according to how much smoke the enclosed balcony was holding. In the morning, it was a gentle mist of grey. By lunchtime, the smoke would have acquired its own twisting logic, pressing against the glass like freshly shorn strands of sheep's wool. By evening, the balcony was a choking-hole filled with toxic dry ice.

Esme gets to her desk and logs on. Sanjay is already at his seat, directly opposite her, his face half obscured by the large Mac screen.

'Morning, sunshine,' he says, without taking his eyes from the computer. 'Nice weekend?'

'Yeah, thanks, um . . . what did I do?' Esme puts her jacket on the back of her ergonomic chair, adjusted by Occupational Health to precisely the right height in order to avoid repetitive strain injury. 'Can't remember. But it was nice, whatever it was. You?'

Sanjay nodded.

'The boyfriend was over from Rome,' he said. 'We stayed in and watched *Breaking Bad* because we're exciting like that.' He sipped from a giant Starbucks cup. Esme knew it would be a Green Tea. Sanjay had given up caffeine for a new year's resolution and was still sticking to it with all the puritanical zeal of a *Mayflower* pilgrim.

'Have you got stories?' he asked.

She shook her head.

'Me neither.'

There was a special rhythm to Sunday newspapers. Tuesday mornings were tense and mildly fractious as everyone tried to cobble together something for conference. By lunchtime, a relaxed bonhomie had set in. When Esme had first started at the *Tribune*, most of the newsroom then disappeared to lunch 'contacts' while secretly lunching each other and racking up considerable wine bills that they then claimed on expenses. Those days had long passed and she wasn't entirely sad to see them go. There was a limit to how effective she could be after several large glasses of Sauvignon blanc in the middle of the day.

Wednesdays were for faffing around – doing the odd telephone interview to stand up a story and surreptitiously booking holidays online when Dave wasn't looking.

By Thursday, you needed to have at least one concrete story for that weekend's paper so that Dave could add it to the news list and present it to the editor. If you didn't, then you were in the perilous position of being sent out to cover running stories like murder cases or political scandals and that involved a lot of standing around with other journalists in the rain, waiting for an important person to comment, then elbowing your way to the front when they did so.

Friday consisted of long hours, frantic typing and last-minute changes of mind from the desk. You were lucky to get out by midnight. Then on Saturday, the misery of working on a weekend gave rise to a shared solidarity of spirit that left you feeling strangely cheerful. When the paper went off stone at 7.30 p.m., almost everyone decamped to the pub (apart from Rita, the part-time sub, who was older and wore the perpetually harassed expression of a working mother whose needs were conspicuously not being met).

Sunday started with a hangover and a nervous feeling in the pit of Esme's stomach about where her article would appear and whether she'd got any fact or quote horribly wrong. The first thing she did was to walk round the corner from her flat to buy the papers from a shop on the Uxbridge Road. Every week, without fail, the newsagent would make the same joke as he totted up the total on the cash register.

'Light reading?'

Every week, Esme gritted her teeth and smiled politely at this charmless imbecile then went home and flicked straight to her pieces. Some weekends, the article she'd expected to see wasn't there and she realised it had been spiked and no one had bothered to tell her. Those were the worst days. She found it hard to pull herself out of a bad mood when she had no byline in the paper. It felt as though she didn't exist.

It is just as she is typing 'academic study' into Google News that Esme feels a looming presence behind her chair.

'Try "Watergate",' Dave says, smirking. 'See if anything comes up. I've heard, on the down low, that geezer Nixon might be up to something.'

Esme flushes. Across from her, Sanjay is busy looking busy.

'Can I have a word?' Dave asks ominously. 'In my office.'

She follows him into a glass-partitioned box that Dave has clung on to, in spite of the owners' constant attempts to make everything into an open-plan, twenty-four-hour, internet-focused news hub. It is an airless room: the windows overlook the building's interior atrium and the walls are lined with bookcases stuffed with out-of-date editions of *Who's Who*, lever-arch files and long-ago awards certificates encased in dusty Perspex. On one wall, there is a framed picture of the *Sunday Tribune* wall clock from the glory days of Fleet Street, set perpetually to ten past two: a civilised time, Esme always thinks, for a more civilised era.

'Take a seat,' he says, gesturing to a chair covered in back copies of the *New Statesman* and old Snickers wrappers. Esme removes the detritus and sits, opening her notepad to a fresh page and readying her pen in an effort to look on top of things.

'Nice piece on Sunday,' Dave says, chewing his thumbnail.

Esme is surprised. The optimism study was precisely the kind of thing Dave usually hated: no investigation, no titillation, just a space-filler to keep the readers happy while they ate their Sunday morning croissants and muesli.

'Sir Howard complained,' he says.

'Howard Pink?' Esme jots down his name for no reason.

'Yeah. We used a picture he wasn't happy with.'

'Well that was the picture desk, not me . . .'

Dave waves her objections aside. 'Yeah, I know that, obviously,' he says, over-enunciating each word to underline her frustrating slowness. He looks at her levelly across his desk. His skin is weathered and pouchy and he has a patch of eczema on one corner of his mouth. The backs of his hands are smattered with faint brown hairs. He's only forty-seven but seems older, more weary. Esme realises she is staring and drops her gaze. Her mouth is dry.

'I wondered why Mike used it actually,' she says. 'Given all the stuff that happened to Sir Howard. It didn't seem exactly right for a light-hearted . . .'

Dave cuts across her. 'I told Mike to use it.'

'Oh. Right. I just thought, what with Sir Howard's daughter going missing all those years ago . . .'

'Yeah, I know, all very sad,' Dave says, not seeming remotely perturbed. 'But life goes on, doesn't it, and Sir Howard hasn't exactly been the shy and retiring type since then, so we were perfectly within our rights to use the picture, but . . .'

She waits. Dave stands up, flexes his arms and takes up the imaginary 4-iron, swinging it back and forward, warming up to hit some non-existent ball. 'Well, his PR guy had asked newspapers not to use that particular photo. Pink doesn't like it, apparently. Thinks it makes him look like a buffoon which is, of course,' Dave takes aim somewhere near the under-watered rubber plant on his bookshelf and swings, 'true.'

Esme suppresses a groan. She finds this display extremely tiresome. It is what Dave believes to be a show of masculinity, the news editor's equivalent of a peacock displaying its plumage.

Every time she thinks she might properly fancy Dave, that it might be more than a workplace crush, he goes and does something that shatters the idea completely.

'Right, so why did you use it then?'

Dave grins. 'Because he told me not to.'

Esme smiles in spite of herself. 'And what I'd like you to do, young lady, is to call Pink up, apologise, say it's not your fault, beyond your control blah, blah, blah but that the least you could do is take him out for lunch to say sorry.' Dave flicks through a Rolodex on the desk in front of him. He is the only person she knows who refuses to get an iPhone or a BlackBerry and keeps all his contacts on a series of battered index cards. 'Take him to Alain Ducasse at the Dorchester, he'll love that,' he says, handing over a card which has several numbers on it, all but one of them scribbled out in red ballpoint pen.

'Thanks, I can look the number up . . .'

'Take it.'

She reaches across, accidentally touching his fingers as she takes the card. She feels a small internal spasm as she does so.

'You'll need to speak to his PR man first. Rupert Leitch. He's a mate of mine from university days. I'll let him know you're calling—' Dave hands her another dog-eared card. 'Well sod off then,' he says, clicking on his computer mouse. 'Look lively.'

Esme returns to her desk, closing the door to Dave's office as she leaves.

'What was that about?' Sanjay asks.

'Howard Pink,' she says.

'The guy whose daughter went missing?'

Esme nods.

'What was her name? It's on the tip of my tongue,' Sanjay continues. He has an astonishing recall for current affairs-based trivia. 'Ada. That was it. Ada Pink. Sweet-looking girl. Weird that she was never found.'

She lets him burble on, murmuring at intervals to appear interested. Sanjay was perfectly capable of talking for half an hour about the kind of sandwiches he was going to have for lunch that day. The weekly appearance of 'Pizza Thursday' in the canteen was a cause for conversational frenzy. After a while, his train of thought peters out and he falls silent. Esme glances at her watch. Only ten minutes till conference. Back to the nudists, then. She'll deal with Pink later.

CAROL

CAROL WAKES IN THE early hours when there is a heavy, pressing sensation on her lower legs and she knows that Milton has jumped onto the bed. Milton paws at the duvet, kneading the feathers like dough before settling himself into the curve shaped by the crook of her right knee, which happens to be precisely the most awkward position for Carol.

Why does he always go for the least convenient option? Carol can barely get through the newspaper these days without Milton walking all over the pages, pushing his head against her face, purring and mewling until she pays him the necessary attention.

She shouldn't be so hard on him. He misses Derek of course. Derek had always been the softer touch: spooning jellied chunks of Whiskas into the feeding bowl when he thought she wasn't looking and tickling Milton's chin until the cat was rolled over, eyes closed, whiskers trembling with pleasure.

Unwilling to disturb him, Carol waits to see what the cat will do next, her senses pricked with the peculiar alertness that comes with the density of darkness after midnight. There is a bit of shuffling, then the sound of conscientious licking.

Oh Lord, she thinks, he's washing himself. We'll be here all night – or what there was left of it. She wonders what time it is. It feels like 5 a.m. but she refuses to look at the clock on the bedside table in case it confirms her fear there is even longer to go until daylight. Sleep is such a nuisance these days. The doctor has given her pills but she doesn't like to take them in case she never wakes up. Besides, she knows what the problem is. She's not used to the absence on the other side of the bed, not yet anyhow, and there's nothing anyone can do about that. She edges her left foot to the side, like a bather testing the water. For a moment, she convinces herself that her toes are going to make contact with the warm cotton of his pyjamas but instead her foot grazes against the coolness of the sheets where Derek should be.

She shivers, withdraws her leg, wonders how many minutes have passed.

Eventually Milton settles down and starts purring, gently at first but then rising in volume until it becomes impossible for her to ignore. Carol sighs loudly, exactly how she used to when Derek was snoring, hoping he would wake up, be apologetic, give her a cuddle and allow her to sink back into the uninterrupted sleep of one who knows she is loved. But of course Milton would never respond to such passive-aggressive tactics. He is, after all, a cat.

She tries to slip her right leg out from underneath his bulk, but Milton stirs and she is caught between wanting to get back to sleep and needing his company. She lies there, eyes open, legs twisted at odd angles. If she just keeps still and tries to relax, then maybe a tiredness will 'wash over' her like it always does in books.

A dull glow from the street lamp outside filters through the curtains, casting a buttery grey light over the bed. She traces the beam of it as it dips and curves across the crumpled duvet and imagines the slopes and valleys of a vast desert, the sand poured across her by some unknown hand as she slept.

She had been to a desert once, with Derek, in Tunisia. It had been a package holiday a few years back, one of those deals he found on the web. He was ever so good on the computer, was Derek. He had always been able to find nice places to stay whereas she never knew where to look. He'd tried to teach her how to do the grocery shopping online at Tesco once but she'd never got the hang of it. And part of her didn't trust the idea of it anyway: she liked to touch her fruit and veg. You couldn't smell a cantaloupe melon through a screen, now could you?

The Tunisia deal had been ten days fully inclusive in a four-star hotel on the island of Djerba. Neither of them had a clue what to expect: all they had wanted was guaranteed sunshine, a ground-floor room for easy access and a swimming pool that Carol could lie by and read her books.

When they got there, ashen and sweaty from the flight over, the hotel had exceeded all expectations. It was an enormous white building with marble floors and balconies layered on top of each other like a wedding cake. The staff had been impeccably efficient and polite. Their room overlooked the pool and was only a short walk from reception which was good for Derek, given how bad his leg was.

For the first couple of days, they hadn't done much, which suited them fine. They'd wake every morning at 7.30, like they did at home, then go to the restaurant for breakfast. The buffet was laden with every type of food: pastries, cereal, cheese, flat-breads, muesli, little bowls of chopped-up dates and several trays of cured meats (there were a lot of Germans, Derek pointed out with slight displeasure. Carol told him to stop being narrow-minded. 'The war's over, Derek, in case you hadn't noticed.' He'd had the grace to look shamefaced).

After breakfast, Carol would set up her sunlounger under-neath a parasol by the pool, slather herself in lotion and take one of her thrillers out to read until lunchtime. For hours she lay there, stately as a galleon, while Derek pottered about indoors doing heaven knows what with his crosswords and his gadget-instruction manuals he'd brought over especially from England.

'What do you want them for?' she'd asked when she spotted him packing the leaflets into his leather satchel. 'How to' manu-als for digital radios, microwaves, dishwashers, broadband connections and the like.

'I don't get a chance to concentrate properly when I'm at

home,' he explained, turning to look at her with an affronted expression. 'I like to know how things work. No harm in that, is there?'

She smiled, patted him on the shoulder.

'No love, none at all.'

At lunchtime, still full from breakfast, they'd waddle over to the poolside bar and have a salad or some fresh fish. Derek would drink a bottle of the local beer. Carol would order a fresh fruit smoothie. They'd retire to their room for an afternoon nap and then, in the early evening before dinner, they'd watch a DVD from one of the selection the hotel had on offer. *On Golden Pond* was a favourite. Carol cried when she saw Katharine Hepburn and Henry Fonda, all shaky with age and set in their ways. There was something so moving about people in love growing old. It's a future you never imagine for yourself when you're young. And yet she knew, without quite admitting it out loud, that the characters in the film weren't that much older than her and Derek.

But on the third day, one of the hotel staff had asked if they wanted to go on an organised excursion to the desert and Derek had signed them up, even though Carol wasn't sure.

'It'll be an experience,' he said, holding her hand. She noticed the thinness of his fingers, the brittleness of his pale nails.

'That's what I'm afraid of,' she said. She was nervous of the unexpected. Derek thought it was one of her failings. No sense of adventure. People were always talking nowadays of the need to 'get out of your comfort zone' but Carol would really rather stay inside it, thank you very much. If you were already comfortable, why would you choose not to be? That would be like deciding to sit on a hard wooden chair rather than a big soft sofa. It wouldn't teach you anything apart from the fact you didn't like hard wooden chairs and she knew that already.

'Come on, poppet,' Derek cajoled. 'It might be fun.'

His eyes were bright at the thought of it. She saw that he'd caught the sun without even trying: his cheeks were pinkish-brown and the tip of his nose was beginning to peel. He was still a good-looking man, she thought, even now, two years shy of his seventieth birthday. His face had filled out as he got older and the extra weight suited him, made him look dignified.

He was five years older than her. When she first met him, at her friend Elsie's twenty-first birthday party, he had reminded her of a dark-eyed bird: rapid and precise in his movements, his face a combination of angles and planes, his nose beaky, and with a shock of brown hair that seemed to blow about even when there was no wind. He had been skinny, almost too thin, and yet she had seen something comforting in his shape as soon as he walked through the door, bending to fit his gangly height into the small, smoky room. She had felt, even then, that she could tell Derek anything and he would understand. He didn't need to say anything and still he would be in tune with everything she thought.

'All right then,' Carol said, kissing her husband lightly on the tip of his peeling nose. 'Let's go to the desert.'

And in the end, it had been amazing. They'd been driven in an air-conditioned jeep across a Roman causeway that connected the island to the mainland and then on to Ksar Ghilane, an oasis lined with date trees and criss-crossed with shallow drainage ditches. The night had been spent in a spacious tent and, although Carol had been worried about the heat, the temperature dropped, and she found that she slept deeply, her dreams accompanied by the rhythmic tautening and loosening of the linen canopy.

The next day, the tour operators had laid on an evening camel ride into the desert.

'Are you sure this is a good idea?' Carol asked, spearing a fresh chunk of pineapple on her fork over breakfast. 'You know what you're like with your leg.'

Derek smiled at her. 'I'll be fine, sweetheart.' He leant back in his chair and stretched his arms out wide. 'I feel like a new man.'

Getting on the camel had been the hardest part for both of them. The animals were trained to sit still while clueless tourists attempted to clamber on to the saddles, but then there was a moment as each camel stood up when you felt as though you were going to be pitched over and thrown onto the ground below. Carol shrieked loudly, much to the amusement of the Berber guides. But Derek took it all in his stride. He'd grown up on a farm, Carol reminded herself, feeling a little foolish at all the fuss she'd made.

They'd trekked for an hour, just as dusk was beginning to creep in across the flat horizon, giving the smooth, sandy slopes a reddish hue, lit up from the inside like paper lanterns. The desert light resembled nothing she'd ever seen: translucent, shimmering, as though the landscape had been freshly painted that morning and they were the first to walk through it.

Neither of them spoke for the length of the trek. They didn't need to. They could sense, without talking, the calm happiness radiating from the other.

Later, they sat around a campfire and were given delicious couscous to eat in clay bowls. The Berber guides sang and played drums and encouraged the others to dance. Derek, exhausted from the ride, declined but Carol found herself wiggling and jiving and clapping her hands along with a pair of dreadlocked Scandinavian backpackers.

They slept in sleeping bags underneath the open sky. The stars, like everyone had said they would be, were brighter but Carol was most taken with the blueness behind them, which was clearer, deeper than at home. She sensed, if only she could reach out and touch it, the sky would feel like velvet against her fingers.

When they got back and printed out their photos, none of the images did justice to their shared memories. It is one of the things that makes her most sad, she thinks now, shifting uneasily underneath the duvet: the knowledge that there is no one else alive who would have experienced the same things as she had, with whom she could lean across the table and say, 'Do you remember when . . . ?' and be assured of a complicit smile, a nod of the head, a hand patted with familiarity and love.

Milton has stopped purring and fallen asleep. Carol, shifting her right leg, feels the jab and tingle of pins and needles. There is a moistness on her cheek. When she wipes at it with the back of her hand, she is surprised by the confirmation of tears.

Stupid, really, she tells herself. Stupid to cry over something that you can't do anything about. She takes a deep, raggedy breath. She feels wide awake.

Admitting defeat, Carol looks at the alarm clock. It is one minute past five in the morning.

BEATRICE

*B*EATRICE SITS ON A plastic bench in Trafalgar Square, waiting for the night bus to take her back to Bermondsey. Her legs are aching from an eight-hour shift of cleaning and folding, wiping and sponging. But the most tiring part, she finds, is the endless tramping up and down the long, windowless corridors that wind through the hotel, each one identical to the last so that it would be easy to forget where you were unless you had the room numbers to remind you. At work she misses the daylight most of all. The building seems hermetically sealed, kept alive only by recycled air. At Catholic school back in Uganda, she'd read a book by Virginia Woolf that talked about a hotel being a place where even the flies that sat on your nose had been on someone else's skin the day before. That is how the Rotunda felt: arid, stuffy, loveless.

Normally, she didn't mind it too much. She had been a waitress for a short time at the Hotel Protea in Kampala when it opened, serving ladlefuls of posho to rich tourists and Kenyan businessmen, and she had got used to the peculiar rhythm of hotel etiquette, the small niceties that would ensure a bigger tip. Once, a white man had left her a $50 note simply because she had brought him a citronella candle when the mosquitoes started buzzing. She had noticed him when he walked into the restaurant, skinny and worried-looking, wearing a beige money belt and two mushroom-coloured bands round his wrists that were meant to protect tourists from insect bites except they never did. His face had been flush with relief when she brought the candle. It gave Beatrice pleasure to see it and, for a brief moment, she had felt valued.

The Mayfair Rotunda was different because she worked behind the scenes and hardly ever got tips. Every day, she cleaned up after people, emptying their bins of used condoms, scooping out their hair from the plugholes, wiping the mirrors free of toothpaste flecks. It was draining work with minimal satisfaction. Beatrice liked things to look clean but then she would come back the next day and the room would be in disarray, as if she had never been, as if she didn't exist.

Today had been particularly bad. The man in Room 423 . . . she shudders to think of him, pressed up so close against her she could feel the bristle of his stubble against her neck, could smell the rottenness of his breath. A coil of anger tightens in the pit of her stomach. How she hated men like that, men who believed they could take what they wanted and treat her like meat. She feels humiliated – not for herself but for them, that they could be so pathetic.

It is part of the job, she has come to realise. Bitter experience has taught her it is better not to resist but to be pliant, to allow them to do their silly business and get it over with. All the maids have the same problem: oversexed businessmen and adulterous foreigners. They tend to clean in pairs now, each one doing an adjoining room, so that if anything ever gets nasty or goes further than you want it to, you can scream out and bang the walls. Otherwise, if you're not being asked to do anything you don't want to, it can be a handy way to make extra money. Some of the girls have regular clients. Ewelina, from Poland, has a guy called Franz who comes over from Austria every month and has given her a Rolex watch. Beatrice is pretty sure it is fake but hasn't the heart to tell her.

But the man today – the fat one in the robe, with hairs growing out of his nose – had not paid Beatrice. Once it was over, he'd tightened his belt, patted her on the bottom and leered at her, as though she had been a willing participant, as though she had wanted him to rub against her until he came. Stupid idiot. Beatrice had stared at him sullenly until he'd been forced to look away. She left the room without replacing his bottle of Chablis or drawing his curtains. She hoped she wouldn't get in trouble for that.

She glances up at the digital display board to find out how long the next bus will be but it is broken so she has to sit here, patiently, waiting for a bus that might or might not come in the next half-hour. Waiting always seems to take so much longer when you don't know how long it will be for, she thinks.

Mrs Dalloway, that was what the book had been called. It had seemed so far removed from her own experience and yet here she is, living in the same city it described, all those years ago. London wasn't recognisable to her when she first arrived, despite having read so much about it. It was so much bigger than it had appeared on the page, so much more foreign, and although Beatrice should have been intimidated by this, she found instead that she took a kind of comfort from the hugeness of the city. She craved London's anonymity, the constant reinvention of the streets, the silence of strangers that would, in any other context, have been unfriendly but which gave Beatrice space to breathe for what felt like the first time in years. She grew to love the overlooked beauty of the urban sprawl, the mismatched things you wouldn't expect: the evening sunlight glinting against a steel girder on the Westway, the flat sheets of cardboard in the Waterloo subway where people slept huddled against the wind, the angry graffiti scrawled across a tube carriage, the flaking paint on advertising billboards, the tin-foil glimmer of a flickering street-lamp bulb against white birch bark. All of it felt to Beatrice like freedom.

She wonders what happened to her copy of *Mrs Dalloway*. She'd had to leave it behind, like everything else. She had been good at school. She wishes she'd been able to stay at university. Hard to remember now but she was studying to be a lawyer.

Across the street from her, there is a bulky shadow, hunkered down in the doorstep of a gentlemen's outfitter's. Her eyes adjust gradually to the dark and she realises the shape conceals a person, coddled tightly in a sleeping bag like a caterpillar snug in its cocoon. She can just make out the tip of a head, covered in a beanie hat, and a flash of skin beneath.

A drunken group of men in matching rugby shirts are trailing their way through the Square, slapping each other's backs, loudly reciting the course of the evening to anyone who happens to pass within earshot.

'Gagging for it, mate,' she hears one of them shout. 'Fucking all over you.'

Men. All after the same thing.

Up on the fourth plinth, Beatrice's attention is caught by a dull strip of gold, picked out by the soft moonlight. She read in the *Evening Standard* that some artists have put an oversized boy on a rocking horse there, where normally you would expect to see grave-faced generals on horseback. She likes the idea of this. It makes her smile. There is something in the rocking-horse boy's carefree attitude – one arm raised aloft in pure, unencumbered happiness – that reminds her of John, her little brother. He would be ten now, she thinks, and a heaviness tugs at her heart.

After a quarter of an hour, a Number 47 swings into view. Beatrice stands, feeling the stiffness in her shoulders and her calf muscles. She slips her Oyster card out of the fake-leather handbag she bought in the Primark sale last year and swipes it across the reader as the driver looks at her with tired eyes. He has light, youthful skin and wears a turban.

He nods at her, just the once, just to let her know that he feels the kinship of the night-worker, that he understands what it is to be one of those silent, uncomplaining people who clean rooms and drive buses and stack shelves and sweep streets into the early hours, who fuel this vast and friendless city, who feed its pavements and drains with sweat and silent submission, who stay hidden from view, passed over by richer residents who believe it

44

all happens without any effort. She sees the bus driver convey this in the smallest inflexion of his head, in the tiniest upturn of the corners of his mouth. She wants to lean over and hold his hand, through the gap in the screen, simply so they can reassure each other that their blood runs warm, that life still pulses in their veins, but she stops herself – just. She smiles at him, then moves to the mid-section of the bus, sliding into the window-seat. The grey upholstery smells faintly of curry.

She leans her head against the glass and dozes, lulled by the juddering of the engine and the tinging of the bell for request stops. A man behind her is burbling to himself, talking in a stream of swear words and furious rejoinders to an imagined opponent. When she turns round, she sees he is swigging from a clear bottle, the neck of it protruding from a brown paper bag.

'What are you looking at, you fucking nigger?'

Beatrice scowls at him. She is neither afraid nor shocked. You get used to such things, living in this city. It is the price you pay for safety. Besides, she has known worse abuse. The police at home had stripped her, forced her to walk through her village naked, then beaten her unconscious and left her on a concrete floor for days without food. Verbal abuse was nothing compared to that, to the humiliation of it.

And then there was the bigger pain, the one she chooses not to think about. Every time she senses the ugliness encroach, she makes herself imagine something else, something easy and sunny and smooth and clean-smelling like bleach in a bath-tub.

But sometimes, in spite of her best efforts, a flash of it will come back to her when she least expects it. She will hear the echo of a muffled scream while she is waiting to cross the road. The traffic lights will slip from amber into red and she will blink, forgetting where she is, finding herself back there, back in the faraway bedroom with his weight on top of her, a bead of his sweat dropping into her open mouth. Or she will be doing her weekly load at the launderette and she will suddenly remember the sour-cream taste of him in her mouth and she will have to sit

45

down to gather her breath before she finds enough strength to continue pushing the clothes into the washing machine's metal drum. Or she will simply be sitting, staring into space, and a splinter-clear piece of remembered past will slice into her mind's eye and it will come back to her in its entirety: the force of it, the mass of him, the sickness that followed, the sense of betrayal and the shame she was angry with herself for feeling.

By the time Beatrice gets back to her flat on Jamaica Road, it is after 1 a.m. and her legs feel so heavy she can barely make it up the four flights of stairs. She slides her key into the lock with relief and goes straight to the electric heater to plug it in. Five years in this country and the cold still seeps into her bones.

Beatrice flicks on the light. Her flat is small and basic. There is a bed-sitting room with a single mattress that doubles up as a sofa and, to one side, a galley kitchen with two gas rings and a rickety grill. A grimy bathroom is situated behind the front door, the tiles spotted with black along the grouting, the shower head covered with a rash of limescale. A smell of damp pervades. When she hangs up wet clothes, they never seem to dry.

She rents the flat from Mr Khandoker, a Bengali man with heavy eyebrows and a permanently sour expression. Mr Khandoker owns several properties in this block, including the ground-floor porter's flat which for months has had sagging cardboard pressed against empty window-frames. The cardboard has the word 'Shurgard' spelled across it in black block capitals and there is a rip at the base of the letter H through which Beatrice can sometimes catch a glimpse of movement: a rapid shifting through the shadows. She is never sure if the movement belongs to humans or rats and has never wanted to find out. It is better, in this block, to keep your curiosity to yourself.

Beatrice tried not to have too much to do with Mr Khandoker. He would turn up on her doorstep every week wearing a pale yellow salwar kameez dotted with oily stains which she assumed were from the spit and fizzle of a too-hot frying pan and she would hand over her rent money in worn £10 notes. Once, Mr

Khandoker had offered to cash a cheque for her and when he returned with half the amount she had been expecting, he explained to Beatrice that of course he had to take interest and did she think he was a charity, handing out free money to worthy causes? No, he said, he was a businessman: one of Thatcher's children.

She didn't make that mistake again. And really, she has cause to be grateful to Mr Khandoker. He is nowhere near as bad as some of the private landlords Beatrice hears about. If she pays him on time, he leaves her alone.

She tries to remind herself of her luck but her mood remains heavy and listless. Beatrice makes herself a slice of toast under the grill, waiting for the corners of the white bread to curl with the heat. She butters the toast thickly from a tub of Flora then rips open a packet of sugar taken from the hotel and sprinkles it generously across the margarine. She bites into it, feeling the sweetness hit the back of her throat.

She wipes the crumbs from her mouth and sits on the bed to take off her clumpy flat shoes. Then, as she allows herself to do for a brief period every single night, she starts to cry. Her shoulders slump forward and she holds her head in her hands, her breath coming in gulps, tears dropping onto the bare floorboards. For five minutes, she summons all the stored-up pain and buried memory and lets the sadness wash over her. She will not let anyone else see her do this, ever. She will not allow them – the man in Room 423, the drunk on the bus, the police back home – to know her weakness. This sadness is hers alone. A precious, shielded thing.

After the tears, Beatrice feels lighter, more herself. She strips off her black clothes, hanging them carefully over the back of a wooden chair without creasing so that she can wear them again tomorrow. She is saving up to buy an iron.

As she goes through to the bathroom, she catches sight of the photograph of Susan, hanging on the wall from a crooked nail. Susan is smiling and the sun catches her hair. Her cheeks are sweating lightly – Susan always hated her cheeks and said they made her look fat but Beatrice loved them. They reminded her of plumped-up pillows. She'd taken the photograph in the café they went to on their first date, although, of course, neither of them would admit what it was until later.

In the photo, Susan is holding a glass of Coca-Cola with a straw. She always drank full fat, never Diet. Said she didn't like the taste.

Beatrice kisses the tips of her fingers and lets her hand rest on the frame for a few moments. She has no idea whether she'll ever see Susan again. The two of them had been split up, shortly after they'd escaped over the border to the Congo and paid a human trafficker to take them to the UK. It had cost Beatrice £21,000. She'd given the trafficker a plot of land her father owned. For the first and only time in her life, Beatrice had been grateful her father was dead and that she'd inherited a share of his fortune.

'It's not safe for both of you to go at the same time,' the trafficker had said, chewing on one end of a cocktail stick. He had grubby fingernails and wore a T-shirt with the sleeves ripped off. 'One of you only. The other will follow.'

They'd had no choice. Susan squeezed Beatrice's hand.

'You go,' she said. 'I'll follow.'

'But . . .'

'You're ill. You should go first.'

Beatrice was still recovering from the effects of the police beating. Her back was pitted with sores. The cuts on her arms were not healing. The corner of one eye was still tender from a brutal punch.

If she had been stronger, more like herself, she wouldn't have let Susan stay behind on her own. She would have thought of something to keep the two of them together. Because what was the point of any of it if they were separated? Why had they fought so hard if they were going to end up alone?

They couldn't be together in Uganda. They'd be arrested or murdered before the year was out.

'Devil-child', that's what Beatrice's mother had called her. Her own mother.

She'd looked her eldest daughter in the eyes and said it.

But by then, Beatrice hadn't cared, had only had space in her head for thoughts of Susan. She'd been obsessed, crazed. And Susan . . . she had been in love with her too, of that she was sure. And yet . . . she'd never followed her to London.

They'd made a plan to meet outside Buckingham Palace, which was silly looking back, but it was the only landmark they could be sure of. On the appointed day, Susan hadn't come. For twelve hours, Beatrice had waited in the drizzle, hugging her too-thin coat closer with every passing minute, not wanting her teeth to chatter. Her toes had grown numb, her legs ached with standing but, almost from superstition, she refused to move. She would not shift from her spot by the dour-looking statue of Queen Victoria, facing the gates and the flag, where they'd agreed they would find each other. She told herself that, if she moved, even just an inch to the left or right, Susan wouldn't come. She made a deal with God in her mind: if I stand here, stock-still, for another hour, Susan will appear.

Beatrice waited until all the tourists had dispersed and the light had changed from rosy pink to sludge-grey and then slipped into dark blue dusk. Still no sign of her.

She'd gone back the next day and the one after that, thinking to herself that Susan must have got delayed or confused or was trying desperately to get a message to her and that she should be there, just in case, to welcome her to this strange city. She should be there, as promised, to prove her love.

But Susan never came. The drafts folder in the email account they'd set up in case either of them needed to communicate remained resolutely empty. Days, then weeks, then months and Beatrice never got word from her. Something must have gone wrong. The trafficker had gone back on his word. Her family had found her and dragged her back to Uganda against her will. Or she'd been taken by the authorities and thrown into a detention centre and it was only a matter of time until they were reunited. Surely that was it? Surely there was some sense to everything they had been through, some reason why?

Beatrice turns away from the photo. It is not good to think like this. Too many futile thoughts and she will become depressed again and when she is depressed, she cannot work, cannot so much as crawl out of bed for fear of the sky collapsing on her and the heavy grey clouds pinning her to the floor. When she gets like that, everything acquires a new, horrifying edge. The world around her sweats with an alien light. Buildings and roads and cars slough off their skins and become unfamiliar beings and Beatrice can't leave the flat through sheer terror of what she might find on the other side of the door.

She must not let that happen. She needs the money to survive. She needs to buy an iron.

She brushes her teeth thoroughly, splashes soap and water on her face, then gets into bed. Something crinkles under her pillow and, when she slides her hand underneath, she realises it is that weekend's paper. She'd picked it up on a bus for the TV listings. Beatrice throws it to the floor. The pages fly open and a photograph catches her eye, along the bottom of page seven.

Her gaze snaps into focus. It is the man from Room 423. He is much younger in the picture but she recognises his piggy little eyes and florid cheeks. Beatrice props the paper up on her knees to read it more closely. It is an article about optimism written by a girl called Esme Reade and the photograph caption identifies the man as 'self-made millionaire' Sir Howard Pink.

A millionaire, Beatrice thinks. She narrows her eyes. He should have paid her.

Howard

HOWARD HAD BOUGHT EDEN House in the mid-1990s, as London property prices were rocketing skywards and when just about anyone with a 5 per cent deposit could find themselves with an interest-free mortgage and a substantial duplex in Chelsea before the day was out. Eden House was a sprawling Victorian-era mansion behind High Street Kensington, built for a painter Howard had never heard of, at a time when moneyed bohemians liked to believe they were re-creating a pastoral idyll in the heart of the city. Luther Eden had aspired to be William Morris but had never quite made it. All that was left of him was a garish oil painting full of impasto brushwork and overenthusiastic representations of hellfire, hung in an ignored corner of Tate Britain.

As a result of Eden's arts and crafts fascination, the house was set back in a large walled garden and dotted with stone-carved representations of forest nymphs and sprightly animals every which way you looked. A goat, curled in on itself with a dazed expression, was to be found at the intersection of a piece of guttering. A charming elfish figurine, complete with a quiver of arrows, peeked out humorously from beneath the window ledge of one of the first-floor bedrooms.

Inside, the house was a mess: higgledy-piggledy staircases, winding this way and that like a drunken Escher sketch, and leading to dozens of small rooms which Howard had attempted to knock through only to be told it was structurally impossible. The saving grace was the room on the top floor, once Eden's studio, which had double-height ceilings and windows on three sides. Howard promptly converted it into the master bedroom, insisting that a four-poster bed with purple velvet swags be placed on a specially constructed platform in the centre of the room, much to the horror of the chi-chi interior decorator he'd hired who called the idea '*de trop*, Sir Howard, *de trop*'.

'Darling, I am *de trop*,' he'd replied. 'Hadn't you realised that?'

It is in this cavernous bedroom that Howard now sits, watching the Formula 1 racing on a giant flat-screen television that slides in and out of a plumply upholstered stool at the foot of his king-size bed. The detritus of his breakfast lies on a tray beside him: slivers of orange flesh lining an empty glass; a white linen napkin smeared with brown sauce; a rind of bacon on a glistening china plate (today is a non-kosher day, Howard has decided). He presses a button on the wall to get someone to clear it away.

As he does so, the phone on the console table at the side of the bed starts to ring.

'Yep,' Howard says, picking it up, eyes still trained on the screen.

'Good morning, Sir Howard,' says Tracy, her voice trilling. 'And how are we today?'

'Fine, fine.'

'Just to remind you, Sir Howard,' she continues, 'that you have a charity luncheon.'

'Fuck.'

Tracy lets the swear word pass. After twenty-odd years, she knows him better than most people. She laughs lightly.

'I've told Jocelyn to have the car ready for 12.30.'

Howard glances at his Cartier. It is already 11.45.

'Fuck.'

'We discussed it last week, you remember,' Tracy says, assuming the manner of a patient nanny. 'It's Action for Elephants. Imelda's charity.'

'Elephants?' says Howard, incredulous. 'Why the fuck do we care about elephants?'

Tracy replies as though he's asked something incredibly insightful. 'It's a pet project of hers, Sir Howard. She went on holiday to Kenya and was moved by the plight of these – hang on, let me get the wording right –' There is a rustling of papers on the other end of the line. 'Ah yes, that's it, "These beautiful and noble masters of the earth". She's got all her family involved – you remember, the Wallis-Parkers. Descendants of the man who founded the London Stock Exchange, I believe. They've got a granddaughter who's a model, always on the front of *Grazia* – you know the one, I'm sure. You'd recognise her if you saw her anyway.'

'Christ.'

'The point being, Sir Howard, that Imelda knows everyone worth knowing,' Tracy concludes crisply. And then, a touch more coldly, she adds, 'Has Claudia remembered?'

Tracy and Claudia don't get on. Claudia thinks Tracy is patronising and dowdy – a fatal combination. Tracy believes Claudia to be little better than an ageing tart with pert breasts (fake) and pound signs in her eyes (lasered).

Howard thinks they both have a point.

'I'll tell her,' Howard says.

'Also, Rupert's asked me to get you to call him about setting up lunch with a journalist from the *Tribune*. He said you'd know why.'

'Thanks, Tracy.'

'Not at all, Sir Howard.'

He puts the phone down and feels a stirring in his nether regions. There's always been something about Tracy, with her buttoned-up manner and clipped efficiency. She'd be a challenge, Howard thinks, unlike most women. Yet he's never been brave enough to follow this thought through, perhaps because he knows the fantasy Tracy (voraciously available once you've mussed up the neatly bobbed hair) is more sexually appealing

53

than the real one. And he's intimidated by her too, if he's honest. Nothing like a woman's self-evident superiority to make your cock shrivel to the size of a deflated balloon.

He groans as he levers himself out of bed and pads across to the dressing room to put on a Paisley silk robe. He goes downstairs to try and find Claudia but after a futile few minutes, peeking in and out of half-hidden sitting rooms and squeezing his cumbersome frame through narrow passageways leading nowhere, he feels his impatience rising. The house had seemed so charming when Howard bought it. He'd believed it embodied a shambolic, semi-aristocratic way of life, unlike all those dreadful new-build mansions in Essex everyone expected a man like him to buy. But, after two decades of living here, he finds himself lusting after the clean lines of a modern house with a double garage and excellent central heating. He knows now that the business of acquiring good taste, as represented by Eden House, means comfort must some-times be sacrificed. Still, he wishes he hadn't bought the house purely on the basis of it looking like something out of a period drama. Howard has learned, through the years, that what he thinks looks nice is almost always the wrong instinct to pursue.

He includes his second wife in that.

'Claudia!' he bellows.

One of the Filipino maids scurries towards him and whispers discreetly that Lady Pink is in the gym before scurrying off again, duster in hand. He should know their names but Claudia gets through staff so quickly he loses track. Howard, wheezing, walks all the way down to the basement where he finally finds Claudia sitting, legs akimbo, feet pressed into cable handles that are attached to tightly stretched wires emerging from a space-age piece of equipment that looks like a shaking treadmill.

'What the fuck are you doing?'

Claudia grimaces at him. Her dyed blonde hair is tied up, revealing an expressionless forehead smooth as eggshell thanks to regular injections of botulin administered by one of the most sought-after dermatologists in London.

'Powerplate,' she says, her voice vibrating, the tremors reminding Howard of a colleague who has just been diagnosed with
early onset Parkinson's. 'It's good for toning up and core strength.
You should try it.'

'No thanks.' He looks at her, taking in for a moment the
slinky lines of her legs, the unnatural buoyancy of her breasts
under black Lycra, and he feels nothing. He analyses this lack
of sensation and is depressed by it, by the recollection of how
passionate he used to be, how crazy she used to make him. The
mere sight of her red-lacquered fingernails around a champagne
glass stem had been enough to send him into paroxysms of
sexual obsession.

He'd met her at a vulnerable time, of course. Ada had just
gone missing and his marriage to Penny, his first wife, was showing the strain. You couldn't ever recover, as a couple, from
something like that, from the hopeless uncertainty of unanswered
questions when your only child goes missing.

All the police could tell them was that Ada, their beautiful,
edgy, neurotic nineteen-year-old daughter, had walked out of her
halls of residence at Birmingham University one Friday evening
in February 2001 never to be seen again. That was it: the slender
filament of knowledge they'd been left with after weeks and
months of fruitless searching.

There had been a thorough investigation. Even now, eleven
years on, Howard gets queasy thinking about it. The questions.
The interviews. The fingerprints. The murky cloud of suspicion
that hovered over the parents, no matter how obvious their devastation. The constant harassment from the press: phone calls,
door-knocks, carefully worded entreaties pushed through the letterbox. He'd hired private detectives – eight of them, through the
years. He'd spoken, personally, to her friends, lecturers, ex-
boyfriends. He'd travelled up and down the country looking for
something without knowing what. He'd taken the best part of a
year off work. He couldn't sleep, was drinking too much, jumped
at the sound of a door slamming.

Penny wanted him to see her therapist, said he was showing all the signs of post-traumatic stress and that he needed help. Howard ignored her. He didn't want to get better. He wanted to pick away at the wound for the rest of his life. He felt, in a way he realised was illogical, that this was what he deserved.

No one knew anything about what had happened to Ada that night. Or if they did, they weren't letting on. There had been rumours of drug-taking and petty crime: a patched-together picture of their daughter that neither Howard nor Penny recognised. The police found tin-foil wraps and teaspoons burned brown in Ada's room. One night, he'd looked up heroin on the internet and the resulting information had sent him into a dark spiral of depression. It was the closest he'd come to suicide.

After a while, he had to ask himself whether it was worth pursuing such hurtful lines of inquiry. Wasn't it better, if Ada was never coming back, to remember her as they knew her? To remember the serious little girl who had to kiss each one of her teddies goodnight before she went to sleep.

Or the dark-eyed seven-year-old in a brown school uniform, her front teeth missing, rucksack straps worn sensibly over both shoulders.

Or the teenager who'd looked at him once across the kitchen table and asked, 'Dad, what did you do in the war?' and when he roared with laughter and said he hadn't even been born, she'd blushed all the way from the base of her throat to the tip of her hairline.

The girl on her father's knee, laughing uncontrollably as he tickled her, pleading with him to stop.

Because if they didn't have memories, if they could no longer believe their cherished girl was who they thought she was, then what were they left with?

There were bleak times, now, when Howard thought it would have been easier to cope with had there been a body to bury, a focal point for their grief. As it was, he and Penny were left in limbo, increasingly unable to bear the sight of each other because it reminded them of the gaping hole in their hearts, the absence that could never be named, the loss that could never be laid to rest.

The decision to divorce was mutual. He'd met Claudia by then and his affair with her had been a deliberate, doomed attempt to counteract profound unhappiness with its antidote of undemanding superficiality. His lust for Claudia had always, peculiarly, been grounded in hatred for all that she stood for. He needed her brittleness, her dead-eyed ambition, her naked desire for status and wealth, as affirmation of what he had always suspected of himself: that he was worth no more, that if you drew back the curtain there was nothing there but a small boy, threading a needle, afraid of being found out.

Shortly after they'd got married at Chelsea Register Office, Claudia had encouraged him to pack away all of Ada's belongings. He'd been keeping his daughter's room like a shrine and would sit there in the evenings, as if inhaling the dust could bring him closer to the air she had breathed. The air she might still be breathing, for all he knew.

Claudia had been right that it was time to move on. She was a hard woman and, for a while, Howard found himself latching gratefully on to her unsentimentality as though it were a life-raft that would bring him, at last, to the edge of the wild ocean. But it hadn't. He'd simply grown more distant from his second wife with every box of Ada's belongings he packed and put into storage. He'd closed off his memories and shut down his thoughts one by one. Thinking, he realised, was too dispiriting. The only time he allowed himself to dwell on his grief and indulge his unhappiness was once a month, at the Mayfair Rotunda Hotel, when his bottled-up sadness made him act in unpredictable ways, surprising even to himself.

At the age of sixty-five, he had discovered a taste for grubby sexual encounters. Sometimes, he thought, the only way to forget about love was to bury it in spadefuls of self-loathing, to make oneself ultimately unlovable, to ensure one's soul was inviolate.

It would surprise almost everyone who knew him that Howard had such thoughts.

The exercise machine beeps and the humming vibrations halt abruptly. Claudia wipes a sheen of sweat from her brow and takes a long sip of water from a bottle of Evian, eyes closed, the lashes coated with several layers of black mascara.

'Have you remembered we've got this charity lunch?' Howard asks. 'Imelda's elephants.'

'Yes, Howie.' She raises her eyebrow patronisingly. 'Have you?'

He ignores her. 'Jocelyn's coming with the car at 12.30.'

'Great. I'll slip into something less comfortable.' She saunters across to him and plants a light kiss on his nose. 'You should wear that tie I bought you. The green one.'

'All right, sweetheart,' he says, pacified by her brief show of attentiveness. He pats her on the bottom. Her buttocks are as hard as an overcooked piece of steak. 'See you in a bit.'

Howard wends his way slowly back upstairs, his lungs getting tighter with each step. He must cut back on the cigars, he thinks. He should take a leaf out of Claudia's book and try to get healthy.

When he gets to the bedroom, he sees the breakfast tray has been removed, the bed neatly made. Propped up against the pillows is a small white bear, paws sewn onto a red heart embroidered with the words: 'I love you Daddy'. It is the only thing of Ada's he could not face packing away.

Esme

'WHERE ARE YOU OFF to?' Sanjay says, sitting up straighter at his keyboard so that the top half of his head is visible over the Mac screen. His eyebrows are looking especially well groomed and Esme wonders if he's had them waxed. Automatically, she runs a finger over her own unruly brows. They are due a plucking but she just hasn't had time this week. She's been frantically dealing with the fall-out from the nudists piece: dozens of complaints from assorted Women's Institutes, cider-pressing clubs, donkey sanctuaries and the Malvern Link Fire Brigade, all of whom are eager to put the record straight about the good work achieved by sales of naked charity calendars.

Online, a vociferous war of words has broken out between anonymous commenters, one of whom has called for the boycott of the newspaper: 'Until such time as the editor of the *Tribune* takes down this pornographic filth and signs a pledge never to post such images again where they can be seen by children or adults of a vulnerable disposition. I, for one, will be cancelling my subscription.'

This comment alone attracted forty-three 'Recommends'. Below it, someone calling themselves 'Satansrib' has added: 'I stopped buying the paper years ago. Too many darkies in the news pages for my liking. Political correctness gone mad.'

Another calling themselves 'Arafat2000' has expressed their opinion that the popularity of nude charity calendars is a symptom of some obscure Zionist conspiracy involving WikiLeaks and the failed extradition of Julian Assange.

Esme sighs. She knows she is meant to embrace reader interaction, but the thought of it makes her depressed. When she first started on newspapers, it was fairly easy to ignore the green-ink obsessives: those twenty-page letters from readers detailing government attempts to assassinate them through secret radio-waves emitted from television aerials and packets of aluminium foil. Nowadays, everyone spewed forth anonymously online and the resulting bile was left for ever suspended in the ether of cyberspace. There is one man – she assumes it is a man – who keeps posting that he's heard 'from friends in the media that Esme Reade only got where she is today on her knees'. She'd spoken to Dave about it and he'd been unexpectedly sympathetic and told the online moderators to take it down.

'Don't let it get to you,' he said. 'You've got to have a thicker skin.'

Which is true, of course, but she can't help taking things like that to heart. When she told Sanjay, he'd bought her a latte. 'If you've only got you this far, you're obviously rubbish at giving head,' he said, which made her laugh.

And then there's all the social networking you're meant to do. Real-life networking is bad enough: tepid white wine and exchanging business cards over the chicken satay skewers but now they've all got to be on Facebook and LinkedIn and editing sixty-second Instagram videos to 'go viral' and 'get more page hits'.

'You need to develop your own brand,' the marketing department had told the *Tribune* newsroom during one of their god-awful 'Multi-Platform Future' briefings, hastily convened to introduce a dwindling group of weary old hacks to the idea of an iPad app and 'data-blogging'.

She has only just set up a Twitter account and is baffled by what to do with it. Reducing the entire day's news to a series of 140-character bullet points seems to her to be an exercise in pointlessness.

'I'm taking Howard Pink to lunch,' she tells Sanjay, buttoning up her jacket, bought from the L.K.Bennett sale two years ago and still wearing well.

'Ooh, anywhere nice?'

'Alain Ducasse at the Dorchester.'

'Blimey,' Sanjay says, sputtering on his coffee. 'I thought that kind of wining and dining went out with the Ark. Who are they going to sack to finance it, one wonders?' He slumps back behind his screen. 'Well you enjoy it while you can. Some of us have real work to do,' Sanjay adds with a meaningful twist of the mouth.

He's joking, of course, but Esme wishes he didn't always make her feel like such an amateur. Walking out into the atrium, she takes out her BlackBerry and logs on to Twitter. 'Off 2 lunch,' she types with her thumbs. 129 characters remaining. She chews her lip. 'Meeting Sir Howard Pink.' 104. 'Hoping to persuade him to give me Fash Attack discount card!' She hates exclamation marks as a rule but Twitter seems to require this kind of enthusiastic repartee. She still has 44 characters left and supposes she should add in some smiley-faced emoticon or semi-ironic hash-tag but she can't be bothered. She presses down with her thumb and sends the Tweet.

In truth, she wouldn't mind a Fash Attack discount card. Sir Howard's chain of teen clothing stores has gone from strength to strength in recent years, after ingeniously persuading top-end designers to collaborate on cheaper ranges for the mass market. The one they'd done with Dolce & Gabanna had sold out in under twelve hours. There were pieces on eBay for triple the asking price within minutes of the doors opening on High Street Ken.

She'd never been particularly good with clothes. Her mother was always going on about Esme needing to look 'put together'.

'A good bag and good heels will lift any outfit,' her mother likes to say. 'Those are the key pieces worth investing in.'

Lilian Reade considered herself something of a sartorial expert, having once enjoyed a short-lived stint as a fashion model in the 1970s after her colleagues in the Ministry of Defence had encouraged her to enter Miss Whitehall. She'd won the competition and signed up with an agency where her most high-profile job had been modelling for a knitting pattern company based in Slough. But the way she talked about it, Lilian's glory days had been a jet-set whirlwind of catwalks, male admirers and parties in St-Tropez.

'Girls had more meat on them in those days,' she is fond of saying. 'No skinny minnies. And I was naturally slender so my agency kept telling me, "Lilian," they said, "You've got to try and put some weight *on*, dear." I mean, can you *imagine*, darling, can you?'

Lilian would give a light spray of laughter while Esme would shake her head dutifully. 'No, Mum, no I can't.'

There is a black-and-white newspaper clipping of Lilian as Miss Whitehall in a shockingly short houndstooth dress standing outside Big Ben, posing as if her life depended on it. Lilian is prone to fishing it out from a conveniently placed scrapbook any time she wants to make her daughter feel inadequate.

Esme thinks of it now as she hops on a bus to Hyde Park Corner, wincing as the skin on the back of her ankle catches against the back of her high-heeled shoe. Her mother, needless to say, swears by high heels but the soles of Esme's feet are already prickling with heat. She hopes she won't have to walk too far at the other end.

But by the time she makes it to the Dorchester – which is further up Park Lane than she had remembered – she is already five minutes late. Her ankles are red-raw, her toes uncomfortably squashed. A silver-haired Frenchman greets her at the door of the restaurant, eyeing her up and down as if she is a piece of second-hand furniture, before suavely sashaying across the plush carpet, leading her past a shimmering pillar of glass that falls from the ceiling like a divine shower curtain and then on to a corner table at which Sir Howard and his PR man, Rupert, are already seated.

'Shit,' Esme says under her breath. Turning up late is not a good way to start the Howard Pink charm offensive.

'Sir Howard,' she says, with as much confidence as she can muster. 'I'm so sorry to have kept you waiting.' She extends her arm. Sir Howard tries to stand but only gets three-quarters of the way out of his chair before his considerable stomach makes it impossible for him to continue without toppling over. He shakes her hand. His palm is cool and surprisingly smooth. A floral scent wafts from his open-necked shirt and she recognises it instantly as Roger & Gallet soap, of the kind once used by her grandmother.

'You're here now, I suppose,' Sir Howard says, unsmiling. She can sense displeasure radiating from him.

Rupert leans towards her and introduces himself. 'Good of you to come, Esme,' he says, as though she is doing them a tremendous favour. He is well-spoken and conventionally handsome, like one of those men in the Gillette adverts. He looks much younger than Dave even though she knows they are contemporaries. She wouldn't imagine the two of them as friends. 'Dave said you're one of his star reporters,' Rupert continues, motioning to her seat. 'I must say, I thought you'd be older. It's a sign of age, isn't it, when policemen and doctors start seeming like children . . .'

Esme notices Sir Howard staring fixedly at a point in the mid-distance throughout Rupert's oleaginous patter. In person, the Fash Attack millionaire looks both smaller and more imposing than his photographs would lead you to believe. His face is dominated by a bulbous nose, framed by a receding hairline that is emphasised by a copious amount of gel, employed to slick the few remaining follicular wisps severely backwards. He is not wearing a tie and the collar of his white shirt lies open to reveal a sprouting of dark chest hair. For a titan of industry, he seems remarkably unintimidating but then she spots his eyes: brown and pinprick sharp, the pupils darting this way and that, trailing the waiters, taking in the other customers, analysing everything that comes into his field of vision. He is leaning his head against one perfectly manicured hand, the tips of his fingers so close to his nose he might be smelling them. He appears almost entirely uninterested in her.

'I've been at the paper for eighteen months,' Esme is saying as a waiter unfolds her napkin and casts it out over her knees. 'Sir Howard, it's very kind of you to take time out of your busy schedule,' she adds, trying to get his attention. She is not used to middle-aged men disregarding her so flagrantly.

Sir Howard turns his head, lizard-like. His voice, when he speaks, is pointedly quiet.

'I was led to believe you were going to apologise,' he says.

Esme flushes. 'Oh, yes, well, of course, Sir Howard. We – I mean, the paper – are really incredibly sorry for the oversight . . .'

Rupert waves her apology away with a flap of the hand. 'It's quite all right. I've explained to Sir Howard that it was the picture desk who messed up. Dave tells me it won't happen again.'

'It won't,' says Esme, although she has absolutely no way of ensuring this.

'I hate that fucking picture,' Sir Howard says, launching the swear word across the table just as the waiter arrives bearing three identical egg-shaped bowls.

'To start the meal, we present to you an amuse-bouche of shrimp and lobster ravioli with a ginger consommé.'

There is a slight pause.

'Well get on with it then,' says Howard. 'We haven't got all day.'

The waiter looks suitably apologetic but then takes a small age pouring the consommé into each of their dishes from individual white jugs. Once this is done, he stands back for a moment as if awaiting plaudits for the culinary genius on show. When none is forthcoming, he gives a simpering smile, bows and clasps his hands together.

'*Bon appétit,*' the waiter says, retreating backwards like a royal footman.

'Christ,' says Howard. 'I thought we'd never get rid of him.'

Esme laughs. He looks at her, his eyes suddenly twinkling.

'I didn't catch your name.'

'Esme.'

'Are you Scottish?'

'No, my Dad was.'

'Was?' Howard fires back.

'Yes, he died when I was eight.'

He puts his spoon down and seems genuinely taken aback. Esme is used to all sorts of reactions when she tells strangers: shocked intakes of breath, sympathetic squeezes of the arm, patronising assurances that 'time's a great healer' but, perhaps because he's had to deal with his own loss, Howard's appears oddly sincere.

'I'm sorry,' he says finally.

Rupert grimaces and wrinkles his brow, to show that he is terribly sorry too.

'It's all right. It was a long time ago.'

'You never get over something like that,' Howard says. 'How did he die?' he asks bluntly.

'Drink driving.'

'Christ. Did they catch the bastard?'

'They didn't need to. My father was the drunk driver.'

Howard sits motionless, a spoonful of soup hovering dangerously over the tablecloth at a midway point between bowl and mouth.

She tries not to think of her father too much but now, having mentioned his death without exactly wanting to, broken fragments of an unasked-for memory coalesce in her mind, each tiny element shooting towards a central point like a series of magnetic filings. The image is of Esme, standing at the threshold to her parents' bedroom when she was eight years old. She is watching, frightened, as her mother kneels in front of the bed and clutches at her hair, sobbing as she grabs fistfuls and pulls at it until small piles of ash-blonde litter the sheepskin rug beneath her knees.

'Mummy?' she says, this child version of herself.

Her mother stops crying, the effort of it causing her to hiccough. She turns her ravaged face towards Esme and tries to smile, her lips rubbed raw of lipstick, her cheeks veined with black, and it is this – the strangeness of her half-tragic, half-comic face, the disarray of her make-up – that affects her daughter most of all, that will stick with Esme for years.

Her memories of her father are more indistinct. A strong arm, lifting her onto his shoulders. A loud expressive laugh. Terror mingled with affection in his presence. A knowledge, even at that young age, that her father was good-looking, a charmer, a man others liked to be around.

At the time of his death, her brother Robbie was too young to know what had happened. For a few years after the police knocked on their door one drizzle-dark November night, interrupting *Jim'll Fix It*, Robbie kept asking her what their father was like and she would try to answer as truthfully as she could.

'He was fun,' she said. 'He told good stories. He made Mummy laugh.'

But, looking back, Esme is not sure, any more, how much of what she told Robbie was her true recollection and how much of what she remembers was a story she told herself from faded photographs, a desire to make the best bits real by saying them out loud. She doesn't know. She doesn't know if it matters.

Esme smiles brightly, breaks off a lump of bread from the warm roll on her side-plate and butters it, re-positioning the knife in a precise, straight line. She taps the knife handle three times with her index finger. The number three, she has convinced herself, has mysterious talismanic qualities that keep her safe.

Howard has finished his soup. Rupert coughs drily and conversation is temporarily suspended. In the uncomfortable semibreve of silence that follows, it is Howard who speaks first.

'You've read about my daughter, I suppose?'

Esme nods. She glances anxiously at Rupert who had made it abundantly clear on the phone that she was 'on no account

66

whatsoever' to mention Ada Pink's disappearance over lunch. But of course, she has read the press cuttings, has seen the smudged newsprint image of Ada Pink's features staring out at her from bygone front pages: the same passport photo used again and again, depicting an unsmiling, frail-looking girl with hollow cheeks, a prominent brow and hair scraped back like a ballerina.

Esme had been in her first year at university when Ada Pink disappeared and the story of her vanishing had seemed little more than a backdrop to diluted Red Bull cocktails and pyjama-themed pub crawls. But now, meeting Ada Pink's father, she is struck by the force of his unhappiness. After all these years, she thinks, his devastation is fresh as new snow.

She fiddles with the corner of her napkin.

'She'd be about your age by now,' he carries on. 'Ada. That was her name.' A pause. 'Or is. I'm never sure what tense to talk in.'

He gives a bark of bitter laughter, shattering the strange atmosphere that has settled around the table. She wonders whether to say something about how sorry she is but, at the same time, doesn't want to sound bogus. She has, after all, only just met him. She's a journalist, not a friend.

'Well, I suggest—' Rupert starts, but Howard interrupts him. His gaze is glittery, unfocused; his smile twisted.

'Let's order some plonk, shall we, Esme?' he says, picking up the heavy bound wine list. 'Toast absent friends.'

She nods her assent, surprised, all at once, to find she has the beginning of tears in her eyes.

Over a starter of artfully arranged radishes and crisp lettuce leaves that costs more than anyone could reasonably have antici-pated, an equilibrium of sorts is established. Howard, warmed up by a full-bodied Pauillac (he had been politely conscious of the fact that the *Tribune* was paying), allows himself to relax. He regales Esme with riotous stories about famous people he has met, including the time he hosted Elizabeth Taylor on his private yacht and she lost one of her diamonds in the shower.

She glances across the table at Rupert, wondering if they are teasing her for sport, but he appears perfectly relaxed. He catches her looking and grins wolfishly, as if implying he's heard every one of these anecdotes a thousand times before. Rupert really is very handsome, albeit in a rather boring way: the male equivalent of a neatly ironed shirt. But there's something about him she can't quite ignore, as if his very blandness poses a challenge. She wonders what he's like in bed. Filthy, she imagines. Probably has a thing about spanking.

At the end of the meal, they order coffee. It comes in pretty china cups. Sir Howard picks out three lumpen brown sugar cubes with his fingers and drops them in his coffee, causing a small splash of liquid onto the tablecloth.

'Well, Esme, I don't mind saying that I wasn't looking forward to this lunch. Thought Rupert was a bloody idiot for setting it up.'

Esme stirs in her milk. She has already realised Sir Howard is the kind of man who doesn't want to be interrupted in full flow.

'But I'm glad to have met you, sweetheart.'

She swallows her indignation. With men like Sir Howard, you just had to go with it. That was how you got the best contacts. Journalism taught you all sexism was relative.

He leans over and pats her hand paternally.

'We should be going,' Rupert says. 'We're already late for our 2.30.'

'Sure, sure,' Howard replies, pushing back his chair. 'Rupe, can you sort out a Fash Attack discount card for this young lady?'

'Oh, really, there's no need,' Esme says, without meaning it.

'Nonsense. You've given me a couple of hours' diversion in the midst of an otherwise painful day of shareholder meetings and buying concerns,' he says jovially. 'It's the least I can do. Besides, it's all part of bolstering our relations with the press.' He wags his finger at her. 'No more unflattering photos, eh? Are we agreed?'

'Agreed.'

He buttons up his jacket, which sits tightly over his waistband, then leans in to kiss her on both cheeks.

'I'm sorry about your dad,' he murmurs softly into her ear and she wonders at first if she has heard him correctly.

'I'm . . .' Esme grapples for the right words. 'Sorry about your daughter . . .' she says stupidly. Rupert glares at her from behind his boss's shoulder.

Howard smiles. 'I know,' he says sadly. 'I know.'

The two of them walk out of the dining room. Esme sits back at the table and signals for the bill. She is perturbed, without knowing why. Something about Howard Pink has affected her. Perhaps it was the obvious resonance of a father who'd lost his daughter meeting a daughter who'd lost her father. But it was more than that too. He seemed, in spite of all the wealth he'd accumulated, in spite of the anecdotes about yachts and diamonds, to be strangely unsure of himself; to be anxious, all the time, that someone would scrape back the veneer of success and see him for who he really was.

Esme could relate to that. Most journalists – and she was no exception – did what they did to prove somebody wrong, to validate their own worth by seeing their name in the paper. She wonders if she could persuade Sir Howard to talk to her. He had never given an interview about his daughter's disappearance but perhaps now enough time had passed. Perhaps he'd just been waiting for the right person.

She can see it now: a sit-down interview across a double-page spread. Millionaire clothing retailer speaks for the first time about his daughter's disappearance. Headline: 'Sir Howard's Private Torment – "Why I can never let go."' There would be a write-off on the front page. Nominations for the Press Awards. Dave would be impressed. He'd take her out for a drink to celebrate. He'd look at her tenderly, push a lock of hair behind her ear and tell her he loved her and was leaving his wife . . .

'Everything was to your liking?' The waiter's persistent solicitousness interrupts her reverie.

'Yes, thanks,' says Esme, embarrassed. She punches the four digits of her pin into the card machine with unusual force and hands it back to him. Get a grip, she tells herself. Having a crush on the news editor is such a cliché. The waiter returns with her receipt, folded into a charcoal-coloured card. She slips it into her wallet, along with a thick batch of other paperwork denoting taxi rides taken and train tickets bought in the name of work. She is overdue filing her expenses, put off doing so by the thought of the laborious new computer system they've brought in back at the office. Sanjay is convinced they've only done it to make it so difficult that no one bothers.

A sluggish pall descends on her as she walks out of the restaurant, back through the lobby to the revolving doors and past the top-hatted attendants on the steps outside. Hotels are such peculiar places, she thinks, full of people not feeling entirely comfortable, either because they're passing through on business and don't want to be there or because they are spending a small fortune on 'getting away from it all' and are worried about not appreciating everything enough. She is relieved, when she gets outside, to breathe in the fresh air again, to see the tall, budded trees of Hyde Park.

On her way back to the office, she tries not to think of her father or the lost Ada Pink, staring out at her with yearning eyes. Instead, Esme takes out her BlackBerry and updates her Twitter feed. 'Stuffed after lunch at Alain Ducasse,' she types with a breeziness she does not feel. 'Feet killing me!'

Carol

CAROL IS LYING ON a massage table having her shoulders pummelled by a nice girl called Stacey. The problem is she has forgotten how to relax. She used to love being pampered. Once a year, for her birthday, her daughter Vanessa would arrange a spa day in a hotel in the New Forest and the two of them would get the train down from Clapham Junction, wheeling their overnight suitcases and anticipating the fluffy robes, a haze of essential oils and glasses of iced water delicately flavoured with cucumber slices.

Whoever came up with the idea of putting cucumber in jugs of water, Carol always wondered. Or lemon, for that matter. Because you wouldn't dream of flavouring water with banana slivers, would you? Or carrot sticks. But somehow lemon and cucumber worked.

The massage had been Vanessa's idea.

'Do you good, Mum,' she said on the phone. 'You deserve some R&R.'

Carol was sitting in the front room, staring at her slippers. She hadn't got dressed yet, even though it was past ten in the morning.

'R&R? What's that when it's at home?'

There had been a suppressed exhalation on the other end of the line.

'Rest and relaxation, Mum.'

'Oh. Right.'

But since Derek died, Carol has found it almost impossible to stop thinking. She'll be drinking a cup of tea in front of *Bargain Hunt* and she'll notice that all her muscles are tightly wound, her shoulders up by her ears, and instead of concentrating on the discovery of some valuable ashtray in the attic of an old-age pensioner from Basingstoke, her head will be filled with the image of a coffin and service sheets and dying flowers and she'll realise that she hasn't been relaxing at all. She seems to have lost the knack.

'Relax, Mrs Hetherington,' the therapist says but the more Stacey tells her to relax, the less she feels able to. Carol's face is pressed through the cut-out circle on the massage table, like one of those seaside paintings where you pose for photos by peering out from underneath a frilly bathing cap or a pair of donkey ears. The hole is slightly too small to contain her features and she can feel the edges of the lavender-scented padding digging into her cheeks. She wonders if there will be marks there when she turns over. Her skin has lost its elasticity of late. She can be pottering around the supermarket, picking up things for lunch, and the side of her cheek will still be stippled with red-pink indentations from where the sheet left its mark over an hour earlier.

Stacey folds the towel neatly to one side, uncovering Carol's leg and prompting a spray of goose-bumps to prick up along her calf. Carol is worried that her feet are ticklish and she won't be able to stop twitching when the therapist touches them.

'Relax,' Stacey says. 'Just think of something soothing.'

Carol tries to imagine faraway beaches and gently lapping waves but instead finds her mind wandering. As Stacey's fingers knead against her calf muscles and the herby, sweet scent of the aromatherapy oil floats around the room, she wonders whether the amount you love someone dictates the nature of their death. Whether, if you loved a person – if that person made you happy and you got to enjoy life more because of them – the punishment for this is to make their death as cruel and painful as possible. A cosmic joke, she'd heard someone call it. Like karma, but inverted.

She'd never believed in God. If He existed, Carol thought, He was a right old so-and-so. All those starving children and poor people with AIDS. What kind of person would allow that?

Whereas she's noticed that if someone hasn't been loved at all and has brought nothing but pain and misery to those around them, they seem to slip easily into oblivion at the end of their lives with the minimum of fuss. Because there's no one to mourn them, is there? And Carol is for ever being told – by magazines, by Sunday-morning TV shows, by well-meaning friends who bring her spiritual self-help manuals called things like *The Day After Grief: Finding and Overcoming your Inner Sorrow'* – that there is a sort of dignity in mourning; that by accepting the death of a loved one, you accept your own mortality and come to a greater understanding of life. That's the theory, anyway.

Load of old claptrap, Carol thinks.

She only poses the question because Connie's husband Geoff has just died peacefully in his sleep of old age and a nastier, more narrow-minded little man you couldn't imagine. Even Connie couldn't wait to be rid of him by the end. And yet for all Geoff's vindictive, ignorant and penny-pinching ways, he had been spared the wretchedness of a terminal illness. No incontinence nappies for him.

'It was a blessing,' Connie said at the funeral. It was also, Carol couldn't help but feel, hugely unfair.

Because Derek . . . well, Derek was the shining love of her life, a man with whom she spent forty-odd years of married content-edness, with whom she never had to explain, only to be, a man who still made her laugh, who could make everything all right just by squeezing her shoulders and calling her 'pet'.

Oh, he had his failings, of course he did. He snored loudly, left teaspoons on the counter, never wanted to go to the cinema because 'it will come out soon on video', but now that he's gone, Carol sees these petty irritations as lovable quirks. His snoring used to keep her awake. Now she finds she can't sleep without it.

Everyone loved Derek: the postman whose name he remembered, the shop assistant at Sainsbury's on Garratt Lane whose grandchildren he would always ask after and the dozens of friends and colleagues he'd got to know in and around Wandsworth through the years. It wasn't just old people either. Their grandson Archie could spend hours building model aircraft with him in the back room.

The two of them were like cuttings from the same plant. She'd catch them sometimes, heads bent over a Spitfire model in the dusky half-light of a weekend evening, and when she asked if they wanted a sandwich, they would look at her in exactly the same way – heads slightly to one side with a quizzical squint of the eyes.

'I'll take that as a no then,' she would say, closing the door behind her, unable to stop herself from smiling.

Even the kids on the council estate opposite would nod at Derek in the street. She never understood how he did it, how he made friends without seeming to try. The day of the funeral, a couple of them came round and rung the bell at Lebanon Gardens while the wake was in full swing. Carol could make out the looming shadow of two hooded figures and had been afraid to open the door at first. She kept the chain on and, peering through the gap, saw two bulky teenagers standing on the front step, wearing bright yellow-and-black trainers and jeans that seemed to be falling off their waists.

'Mrs Hetherington?' one of them said and his voice, when he spoke, was timid. He had chubby cheeks and his right eyebrow had thin stripes sliced through it. They must have been done with a razor, Carol thought.

'Yes,' she said, bracing herself. She honestly believed they were going to mug her. There'd been a gangland murder on the estate last year and she kept expecting to see them pull a knife.

'We wanted to pay our respects,' said the one with the fat

cheeks, the phrase sounding stilted, as though he had been told what words to use.

His friend hung back, face shrouded by a baseball cap pushed low on his forehead. 'Sorry for your loss.' He handed over a beautiful bunch of hyacinths, wrapped tightly in Sellotaped brown paper. In the fleshy part between his thumb and forefinger, there was a small tattooed circle: half black, half white.

'Thank you.' She was so surprised she forgot to ask them in.

She still feels bad about that. She knows Derek would have ushered them in, told them to join everyone in the front room and got them to tell him about their lives. He was like that. No prejudice. Treated everyone the same.

When Derek was diagnosed with prostate cancer, it was the most awful thing that had ever happened to her. They were worried about how Vanessa would take it, of course, and about Archie, about how they would cope, but mostly they were pitched into a feverish, gnawing anxiety about what was going to happen when the two of them were parted. They had grown so used to each other, you see. Never been apart for more than a week.

'Just relax, Mrs Hetherington,' Stacey says again, her voice soft against the rising and swelling of tinkling water and rainforest sounds, piped in from the iPod in the corner of the room. 'You're carrying a lot of tension.'

As if tension could be carried. As if it were a bag of shopping, Carol thinks.

Derek had died in hospital. They hadn't wanted it to end like that and she still can't forgive herself for it. He'd asked to be discharged so that he could come home and die in his own bed and Carol had rushed back to Lebanon Gardens to get the house ready. She'd wasted her time doing silly things: putting flowers in a vase on the chest of drawers upstairs, cleaning the windows so that he'd have an unobstructed view of the tree-tops outside, buying a special tin of Fox's chocolate biscuits even though he was hardly eating by then.

75

Why had she done all that? Why hadn't she realised that the time they had left was so precious that she couldn't afford to waste a single second of it?

Because, by the time she got back to the hospital, Derek had died. The Irish nurse, the nice one with the curly hair and fat arms, had been the one to tell her. And although, of course, she'd been expecting it, had been told again and again that Derek's illness was terminal, that the chances of recovery were nil, that she had to prepare herself for the worst . . . when it happened, she was shocked.

'He's gone,' the nurse said. 'He died half an hour ago.'

Carol's stomach curved in on itself, punched by some invisible hand. The beige-green hospital walls seemed to slide towards her, squeezing the air out of the strip-lit corridor. She tried to walk towards Derek's bed but, instead of the solidity of the linoleum floor that she had been expecting, her foot slipped into nothing and she felt herself spiralling into space. The nurse steadied her, sat her down and told her to take her time but she couldn't rest. She was desperate to see Derek, to hold his hand and tell him she loved him. Tell him she was sorry for not making it in time.

She pushed the nurse away, refusing the offer of sugary tea. She walked hurriedly down the corridor, balancing one hand against the wall to keep herself from falling. She convinced herself that if she got there quickly enough there would be something of him still alive, a hovering sense of Derekness, a lingering warmth in his heart like the coal-hot embers of a night-time fire. If she got there quickly enough, surely his soul would be waiting for her, resting for a while by the hospital bed until she arrived? She would still be able to feel Derek, wouldn't she? Her love was too strong for him just to disappear, wasn't it?

But when she saw him, she had to put a hand over her face to stop herself from crying out. She'd never seen a dead person before, never understood what it meant.

Because the figure in the bed looked like Derek but the essence of him, all those tiny movements that she'd never noticed before – the flicker of a look as she entered a room, the almost indiscernible curl of the lip, the placid sound of his inhalations, the steadiness of his touch as he reached out to take her hand – all of them had stopped, just like that. She realised – for the first time, she properly took it in – that she would never see any of it again.

And outside, birds cheeped, sirens sounded, a wind continued to blow and the world went on as normal without realising what had been lost. The enormity of it.

She stared at him and although she should have been devastated, although the tears should have been running down her cheeks, she caught herself thinking: So this is what a dead body looks like.

It was the shock, of course. It took a while to sink in.

Derek lay on his back, his mouth gaping open to reveal a black, still hole. His eyes were closed, the lids thin and papery. His skin had acquired an unnatural, waxy sheen. Liver spots crept across his naked scalp like lichen on a rock. She wanted to take his hand and yet something stopped her. This strange, stony presence was no longer her husband.

Part of her felt relief. She had been worried about burying the body, sending it into the ground and crushing the frail bones under 6 foot of soil. But she saw now that the physicality of Derek was relatively unimportant. It was what had been cradled within that counted.

'OK, Mrs Hetherington, if I could just ask you to turn over onto your back . . .' The therapist's voice interrupts her thoughts. She shakes the idea of Derek from her mind. It is not good for her to dwell on the past, on what can't be changed. Vanessa has been encouraging her to pick up her hobbies again and ring round a few of her Book Club friends. Her daughter has started staring at her sideways, with a crinkle above her nose and a concerned gaze. It is as if Vanessa is looking after her, whereas it should by rights be the other way round and Carol can't get used to it. She feels patronised and quietly furious when she knows Vanessa is only trying to help.

'It'll do you good, Mum,' has become her regular refrain. It's what Carol used to say when Vanessa was a teenager, lolling about on the settee complaining she was bored, flicking through the TV channels even though it was a blazing sunny day outside.

Whenever she remembered the 1970s, it always seemed to be hotter.

'Why don't you go and play in the park?' Carol would say. 'Do you good.'

She's dreading Archie becoming a sullen, moody adolescent. At twelve, he's just on the cusp of it, but so far he is still the shiny happy boy he has always been. She worries, with Derek gone, that he'll feel the lack of a male role model in his life. Vanessa is a single mother. Carol has never met Archie's father – has never so much as heard mention of his name.

The main thing is that he seems to have settled into his new secondary school. Vanessa showed her Archie's first report the other day and Carol couldn't make head nor tail of it.

'He's got a lot of Cs, hasn't he? That's not like him.'

Vanessa bit her lip. She was impatient by nature, but her mother's slowness always seemed to set her even more on edge than usual. 'It just means he's performing at a competent level. They don't give As and Bs any more.'

'Don't they?'

'No, Mum. It's all numbers now. And a 7 is really good.'

She looked at the report more closely. When she held it, her fingers trembled slightly. She'd noticed the shaking more lately. She steadied her hand. There were 7s all the way down the page. She grunted, satisfied. That was her Archie.

The therapist is smoothing the palms of her hands across Carol's collarbone, sweeping them up all the way to her earlobes and back again. It feels good when she pulls firmly at the base of Carol's neck, easing the muscles gently towards her and then releasing.

'Oh that's lovely,' Carol murmurs.

The therapist laughs lightly.

'Good. Just relax into it.'

She takes a few deep breaths, trying to concentrate on the pleasurable sensation of the massage while at the same time worrying that her inability to relax means she is not enjoying it enough. She wonders if she could set Vanessa up with somebody. Speed-dating, wasn't that meant to be the latest thing? Maybe she should suggest it to her. She didn't want Vanessa to see her as a new project: putting her mother back together again in much the same way as she might renovate one of her flats.

And then, the solution to the problem comes straight into her mind, bubbling up to the surface like a lifebuoy. Alan, she thinks, triumphantly. Her next-door neighbour. He seems nice enough – a bit quiet, but that might just be shyness. Why had she never thought of it before? He'd be good for Vanessa, she is sure of it.

Alan had moved in over a year ago after coming down all the way from Glasgow to make a new life for himself. He'd never been married, he told them when they first met. He was unloading furniture from the back of a rental van at the time. A long-term relationship had just broken up, he explained – even though they hadn't been prying.

'Oh I'm sorry,' Carol said.

He smiled at her, bending his head so that he did not meet her eyes. His cheeks blushed pink.

'Not to worry,' he said, his voice accented with a vague burr that she couldn't place. 'These things happen.'

He had strong forearms, Carol noticed. She liked arms: it was one of her things. Alan's forearms, visible beneath a rolled-up sleeve of a red-and-black lumberjack shirt, were tanned and thick veins ran down from his elbow to surprisingly fine-boned wrists. She discovered later, once she'd got to know him a bit, that he was a keen amateur gardener, which explained the tan and the muscle definition. Derek used to tease her about her crush on 'that fancy-man from next door' but he didn't mind. Within a week of Alan moving in, he was giving their new neighbour hydrangea plant cuttings for his flower beds and unwanted advice on the acidic soil content of SW18.

'You want to watch that, Alan,' he said one morning, leaning across the garden fence. Alan nodded silently, rubbing the back of his neck, not wishing to be rude because he probably knew it all already. Derek shrugged his shoulders and left him to it.

'Not a talker,' he said, on coming back into the house, and that had been that.

How old would Alan be, Carol asks herself as the therapist moves from her neck to her scalp, pressing her fingers down, twisting her hair this way and that so it will probably be an awful mess when she leaves. Mid-forties perhaps? It was so difficult to tell nowadays. He wasn't a looker, that's for sure. His face had a pudgy quality, like an uncooked loaf of bread, and his eyes were on the small side. But then looks don't last, as she was always fond of saying. Vanessa's at the stage in her life where she should be settling for someone reliable and kind.

Yes, that's what she'll do. She'll invite Alan round for a cup of tea, one of the days that Vanessa just happens to be popping in. With this resolution made, Carol feels happier. For the first time since she stripped down to her knickers and lay on the massage table, she starts, cautiously, to relax – just like she's been told.

Beatrice

ON MONDAY MORNING, BEATRICE wakes up with a lovely, leaping sensation in her stomach. It is her day off: twenty-four hours of concentrated freedom without a single bed to make or toilet bowl to clean. She smiles at herself in the bathroom mirror as she slicks her hair back with wax and rubs cocoa butter into her elbows, making them soft. Then she catches herself grinning like an idiot and stops abruptly. Her teachers always said she had a happy nature but it seems silly to smile when there's no one else around.

'Beatrice always looks on the bright side,' one of the nuns had written in a school report. She remembers her father had been pleased by that.

'It's good to accentuate the positives, Beatrice,' he said. He was wearing his fancy suit and tie. 'Life is a big adventure.'

She looked up at him, blinking. She loved her father but was also in awe of him. He was so tall, she thought, that his head almost touched the sky. She was too shy to answer him that day and hid her face in her hands, glimpsing at the retreating shape of him through interlaced fingers. He laughed and walked out of the door, his slim briefcase swinging from one hand. In all of her memories, he is laughing.

He died when she was fifteen of an illness she hadn't known the name of until she was older. And even then she hadn't understood. They said it was sexually transmitted, the thing that made him lose weight until his flesh had sunk into his bones, that scarred his conker-smooth skin with scab-sore marks the texture of sandpaper.

AIDS. An odd label for a disease, she always thinks, when, according to her big, red English dictionary, 'aid' is a synonym for 'help'.

Would her father still have loved her had he lived to know the truth of who she was? When the police discovered her and Susan in bed together, tipped off by a surly-faced villager, was her mother right when she said Beatrice had brought disgrace on the family? Would her father have disowned her too?

She will never have the answers. She likes to think he would have understood but people can surprise you. Even the ones you think you know better than anyone. Even the ones who are meant to love you.

She pours a sachet of Mayfair Rotunda instant coffee into a mug of boiled water for breakfast, then gets dressed in deliberately bright colours. After ten days of black uniform, Beatrice is desperate for a change. She picks out a neon-yellow T-shirt from TK Maxx and jeans that she found in a charity shop. They are a bit too tight, but the T-shirt is long enough to cover the slight flabbiness of her stomach. She zips up a red puffa jacket because she knows, even though it is sunny outside, she will still feel the cold. It is one of the things she fears she will never get used to in this country. That and the dark evenings. When she first arrived in London, at the B&B in Manor Park arranged by the trafficker, it had been winter. She did not know what to think when the sun disappeared at 4 p.m. and the temperature dropped. It was as if God had turned off the lights.

It had taken her a long while to acclimatise to the darkness and the damp. She felt as though every breath she took of London air was soaked through with a moisture that blocked her nose and thickened her throat. And then there had been the fog. Beatrice had read about the city's opaque, settling mists in Dickens, but still her first experience of London fog took her unawares. When it had swept up from the banks of the Thames, rolling through the streets like smoke, she had felt unanchored from her surroundings, cocooned in a strange cotton-white numbness that served only to make her feel more alone. The fog seemed to settle in her chest. She had wheezed for days and when she coughed it sounded as if a small rattling ball had lodged itself in her windpipe.

Beatrice grabs her Primark bag and puts her wallet, the newspaper cutting and her mobile inside. As she leaves, she presses her fingers against the frame of Susan's photo, and checks her fingertips for dust, automatically. Clean as a whistle, she thinks, proud of the colloquial turn of phrase.

Once outside, she walks up the Jamaica Road to a small stretch of shops: a chemist, an internet café, a Halal grocer and a Chinese takeaway. When Beatrice makes extra tips from work, she likes to treat herself to Peking duck pancakes. Just thinking of the sweet-salt taste of the glutinous plum sauce and the cooling slivers of spring onion is enough to make her mouth water. She doesn't have enough money this week. Tonight, it will be her regular meal of white bread smeared with tomato ketchup, accompanied by a few Tesco Value chicken nuggets on the side. She isn't much of a cook and doesn't particularly like the nuggets but she knows it's important to eat protein to keep her strength up. And that's the cheapest way she can do it. She thought she'd miss Ugandan food when she first came here but her taste buds have changed. Or maybe it's just that she doesn't want to be reminded of home, of her mother's matoke and juicy pineapples and the nutty sweetness of a freshly picked banana. Better to have no memories. Better, after everything that happened.

Beatrice pushes the door of the internet café. Manny, a tall, bespectacled Somalian, is standing behind the counter, tinkering with a screwdriver and a laptop. He glances up when he hears the door.

'Hey, Beatrice! How are you doing, my friend?'

He leans across the counter and does his special handshake: bent fingers, knuckle pressed against knuckle, a sweep of palm. His hand is dry. Beatrice smiles. Manny was the first friend she made in Bermondsey and has been a fund of useful information about housing benefits, community grant applications and government welfare schemes over the years. He has an extraordinary aptitude for making sense of complicated things, whether it be a computer chipboard or an eight-page form from the council, needing to be filled out in block capitals. It was Manny who had given her a mobile phone, handing it over one day with a sheepish smile.

'I can't take this, Manny . . .' Beatrice had said.

'Sure you can, sister.'

'Where did you get it?'

Manny had ignored her and she knew, without him having to say anything more, that she was not to ask too many questions. In the end, she'd accepted the gift gratefully. One day, she knew, Manny would call in the favour. She was ready for it.

'I'm good, Manny, good. How's business?'

'Oh you know what they say: Can't complain. Mustn't grumble.' Manny throws his head back and roars with laughter, his mouth wide open so that she can see the startlingly red tip of his tongue. 'How's the hotel?' he asks.

Beatrice shrugs.

'Hey, listen. Do you mind if I use a computer?'

'Be my guest,' Manny says, gesturing towards the nearest terminal. 'Number 4. Anything I can help you with?'

'No. Thanks, Manny.'

He stares at her lazily. His pupils are dilated and his breath smells of marijuana smoke. She always wonders how much of Manny's laid-back demeanour is the result of generous self-medication. Sometimes, on her way to a late shift, she'll see Manny sitting on the low wall just outside the tube station, brazenly smoking an enormous spliff without any concern that he might be seen or arrested. He gathers waifs and strays around him, greeting them all with the same approachable smile, and if you didn't know him, you'd think he was the nicest, softest person you'd ever seen. But she's seen Manny turn, his temper gleaming and rapid as a flick-knife. You didn't want to get on the wrong side of him. So far, Beatrice had managed not to.

For some reason, Manny had liked her from the start. She'd walked into his internet café one day on the edge of tears because she'd just heard her refugee status was up for review and needed to do some research but was struggling to understand the Home Office's impenetrable bureaucratic language.

'Why are you so sad?' he'd asked, as if it were the most natural question in the world. And because it was the first time in months that a stranger had asked her how she was, the whole story had tumbled out of her.

Almost the whole story.

She hasn't told Manny she is a gay. She still hasn't been able to find the words. Suppression does that to a person. Besides, she doesn't kid herself: she knows that, if Manny is attracted to her, he will be more willing to do things for her. She is caught, internally, between thinking this is a dishonourable way to behave and believing, bitterly, that it is the least the world owes her. If she is to be forced to live a lie about her sexuality, Beatrice reasons, then at least she will live it to her own advantage.

None of this is Manny's fault, of course. But he is a man. An African man. She has heard him talk about women. Sometimes, when she is in the internet café, the electronic bell will ring and it will be one of Manny's many friends. They will saunter up to the counter, these friends, with their sleazy smiles and lazy gaits, with their hair close-cut to their scalps, their muscles slicked with the sweat of the night before. They look like young boys playing dress-up in jeans that are too big for them, slung low on their waist with their underpants on display for anyone to see.

These friends do not notice Beatrice sitting there, like a small, unimportant shadow of someone who used to be. Nor do they acknowledge the sullen, tattooed girl in the corner, tip-tapping on the keyboard with gel-tip nails to update her Facebook page. They do not notice the woman in a hijab, silently typing up her CV. They do not register any woman who has not expressly packaged herself to attract male attention. Instead, these friends walk straight up to Manny who stands there, like a king awaiting his courtiers, his face emerging from behind the refrigerated drinks shelves that are always optimistically stocked with faded cartons of exotic fruit juice: lychee, mango, papaya.

Yes, Beatrice has heard Manny talk about women: she has heard his dirty laughs and his whispered jokes and the slap of the palm of his hand in a congratulatory high-five. She knows men like Manny, who need sex and power like most people need bread and water. Even his name is a distillation of masculinity. She wonders, occasionally, whether Manny is a nickname, given to him by an admiring coterie of young men in acknowledgement of his sexual prowess. Or perhaps it genuinely was the name his parents gave him and the way he turned out was a fateful coincidence. 'Nominative determinism', they called it. She'd heard a discussion about it on the breakfast radio after a man called Mr Diamond had been forced to step down from his position as head of a failing bank, only to be replaced by a colleague called Mr Rich. She smiles at the thought of this.

'Now that's what I like to see!' Manny reaches into the refrigerated shelves and hands Beatrice a carton of lychee juice. 'A lovely smile on a beautiful woman.'

He winks. She rolls her eyes, accepts the juice and takes her seat at the computer.

'Hey, Beatrice, one day you'll realise we're meant to be together.'

'Yes, Manny. And one day pigs will take to the sky with wings.'

He guffaws then disappears into a back room to turn up the radio. A thumping reggae beat rings out just as Manny re-emerges and starts to dance, swaying his hips suggestively, eyes half-closed as he clasps an imaginary partner to him. An unlit joint is tucked behind his ear. She can't help but laugh. Yet she tilts the screen ever so slightly away from the counter so Manny can't see what she's doing. There are elements of her life that Beatrice knows it would be wiser to keep private. Howard Pink, for instance. That was something she wanted to do on her own.

She logs on to the computer, double-clicking on the internet icon. She types 'Sir Howard Pink' into the Google search bar. Rapidly and methodically, she clicks through the relevant documents, assimilating information. It feels good to be using her brain again. She finds out that Sir Howard had started in business at the age of fifteen, selling clothes from a market stall. At twenty-one, he'd bought his first shop. By thirty, he was a millionaire. By thirty-five, after an aggressive corporate takeover, he had bought out the Paradiso Group of clothing shops. He was routinely in the top fifty of the *Sunday Times* Rich List, with an estimated fortune of £3.3 billion. He has a reputation for throwing lavish theme parties, which turns up a number of unexpected images: Sir Howard in an Hawaiian shirt and grass skirt on his fiftieth birthday, celebrated on a private Greek island with six hundred of his closest friends (and a performance by Stevie Wonder); Sir Howard laughing riotously while dressed up as a medieval pope; Sir Howard sporting a giant sombrero accompanied by an unsmiling blonde woman in a nurse's outfit. Then there was all the stuff about his daughter, Ada, who had gone missing at the age of nineteen in mysterious circumstances. Beatrice skims over these stories. They aren't what she needs to focus on. Everyone has sadness in their lives. It does not elicit her sympathy.

After twenty minutes or so, she has all the information she needs, including an email address for the chief executive's office at Paradiso. She opens up a new Microsoft Word file. The screen fills with a blank white page, like a fresh sheet pulled tight on a hotel bed.

'Dear Sir Howard,' she writes in Arial 12-point. The animated paperclip pops up in the corner of the screen. 'You look like you're writing a letter,' a speech bubble says. 'Would you like some help?' Beatrice scowls. No, she thinks, I don't need anyone's help. Not any more. This, I'm doing for me. She takes a deep breath, then types: 'You won't remember me but we met in Room 423 of the Hotel Rotunda in Mayfair.'

Howard

H E'S NEVER SEEN THE point of opera, to be honest. All that faffing about on stage, those fat people singing declarations of love in a foreign language while everyone in the audience sits puffed up with their own pretension, fanning themselves with programmes that cost more than an hour's wage for the Polish babysitter back in SW3. No, if he had a choice, he'd rather go to a musical. A couple of hours of Andrew Lloyd Webber with an ice cream in the interval and he's happy as a clam. As he reminded Claudia on the way to the Royal Opera House this evening: it's a fraction of the cost for essentially the same form of entertainment.

'No, Howie,' she'd said, inspecting a fleck of dirt caught in the edge of a long acrylic nail. 'No, it's not.'

'It's all singing, isn't it?' He knew, of course, that he was being impossible, that he didn't fully believe what he was saying. But the temptation to wind Claudia up by playing the ill-educated buffoon was irresistible. He caught Jocelyn eyeing him in the rear-view mirror with a carefully neutral expression. Sometimes – not very often, admittedly – Howard wondered what his driver thought of it all. Jocelyn was a miner's son from the Welsh Valleys. He would probably be horrified to learn they had spent the best part of £600 on a couple of tickets to the Royal Opera House when neither of them really cared about the art form. Because although Claudia pretended to read the programme notes, she wasn't interested in the performance. The most important thing for her was to be seen and, preferably, photo-graphed by one of the Society magazines. He could already imagine the caption: 'On Monday, Lady Claudia Pink enjoyed a night at the opera. She was dressed in a discreet black-lace sheath dress by blah blah blah, accessorised with diamond drop earrings by blah blah blah, and accompanied by her husband, self-made millionaire Sir Howard Pink, CEO of the Paradiso Group.'

Self-made, my arse, Howard thinks.

Jocelyn indicates left into a side-lane, just off Bow Street and pulls up in a disabled parking bay.

'What is it we're seeing tonight anyway?' Howard asks.

'*La Bohème*, dear,' Claudia replies, the 'dear' dropping down his back like ice.

'What's the story?'

'Penniless writer falls in love with charming flower girl. They split up. Get back together. Flower girl dies of tuberculosis. Or consumption. Are they the same thing? I never know.'

Claudia takes out her compact to powder her nose, then clicks it back into place, slips it into a sequinned clutch bag and waits for Jocelyn to open the door without glancing at her husband.

'Sounds a right laugh,' Howard says, getting out and stepping directly into a shallow puddle which leaves a faint tidemark on the toe of his polished black shoes. He walks round and proffers his arm to Claudia. As they move along the pavement, he hears the soft silky friction of her stockings and is aroused in spite of himself. He gives her a friendly squeeze on the hand. She smiles at him, briefly, then allows the smile to slide from her face so quickly it leaves no mark on her features. He is reminded of his mother, wiping the kitchen table clear with a dishcloth, catching the crumbs in one cupped hand.

They are ushered up two flights of stairs and directed along the red-carpeted corridor towards the Royal Box. Howard likes to sit here despite the fact that the view is obscured. He gets off on the thought that he is sitting in the same place as the Queen, even though the gilded chair with rococo swirls where Her

Majesty actually takes her seat for a performance remains roped off in the corner.

You can always get close, Howard thinks as a member of staff takes his coat and gives him a glass of champagne in one swift motion, but never close enough.

He and Claudia have invited three business associates and their partners to join them this evening. It's a good way, he finds, of getting people on-side. A night at the opera still carries a certain *je ne sais quoi*, especially for the Yanks.

'What does that mean anyway, "*je ne sais quoi*"?' he had asked Claudia, way back when they first met. They were sitting in her apartment overlooking Battersea Park, all thick white carpets and damask Laura Ashley curtains. Claudia was snuggled up against him on the sofa, swathed in a cashmere cardigan. Silver-framed photographs of her children from her first marriage lined the faux art deco mantelpiece.

'I don't know what,' she said.

'Oh, I thought you spoke a bit of French.'

She laughed. 'No, that's what it means: I don't know what.'

He'd been amused by the exchange. Then Claudia had got that naughty look in her eye. She undid the zip on his trousers, knelt down in front of him and gave him the most fantastic blowjob. He looked down on her highlighted blonde hair, feeling his penis grow larger in her wet, tight mouth, and he thought he'd finally met a woman as desperate to make it as he was. And although he'd known, deep down, she wouldn't make him happy, Howard had ignored his dissenting internal voice and gone and done it anyway. Divorced Penny. Married Claudia. Told himself he didn't want softness in his life, not any more. He wanted strength and brittleness and a bottle-blonde who gave him head whenever he asked for it (and sometimes when he didn't, although those occasions had been less frequent of late). Back then, he had wanted never to have to think about the real, painful, deep kind of love ever again.

'Bradley, great to see you,' Howard says, shaking the hand of

91

Bradley Minchin, the American businessman who had made his fortune by setting up a chain of organic groceries across the Midwest. 'So glad you could come.'

'Wouldn't have missed it,' Bradley says, flashing teeth so white they might have been Tippexed.

'You know my wife—' Claudia shimmies up, extending a tanned, toned arm. Bradley takes her hand and kisses it with a flourish.

'You get younger each time I see you,' he says. Claudia giggles becomingly. If only you knew, Howard thinks, just how much that varnish of youth was costing him each month. Still, on nights like this there was no doubt that she was in her element. She carries out her end of the bargain, that's for sure.

They walk across a thin strip of corridor to the private dining room where a table has already been laid for dinner. The plan was to have the starter before the opera began at 7.30 p.m., then to eat a subsequent course at each interval. The one good thing about opera being so bloody long, thinks Howard, is that at least you got a chance to eat and drink properly.

The waiters bring out the starter on oblong plates bearing miniature Scotch eggs and three artfully arranged asparagus spears. When Howard cuts into the egg, yolk trickles out onto the white china. He grunts, satisfied.

'So, Howard.' Bradley leans into him, as though about to reveal some juicy personal secret. 'How's tricks?'

'Good, thanks, yeah. Bit of trouble earlier this year with the shareholders and the remuneration packages, that kind of thing, but it's mostly blown over. To be expected.'

Bradley arches his eyebrow.

'Word is the UK government wants to tax the shit out of successful capitalists.'

'Well when I spoke to David the other day—' Howard says, casually dropping the first name of the Prime Minister into the conversation and watching the studied casualness with which Bradley disguises the fact he is impressed. 'He assured me that his

92

party was very much in favour of wealth creation. He's well aware that without people like me contributing over the odds through our taxes there'd be no way of even beginning to tackle the deficit. None at all.'

In fact, his intimate tête-à-tête with the Prime Minister had taken place over six months previously and had consisted of a few polite words exchanged over canapés at a reception in Number 10, but he wasn't about to let on. It did no harm to remind those who needed reminding of his status.

'Wow,' Bradley replies, covering the mouth of his wine glass as the waiter proffers a bottle of Puligny-Montrachet. 'I'm impressed you have the Prime Minister's ear.'

Howard lets the thought lie, silent, between them. He is already bored and glances across the table to get Claudia's attention. She is throwing her head back, laughing, and the soft, freckled indentation of her neck glints in the light. Looking at the softness of her throat, he thinks how easy it would be to slit it.

He motions to the waiter to refill his glass and drinks more swiftly than he should. In a few minutes, the lights start to dim and the assembled crowd is ushered through to the Royal Box for the performance. There is a heady waft of Coco Mademoiselle and he realises Claudia is by his side. She taps his elbow and strains upwards to whisper in his ear.

'Remember to turn your phone off, Howie. I know what you're like.'

'Already done it,' he fibs, then surreptitiously fumbles inside his jacket pocket and switches his BlackBerry to 'silent'.

He takes his seat in the front row of the box, edging forwards over the balcony to look at the crowds, squinting to see if he recognises anyone. Claudia places herself bolt upright on her seat, fixing her face with a vague smile. He catches her out of the corner of his eye as the curtain goes up and he wonders, not for the first time, what on earth she might be thinking.

The first act passes. There are the inevitable soprano trills and rumbling bass notes, all stitched together pleasantly enough by the swellings of the orchestra. An inventive set designer had transposed the action from a garret in nineteenth-century Paris to a 1950s loft apartment in Manhattan, complete with low-slung Danish side cabinets and Martini glasses. The female singers were trussed up tightly in the kind of dresses his mother used to wear: nipped in at the waist, full-skirted, an elegant neckline.

They were all so fat though, weren't they? Why are opera singers so large, he finds himself wondering? Was it something to do with having to accommodate the extra lung capacity? Or was it a convention that had set in, so that the profession of opera singer attracted people with good voices who also happened to like their food? Whereas pop music tended to suck up all the chisel-jawed men and neurotic anorexics.

Anorexia. Terrible disease. He'd previously always been minded to dismiss it as a psychosomatic self-indulgence. But that was before Ada.

He finds his thoughts hovering, dangerously, over an image of Ada, her hip bones jutting out, her ribcage pressing through skin as translucent as airmail paper. She had been sixteen and studying for her GCSEs when the teachers at her boarding school had noticed she wasn't eating. They'd called Howard and Penny in 'for a chat' and had asked them both whether there were any tensions at home they should know about – as if it were any of their bloody business.

The headmistress – a colourless woman called Miss Dunn, dressed in a tweedy two-piece, her hair set in dull grey curls – had sat them in her office and talked at them for the best part of twenty minutes.

'We find that a lot of girls tend towards eating disorders when they're seeking to re-establish control over some area of their life,' she had said. The expression on her face tried to be sympathetic but stopped just short of being successful. 'Sometimes this can be because they're falling behind in their studies. Or a friendship group has splintered. Or' – she lowered her voice with

94

meticulous understanding – 'it can be because her parents are going through some difficulties. Separation, for instance. The prospect of divorce. Adolescent girls are terribly sensitive. They pick up on the smallest things.'

Howard had been dumbstruck by the cheek of the woman. He hadn't trusted himself to speak. It was Penny who had stepped in to salvage the situation.

'No, Miss Dunn, there's nothing like that going on,' she said in a small, calm voice. 'Howard and I are very happily married and we love Ada dearly.'

Looking at his wife then, with her upturned nose, her pink cheeks and tiny hands – all of her so neat and precise like a matchbox doll – he had felt a wash of love for her so acute that it stopped the breath in his throat.

'I should think, if Ada is unhappy,' Penny continued, 'it's because she doesn't like this school.'

The headmistress fidgeted with a string of pearls at her neck. Penny stared directly at her, her hands clasped on her lap, holding tightly on to the strap of her leather handbag. 'And having spent half an hour in your company, Miss Dunn, I can't say I blame her.' She said it just like that, in the same small voice, as though she'd been pointing out a loose thread on the teacher's cardigan.

Then Penny stood up, swept down her skirt and held out her hand until Howard took it in his. They left the room together without another word.

They'd taken Ada out the same day and found her a place in a local private school. He remembers looking at her in the back of the car as Jocelyn drove them back to London. Her dark eyes had acquired a wariness that wasn't there before. She jumped at noises like an animal twitching at the crackling of twigs. Her face was sallow and the hair on her arms had grown thicker. The maroon school uniform hung loosely on her bones. Her socks gathered around her ankles like discarded snakeskins and he could see a blue twist of vein pulsing at her wrist.

He couldn't bear to touch her. She seemed shrunken, her sense of self lessened by the physical loss of flesh. But at the same time, she was frighteningly alive. There was something about her, some vital energy that pressed to the surface of her skeletal appearance, as though her rejection of the primal need to eat had left her stripped back, blessed with a total purity of thought, an ability to see through everything for what it was. The way she looked at him . . . it was like he had no secrets left. He was reminded of those stories of religious fanatics who fasted for days on end, believing it was only through divesting the body of its bestial urges that one could attain spiritual enlightenment.

Physically, she was at her most vulnerable and childlike. But her eyes . . . her eyes were so old. They were his mother's eyes.

When they got her home, Penny had lifted her onto the scales and she weighed a fraction over six stone. Standing at the bathroom door, still unable to talk, Howard flinched. It had required such self-control to get to that state and he was horrified, but one of the most disturbing aspects of it all was that there was a sliver of recognition within him. He couldn't help but admire the mental strength it displayed. The tenacity of it.

Howard tries to concentrate on the opera and focuses on the English subtitles, scrolling across the miniature screen in front of him. A warbling woman on stage is singing about a restaurant bill.

He leans across to Claudia and whispers in her ear.

'Not much of a story, is it?'

He can feel her roll her eyes even though it is too dark to see the detail of her face.

'That's not the point, Howie. It's the music. The music's so beautiful.'

He sighs, more loudly than he'd intended, and tries to make out the time on his watch. For the rest of the act, he thinks about the latest balance sheets. The Paradiso Group was doing well, in spite of the economic crisis. He's noticed that women keep buying clothes, even when money is tight. They want to look their best, even if everything is unravelling behind closed doors. It's a lesson he learned on Petticoat Lane: when Mrs Foster's husband was sent down for armed robbery and she had barely a penny left to scrape together, she would come to the stall every Friday and buy herself something – anything, really, it didn't matter how small. One week, it was a scarf. The next, a hairpin. The routine of it was important to her. The face-saving.

And he's made sure that Fash Attack, his flagship chain of stores, has a good price point: cheap enough for students to shop there but not so cheap that they were being accused of promoting sweat-shop labour and disposable fashion by the granola-munching, sandal-wearing brigade.

Christ, what a bunch of tossers. They'd march in the street, lob bricks through his windows, accuse him of being a greedy capitalist bastard without ever having the subtlety of mind to realise he was creating jobs and paying a ridiculous amount of tax just so they could go on claiming benefits and sending their children to state-subsidised schools and hospitals. He's sick of the lot of them.

Oxfam approached him last year with a proposal for an 'ethical' jewellery range. Flattened Coke-bottle tops, strung together with beads and brass chains by African villagers – that kind of thing. They'd got some model to lend her name to the whole ghastly enterprise. She'd come into his office wearing a floaty white kaftan and had spoken to him about the need 'to give something back'.

'I give plenty back already, sweetheart,' he'd said.

She gazed at him with vacantly pretty eyes. 'But if you could see these women, if you could see what it means to them to be making these pieces—' That's what she called the sorry-looking bracelets and necklaces – 'pieces', like they were art or something.

'Listen, love. I know you're trying your best. I know your publicist has probably told you this is a great thing to be doing, given you're knocking on a bit and all the M & S campaigns have gone to Myleene Klass and Twiggy . . .'

She smiled.

'But I'm afraid I'm not interested. I already give money to charity. My conscience is clear.'

She was so surprised by his bluntness that she kept smiling at him as he was speaking. At the end of their meeting, she'd even leaned across and given him a peck on the cheek. She smelled gorgeous: sea-salt mixed in with a musky hint of incense. The model had wafted back out onto the street, trailed by half a dozen hipsterish types in trendy spectacles and rolled-up chinos. He'd never heard from her again.

All around him, there is applause. Bradley is clapping noisily and shaking his head, seemingly incredulous at the brilliant operatic performance he's just witnessed. That's the thing with Americans, Howard thinks. They always try a bit too hard. It's the newness of their country. They're overcompensating.

The group rises as one and goes back through to the dining room where the waiters are already standing with the main course. Howard glances at the plates, covered with edible purple flowers and thinly shaved slices of beetroot. His stomach turns. What he wouldn't give for a bowl of chicken soup.

He fishes out his phone from his jacket pocket and glances at the screen, not expecting anyone to have called him. There are five missed calls, all from the same number. Rupert. He checks his email. There is one from Rupert, flagged up by a vivid red exclamation mark and the word 'Urgent'.

'Howard – call me asap,' it reads.

Claudia is standing next to him, her hand on his arm. He thinks she has a quizzical expression on her face although her skin is as immobile as a factory-farmed chicken breast, all swollen with water and hormones.

'I just have to make a call.'

He walks out into the corridor before she has a chance to protest. He feels a thudding panic rising up in his gullet. When he scrolls through to get to Rupert's numbers, the pads of his fingers are coated with a light sheen of sweat. Why is he so tense?

He knows of course. It is always for the same reason: fear of being found out. Fear that someone is going to tap him on the shoulder and say, 'You don't really belong here, do you?' and send him back to Stepney.

The phone rings, once, twice. Before it rings a third time, Rupert picks up.

'Howard,' he says. 'We've got a problem.'

'What is it?'

'Does the name Beatrice Kizza mean anything to you?'

'No.'

'She works as a chambermaid in the Mayfair Rotunda.'

He casts his mind back to the night he'd spent at the hotel. The room. The bath. The curtains drawn. The chambermaid.

'She's claiming you sexually assaulted her.'

His spine tingles. A weight drops onto his chest. His tie feels too tight. A dissonant note sounds from the orchestra pit and at the same time his mind jangles in a minor chord.

'Christ.'

Esme

DOORSTEPS.

In her previous, non-journalistic life, she'd innocently assumed they were inanimate objects. She'd never realised 'doorstep' was also a verb. She hadn't ever done one before starting at the *Tribune*. There wasn't much call for them on *Trucking Today*.

Esme had first read about doorsteps in the second-hand journalism manual she'd bought off Amazon when she got the Hunter Media traineeship. The manual was written by someone called Geoffrey Beechcroft and had a grey-green cover with the title picked out in white italics: *A Guide to Newspaper Journalism*. It had been published in 1985, which didn't bode particularly well for its accuracy in the modern age and, when she'd Googled the author's name, it turned out he'd never actually been a newspaper journalist – or at least, not on any publication she could find. His Wikipedia entry, written in suspiciously self-congratulatory language, described him as 'an auteur and academic, with a particular interest in cultural interconnectedness'. Whatever that was.

The previous owner of Beechcroft's *Guide* had clearly used it a lot: the pages were dog-eared and heavily annotated and there was a strange stickiness on some of the pages, as though something had been spilt on the book and forgotten about. Or worse.

In the weeks leading up to her first day at the *Tribune,* she'd pored over Beechcroft with the feverish conscientiousness of an eager new student. She remembers turning down the corner of the page on doorstepping, to remind herself of what it meant. It had come in useful over the last eighteen months. In fact, she had read Mr Beechcroft's analysis so many times, she could recite the definition by heart:

"'Doorsteps are events where journalists make calls on people at their homes, businesses or leisure activities that have not been previously agreed with the individual. These calls are usually made with the intention of asking questions or getting a reaction to an event or development. Doorsteps can be hostile and confrontational but are also simply unexpected by the individual with no negative effects.'"

That just about covers it. Apart from mentioning the fact that they're a bloody nuisance.

There are some journalists who actively enjoy them, who think that any excuse to get out of the office is worth it, no matter what they have to do in exchange for a paltry few hours of fresh air. Sanjay is one of these. His job as health editor means that, these days, he spends most of his time chained to his Mac, skim-reading the latest reports from the *British Medical Journal* in the hope of landing a scoop about calcium pills increasing the risk of heart attacks. If Sanjay gets sent on a doorstep (an increasingly rare occurrence, owing to his supposed seniority), he genuinely leaps at the chance – grabbing his jacket from the back of his chair with the gleeful expression of a toddler who has been allowed out of his playpen. Most of the time, Sanjay will come up with a convincing excuse as to why he had to stay out for the whole day. He'll ring up the newsroom and say that no one is in but the neighbours have told him they'll be back soon.

'I think it's worth sticking around, Dave,' Sanjay will say. 'I'm happy to do it.'

And Dave inevitably says yes, knowing full well that Sanjay will be scouting out a suitable nearby restaurant for a spot of lunch as soon as he hangs up, saving up the receipt to claim back on expenses once a seemly interval has elapsed.

Then there are those who take pride in being good at them, who see the doorstep as some hallowed rite of passage into real journalism. These hacks recount their door-knocks like battle-wearied Spitfire pilots might recall a succession of shot-down Nazis. Cathy, one of the longest-serving members of the *Tribune* newsroom, is one of these. A few weeks ago, Esme had been cornered by Cathy on a Saturday night in the pub after the last pages had been sent.

'The thing is—' Cathy slurred, filling up an enormous wine glass with another slosh of the House Sauvignon. 'People want to talk. I should know that better than anyone . . .'

She had gone on to regale Esme with a run-down of all the many exclusive, award-winning interviews she'd snagged for the paper simply by turning up on a stranger's doorstep with a note-pad, a killer instinct for a story and an appropriately earnest expression on her face.

The grief-stricken mother of a dead soldier. The wife of an actor imprisoned for paedophilia. The teacher accused of sleeping with her pupils. The politician embroiled in a corruption scandal. Cathy had, apparently, done them all.

'That's what journalism's about,' she said. 'Real people.' She pointed at Esme, extending one finger, her hand wobbling. 'Don't you forget it, missy. I've seen your type before. Straight out of university, think you know it all . . .' Cathy patted Esme on the hand. 'No offence.'

Esme looked at her older colleague, taking in the carefully blow-dried hair and the rheumy, unfocused eyes. Cathy must have been in her fifties but she looked trim, with sculpted arms and a neat, attractive way of dressing. She'd never married or had children: her entire life had been devoted to scoops and deadlines, to proving that she was as good as the men in the office, that the casual misogyny of Fleet Street didn't bother her, that she could banter along with the rest of them. She had succeeded, in a way. She was the chief feature writer on the paper and Dave rated her highly. But Esme couldn't help feeling that, somewhere along the way, something integral had been lost, some intangible human quality that made Cathy seem unreachable. She was – not unfriendly, exactly – but hyper-aware of her own position, constantly on the defensive in case someone was making fun of her.

She wanted Esme to be her ally. But Esme shrank away from Cathy's overtures without quite knowing why. Partly it was that she couldn't compete with Cathy's prodigious drinking and Esme's failure to match her glass for glass was seen by the older woman as yet further evidence of her prissiness and naïvety when in fact it came from a deeper-seated mistrust of alcohol. Partly it was that the other reporters were wary of her. There had been more than one occasion where Cathy had removed a junior's byline even though they had done all the spadework. Mostly, it was that Esme couldn't make her out. Cathy was capable of immense charm and friendliness but without ever sharing a confidence that would show her in a bad light. You came away from a conversation with her fearful that you'd said too much, that you'd shared too many secrets, and realising that Cathy had given nothing in return.

Of course, that's what made her such a good journalist. And so gifted at doorsteps.

Unlike Cathy, Esme hates doorstepping. The problem is that she seems to be good at them. People warm to her, she has discovered, possibly because her distaste for the direct form of attack marks her out as someone who is unlikely to screw them over. Either that or she's a good listener.

'People love to talk,' is one of Cathy's favourite maxims. 'Give 'em half a chance and they're spewing out their whole life story. Cheaper than therapy.'

Maybe, thinks Esme. But she wanted to be a reporter, not a psychiatrist.

When Dave had called her across this morning, signalling to her with a look that made her stomach twist, Esme thought he wanted to ask her how the lunch with Howard Pink went. No such luck.

'Ever heard of Jo Feenan?' he said, running his extended fore-finger across his right eyebrow, smoothing down the wayward hairs.

'Yes,' Esme lied. What was it about men of a certain age that made hair grow in the most unexpected places? A broad thicket sprouting out of an earhole. Shivering wisps protruding from the nasal passage. Wiry curlicues winding through eyebrows . . .

'He's a writer of humorous novels,' Dave continued. 'Big in the '80s. We've had a tip-off that he had an affair a few years ago and fathered an illegitimate daughter.'

'Who's the tip-off from?'

'None of your beeswax,' Dave said, tapping his nose.

Who says that, thought Esme. Who, actually, in real life, says 'beeswax' like they're a character from some jolly 1970s sitcom?

'It's a good source, that's all you need to know,' Dave said. 'We've got an address for the woman. She lives in Winchester. Short train journey out of Waterloo. Check it out, would you?' He passed her a torn slip of paper with the address, written in Dave's recognisable scrawl of capital letters. A graphologist had once told her only egomaniacs or psychopaths wrote entirely in capital letters.

Which one was Dave, she wondered?

'OK,' Esme said, her heart plummeting at the thought of a wasted day on public transport. 'I had a page lead I was working on, about the House-builders' Association—'

'Forget it.'

'But—'

He stared at her blackly.

'I want you to concentrate on this.' A pause. 'Are we clear?'

She nodded. Dave could switch from light-hearted to brutal in the space of a breath. It was one of things she both disliked and admired. She found herself wondering, not for the first time, what he was like at home, when he argued with his wife. She couldn't imagine him ever giving ground or admitting he was wrong.

'Lucky bitch,' Sanjay says when she tells him she is off to Winchester. 'Lovely cathedral. Nice little craft shops.'

'I wish you were going instead. I can't be arsed today, I really can't.'

She sits down and takes her trainers out of her bag, sliding her feet out of her high heels.

'Ugh,' Sanjay says, wafting a hand in front of his nose. 'Can't you invest in a more glamorous pair of sensible shoes?'

She laughs. 'These are comfortable.'

'Comfort is the death of chicness.'

'Who said that?'

'No one, darling. Just one of my off-the-cuff bons mots.'

He turned back to his computer, typing frantically with two fingers. It was one of the things she'd been most surprised by when she started here: the sheer number of journalists unable to touch-type. Beechcroft had informed her the skill was essential.

She left the office with a clutch of cuttings, rapidly printed off from the online archive, a headache and a nagging sense of dissatisfaction. What was she doing with her life? Going to ask some poor woman whether she'd had an affair with a writer no one had ever heard of. Who cared, really? She spent most of the tube journey to Waterloo sighing loudly at the pointlessness of it all. She wonders if everyone feels like this or whether existential gloom is the particular preserve of journalists, a species unforgivably prone to questioning everything. Occasionally Esme catches herself thinking she'd love an undemanding office job as someone else's PA. No responsibility. A lunch hour. Clocking off reliably at five every day. Getting to wear impractical but sexy tailored suits and high heels.

Waterloo Station is filled with criss-crossing commuters, walking with shut-off eyes as though pulled by an invisible string from one side of the terminus to the other. She is fascinated by commuters, by their sense of self-importance. They do not deviate from their course for anyone, these grey-suited men and women with their harried expressions and fly-away hair and dirt-bled shirt collars and click-clicking shoes in need of reheeling. They move with a purposeful sense of their own superiority, wordlessly conveying the extreme necessity of wherever it is they need to be, whatever crucial appointment they have to make. In their hands, they brandish the blue square of a prepaid Oyster card as simultaneous talisman and symbol of identity – proof of belonging to the big, messy rush of the city. They tsk-tsk at tourists taking too long to understand the tube map and quickstep with disapproval around the groups of schoolchildren loitering with intent in WH Smith. Everyone else seems to be in their way, Esme notices, and she forces herself to slow down and dawdle so as not to be one of them.

A man in a bulky anorak shoves past her, his shoulder colliding into hers as though tackling her for possession of some unseen ball. Her bag swings back against her waist as he passes. She swears at him, the rapid dart of the expletive ripping out of her with unexpected force.

On the train, still angry at Dave and the rugby-tackling man, she reads a magazine out of spite. Then her natural conscientiousness takes over and she takes out the cuttings. When the buffet trolley comes through, Esme treats herself to a coffee and a flapjack. By the time she arrives, she feels almost normal.

Now here she is, with a printed-out map of the woman's address in one hand, trying to work out her bearings. Spatial awareness has never been her strong point. When Esme had done her Bronze Duke of Edinburgh, she was the only one in a group of six schoolgirls who had been absolved of all map-reading duties. She should use the maps function on her iPad but can never work out how to turn it round without the streets melting confusingly in the wrong direction.

After several minutes, she admits defeat and asks a passer-by the way to Parchment Street. It turns out to be only a few hundred yards away and, when she gets there, she discovers a pleasing row of terraced cottages, each one painted in a contrasting pastel colour, the front doors set back slightly from the road. Does everyone on the street get together and agree on the colour scheme,

Esme thinks, or is it just fortuitous good taste that they all want to paint their houses in complementary shades? She can't imagine that ever happening in Shepherd's Bush. The house three doors up from her is a crack den.

When her brother Robbie came round to her flat for the first time to help her assemble an Ikea wardrobe, he'd looked at the meagre proportions of the sitting room and the black patches of damp on the kitchen walls, then given a sly smile and said, 'Nice to see you've gone down in the world, Es.'

She glances at the scrap of paper Dave has given her: 'Clarissa Treherne, Number 16'. Esme takes a few deep breaths, half hoping that Clarissa Treherne is not there and she can leave a carefully worded letter instead of having to face her in person. How do you ask someone you've never met if they've had an affair? Beechcroft is frustratingly silent on this point of etiquette.

Esme walks up the short pathway to Clarissa Treherne's front door, shoes scrunching against the gravel. She presses the doorbell firmly. No turning back now, she thinks grimly. Her senses are on high alert, ears pricked for the sound of footsteps in the hallway.

The door opens. A tall man with a wide, tanned face and sun-bleached hair stands in front of her, one hand on the latch.

'Yes?' he says. He is wearing a checked shirt and shorts with grass stains on the seams. In his arms, he carries a small girl in a pink dress.

'Sorry to bother you.' Esme is thrown. For some reason, she hadn't anticipated anyone but the woman in question opening the door. 'I was looking for Clarissa Treherne.'

'She's just in the garden,' the man says. The girl starts to squeal. 'Shh, sweetie. Daddy's talking.' He gently moves the girl's podgy fist away from his face and Esme catches the silver gleam of a wedding ring on his fourth finger. 'Who should I say it is?'

She hesitates.

'It's Esme Reade, a reporter with the *Sunday Tribune*.'

He looks baffled. 'Oh. Right. Can't say we read it ourselves. We tend to get the *Observer*. What's it about?'

Thinking fast, she says, 'We're doing a story about young mothers in the Winchester area. A new study has found that Winchester has the highest rates of . . .' She falters. 'Of postnatal depression.'

The man's face clears. 'How interesting. Well Clarissa didn't have PND—'

'No, that's fine. It would be good to get a broad range of voices.'

He nods, then disappears into the gloom of the house, leaving Esme nervously standing on the threshold. Reflexively, she wipes the toe of her right shoe against her tights. She can hear the murmur of chatter, punctuated by the plaintive cries of the child, then the echo of heels on wooden floorboards.

'Hi, I'm Clarissa Treherne.'

'Esme Reade, *Sunday Tribune*.' They shake hands. Clarissa Treherne is a tall, elegant blonde, dressed in floaty linen and tight jeans. She looks like she should be advertising eco-friendly laundry powder in a field of wild daisies.

'I'm so sorry to bother you,' Esme says, lowering her voice, already hating how underhand she sounds.

'It's no bother,' Clarissa Treherne looks at her, absent-mindedly.

'I've been sent to ask you something a bit delicate.' Esme is hoping the woman will sense the urgency in her tone and close the door so that her husband won't hear, but there is no movement. 'As I said, I'm from the *Sunday Tribune* and we've got it on very good authority that you had—' She stumbles. 'A liaison of sorts with, um, the writer Jo Feenan.' The sentence sounds scrambled. She wonders, too late, whether she has got the words in the right order. Her eyes feel dry and scratchy. Her throat is parched. She senses her cheeks burning and hopes her discomfort is not obvious.

No one says anything. A low murmuring breeze lifts a few

strands of blonde hair from Clarissa Treherne's forehead. The weather has shifted. The tang of rain is in the air.

Finally, she pulls the door to. Esme scrutinises the woman's face. A thin vein at her right temple presses against her skin, the violet-blueness of it matching both the colour of her eyes and the precise shade of Number 16's exterior walls.

'You've got a bloody nerve,' Mrs Treherne says and although her teeth are bared and glinting, her voice is absolutely level. 'Showing up here unannounced, spreading unsubstantiated rumours . . .'

'I'm sorry. I can see it's not a good time, but—'

'You're damn right it's not a good time,' she hisses. 'My husband and my two-year-old daughter are on the other side of that door.'

She glares at Esme.

'What business is it of yours what I do with my private life?'

There is no good answer to this.

'You're right,' Esme concedes. 'It isn't any of my business. I was sent here by my news editor—'

'Only following orders, were you?' snaps Mrs Treherne. 'Jesus, how can you live with yourself?'

Mrs Treherne grips the door handle so tightly her knuckles turn white. She has tears in her eyes, Esme notes. They wouldn't be there if she had nothing to hide. If this were simply a malicious fabricated story, the chances were she'd be laughing it off. She certainly wouldn't be this defensive.

'Listen, if you're denying it . . .' Esme starts.

Clarissa Treherne turns to go back into the house but there is something half-hearted in her movement. She is dithering.

'Mrs Treherne, there's absolutely no reason why you should listen to me, of course there isn't. But it's only fair to warn you that the story is going to get out somehow. Isn't it better to have a chance to put forward your version of events, the way you want it to be told?'

Clarissa Treherne stands unmoving, her gaze downcast. Her

shoulders are jagged peaks of tension beneath her blouse. She appears to be listening.

Esme has no idea where these turns of phrase are coming from. 'Fair to warn you'. 'Your version of events'. She is reminded, briefly, of those television detective programmes her mother used to watch on weekday afternoons, the ones featuring a grizzled man in a beige mackintosh, doggedly knocking on doors and asking questions until he broke down the suspect's resistance.

She is shocked how easily the patter comes to her. Shocked, also, that now she has Mrs Treherne's attention the thought of getting an admission makes her blood pump faster. She can taste the story. She can see it take shape in her mind, its vaporous edges becoming solid, each fact unpacking itself in a beautiful preordained sequence. She can imagine the drop intro, the drawing in of the reader, the careful way she would describe the street. She feels the power of her position and, for a brief moment, she forgets the tawdriness, the shame she should be experiencing, the social embarrassment her mother would expect to find within her, and she breathes in the scent of conquest. Of release.

So this is why Cathy loves a doorstep, she thinks. The purity of it. Person to person. Lies. Truths. Reveals. All of it – a big, messy tangle of human folly.

'I can't talk now,' Mrs Treherne says, her eyes darting sideways. 'For obvious reasons.'

'No, of course. I quite understand your predicament.'

Clarissa Treherne looks at her. 'I don't think you do.'

Esme does not respond. A small smile plays at the corner of her lips. She already has her prey hooked. It's time to reel her in.

'We can do this any way you want.'

Mrs Treherne scowls, then wipes her forehead with the back of her hand. 'OK. Leave me your number and I'll call you later once I've sorted things out here.'

Esme fishes a business card out of her handbag and passes it over. 'Would you be able to give me your number, just in case . . . ?'

She shakes her head, her blonde hair mussing itself up prettily. 'You can have my email.' Esme hands her the spiral-bound note-pad she has been carrying. Mrs Treherne scribbles down an email address.

'I'm really sorry to have burst in like this,' Esme says. 'I know you probably don't believe me but—'

'You're right, I don't believe you,' Mrs Treherne says. 'Why should you care if I've messed up my life? We've only just met.'

'I know. I just – I'm not going to . . . I promise. It'll be your words, the way you want to explain things. Your side of the story.'

Clarissa Treherne snorts. 'Maybe.' She seems about to say something and then to reconsider. 'Whatever. I might as well talk to you as anyone else.' She examines Esme's face intently. 'If Jo Feenan thinks he can treat me like dirt, he's got another think coming.'

And there it is, thinks Esme: the gem-like glimmer of certainty, the undercurrent of scores needing to be settled, of wrongs need-ing to be righted. She's going to talk, Esme is sure of it.

Clarissa Treherne slips Esme's card into the pocket of her jeans, then turns and shuts the door forcefully. Low grey clouds are veiling the sun like cataracts. Esme pulls the belt of her jacket more tightly around her.

She retraces her steps back up the street, taking out her mobile to call Dave. Mrs Treherne has as good as admitted it. There'll be a nice double-page spread for her out of this if she gets the inter-view. Part of her feels elated that she has done her job well. The other, unspoken, part knows that she has done something grubby.

She thinks of Cathy, her lipstick marks on the rim of a wine glass, her box of Vogue cigarettes on the pub table.

'Everyone wants to talk,' she imagines Cathy saying. 'You just need to find the right question.'

On her way back to the station, Esme passes a Fash Attack

store. She glances at her watch: more than enough time to indulge in some retail therapy. She leaves a message for Dave then gets out her wallet, checking to see if she'd remembered to bring the Fash Attack discount card she'd been sent by Howard Pink's PR man. There it was, nestling between a pile of taxi receipts: a shiny pink square with her name picked out in gold lettering. No harm in using it, she thinks. This job has to come with some perks, after all.

Carol

SHE IS SITTING ON the sofa in her dressing gown with a cup of cooling tea in one hand when the doorbell rings. She has grown more lax about getting up of late. It is already gone eleven and she has been watching television for a good couple of hours. She generally kicked off with a smattering of *Daybreak* – Carol liked the Northern Irish girl they used to have on, but she'd left to go and marry a footballer and the show had never been the same since – followed seamlessly by *This Morning*, because the recipes were so good and she always learned something from the agony aunt phone-ins. On particularly lethargic days, she'd allow herself to slide into a few minutes of *Jeremy Kyle* on ITV, even though she suspects the constant stream of shouting adulterers, anti-social teenagers and DNA tests for absent fathers is rotting her brain.

The doorbell rings just as the *This Morning* theme tune is starting. She switches the television off quickly, directing the remote control in the general direction of the screen and waving it about a bit. Since getting the satellite dish installed, she's never sure which button to press. There are too many of them and she can barely see the tiny white lettering on each pad without her glasses.

The doorbell is followed by a knock. 'All right, all right, I'm coming,' she mutters under her breath. 'Keep your hair on.'

Carol pushes herself up off the sofa, tightening her dressing gown belt and ensuring that no scrap of her winceyette night-dress is visible. She feels caught unawares and embarrassed. It's probably the postman, delivering a letter that needs a signature. She's noticed an upsurge in administrative paperwork since Derek died. She'd never previously realised that death was measured out in pre-addressed envelopes. It seemed undignified, somehow, that a man such as Derek could be reduced to typed template letters and meaningless forms in triplicate. In life, his physical presence had been so tangible, so reassuringly large. At parties, she always knew where he was in the room without looking, as though the simple fact of him somehow redistributed the air, squeezing the molecules of it aside to let him pass. Now that he is gone, all that is left of him is scraps of paper, torn-up fragments of memory, an absence around which she shapes her days.

On holiday in Tenerife a few years ago, they had driven in the rental car from the hotel to a local winery. Glancing out of the passenger-seat window, Carol kept seeing signs for a 'Butterfly Zoo'. As Derek drove, she wondered what a butterfly zoo would be like. Would the butterflies be held in mesh cages, trapped wings fluttering without purpose? Or would they be dead, their small bodies pinned against the wall and shielded by glass from sticky hands? She had never liked zoos: the illusion of freedom contained within nasty confinement. But the idea of dead butterflies was even worse.

They'd never gone to the Butterfly Zoo. Carol wishes they had. Now, in her head, she sees death as a lifeless insect. A creature with wings studded against velvet; a stillness where once there had been vibrant, jittering life.

When Carol gets to the door, she sees that it is not the postman but her neighbour, Alan. Fancy that, she tells herself. I was only thinking of him yesterday and now here he is. Looking through the spyhole, she can see him distorted and looming, leaning towards the door, his hands behind his back, staring through at her. For a split-second, she is sure that their eyes have locked and she shrinks back from the wobbling image of his blackened pupil, afraid of being caught staring. She shakes her head. 'Stuff and nonsense,' she says softly to the empty hallway. 'Silly old bat.'

She undoes the chain and opens the door. Sunlight streams in and an unexpected warmth rises from the stones of the pavement. She hadn't realised it was such a balmy day.

'Alan,' she says. She has to remind herself to smile. Her normal responses to social situations seem to have dulled over the last few months. A lot of it feels like too much effort. 'Well this is nice.'

Alan grins, shifting from one foot to the other like a small boy about to ask for his ball back.

'Nice to see you too, Mrs Hetherington.' He glances at her dressing gown. 'I'm sorry to disturb you—'

'You're not disturbing me, Alan. Why don't you come on in off the street? I'll put the kettle on.' She pads back down the corridor, leading the way to the kitchen at the back. 'I haven't had a chance to get dressed yet. Such a busy morning, what with one thing and another.'

White lies. They come easily to her these days.

'Time flies when you're having fun,' Alan says, his voice monotone. Carol pulls out a seat from the kitchen table and motions for him to sit.

'Yes,' she agrees, even though she has always thought it a particularly stupid expression. Still, he's just trying to make small talk. 'Yes, it does.' She fills the kettle from the cold tap, putting in too much water just because the sound of it soothes her. She does not sit, not straight away, but instead looks at Alan and takes him in, evaluating him for the first time as a potential suitor for her daughter.

He is wearing a crumpled blue flannel shirt, rolled up to the elbows, and faded blue jeans. His Timberland boots have a crust of mud around the soles. Through force of habit, she glances at the lino to see if he's trailed any of that dirt into her house and sure enough, the white-grey checked pattern is speckled with dots of black like rabbit droppings. The kettle starts to boil, so noisily that any chatter proves impossible.

Alan's face has an unhealthy sheen to it: he is pale and his cheeks look sallow. There are purplish smudges beneath his eyes and he seems uneasy, picking at his fingernails, one knee juddering up and down underneath the table. He is a large man and yet something about him remains unformed, almost wilfully youthful.

He looks too big, sitting there squeezed into her Ercol chair, his lumbering arms pressed against the spotless pine table like pieces of roasting meat. His neck is thick and brown and there is a suggestion of coiled muscle beneath his shirt, the tendons packed tightly into his torso. Not tall, Carol thinks, but imposing – yes, that's the word she'd use to describe him. Vanessa normally goes for wiry, thin types whose complexion denotes a life of libraries and air-conditioned offices – like they'd not seen a day of sunshine in their lives. All of her previous boyfriends have been a bit wet, to be honest. A change might do her good.

'What can I do for you, Alan?' she says when the noise from the kettle finally subsides.

'I was just wondering, Mrs Hetherington—'

'Carol, please.'

He grins, showing the prominent gap between his two front teeth.

'Carol.' He draws out the two syllables, playing with the word in his mouth, tasting it. 'Carol,' he says again. 'Could you do me a favour?' There is a mild West Country tone to his voice that Carol finds appealing. It accentuates the childishness of him, makes it seem like he needs looking after.

'That depends what it is!' she replies cheerily but it comes out more accusingly than she'd intended. She can't seem to strike the right conversational notes any more. Everything she says sounds off-key.

Alan's knee jiggles. Biscuits, she thinks suddenly. They must have biscuits. She's sure she's got some somewhere, even though it was Derek who'd always been more partial to them. The older he got, the sweeter his tooth had become. He was quite capable of demolishing half a packet of chocolate digestives sitting in front of *Newsnight* of an evening. But then, with the chemotherapy, he'd lost his taste for sugar. Just like that. Overnight, he'd started craving pickled things: hard-boiled eggs preserved in gloopy jars of vinegar, capers, big tubs of sauerkraut that Carol had lugged home from the Polish shop in Southfields.

Funny what terminal illness did to you.

She catches herself. No, not funny. Not funny at all.

She turns her back to Alan, rummaging in the cupboard for the biscuit tin. Her fingers brush against its cool edges and she slides it out with a sense of triumph. It is the same tin she's used for years: a commemoration piece from Charles and Diana's wedding, their two young faces staring out at her in faded colour. Diana is smiling shyly, her eyes cast down over her pussy-bow blouse.

A tragedy, what happened to her, Carol thinks. And those two lovely boys. A tragedy. Her eyes moisten and she busies herself arranging fig rolls on a patterned plate so that Alan won't notice. When he takes one, the biscuit looks small as a postage stamp in his hand.

'Thank you,' he says. He chews on the fig roll and carries on speaking, so that a patch of table in front of him becomes covered in a light spray of crumbs. Carol tries to ignore this and then, when she can't, finds herself making excuses for him. Perhaps he's lived on his own too long, she thinks. Having a girlfriend would do him the world of good.

'I'm going away for a few days and I wondered if you'd mind watering my plants,' he says, the words coming out in a sudden, nervous rush.

She laughs.

'Oh, I thought it was going to be something serious.'

'It is.' Alan meets her gaze, his face unsmiling. 'I love my plants. I do.'

She chuckles. Alan doesn't respond. She has offended him somehow. 'Of course I will, dear.' Carol takes the tea bags out and passes Alan a mug. Too late, she realises it has 'World's Best Dad' emblazoned across the front in vivid blue lettering. It had been a Father's Day present for Derek some years ago from Vanessa. Not that they had marked the occasion – the sentimentalisation of random days of the year for commercial profit had been one of Derek's particular bugbears.

'It all comes from America,' he would say, any time he saw a padded Valentine's heart or an inflatable Hallowe'en pumpkin. 'Tat, the lot of it!'

But he'd loved the 'World's Best Dad' mug in spite of himself. When Vanessa had handed it over, all wrapped up prettily with a spotted red fabric bow, his face had been a picture.

'What's this for then?' he'd said.

'Father's Day, Dad,' Vanessa answered, even though she'd never got Carol so much as a bunch of flowers for Mother's Day. Not that she was going to say anything, mind. Not that she cared. Well, not much, anyhow Derek had always been her daughter's favourite. Vanessa could wrap him round her little finger when she wanted to.

Derek had opened the box and eased out the mug with the tips of his fingers, holding it up to the light as if it were a precious antique. He was delighted with it and, as soon as he'd given Vanessa a hug, went to make himself a cup of tea. He insisted that the tea tasted better in that mug than any other. Over the years, the white china inside had browned with repeated use. Now, as she passed 'World's Best Dad' over to Alan, Carol hoped he wouldn't notice the rust-coloured ring-stain around the top.

'I promise I'll do my best to look after them, Alan,' she says. He looks so disconsolate that she leans forward, about to pat the back of his hand, but she stops herself, just before making contact. She wonders why she does that.

'Thanks, Mrs Heth – Carol.' He grins shyly. 'It's my pride and joy, that garden. I've put a lot of work into it.'

'I know you have. We always used to see you out there, planting things.'

Alan looks worried. 'Did you? I hope I wasn't making too much noise.'

'No, love. Not at all. You're a very considerate neighbour.'

He glances at her and she notices his eyes fall downwards towards the V-shaped cleft where her dressing gown is gaping open. She draws the neck of the gown closer to her and makes it obvious she has seen him looking but he doesn't shift his gaze, does not, in fact, seem remotely embarrassed.

'Anyway—' she starts, feeling uncomfortable.

'I've built a patio,' Alan says, almost simultaneously. 'I researched how to do it all online and it wasn't much trouble. I got the paving stones from a reclamation yard. They were throwing them out. Got a good price.'

His dark brown eyes are gleaming. Before, she'd thought there was a kindness in his features but now, examining him more closely, Carol realises that it is more a sort of slowness, as though his thoughts take longer to come to the fore than other people's. He seems to be several steps behind. In fact, she thinks uncharitably, he's what her mum would have called 'a bit simple'.

No, she realises with sudden clarity, he wouldn't be right for Vanessa at all.

She'd never had much chance to speak to him before. After that first brief chat when he moved in, it had all been smiles over the garden fence, a shared nod of the head when the weather was nice, an exchange of chit-chat that skimmed the surface of civility, but nothing more. She begins to think she might have got him wrong.

'That sounds lovely, Alan,' she says.

He slurps the rest of his tea and takes another fig roll from the plate without asking.

'You'll have to come over when it's built. Have a cup of tea, or—' and here he breaks off, cocks his head and winks at her.

Carol swallows drily. 'A gin and tonic. A sundowner. That's what they call them, isn't it? In posh restaurants?'

She nods, in what she hopes is a motherly fashion: encouraging but not flirtatious. She doesn't want Alan to get the wrong idea. Carol wishes she weren't in her dressing gown. What had possessed her to open the door in this state of semi-undress? She feels vulnerable and exposed without her usual armour of clothes.

'When are you off on holiday, Alan?'

'Thursday, just for four days. There's a tap in the back garden so you can fill the watering can out there. No hoses allowed, of course.' He grins. 'Wettest drought I've ever known,' he says, but it sounds like a joke he has overheard and stolen from someone else. Besides, it's still only May. There's been no talk of a hose-pipe ban as far as Carol knows. Not since last year, when the news headlines were full of talk about a drought because the reservoirs were so low. It was strange of him to mention it.

'That'll be no trouble, Alan.' Carol picks up the empty mugs and stands up to put them in the sink, hoping he'll get the message. Normally she'd ask where he was going but she is unwilling to prolong the conversation. She stays there, her hands pushed against the damp rim of the steel moulding.

Alan looks at her, silent, for a few seconds. Then his face cracks into a grin again and he pushes his chair back.

'Right, I'll be off then, Carol. Thanks very much for – you know—' He gestures towards the table and the plate of biscuits. 'My plants will be in good hands!'

She smiles, half-hearted. He walks down the hallway, his feet clomping against the carpet, his shoulders stooped as if afraid he might knock against the ceiling. At the door, he turns to her and rapidly, before she has a chance to move away, he bends down and kisses her on the cheek. His lips are warm against her face, his breathing close.

Carol is so startled she doesn't have a chance to react until he's out of the door, waving at her jauntily.

'Bye then,' he says, raising his voice a fraction too loudly.

She holds a hand up, speechless.

It is the first time a man has kissed her anywhere since Derek died. As soon as she closes the door, she rubs her cheek frantically, trying to rid herself and the house of Alan's presence. But even as she goes upstairs to get dressed, she can feel the shadow of him: a darkness lingering like a cat in the corner, waiting to pounce.

Beatrice

*I*T HAS BEEN FORTY-EIGHT hours and Beatrice still hasn't heard back from Howard Pink. All she got was an automated response in her email inbox, thanking her for her correspondence to the Paradiso Group and reassuring her that the matter would be attended to 'at the earliest opportunity'.

She hadn't expected a swift and easy resolution, of course, but she is disappointed. She doesn't especially want to make life difficult for Howard Pink or that tough-looking blonde woman in the gossip magazine photographs, she assumes is his wife. At the same time, she doesn't want to let him get away with it. There is a fire in Beatrice that has yet to be quenched. The experience of her life so far has left her not jaded but hungry. She wants to prove herself, to show that she isn't to be taken for granted, that all the humiliations and loss and pain and wrongness that have beaten down on her like sharp hailstones from the sky, that all of it is for a reason, a purpose.

She knows she is an oddity in this respect. Every week, she drops in to the Refugee and Asylum Seeker Support centre in London Bridge, and she sees other men and women arriving through the doors with hollow eyes and a glazed expression, sagging with a sense of defeat. When Beatrice first arrived, she was like this too: a mere outline of herself, as though all the scribbled colour of her had been rubbed out. She had barely been speaking, could not find the words to express herself, and was terrified, if she did, that the British authorities would be disgusted by her and would send her back home.

A volunteer had led Beatrice inside, seating her at a small kitchen table in the back office while she made her a cup of instant coffee. She had given Beatrice a coat. Beatrice put it on, sliding her arms through the sleeves and feeling the soft graze of material against a trail of goose-bumps. And then, instead of asking questions, this woman had waited for Beatrice to talk.

Eventually, Beatrice had found her voice. The first thing she said was, 'Thank you.'

The lady smiled. 'What for?'

'Being kind.' And then, bit by bit, over the course of several months, Beatrice was able to tell the woman, whose name was Emma, the bare bones of what had happened. She talked about Susan as a friend and skated over some of the more intimate details. She was scared, of course, but it was also that she simply didn't have the language. All her life, she had been taught not to admit what she was.

But then, after Beatrice had been dropping in to the centre for a few weeks, Emma leaned across, patted her hand and asked:

'Was Susan your lover?'

It was so simple, the way she asked it. As if there were nothing to hide.

'Yes,' Beatrice said.

Emma nodded. 'Well that's what we need to tell the Home Office.'

That's when Beatrice had started fighting again. And it felt good to take them on – all of them; all of the blank, expressionless civil servants who interviewed her; the judges who ruled against her; the solicitors who asked the same questions over and over again. Some people got broken by the system. Some people said the trauma of dealing with it was worse than the terrors they were fleeing from. Some gave up. Some were deported when all the life had been squeezed out of them. Some paid money to set up fake marriages. Some turned to crime because it was easier.

Some killed themselves, jumping into the brown, pounding currents of the Thames, arms spiralling, mouths gasping, the ferocious rush of wind snatching their screams away as they slammed against the water with a crack of snapping bones.

Others, like Beatrice, found a determination so profound it bordered on the obsessive. She began to believe again in her own strength. So when a man in a brown suit sat across a table from her in an official interview and asked her, in his nasal voice, what kind of sex she liked, whether she'd ever slept with a man and how could she prove she was a lesbian, how could he believe her, Beatrice was able to look him directly in the eye and laugh.

'I don't need to prove anything to you,' she had said. The man had looked shocked, then affronted, then confused.

And it felt good. It felt like watering a patch of dried-up soil and watching green shoots rise again. She got refugee status after that. She had fought the system and, in a small way, she had won.

So now, when Beatrice sees new arrivals slinking unsurely through the doors at RASS, she feels frustration. She wants to shake them, tell them to wake up and fight. The best bulwark against desperation, Beatrice has discovered, is having something to rail against.

Injustice rankles. The casual arrogance of privilege angers her like nothing else. And Howard Pink had got to her more than the others. Because of what he did. Because he had not looked at her once and that, when it was over, he seemed so complacent, as though he believed she had enjoyed it, had actively sought his grubby attentions.

It reminds her of another time, another room, another man. A viciousness she never imagined. The bead of sweat in her mouth. The taste of must and salt. The dampness of the sheets. The disgust rising in her gullet – disgust at herself or at him she has never been sure.

Beatrice glances at her watch: 11.30. Her shift starts at 2 p.m.

She decides to go in early and visit the National Gallery. It astounds her still, after five years in London, that she does not have to pay to get in. She is caught between enjoying the freedom this gives her and thinking it absurdly wasteful of the UK government. In Uganda, she never went to art galleries. It had never even crossed her mind that it might be a pleasurable thing to do. At school, the nuns occasionally showed slides of great religious art: a succession of gold-leaf Madonnas with plain white faces and an overgrown man-child in their arms, their beatific skin imbued with an oddly greenish tinge. But in the National Gallery, Beatrice has found herself drawn to the later paintings – the eighteenth- and nineteenth-century oils, with their glassy surfaces. She admires the way the large canvases are hung imposingly on the walls, contained by swirly gilt frames, all in careful order.

She finds peace in the glazes, in the translucent rendering of fabric: a curtain swag in the background of a Vermeer, a flower-patterned fold in the dress of Madame Moitessier. The smallness of detail appeals to her. It is the portraits that draw her in. The landscapes, with their earnest reimaginings of Roman pastures and sun-blessed waterways, leave her cold.

Today, with her mind unsettled, she thinks half an hour of staring at the paintings will restore her calm and make her ready for a long shift at the hotel.

She catches the bus into town. When she first arrived, she hadn't been able to afford the bus. Even now that she earns a good enough wage, she feels guilty doing so. Shortly after meeting Emma, Beatrice had applied, on her advice, for an English Language course at Southgate College. Her spoken English was already fairly fluent but she had wanted to improve. More than that, she had wanted something to do.

The College invited Beatrice for an assessment. It was January and very cold and Beatrice had no money so she'd left early in the morning and walked there from Bermondsey. It had taken her two hours. After the interview, one of the teachers gave her £10 to cover her travel expenses. Beatrice took the note in her hand. It was crisp and smelled lightly of tobacco, but she hadn't wanted to waste it and in the end, she walked all the way back, putting the £10 in an empty jam jar in her kitchen cupboard and screwing the lid tightly on top, saving the money for some day when she really might need it.

The £10 note is still there in the cupboard, like a charm. The red-and-white-checked jam jar lid now has a patina of dust. Beatrice is saving it, just in case.

In Trafalgar Square, several dozen American schoolchildren in brightly coloured anoraks are sitting around the fountain, unwrapping cling-filmed sandwiches and playing tinny music on their mobile phones. Their voices seem to exist on a higher frequency than anyone else's, self-confident and brash, easy laughter bubbling under each elongated vowel. Beatrice frowns at them as she passes and hunches further into herself, wrapping her arms tightly across her torso. She knows they won't notice her as she walks past. She moves beyond the reach of their understanding, slipping by in the shadows. And yet, she reminds herself . . . and yet I exist.

Then, just as she reaches the stone steps leading up to the Gallery entrance, she thinks she sees him and her breath stops. He is standing at the edge of the group of schoolchildren with his back to her, head stooped slightly forward, tight black curls close-cut against his scalp. He is tall, much taller than her, and there is something about the set of his shoulders, the way they slope off sharply into muscular arms, that makes her wince in recognition. He is wearing a navy-blue hoodie and bright white trainers. Box-fresh, he would've said, grinning so that she could see the glint of gold filling at the back of his mouth.

The sight of him makes her shake. She feels the ground warp and contract and dissolve and, just as her knees buckle and she realises she is about to fall, she reaches out blindly for something solid to grab hold of.

'Are you all right?' The voice comes from far above her and

when she looks up she sees it belongs to a man in a dark brown suit and a pink tie clutching a package wrapped in greaseproof paper. He moves towards her and she is assailed by the overpowering smell of tuna fish and for a moment she thinks she will be sick. The man is still talking, his words sliding into each other. She can make out the odd phrase, 'feeling faint . . . wait here . . . too hot . . . take off your coat . . .' and she tries to say that she's fine but soon she is sitting on the cool grey stone and the man is crouching in front of her, peering into her face and offering her a white plastic cup.

'Just take a drink of water and you'll feel much better,' he is saying.

She takes the water and drinks it gratefully. The empty cup makes a crackling sound when she flexes her fingers. She glances at the man in the brown suit and attempts to smile.

'Thank you. I just . . . I thought I saw . . .'

She twists her neck and looks at the crowd of students, the blood in her head pumping wildly. If it's him, she thinks, I need to get away from here right now. I need to start running. If it's him, it means he's followed me. It means he's still angry.

And then the boy in the navy-blue hoodie turns round and she realises with a cool wash of certainty that it isn't him at all. His face is too narrow, his eyes too close-set. The boy is fiddling now with his phone, swiping at the screen with rapid fingers until an unrecognisable rap tune starts to play and he begins to bop his head in time with the beat as his friends look on. He is a teenager. Too young.

'I'm fine now,' Beatrice says, breathing deeply. 'I'm sorry for the bother.'

The man looks concerned. But then he checks his watch, takes his sandwich and brushes down his trousers with the palm of his one free hand.

'If you're sure . . . ?' He leaves before she has a chance to answer.

Beatrice gets up slowly, allowing the bright dots in front of her

127

eyes to disperse. She looks straight ahead, breathes. It wasn't him, she tells herself. It wasn't him.

She climbs the stairs and wends her way automatically through the crowds to her favourite painting. It will calm her to look at it. The painting is tucked away in one of the larger halls, hung almost as an afterthought because there is no name attached to either subject or artist. It is called *Portrait of a Lady* and all the information card can impart is that it is French, nineteenth century.

'This was once thought to be a portrait of the singer Madame Malibran, but there is no evidence to support this identification,' the neat, typed font reads. 'The work has been attributed to both Ingres and John Vanderlyn (1775?–1852), but neither suggestion is satisfactory.'

The brusqueness of this summary usually makes Beatrice smile, as if whoever wrote it was unable to disguise their frustration at not being able to work out anything more about the painting. That single word – 'satisfactory' – redolent, as it was, of uninspiring school reports, amused her. But today, the painting does not have its usual soothing effect. Her thoughts are in too much disarray.

Breathe, she reminds herself. Just keep breathing.

Beatrice stands about a foot away from the painting. She likes to be close, but not so close that she is peering across the rope and has to be motioned back by a security guard. The lady in the portrait is wearing a white dress and a velvety stole. She has delicate features and is leaning forwards slightly, looking at something to one side of the artist, her eyes darting out of the frame as though caught deep in her own imagination. There are gold-ringed diamonds on each earlobe. Her hair is tucked behind her ears on either side of a central parting.

When Beatrice was a little girl, she had always wanted hair like that: white woman's hair that was shiny and fine and straight, dropping like a waterfall over her shoulders when she let it down. Instead, her own hair was wiry and frizzy and had a wayward mind of its own. In Uganda, she used to sleep with a silk scarf to keep the moisture in. She'd lost the scarf somewhere along the way. It had been purple, she recalls, with swirling yellow butterflies.

The lady in the painting has an ambiguity that Beatrice finds appealing: the freshness of her skin and the simplicity of her dress give her the innocence of a newly plucked flower. But there is mischief in the tiny upturned corner of her mouth, the gentle arch of her face that makes you think it would be foolish to underestimate her.

Looking at the portrait, Beatrice feels that the artist – whoever he was – wanted this woman and that she, in return, had toyed with his emotions. Not because she was flighty or heartless but because power, for a woman, could only be exercised in certain limited ways. It was a sexual power. A tacit acknowledgement that a man could be undone by the uncontrolled nature of his desire while a woman could look on, with laughter in her eyes, at his self-debasement.

Beatrice looks at the woman in the painting for what feels like a long time. It would have been easier for her, Beatrice thinks, with her inherited wealth and her position in society. She wouldn't have understood what it was to be powerless, wouldn't have known what it was to be cast aside even though all you had ever done was allow your heart to love freely, even though you didn't think of the way you loved as an unnatural mutation. The woman in the painting wouldn't have allowed herself to be abused. The woman in the painting would have stood up for herself, Beatrice is sure of it.

And that, she thinks in a burst of clarity, is what she has to do. She must stop being chased by ghosts and move forward. She has to remind the world she is worth something – and it starts with Howard Pink.

Howard

*H*OWARD SITS, WITH HIS head in his hands, his elbows on the gleaming surface of the conference table. He has read a few novels in his lifetime – generally thrillers bought in airports with big gold lettering on the front – and he has always thought the idea of someone putting their head in their hands to denote desperation was lazy writing. But now, here he is, doing exactly that. Sometimes, he thinks grimly, a cliché is a cliché because it's true.

'Howard.' A voice that he recognises echoes across the expanse of shiny black granite. He remembers ordering this table five years ago when black granite was a marker of exorbitant wealth. They'd had to winch it up through the window. It had taken six workmen the best part of a day. By the time it was *in situ*, a heavy rectangle propped up on eight leviathan-sized table-legs hewn from substantial blocks of stone, even Howard thought he was mad. The black granite stared back at him now: a vast, static lake, seeping like oil to the corners of the room.

'Howard, are you OK?'

He lifts his head and forces himself to meet Rupert's eye. He nods.

'Yeah, fine,' he says. Forcing the two unremarkable words out of his throat feels like pushing a basketball through a tight woollen sock, shrunk in the wash. 'Christ. How could I have been so stupid?'

'Well—'

'It's a rhetorical question, Rupert.' Howard sighs, the breath coming out of his lungs in a clogged-up wheeze. He notices a tiny flap of skin emerging from the corner of his thumbnail like a splinter. It has been bothering him since this morning. It's surprisingly painful for something so insignificant. Why hadn't he tackled it before now? The fact that he hadn't bothered to address this small niggle for over twelve hours, even though it was irritating him and even though it would have been so easy to prise it off with a judiciously applied pair of tweezers, seems at this moment in time to be a metaphor for his entire life.

Ever since his mother died, ever since Ada disappeared, ever since his marriage to Penny broke down, ever since he lost the only three people who believed in his fundamental goodness, Howard has known he is heading inexorably towards disaster with all the ponderous certainty of a hundred-ton trawler bowling into a bank of rocks. Why hadn't he stopped himself? Why hadn't he turned the ship round? Why had he let his life degenerate into this ugly stasis, where he could no longer look at himself in the mirror, where he knew he was acting in ways that were not true to his fundamental nature?

He has found it so easy to convince everyone else of his awfulness. People who didn't know him, and even some who did, thought of him as a man who could take what he wanted – cash, companies, people – who could grab it all like sweets from a jar, just because he thought life owed him.

He had built this reputation and people had begun to look at him with wariness. They had believed in this unlikeable version of Howard Pink. Worse – they had started to respond to it. He was knighted. Claudia married him. He became respected by his peers. He ate in the finest restaurants. He was asked to write opinion pieces for the financial press. Of course he forgot who he was – who wouldn't?

Little Howie Pink, who sewed buttons on waistcoats and sold schmattes from a stall on Petticoat Lane. That kid, with his big ears and spotty skin – what chance did he have? He was pathetic. An innocent in a life where toughness triumphed. After Ada had been taken from him, he'd packed the little boy away in a box. Now, here he was, faced with the nasty reality of who he had become: a dirty old man who wanked over a chambermaid in a hotel room for kicks.

He lifts the edge of his thumb to his mouth and bites off the hangnail, tearing it out with a firm pull of the wrist. A thin plume of blood marks the spot. He feels better.

'Is she taking me to court then?'

Rupert steeples his fingers together. 'No, Howard. As I've explained, Beatrice Kizza has not mentioned a lawsuit.'

'Might as well have.'

'And if she did choose to pursue that particular avenue,' Rupert continues,' she'd have a bloody hard time making it stick. It's her word against yours and, frankly, Howard, no one's going to believe a fucking Ugandan maid. Not only that, but a Ugandan maid who's taking money away from hard-working English folk. Asylum seeker, my arse. She's got a nice little flat we're probably paying for, she's got a job, a steady income. Christ, she's probably using the NHS to get her tits done. Probably wants her whole family to come over here next.'

Howard waves his hand to make it stop. He's always surprised by how vicious Rupert can be, underneath that polished old-Etonian exterior. He wonders what Rupert actually thinks. Rupert's own opinions are as slippery as fish. Howard doesn't even know how he votes. Probably Tory, he thinks, given that he was at school with the Prime Minister. For all Howard knew, he had warmed the future PM's toilet seat with his adolescent bum.

Rupert pours himself a glass of sparkling water from the cluster of bottles at the centre of the table. There is an outline of a green bubble imprinted on the glass. When did everything get so meaningless, Howard wonders? Water. The clear, quenching liquid that is a prerequisite of life itself. The oozing, tidal pull of seas and rivers. The glowering thundercloud. The birthing pool. The NGO-funded wells in African villages. The gleaming stainless-steel taps in First World kitchens. The beads of sweat strung across his brow like bunting. All of it – distilled now into the curved glass bottle in front of him and given the most anodyne, focus-grouped logo a wet-behind-the-ears management consultant could think of. A bubble. Emptiness itself.

'So the first thing to do is make sure this Kizza woman doesn't speak to anyone else about this,' Rupert says, 'and to that end, I've taken the liberty of drawing up a confidentiality agreement. Assuming you're willing to pay to make this problem go away, which I would highly recommend as the most effective strategy, then . . .'

'I did it, Rupert,' Howard says. He is still in his opera clothes: a dark grey suit and starched shirt, fastened at the cuffs with silver cufflinks given to him by his mother on the day he opened his first shop. He had come straight here after Rupert called, making some feeble excuse to Bradley Minchin as to why he had to miss the second half of *La Bohème*.

'Urgent business, I'm afraid,' he'd said, shaking hands and pretending not to notice the guests' startled expressions. Claudia had given him a look that he secretly referred to as her 'Lady Macbeth stare' but he didn't have time to apologise. He knew she'd assume the role of gracious hostess as soon as he left. She was good at that kind of thing.

Jocelyn had driven him to the office, knowing not to ask any questions. The chauffer had tuned into Magic FM for the duration of the journey. It was Howard's favourite radio station but he never admitted it to anyone else – least of all Claudia, who prided herself on being a Radio 3 buff.

When they got to Paradiso HQ, situated in a characterless patch of land behind Paddington Station, Tracy Chapman was singing earnestly about the need for someone to forgive her. Howard felt tears prick the back of his eyes. What had he done?

Now, looking at Rupert, he feels the need to unburden himself.

'I did what she said I did,' Howard continues. 'Didn't even know her name. But I just felt . . . lonely, I suppose. Fucking hell, that sounds pathetic. But you know what? I thought . . . I thought there was part of her that wanted it too.'

He shakes his head. How grotesque he was. What a stupid old man.

'Howard, I think you should stop right there,' Rupert says, holding up one hand. His palm is strangely unwrinkled, like a baby's. 'That's not an avenue you need to go down.'

'What do you mean?'

Rupert rubs the back of his neck.

'First of all, I don't care whether it happened or not. It's not my position to judge. It's my job to deal with what happens next.' There is a pause. 'And, erm, how can I put this? I think it's safe to say Beatrice Kizza was not a willing partner in this . . . this exchange.'

'Well, OK, Rupe, but you weren't there. Just between you and me, it's not the first time I've done this sort of thing. It was a five-star hotel! There's a kind of . . .'

'She's a lesbian.'

Howard stops short. For a moment, he can't make sense of what he's just heard. The words seem jumbled. He waits, allowing them to slot into place in his head until they form a coherent sentence. And then, feeling that his neck is too big for his collar, he undoes the top button of his shirt.

'Fuck.' The expletive hangs in the air between them, a swollen cloud on the brink of bursting.

'Yes, quite,' says Rupert, leafing through several bits of paper and rearranging them on the table. 'In fact, we're in the unusual position of having Beatrice Kizza's sexuality legally verified by the UK authorities. She was given permanent refugee status' – Rupert checks the left-hand corner of a typed sheet – 'in 2009. It says here that homosexuality is illegal in Uganda and punishable by up to fourteen years in prison. So . . .'

Rupert lapses into silence.

'Right. So despite what you said a minute ago, we wouldn't have a leg to stand on in court.'

'Listen, it's not going to court. Her email says simply that she wants to meet and I'm pretty sure that if you make a generous – but appropriate – financial gesture there'll be no more trouble.'

'Let me see that—' Howard leans across and snatches the email from Rupert's hands. His thumb is still bleeding and, in his haste to read the email, he leaves a trace of blood on the page. He tries to rub it off but only succeeds in smearing it further.

'Shit.' Howard takes his spectacles out of his inside jacket pocket.

The email is brief and to the point. He is surprised at its polite, almost chatty, tone.

'Dear Sir Howard,' it goes.

You won't remember me but we met in Room 423 of the Hotel Rotunda in Mayfair. It was Monday 4th May and I was the chambermaid who came to turn down your bed before dinner. My name is Beatrice Kizza. I don't think you know my name because you never asked it.

As I was folding back the sheets on your bed, you came up behind me, took out your penis and pleasured yourself while holding on to me. I felt degraded and humiliated by your attentions. I also feared for my own safety.

I know that you are a rich and successful man. I would therefore like to meet with you at your earliest convenience to discuss ways in which you could compensate me for the above incident.

As yet, I have not told anyone else about what happened. I look forward to hearing from you.

Yours sincerely, Beatrice Kizza.

Howard reads to the end, then folds the paper carefully into quarters. He sits for a while, staring into space, aware that Rupert is looking agitated.

'"As yet",' Howard muses out loud. 'What does that mean?'

His shame of a few moments ago has subsided. In its place is a more familiar sensation: the urgency of tackling a problem that needs to be solved.

Rupert shakes his head.

'I'm not sure, Howard. But reading between the lines, I suspect she's after money. Otherwise, surely, she would have gone to the police.'

Howard checks who the email was sent to: ceo@Paradiso.org.uk. It's a standard address available from the website, designed to fool customers into thinking they've got direct access to the chief executive. But of course, this email address doesn't come to him. It goes to his PA. It goes to Tracy.

His heart lurches forward.

'Has Tracy seen this?'

Rupert looks uncomfortable.

'Yes, Howard. Yes, she has. It was Tracy who alerted me to this, um, this unfortunate, ah, situation. But listen, Howard, there's absolutely nothing to worry about. We've got this under control early enough and—'

'What did Tracy say?' His PA is a woman of unimpeachable morals who has shown him nothing but loyalty for over twenty years and who lives a quiet, dignified life in a terraced house in Epsom with her two cats, Mork and Mindy. For some reason, the idea of Tracy reading about his seedy behaviour in a hotel room on a day when he was meant to have been remembering his long-lost daughter makes Howard feel more wretched than anything Rupert has said up to this point.

'She didn't say anything.'

Howard slumps forward and places his head back in his hands. He stares at his darkened reflection in the shiny granite. A half-remembered flash of Ada as a toddler comes to him, wearing silken shoes and a bridesmaid's dress, carrying her teddy by the ear, stumbling towards him with a naughty smile and shouting, 'Dada, where ARE you?'

He starts to cry. Rupert, as Howard had known he would, pretends not to notice.

Esme

THERE ARE SOME PEOPLE who love going home to visit their parents. Esme is not one of those people.

She's never had a particularly easy relationship with her mother. It wasn't overtly antagonistic – they were both far too well-trained in the arts of silence to give voice to any of their frustrations with each other – but it was tricky nonetheless. A conversation with her mother was an incremental battle of slights and disappointments, all overlain with a prickly sense of martyrdom. When Esme doesn't visit, Mrs Reade will respond with heavy sighs on the other end of the phone line.

'I know you're very busy,' she'll say. 'But it would be good to catch sight of you once in a blue moon.'

And then, when Esme does traipse halfway across the country to come and stay, taking off one of her precious Saturdays to do so (the *Tribune* only allows you two a year as holiday), her mother will invariably make pointed references to how nice it is to see her daughter throughout the course of the weekend.

'It's so rare I get the chance, darling,' she will say. 'I hardly ever clap eyes on you these days.' Laughter. Meaningful pause. 'I mustn't be greedy. Something's better than nothing, after all.'

A sad gaze out of the window, followed by an effortful attempt at a smile.

It's the fact that she's only got one of her parents still living that makes the whole exercise so much more intense. Esme has often wished her mother could meet someone new. The pressure of looking after her would be substantially lessened. But Mrs Reade has never shown much interest in romantic entanglement. She prefers, instead, to take a revisionist attitude to her first marriage.

'I never so much as looked at another man when I was with your father,' she is fond of saying. 'And he *adored* me. Worshipped the ground I walked on.'

Esme's recollections are different. She remembers her parents arguing when she was younger. Not the normal type of arguments you saw on domestic TV dramas, where voices are raised and glasses smashed, but something far more insidious. Their disagreements were always dangerously quiet. The cruellest accusations were the ones left unsaid; the most lethal weapon in their joint armoury an atmosphere of perpetual, unspoken discomfort. But to listen to her mother now, Esme thinks, it would be easy to forget any of it had actually happened.

In any case, Lilian Reade has never found any man who can compete with her hagiographical recollection of her dead husband so Esme is duty-bound to make frequent phone calls and visits. Robbie, by contrast, stays away as much as possible but somehow manages to remain his mother's favourite.

Last year, the two of them had come up for Lilian's fifty-fifth birthday. Esme had searched high and low for a present. Lilian had mentioned in passing having seen a 'darling' pair of jade earrings in a jeweller's shop window in Hereford and Esme had taken it upon herself to hunt for them, presumably out of a sense of guilt, which was her motivation for most things. She'd finally tracked them down in a tiny antiques shop after several hours, handed over an unreasonably large amount of money and presented them with a flourish on her mother's birthday, only to watch Lilian attempt to mask her disappointment as Esme realised they were not, in fact, the right ones. Robbie, by contrast, had forgotten all about their mother's birthday until the day before, when he had rushed out at the last minute to buy a teapot painted with Union Jack flags and an apron emblazoned with 'Keep Calm and Carry On' from a horrible little gift shop round the corner that was famous for never changing its window display. Lilian had been disproportionately delighted with Robbie's gift, calling both items 'charming' and 'jolly' and festooning him with kisses.

'Don't worry about it,' he had said after Esme had unsuccessfully tried to brush it off. 'It's nothing personal.'

'It's entirely personal,' she had replied. And she couldn't help but feel it still was.

At least once a month, out of some negligible sense of duty, Esme does the three-hour train journey to Hereford where Mrs Reade will be waiting in her small red Fiat, her face painted with too much make-up, her hair freshly blow-dried, her pearl necklace accessorised with cream-coloured bangles and a jaunty silk scarf.

Esme plays it all through in her mind as she sits in the train carriage, head resting against the glass. She promises herself, as she always does, that she won't let her mother get to her. Not this time. She will be mature and forgiving and generous. Her mother is lonely and values her daughter's company, even if she has a funny way of showing it. Esme will be the bigger person. She will smile and laugh and compliment Mum's cooking and she'll tell her a bit about her life in London and make it clear that she's doing well, professionally speaking, and she'll field any questions about boyfriends with deft politeness.

But as soon as she steps onto the platform at Hereford and slams the train door shut behind her, Esme feels herself revert instantaneously to the moody teenager she'd vowed not to be. There was no one else in her life who had this effect on her. Did other people have the same problem with their families?

'Darling! Coo-ee! Over here!'

Esme hears her mother before she sees her. Squinting against the sunlight, Esme follows the general direction of her mother's beautifully enunciated screeching (the result of several years of elocution lessons as a child). Lilian is in the far corner of the railway station car park, leaning out of the Fiat's open door and flapping her hand frantically. Esme waves back. She starts walking across, trundling her wheeled suitcase behind her.

'Over here, darling!' her mother shouts. When Esme gets to the car, Lilian envelops her daughter in a graceful hug, their bodies not quite making contact.

'Hi, Mum. Thanks for picking me up.'

The car is sweetly scented with lily of the valley. On the back seat is a neatly folded tartan rug. It has been there for approximately fifteen years and has never, to Esme's knowledge, been used.

'Of course I'm going to pick you up! It's not every weekend I get to see my daughter, after all.'

She turns the key in the ignition and forces the gearstick into first with an agonising clunk. Lilian is a terrible driver.

'Goodness,' her mother says, glancing at Esme's case. 'You've brought enough to stay a week! What have you got in there?'

'Oh, you know, drugs. Crack pipes. Empty bottles of vodka. The usual,' Esme mutters.

Her mother doesn't smile. As she indicates left onto the main road, she mutters, 'All right, I was only asking.'

Esme glances at her watch. Barely ten minutes have elapsed since her train arrived. Already they're annoyed with each other. And that, Esme thinks as they chunter through an amber light just as it starts to turn red, is how it starts.

They stop at Sainsbury's on their way home to pick up some groceries.

'I thought it'd be easier if you came with me because I can never keep track of what you like,' says Lilian, picking up a basket by the entrance and passing it to Esme to carry. 'You keep chopping and changing.'

'Do I?'

'You know you do, darling.' She bends forward to inspect a

bunch of asparagus, wrinkles her nose, then places the vegetable back on the shelf. 'What is it you're having for breakfast these days?'

'I don't have anything.'

Her mother recoils. When she speaks, her voice has a staccato quality.

'You. Mean. To. Say. You. Don't. Eat. Breakfast?'

Esme stays silent, her gaze level.

Lilian shakes her head, as if to get rid of water blocking her ears.

'It's the most important meal of the day, Esme.'

'So people say.'

'It's the key to staying slim.'

Lilian looks pointedly at her daughter. She doesn't add anything else but the implication is already there. Esme glances down at her wrists: they have always been the slenderest part of her. She checks them now to reassure herself that she hasn't put on weight. She is relieved to see they are the same as ever – pale and thin as a strip of silver birch.

'Pâté! I almost forgot,' her mother cries, rushing off to the deli counter. Esme stares at Lilian's retreating figure: a round-shouldered, middle-aged woman trying to make the best of herself in a knee-length navy skirt and court shoes. From this distance, she looks unremarkable. Unremarkable and alone.

Esme reminds herself to stay calm. She makes a deliberate effort to smile.

The tension lifts as soon as they get home. Lilian opens the door to the Old Rectory with a flourish and all at once, Esme can smell the distinct fragrance of family: a jumbled-up mixture of coffee grounds, washing powder and dusty potpourri.

'Home sweet home,' Lilian says. She gestures towards the hall-way with a genteel flourish and waits for Esme to walk in first. 'Welcome back, darling.'

'Thanks, Mum,' Esme says, carrying her case and a bag of

shopping over the threshold. 'It's good to be back.' And she means it too.

Her bedroom is on the right-hand side at the top of the stairs, with a window overlooking the garden. A few months after Esme had moved to London to start on *Trucking Today*, Lilian had unsentimentally announced that she was renovating. As a result, Esme's room, which had once been a hallowed shrine to the musical and aesthetic talents of various boy bands, was now almost unrecognisable from its previous incarnation. The dog-eared posters, each one painstakingly ripped out from music magazine centrefolds and Blu-tacked onto the flock wallpaper, had been the first casualty of Lilian's manic interior decoration. In their place, Esme's mother had sponged rough-edged circles of yellow paint onto the walls in an attempt to give a rustic feel to the room, reminiscent of a Mexican cabana she had once read about in a glossy travel magazine. In reality, the effect was rather slapdash. Every time Esme saw it, she thought not of glorious South American sunsets but of mouldering oranges left to shrink and pucker in a neglected fruit bowl.

The bed is the same metal-framed single she had slept in all her young life. The duvet, with its pattern of dancing penguins, is gratifyingly familiar. Esme sits on the edge of the mattress and slips off her ballet pumps. She unpacks a pair of hotel slippers from her bag and puts them on – her mother doesn't like 'outdoors' shoes to be worn inside. She is pleased to have remembered this.

But then, over a supper of presliced ham and under-seasoned new potatoes, Lilian starts asking her daughter about work and it all begins to slide downhill. Esme feels her hackles rise almost as soon as her mother mentions the *Tribune*.

'It's not my paper of choice, as you know,' Lilian says, slicing a minuscule potato with surgical precision. When she has cut herself an appropriately tiny morsel of carbohydrate, she spears it with her fork and then lets it rest, untouched, on the side of the plate. 'But I must say I've found bits of it very entertaining.'

'That's great. I mean, I know you might think some of it's a bit lowbrow but it's very good at what it does. The editor . . .'

'But don't you think,' Lilian interjects. She lowers her voice as if imparting a confidence. 'That it's a bit *beneath* you, darling?'

Esme flushes. She pushes her knife and fork together, sliding a piece of ham to one side of the plate.

'No, I don't.'

Lilian wipes the corner of her mouth with a frayed linen napkin. Her lipstick leaves a mark on the white material.

'Well that's good.' After a few moments, Lilian lapses into silence. In spite of herself, Esme is goaded into a response.

'I mean, why would you think that?'

Lilian gives a little cough. 'Oh, I'm sure I don't know anything about newspapers but it's just—' She breaks off.

'Yes?'

'Well, I did think you were rather hard on that Treherne woman.'

'Clarissa Treherne? The one who had an affair with the writer?'

Esme has almost forgotten about the pretty blonde on the doorstep in Winchester. She had written up the interview and it had been splashed across two pages, with a full-length portrait of Clarissa Treherne looking chastened and lovelorn in a flowery dress from Marks & Spencer. Chris, the photographer, had turned up with several outfits deemed suitable by the picture-desk. Nothing too black, too short or too slutty. The objective was to make Clarissa Treherne look as Middle England as possible and in that, at least, they had succeeded.

'That's the one,' says Lilian, tapping her fingers on the table. 'I don't see what business it is of yours – or anyone's, for that matter – whether she had an affair or not. They're both consenting adults, aren't they?'

'Yes, but—'

'It just seemed a bit *tawdry*, that's all, dear. And I couldn't help thinking about that poor child. Finding out her father's not who she thought he was.'

Then Lilian adds, 'But I'm sure you wrote it beautifully,' which somehow makes everything worse.

Before Esme can reply, her mother starts stacking the plates and clearing the glasses away. Although her initial response is one of self-righteous indignation, Esme finds that it soon subsides to a vague, unsettled sense that she has done something wrong. For all that her mother can be irritating and hurtful, in this instance she might have a point. And it bothers Esme that, caught up in the triumph of a successful doorstep and the subsequent plaudits from the newsdesk, she hadn't even considered the underlying morality of what she was doing. All she had cared about was getting her name in the paper, getting a good show for her story, getting Dave's attention. And Clarissa Treherne's daughter? She hadn't given her a second thought.

Esme pushes her chair back. It squeaks against the flagstones. She takes the rubber gloves from underneath the sink and puts them on, running the tap until the washing-up bowl is filled with soapy suds.

'I'll do this, Mum,' she says. 'You go and put your feet up.'

Lilian squeezes her daughter's hand.

'Thank you, darling,' she says, padding out of the kitchen in her sheepskin-lined slippers. Esme can hear her walking down the hallway, humming a non-specific tune, and she feels a rush of guilt that she does not love her mother enough, that she cannot hide it and that, underneath it all, this makes her a bad person.

She concentrates on washing the dishes. The soap suds pop and burst. Outside, the light mellows, then darkens. The tinny sound of a television starts up from down the corridor. If she strains, she can just about make out the theme tune to the ten o' clock *News*.

When she goes upstairs, Esme sees that her mother has left something on her pillow. As she gets closer, she realises it is a box of chocolate Brazil nuts, placed on top of a ripped-out page from a magazine. '10 Tips To Stop Back Pain,' Esme reads. She had complained earlier to her mother that long hours in front of a computer had left her with a numb shoulder.

Looking at these offerings, Esme feels a rush of complicated love. Chocolate Brazil nuts have been a favourite since childhood. Lilian always used to save her the special ones from Christmas assortments of sweet treats and jellied fruits. That she has remembered this makes Esme smile. She knows her mother loves her. She should try harder to show her mother that she loves her back.

Esme puts on a pair of socks before jumping into the shivering coolness of the bed. Lilian doesn't believe in central heating after 9 p.m. so the whole house has settled into the usual night-time draughtiness. Even this inspires a feeling of fondness.

'Oh Mum,' Esme murmurs under her breath. She scans the magazine article. Apparently she should take a break from her screen every half-hour and roll her shoulders clockwise, then in the other direction. She tries it now, sitting up against the headboard, and her joints click and snap satisfyingly. Then she switches off the bedside light, snuggles down into the clean sheets and rests her head on the pillow where the chocolate Brazil nuts have left a soft impression.

Tomorrow, thinks Esme. Tomorrow will be good. Tomorrow, I will be a better daughter.

She sleeps soundly, tucked up neatly under the single duvet, and wakes to the sound of her mother scrabbling around in the kitchen beneath her room: the reassuring rhythm of taps being turned and cupboard doors being opened. At precisely ten minutes past nine, just as Esme had known she would, her mother knocks gently on the bedroom door, peeks her head round and says cheerily, 'Morning, darling. Cup of tea?'

'Lovely, thanks, Mum.'

Esme props herself up against her pillow and takes the hot mug of tea from her mother's hands. It has been made just how she likes it: strong but milky. She blows gently across the top, feeling the steamy warmth against her face. Her mother leans across and briskly opens the curtains. The room is filled with a muted light, the colour of an unwashed dishcloth.

If Esme had been left to her own devices, she would have treated herself to a lie-in but she knows her mother sees excess sleep as a sign of weakness, a waste of time that could otherwise be devoted to endless domestic chores (chores that, by dint of their extreme triviality, could only have been invented purely for this purpose: replanting the herbaceous borders, cleaning the fridge, darning an ancient pair of socks when it would be easier to buy a new pair. Because, Esme thinks, who really needs to rearrange their sewing-box? Who genuinely believes their life will be enriched by the effort of it?).

'Not all that nice a day, I'm afraid,' says Lilian, sitting down delicately at the end of the bed, right at the edge. Her mother has a knack of pretending not to want to draw attention to herself while achieving precisely the opposite effect.

Esme pats the bed with her spare hand.

'Come closer, Mum. Get comfortable.'

Lilian shuffles up, head bowed, a small smile on her face. She is already dressed in Capri pants and a striped pink top. The top is made out of stretchy fabric which clings to her, accentuating the single roll of post-menopausal fat that spills over her waistband. The square neckline reveals a sunned patch of neck, skin still glistening slightly from Lilian's daily moisturising routine involving the generous application of Oil of Olay. Her fingernails are painted a glimmering pink.

'I like your nail varnish,' Esme says.

'Oh thank you. I had them done the other day at this new nail bar in town. Terribly nice Thai girls. Couldn't understand a word of what they were saying but it was very good value.'

Lilian glances at her.

'Did you sleep well, darling?'

'Mmm. Like a log.'

'Well,' Lilian says, crossing her legs and cupping her hands around one knee. 'What would you like to do today?'

What she'd most like to do today is buy the Sunday papers and watch trashy American reality shows in her pyjamas. But she knows better than to say this out loud.

'I don't know. Maybe we could go somewhere nice for lunch? Or the cinema . . . ?'

'Oh no, it's far too nice a day for that.'

'I thought you said it wasn't looking that great.'

'It'll probably clear up later.'

Esme takes a gulp of tea. She can feel her cheeks burning.

'What would *you* like to do, Mum?'

Lilian laughs, grabbing hold of Esme's leg through the duvet.

'I don't mind as long as I'm spending time with you.'

'OK,' Esme says, putting the tea to one side and swinging herself out of bed. She is determined this conversation won't beat her. 'Then let's go for lunch at the pub and have a proper catch-up. I might pop to the newsagent's to get the papers before then.'

She bends to kiss her mother affectionately on the top of her head to forestall any further objections.

'I'll jump in the shower.'

'All right, dear,' Lilian says.

'Thank you for the chocolate Brazils. You're so sweet to remember.'

Lilian beams at her and waves her hand dismissively.

'It was just a little thing . . .'

She turns away from Esme and starts to rearrange the bed, pulling the sheets cleanly to each corner, smoothing the wrinkles from the slept-in duvet. Esme stares at her back for a moment, then puts on her dressing gown and strides into the hallway with a purposefulness she doesn't feel. In the bathroom, just as she is about to turn on the shower, her mother shouts after her, 'Your phone's beeping.'

'I'll check it later,' Esme replies, her voice swallowed by the noise of the water tank, jolting itself into use.

Later, when she does look at her phone, scrubbed and fresh, with wet hair trailing down her back, she notices she's missed a call from Dave. Her stomach contracts. If he's calling on a Sunday it's generally because there's a serious complaint about something she's written. She listens to the voicemail message standing in the middle of her bedroom, holding a towel around her with one hand. Her mother's towels are always slightly too small and threadbare to be comfortable and she has to wrestle with the edges of it to keep herself from trembling.

'Hi, Es. Give me a call, would you? Thanks.'

She rings him straight back. Dave answers immediately.

'Esme,' he says, stretching out her name like a piece of melting caramel. 'Sorry to disturb you on your day of rest.'

'That's OK. Anything wrong?'

She can hear a jumble of noises in the background: the faint voice of a teenager, an answering female murmur and the sound of cutlery being laid out on a table. His family, she thinks, and she feels exposed, suddenly, aware of her nakedness underneath the damp towel.

'Not as such,' Dave continues. 'Are you in London?'

'No, I'm at my mum's.'

There is a pause on the other end of the line.

'Where's that then?'

'Herefordshire.'

'Nice countryside there. Lot of hedgerows.'

'Erm, yeah, I suppose there are.'

'Listen, Es, could you get back here for tomorrow. I wouldn't normally ask but it's important.'

Relief floods into her bones. A watertight excuse for leaving early. She smiles.

'Of course, but can you let me know what it's about at least?'

'It's about your mate,' Dave says. He leaves a beat of perfectly judged silence, just enough to whet her appetite.

'Howard Pink,' he says. 'He wants to do an interview.'

149

Carol

*I*T WAS VANESSA WHO had the idea for an excursion.

'I thought we could go to the Wetlands Centre,' she had said, bright and breezy over the phone a couple of nights ago.

'Your dad loved that place,' Carol replied, before she could stop herself. Vanessa was worried she was wallowing. That was her word. Wallowing. Like a seal.

'I know. And Archie loves it too. He can use those binoculars you gave him.'

Last August, when Archie had turned twelve, Carol had got him the binoculars for his birthday. Derek had just started his chemo – long hours spent in a room hooked up to a bag of chemicals. She would go with her husband to the hospital and do her knitting or take some of her magazines: anything to avoid looking at the life draining out of him. The worst part was when he tried to be cheerful. He'd attempt a smile but the crinkles at the corner of his eyes seemed to deepen, as if some invisible hand had dug out a series of tiny ditches on the landscape of his skin. His cheeks sank into themselves, collapsing like badly pitched tents, so that instead of looking reassuring, he appeared only to be losing himself into a succession of empty spaces. It was the emptiness that broke her heart. There were days when Derek's face wouldn't express anything at all.

Archie turned twelve in the midst of it all, so Carol had taken it upon herself to get his present. She'd discussed it with Derek and he'd agreed that a pair of binoculars was 'just the ticket'. Archie loved birds. He'd saved up all his pocket money to become a member of the RSPB after watching a nature documentary on the declining number of sparrows. So Carol did a bit of research online and then pottered down the road to the Southside Centre to order a pair of lightweight, waterproof binoculars from Argos. She paid £61.99 at the till, which was more than she'd usually spend on anyone else's birthday present, but she knew the look on Archie's face would be worth it. Besides, it wasn't as if he had a dad to spoil him. It was only him and Vanessa, after all.

She'd been right about Archie's reaction: as soon as he'd opened the carefully wrapped box, his face got that blurry look around the edges. He was happy as a pig in clover.

Derek, sitting on the sofa, covered snugly in a blanket even though it was one of the hottest days of the year, had chuckled with satisfaction. Archie rushed over, throwing himself into his granddad's arms, burrowing his head into that tender part between the top of Derek's shoulder and the base of his neck.

'Thank you, Granddad,' he said, voice muffled.

'It was your grandma's idea.' Derek patted his grandson on the back. He let his hand rest there, white and frail against the red of Archie's polo-shirt. Looking at them, Carol was struck by their completeness: just the two of them, curved into each other, finding each other's gaps and filling them. She wanted to cry, not from happiness or sadness, but from something in between the two that she couldn't define.

Sometimes, Carol thought to herself as she listened to her daughter's voice on the phone, the simplest things gave you the best feeling.

'I'd love to come,' she said.

On the other end of the line, she could hear Vanessa exhale with relief.

So here they are, walking along the towpath towards the Wetlands Centre near Barnes, just the three of them: Vanessa in cut-off denim shorts and a black T-shirt that makes her look paler than she is, Archie with his binoculars strung proudly round his neck and Carol wearing her sensible walking shoes and a floppy fabric sunhat that presses down too tightly on her hairline. Sweat prickles on her forehead. The problem with getting older, she finds, is that you can't keep up any more. Whenever they walk anywhere together, Vanessa starts off being thoughtful and slowing her pace so that it matches her mother's. But then, after fifteen minutes or so, her daughter seems to forget and slips into her usual briskness and Carol doesn't like to be a stick-in-the-mud, so tries to speed up without saying anything to draw attention to herself. As a result, Carol arrives everywhere uncomfortably hot and out of breath.

By the time they get to the Wetlands Centre, all Carol wants is a nice sit-down and a cup of tea. In the queue for tickets, Archie glances at her sideways. His head is bowed, his face half obscured by hair, but she catches him taking everything in. He is the most observant boy. Wise beyond his years, as she's fond of telling anyone who'll listen.

'Mum,' he says, tugging at the edge of Vanessa's T-shirt.

Vanessa doesn't turn to look at him. She's busy on her phone, Carol sees. As usual. Her daughter went back to work three months after Archie was born. Three months! Carol didn't approve of career women, on the whole. By all means have a part-time job when you're raising kids, just to make ends meet. But what was the point of having a child if you weren't going to mother them? All this talk of women 'having it all'. Stuff and nonsense. Why would anyone want to have it all anyway? You made your choices and you stuck to them.

'Mum,' Archie is saying, determination creeping in around the edges of his voice.

'Mmmm.'

'Can we have a drink in the café first? I'm really thirsty.'

'Oh Archie, I told you to bring some water . . .'

'Please?'

'OK. But we don't want to miss the bird feeding at three.'

While Vanessa pays for their tickets with a credit card, Carol hugs her grandson close to her. He wriggles but she knows he likes it really. She presses her hand tight against his ribcage and feels his slender bones. Over the last few months, he has shot up in height. She worries constantly that he doesn't eat enough. She knows, too, that he won't allow her to hug him for too much longer. Soon he'll be a gangly teenager, introverted and self-conscious. She's seen it all before with Vanessa. In fact, looking at her now texting whoever it is on that Blackcurrant contraption or whatever they call it, Carol is not even sure her daughter has ever grown out of adolescence.

When they're sitting down on the wooden chairs on the café terrace, Carol takes a sip of her tea, looks at Archie sipping his Coke through a straw and fiddling with some setting on his binoculars, and she plucks up the courage to ask, 'Who are you on the phone to?'

Vanessa stares at her blankly.

'Mmm? Oh, no one. Just a work thing.'

Vanessa works for a property company. Letting out luxury apartments to businessmen for short-term stays – that kind of thing. She earns a good salary, but most of it is on commission.

'At the weekend?'

Vanessa rolls her eyes.

'Yes, Mum. Just an email I had to reply to.' She makes an elaborate show of putting her phone back in her handbag, then zipping it up. 'There. Now I'm all yours.' She ruffles the top of Archie's head and he smiles, grateful at last to have his mother's attention.

'How's your tea?'

'Lovely, thanks.'

'And how are things . . . you know, generally? Should we be worried about you?'

Vanessa looks over the top of her sunglasses. Carol can see her pale blue eyes and, beneath them, dark circles the colour of hyacinth petals. She marvels, once again, at her daughter's unexpected beauty. She pats Vanessa lightly on the hand.

'I'm fine, love.' And then, because she knows that Vanessa is trying, that she is really making an effort, she adds, 'Thank you for asking.'

'You know you can always come and stay with us—'

Archie nods. 'Yeah, Grandma. You can have my bed.'

Carol laughs. 'And where would you sleep? No, honestly, I'm very happy on my own. Besides, I've got to water my next-door neighbour's plants. He's off on holiday.'

'That's nice,' Vanessa says distractedly. The phone is vibrating in her handbag, sending out pulsations of sound.

'Yes, Alan. Lives at Number 12,' Carol continues, making a point of carrying on the conversation despite her daughter's attention wandering. 'Odd fellow.'

'Why?' Archie asks, finishing the last of his drink and sucking on the straw until it starts to make a bubbling noise. Vanessa tells him to stop and he does so immediately, with a meekness that makes Carol sad.

'Just . . . I can't put my finger on it . . . just something about him that doesn't seem to fit.'

They lapse into silence. Carol finishes her tea, savouring the sweetness of unstirred sugar at the bottom of the cup. She winks at Archie and he grins at her. There are two small patches of pink on the apples of his cheek. She wonders if Vanessa has put any lotion on his face but can't quite bring herself to ask, knowing that, if she does, a curtain of defensive silence will fall around them and the rest of the afternoon will be ruined. She's ever so sensitive about things.

'Shall we go then?' Vanessa says, checking the time on her watch. 'Bird feeding starts in five minutes.'

A woman wearing thigh-high waders with a jolly, weather-beaten face introduces herself as Sally, the bird-feeder. A small group of parents and children has gathered under a gazebo at the central meeting point. Sally shows them a wheeled trolley containing buckets filled with various pellets and tells them that this is for the birds only and should on no account be eaten by humans, at which point a toddler in a blue Boden dress and tiny Converse trainers leans forward and scoops out a handful with podgy fingers.

'Milly, no,' says a blousy brunette, smiling stupidly as though Milly has just done something terribly charming. 'Put that back, darling. It's for the birdies. Yes, it is. The little ducky-wuckies.'

Carol grimaces. Baby talk. Can't abide it.

The child looks at her mother stubbornly, then lets the pellets drop to the ground.

'It's fine, honestly,' Sally says generously. 'Let's get going, then we can give the birds something to eat.'

Archie stoops to pick up the scattered pellets and his binoculars graze against the gravel path. Vanessa is on her phone again so Carol bends over to help him, feeling a dull ache in her lower back as she levers herself gradually closer to the ground.

'We'll have more to give the birds now,' Archie says, clenching his hand tightly in a fist. He has never liked untidiness.

'Good idea.' Carol is so close she can smell shower gel on his T-shirt, mixed in with the scent of freshly sharpened pencils. She gives him the pellets she has gathered and they set off, trailing behind Sally and her wheeled trolley.

It is a beautiful day. Only the faintest wisps of cloud in a sky shot through with glistening threads of sunshine. The river water throws up shards of refracted light. There is something about parkland that makes Carol feel secure. It is the manageability of scale, perhaps: the knowledge that there is a boundary in the distance, unseen and yet definite. She has always found the idea of untrammelled wilderness frightening. When, in the past, Derek had encouraged her to swim in the sea on holiday, she could never fully relax. She was aware, all the time, that a vast wave could rip her away from land. That she could go under. She relied on Derek to chivy her along, to make her go on a camel ride in the desert and to do things she wouldn't normally because he was there and that meant she didn't need to be afraid. And now he wasn't with her, so she's scared all over again.

'Mum! It's a little ringed plover.' Archie is pointing excitedly at a bird. To Carol, it seems to look just like any other feathered creature. Vanessa squints her gaze and follows Archie's hand.

'Oh yes,' she says, putting her arm around Archie's waist. 'Can I use your binoculars?'

Archie nods. The binoculars are still hanging around his neck. Vanessa leans across and puts them up to her face.

Carol hangs back, just to look at them. From the back, they could be siblings.

'These are great, Mum,' Vanessa cries. 'What a fab present.'

Carol beams at them both. Whatever she might think about the way Vanessa chooses to live her life, her childlike glee can be a wonderful thing. A warmth rises up from the tip of Carol's toes, all the way to her neckline and then to the roots of her scalp. For the first time in months, she remembers what it is to experience the uncomplicated joy of a brief, simple moment of happiness. She is relieved, more than anything, that she still has the capacity, that her heart is still open enough to allow a chink of it through. She had been worried, after Derek's death, that she'd never be able to feel anything again.

Later, they all go back to Lebanon Gardens for tea. Carol makes Archie's favourite – tuna fishcakes with green beans on the side. He doesn't care for junk food. Apart from ice cream, he hardly has a sweet tooth either.

'He's started watching *MasterChef*,' Vanessa says, as Carol is topping and tailing the beans. 'Cooking is his new big thing.'

Carol laughs. 'It's hard to keep up.'

'Yeah,' Vanessa agrees, pouring herself a glass of orange juice. Carol puts a pan of water on to boil. Her daughter has never been one to offer help unless it is explicitly pointed out to her that it might be needed. She wonders why this is, exactly. Had she and Derek spoilt her? Would she have been more thoughtful if they'd had another child?

And yet there were times when Vanessa was extremely loving, as if her affection could manifest itself only in sudden, demonstrative squalls.

'Love you, Mum,' she will say, in the middle of a chat about something entirely mundane. Or she will come up behind Carol and clasp her tightly in a hug, head pressing against her mother's back. Or she will write a beautifully effusive card, after months and months of never saying thank you. The unpredictable nature of these events left Carol vaguely suspicious each time. Why did everyone have to go around saying they loved each other anyway? What was this modern fashion for weeping and wailing at the slightest provocation? In her day, they didn't need to vocalise any of it. They just got on with things. It was actions that counted.

Archie devours his tuna fishcakes in a few rapid bites, then asks if he can get down to watch television. Vanessa stays seated, toying with the food on her plate.

'Not hungry?' Carol asks.

'Sorry, Mum,' Vanessa says with a tired smile. 'Too many sweets at the Wetlands Centre.'

She says that and yet Carol knows she's hardly eaten a thing all day.

'You'll disappear if you're not careful.'

Vanessa suppresses a sigh.

'Mum, I'm forty-six. I can look after myself.'

'Sorry I spoke.'

There is an uneasy silence.

After tea, Carol remembers that she hasn't yet watered the plants next door. She wonders if she can get away with not doing them, just for one day, but her Presbyterian guilt gets the better of her. The last two days have been hot and dry. His hydrangea will be wilting by now.

Archie is curled up on the sofa, watching something that involves adults doing an obstacle course. A ginger-haired man in a Lycra one-piece is attempting to leap onto a rotating rubber wheel, while being doused in water from a series of high-pressure jets.

'Do you want to come and do the plants next door with me?' she says hopefully.

Archie stares at the screen, seeming not to have heard.

'Archie?'

He nods, turns off the television and comes with her, silently. Sometimes she wishes he weren't so well-behaved. He seems too adult, as though the spirit has already been ground out of him.

She takes Alan's keys from the hook in the hallway and goes next door, with Archie trailing a few steps behind. As soon as she opens the front door to Number 12, Archie's curiosity gets the better of him and he bowls past her into the hallway, excitedly looking into each room and comparing the layout to her house.

'He's got a smaller kitchen,' Archie shouts.

'I don't think he's got his side return done, has he?'

'Ugh. His fridge *stinks*.'

'That's not nice, Archie,' she says, but she follows him down the corridor and peers into the fridge. A plastic bag from a super-market deli is on the bottom shelf, filled with pinkish lumps that she assumes are prawns. A gelatinous liquid is seeping out from underneath. She reaches in, takes the bag and throws it in the pedal-bin.

'Eww, gross!' Archie says.

'He must've forgotten they were there.' Carol makes a mental note to empty the bin before leaving. She doesn't want the prawns smelling out the entire house before Alan gets back. She leaves Archie exploring the upstairs and makes her way through the double doors into the garden. She bends to fill the watering can from an outside tap, feeling her knees ache with the movement. Once the can is brimming with water, she has to spend several seconds gathering enough strength to stand upright again. She's so much more tired in the evenings now. As she straightens, Carol emits an unintentional groan, supporting the small of her back with her one free hand. She can remember her mother standing in exactly the same way. It's true, she thinks, I've finally turned into her.

She starts, methodically, in the far corner of the garden by the small apple tree and works her way round clockwise until she gets to the potted plants on the patio. The tiles are evenly placed and scrubbed clean. There are no weeds in the cracks, Carol notes approvingly. Each plant has a small handwritten label stuck into the soil next to it, identifying its genus. There's no doubt that Alan takes good care of his garden.

'Grandma!'

She turns to see Archie leaning out of an upstairs window, waving at her. She smiles, in spite of herself.

'Get down here, nosy parker! And close that window properly. I don't want Alan thinking I've been snooping around.'

After a few minutes, Archie emerges in the garden. She has done most of the plants by then: the rhododendron, the camellia and the mixed herbs in the trough by the window. Her shoulders are tingling with the exertion.

'Oh heavens, I forgot the jasmine bush at the back,' she mutters.

'I'll do it,' Archie says, grabbing the watering can from her.

'All right then, love.' She sits down on one of Alan's outdoor chairs, sighing with the comfort of it. She watches her grandson run to the end of the garden. The back of his neck has caught the sun. There is a strip of paler flesh from where the binocular strap would have been. She should give Vanessa some lotion for that to take home. A drowsiness creeps over her. Her eyelids droop downwards and she is unable to stop her vision from stuttering so that all she can see is the thin sliver of Archie's trainers in the grass. Just a few seconds, she thinks. I'll just shut my eyes for a few seconds.

'Grandma!'

She jerks awake. Archie is beckoning to her, pointing at something in the ground. Still half-asleep, she walks to where he is standing and because everything still seems a bit dreamlike, a bit shrouded in shadow, it takes a while for her gaze to click into focus. When it does, she isn't immediately sure what she's looking at.

'What is it?' Archie is saying and then he is holding her arm, shifting back from the edge of a flower bed where the soil has recently been turned over and there is something in the ground, something that looks like a bunch of twigs but, at the same time, the twigs are too angular, too precise in their delineation and soon Carol is kneeling down, reaching out to clear them away. Just before the tip of her finger makes contact with whatever it is, she stops herself. And suddenly, she knows. She knows, beyond doubt, what she is seeing.

It is a hand. The decomposing bones of a human hand.

The gasp of surprise sticks in her throat.

Beatrice

SHE WAKES SCREAMING. IT is the dream again, the one where she is running down an endless narrow corridor. Someone is chasing her. A man. He has no face but Beatrice knows who it is. The more she runs, the stickier the ground becomes. The man keeps chasing and her feet are sucked under and she is trapped, half devoured by an inky muddiness. She tries to free herself, wriggling her torso frantically to dislodge herself from the thick, gloopy substance, but with every movement, her energy is sapped and her muscles become loose with exhaustion. Beatrice can hear his quickening footsteps behind her and all she can do is raise her arms over her head in a useless attempt to protect herself and then, just as he is about to get to her, she wakes, dripping with sweat and confusion, gasping for air.

She'd had the same dream every night for the best part of a year when she left Uganda. It was particularly bad when she was struggling to get a National Insurance number. Ngozi, an acquaintance at RASS, had persuaded her to use a Nigerian woman's ID.

'But I don't look anything like her,' Beatrice had protested. She had assumed, sensibly enough, that the National Insurance card would carry a photo. It seemed ludicrous to her that it wouldn't.

Ngozi had laughed and sucked her teeth. 'Mmm-hmm,' Ngozi had said, her chest jiggling with mirth. 'Child, even if it mattered, we all look the same to them.'

It didn't take long for Beatrice to realise that Ngozi was right. She found her first illegal job listed in the back of a free newspaper. It was cleaning an office in Docklands, a tall building of steel and tinted glass with nondescript corridors covered in fraying carpet tiles and bathed in harsh fluorescent strip lighting that made everyone's faces look pouchy and dull.

The supervisor had barely glanced at her, let alone her fraudulent National Insurance details. He had simply wanted to know how soon she could start, whether she had a problem with being paid cash in hand, which, of course, she didn't. The work had been stultifying in its repetitiveness. There was a particular kind of boredom, she discovered, that came from carrying out a succession of mundane tasks late at night, when everyone else had gone home and the only sound was the sporadic mechanical whirr of the photocopier shutting down. Occasionally, Beatrice would come across the odd straggler: slack-skinned businessmen shuffling paper and trying to avoid going home. They would never look at her, these men, even when she passed within 3 feet of them, pushing the industrial vacuum cleaner with tired arms and gathering up the looping orange electrical flex behind her. She wasn't sure whether they were deliberately ignoring her or whether they were nervous of reminding themselves of their own realness. She began to think of them as waxworks, like the ones she had read about in Madame Tussauds: startlingly realistic, disturbingly motionless representations of actual human beings. Waxen men.

And then, one night, she found one of them dead. He was hanging from a coat hook in his office, his face purple and distended, eyes bulging like a grotesque tribal mask. She had stood there, with her hand on the door, shocked into a moment of complete stillness. She hadn't wanted to get involved. She knew that if she reported the suicide, the police would probably want to talk to her and then she would be found out and deported. So Beatrice had closed the door, leaving the vacuum cleaner where it was, orange flex still plugged in, and she had walked back down the corridor, into the lift and out of the building's revolving doors into the night air. She hadn't gone back to work the next day or the one after that. The worst part of it was admitting to herself that she hadn't been that upset; that the sight of the man's inert body had not moved her as it might once have done. Was she losing herself? Was her capacity to feel being squeezed out of her?

The relief when she was finally granted permanent status had been palpable. The dream with the man chasing her down the corridor seemed to retreat. She hadn't had it for ages. And now, here it was once more, reminding her of the incident she had tried so hard to forget, the dark, ugly thing that she has painted over in her mind, hoping it would never resurface. But she has come to realise that memories always do. Especially the bad ones, which rise like bubbles of damp through paint.

Beatrice glances at the radio alarm clock. It is 3.22 a.m. The sharp-edged traces of the dream prick against her scalp. If it had been a couple of hours later, she would have got up, convincing herself that she had meant to rise early in order to have a productive day filled with necessary tasks so that she didn't have to think any more. As it is, she feels alone and small. Underneath, she feels scared.

She twists her head on the pillow, trying to shake off the dream, trying to cough up the bitter taste it has left in her mouth. It doesn't work. She stills herself, bracing and clenching her muscles for what she knows is about to come.

The memory sweeps towards her like a wave, stretching up to its full height, looming over her tiny, stick-man form standing on the tideline. In a moment, she will be engulfed in it, pulled down by its magnetic current. The wave rushes towards her. And then it breaks.

Lying in the dark, eyes open, chest tight, Beatrice surrenders herself. She tries to think about it as dispassionately as possible, so that the memory comes back as a series of objective facts, written up for the purposes of historical record and future analysis. She tries not to cry.

It was a day in November. Six years ago. They were in Susan's modest, single-storey house, snatching at a spare half-hour in the late afternoon. Beatrice was lying half-naked in bed. Susan was sitting on the edge of the mattress, the knotted curve of her spine visible beneath a thin cotton shirt. Beatrice can remember smiling at the sight of those familiar vertebrae, poking out like pegs on a clothesline. She wanted to reach out and trace the shape of them but, for some reason never fully explained, she stopped herself just before she touched the taut warmth of Susan's skin.

She had been happy. It is important to remember that because it would be so easy to forget, knowing all that had happened between then and now.

As Beatrice withdrew her hand from the not-quite-touching of Susan's back, there was a brutal explosion of noise. A crack-slash-slice like a bone being broken.

The door shattered and splintered, buckling on its hinges and slamming to the floor, releasing a cloud of red dust.

Both of them started scrabbling to cover themselves with whatever clothes came to hand. But before they had a chance to disguise the bareness of their bodies, Susan's brother was on the threshold wearing big black boots, stamping his feet, breathing heavily so that his nostrils flared with each exhalation.

For a moment, neither Beatrice nor Susan knew what was happening and in that first bout of confusion, they reached for each other, the tips of their fingers grazing too briefly over the bed sheet.

The sight of that small almost-motion, that single half-expression of closeness, seemed to enrage Susan's brother. He shouted, the words slipping into each other so that they were a torrent of gushing sound neither of them could make sense of. He marched into the room, gesticulating wildly, madness in his eyes. He screamed so hard the spittle gathered in bubbles at the corner of his mouth like spattered coconut juice. He accused them of bringing shame on their families. He called them a disgrace. He said the sight of them disgusted him.

Susan sprang out of bed to try and calm him but her brother lashed out with one arm, slapping her cheek with the flat of his muscle and sending her skittering to the ground.

Beatrice rushed towards them, calling out her girlfriend's name. There were tears of panic in Susan's eyes. Beatrice bent over to stroke her cheek without thinking. It was a natural response when you loved someone.

Wasn't it?

Watching them, huddled on the floor, Susan's brother became silent and the silence was worse than the noise. It had more intent behind it.

He walked towards Beatrice, keeping his gaze level with hers, his face slicked with sweat, the veins in his neck standing out. Quickly, so quickly she had no chance to defend herself, he grabbed her arms in his hands, his fingers gripping and pinching her skin like he was wringing the neck of a chicken. With his hands still on her arms, he twisted his leg round, nudging into her kneecap from behind so that, in one swift movement, she was on the bed, with Susan's brother lying heavy on top of her.

He laughed.

'Whore,' he said, his face pressed up against hers. 'You get on your back for anyone, you filthy fucking whore.'

And even in the midst of it, even knowing what was about to happen, even as he took his cock out and forced it into her mouth, Beatrice had time to think that the language surprised her. Because this was Susan's younger brother. The one who had a sweet smile. Who had looked so harmless sitting on the steps of the Endiro Café in Kisementi, drinking Coca-Cola from a bottle through a straw, proudly wearing his box-fresh trainers. And now he was pushing down her pants, unbuttoning his trousers, grunting at her through gritted teeth, all the time leaning on her with his full weight so that, for a moment, she feared she might stop breathing altogether.

He didn't look at her as he was raping her.

Rape. It deserves the word.

Her mind turned white. She tried to focus on something else, something everyday and reassuring, and her thoughts fixed on the image of five potatoes and one onion they had left drying on the step outside in preparation for dinner. Five potatoes and one onion. Five and one.

When it happened, she remembers thinking it wasn't so bad after all. It was the terror of anticipation that had made it so vicious. It was the *thought* of being ripped through, for the first time, by a man that sickened her. It wasn't the actuality of it. Because while he was inside her, she remained outside herself – dislocated, unreachable, inviolate. It was so unlike her acts of love with Susan that it belonged somewhere else entirely, some-where beyond her own sphere of reason, a snow-globe turned upside down with flakes of white drifting towards the sky.

And afterwards, he seemed embarrassed. He left her lying there, the dribbling ooze of him dampening her thighs. He pulled up his trousers and walked out of the house, the tread of his feet sounding heavily on the bare floor.

The last image she ever had of him was of his back receding: sloping shoulders, muscular arms, black boots. It was this image that kept recurring, rising up when she least expected it. She saw him on tube escalators, at café tables, on the top deck of buses. Once she thought she saw him reading a magazine with a film star on the cover on a bench in Hyde Park. The boy in the blue hoodie listening to music in Trafalgar Square had been him too.

On the bed, lying there with a clotted numbness between her legs, Beatrice heard him go. The thud of black boots. The slam of the front door. The silence punctuated by birdsong that seemed, suddenly, obscene.

Susan started crying, rocking backwards and forwards on her

haunches in the corner of the room. Beatrice stayed on the bed, staring for a long, long time.

And the most painful part, more painful by far than what he had done to her, was that Susan didn't come to comfort her. In the days that followed, Susan had acted as though it were some-how Beatrice's fault. And then the villagers found out.

Nothing between them had ever been the same after that.

In her bedroom in Bermondsey, Beatrice wraps the duvet more tightly around her. She turns onto one side so that her cheek lies flat against the cotton of her pillow. She draws her legs up to her chin like a child and closes her eyes. She tries to imagine a field of sheep and then to picture each one of them leaping over a fence in spirited single file. She counts them as they jump. Someone had once told her this is what English people do when they can't sleep. Beatrice thinks it's stupid but, at this point, is willing to try anything.

She gets to twenty-five before her overactive thoughts get the better of her. She begins to visualise the sheep like whirling fluffy clouds and gives them individual faces and different coloured wool. She imagines them bright pink and purple and with yellow polka dots. She plants flowers in the grass that grow big, angry petals with teeth like a Venus fly-trap. She makes the fence higher and higher so that the sheep struggle to clear it. And then, finally, one of the sheep gets stuck on the topmost ledge and he is left there, his feet scrabbling against the wood, bleating uselessly to the flock down below.

She opens her eyes again, shaking her head to rid it of such nonsense.

'Stop your stupidity,' she says out loud so that her words reverberate uselessly into the empty room.

The time on the clock flashes towards her: 3.35 a.m. She switches on her bedside light and presses back her hair with the palms of her hands. She tries to find something to make her laugh or to make her angry or to coax a fieriness from her belly so that she doesn't have to admit what it is she is actually feeling, which is frightened. Because being frightened makes you weak. She will not be weak. Not today of all days. Not the day when she is due to meet Howard Pink.

She swings out of bed and finds her slippers with the tips of her toes. In the bathroom, she turns on the shower so that it has time to heat up properly. She wants to submerge herself in water that is almost too hot to bear. She wants to feel the electric tingle of it on her skin: a purge.

Under the hot stream of water, Beatrice rehearses what it is she wants to say to Howard Pink. She still has trouble believing she will actually confront him, that the email she wrote in Manny's café in a fit of – of what exactly? Frustration? Determination not to be ignored? – has had such immediate consequences.

And yet it seems to have worked. A man named Rupert had got in touch with her a few days after she sent her original email. He had called her mobile from an unknown number. She'd been cleaning one of the bigger hotel suites and was in the middle of emptying a bin full of minibar bottles and spent condoms, knotted at the end, when her phone went off. Beatrice wasn't meant to have it on while she was at work but it was so rare for her to get phone calls that she answered anyway.

'Is that Beatrice Kizza?' a posh male voice said on the other end of the line.

'Yes.'

'Are you in a place where this conversation can be overheard?' Beatrice scanned the room. She was on her own. Ewelina was in the next-door suite. She pushed the door closed, putting the 'Do Not Disturb' sign on the outside handle.

'No,' Beatrice said.

The man spoke.

'My name is Rupert Leitch. I work for Sir Howard Pink. I think you know why I'm calling you.'

His voice was icy and bored. Beatrice imagined him with a white moustache and a purple jacket, sitting in an enormous leather armchair by a roaring fire, like Professor Plum in the old Cluedo game she'd grown up with back home. She stayed silent.

'I'm calling you on Sir Howard's orders to arrange a meeting between the two of you.'

She scrunched up the duster she was carrying, put it back on her cleaning trolley and sat on the end of the bed. She was disturbed to see she was shaking.

'Are you still there?'

'Yes.'

'Right.' There was the sound of the top of a biro being clicked over and over in Rupert Leitch's hand. 'Sir Howard is an extremely busy man but he has a window next Tuesday at 8.30 a.m. You will come to the Royal Garden Hotel in Kensington where we have booked a suite. Do you have a pen?'

Beatrice reached for the notepad underneath the Louis XVI-style lamp on the bedside table.

'Yes.'

Rupert Leitch gave her the address, his tone still terse.

'When you arrive, you will be met by me at reception. Do not give your name to anyone. If you are asked, you say simply that you are meeting a wealthy anonymous client for a job interview as his housekeeper. Do not discuss it any further. Is that clear?'

'Yes.'

'I want to make it absolutely crystal that, as far as anyone else is concerned, this conversation never took place,' he continued. 'Your total and utter discretion is required. If any word of it gets out, if you speak to any person about this – a friend, a family member, anyone – we will . . .' He seemed to gather his force. 'Unleash hell.'

He stopped, then added, as if the thought had only just occurred to him, 'Do you understand? I mean, do you speak English?'

She was too taken aback to be insulted.

'Of course I do.'

'Sir Howard is an extremely powerful man with friends in

169

influential places. I'm sure I don't need to spell it out for you any more than that given the . . .' He paused. 'Well, shall we say, the delicacy of your situation.'

'I understand,' Beatrice said, her throat tight with dislike. She sat up straighter.

'Good.' Rupert Leitch dropped his voice, moistening each syllable with a slight lisp. 'It was Sir Howard's own decision to meet you. I was – and remain – entirely opposed to the idea. Our lawyers tell us we'd have a watertight case against you for extortion and attempted blackmail.'

Beatrice said nothing.

Quickly, as though no threat had ever been uttered, Rupert Leitch assumed the brisk manner of a jolly headmaster.

'Good. See you Tuesday.'

In the shower, she shakes despite the heat of the water. Why had she done it? What had possessed her to send the email? It is quite simple: she is sick of being a nobody.

She is sick of men getting away with it.

She wants to stop being a faceless person among the masses of other faceless people afraid to make a noise, fearful of disrupting the precarious equilibrium of their existence. She wants to rediscover her courage. She wants to remind herself who she was: Beatrice Kizza, the girl who could climb to the top of the avocado tree in her auntie's garden when all the boys were scared.

Because somewhere along the way, she had lost a bit of herself. She tried, each day, to put on a front, to arm herself with a defensive shield that would make her impenetrable, and yet there was a softness, still, at the core of her. And that weakness came from Susan, from the absence of her. Because there were no answers. Because she didn't know, any more, whether Susan had felt the same. Because it had cost Beatrice so much to love her and now there was nothing to show for it.

Perhaps, Beatrice thinks, scrubbing at her skin with soap, Susan doesn't want to be found. In her lowest moments, she torments herself with this thought: that Susan has gone back to her family, to her rapist brother and her wretched parents and forgotten all about her girlfriend. That everything they said to each other was a lie.

She steps out of the shower, dripping water on the cold tiles, watching the imprints of her toes slip into each other and form a larger puddle. She rubs herself dry roughly, punishing herself with the discomfort, and then walks back into the bedroom, throws on tracksuit bottoms and an old T-shirt and picks up her keys. She slams the door behind her, not caring if she wakes her neighbours. From the open balcony, she can see that the sky is still dark, stars studded into the blackness like drawing pins. The lift is out of order, so she takes the stairs. On Jamaica Road, she starts walking, picking up her pace until her breathing is ragged and her thoughts begin to shift and scatter. She pumps her arms up and down, the rhythm of movement helping her mind to become clear. She can feel the sharp tingle of a blister forming on her right ankle. After an hour or so, the blister is all that she is focusing on. The unspoken anxieties disperse.

By the time the sun has risen and the traffic has started to fill the roads, Beatrice is more prepared for what the day has in store. She runs up the stairs to her flat. She puts the kettle on, takes out a sachet of coffee and pours it into a chipped mug, the inside of it stained the pale brown of a mushroom skin. She is too nervous to eat anything, so she takes her coffee back into the bedroom, turns on the radio as loud as it will go and lets the pumping beats of a pop song fill the flat.

The night before, she had carefully pressed her best clothes with her new iron. Hanging from a hook on the wardrobe door is a knee-length grey skirt she'd found in the Trinity Hospice charity shop and which fitted her perfectly once she'd taken up the hem, a white shirt given to her by the volunteers at RASS when she first came over – it has worn out a bit around the cuffs but is still pretty serviceable – and a navy-blue jacket she bought in the sale at TK Maxx to treat herself last Christmas. The jacket is baggy around her shoulders, which have always been slender, but otherwise the cut is flattering. Beatrice tries to make the best of herself, even though nice clothes are a luxury she can't really afford. She has always enjoyed the act of getting dressed. Susan used to make fun of her for it.

'You spend so long getting ready we might as well not go out,' she'd say. And then she'd get that mischievous look in her eye and Beatrice knew that Susan didn't want to go out anyway. She wanted to stay in, to lie on the bed with her and kiss and stroke and tease and lick and hold and love.

Beatrice frowns at herself in the mirror. It is better not to remember. It is easier to cauterise each emotion, to become a shell, a screen, an empty page. It is safer not to allow anyone else in. Not even John, she thinks. Not even her brother. Did he know what she was? Had he been told?

She slips the skirt on over her thighs and breathes in to zip it up. She has noticed a slight bulging around her hips and belly and wonders whether she should make an effort to eat more healthily. But then, almost immediately, she thinks: What does it matter – who will see me anyway? And when she puts on the shirt and jacket, she feels better. She looks at herself critically in the full-length mirror, then nods at the reflection, satisfied. Professional and neat: a person to be taken seriously.

He will pay attention to me, Beatrice thinks.

She shuts the wardrobe door. She must focus her mind, concentrate on what it is she needs to say. There had been a book once, left behind by a hotel guest, that Beatrice had glanced at. It was a self-help manual and she had intended to flick through it only to scorn the contents and reassure herself that rich white people will believe any old nonsense. But she had been drawn into the first chapter in spite of herself. The book had a purple-and-blue cover and was written by someone called Dr Aaron Toll-Furstbender. The author picture on the back showed Dr Aaron to have a neatly cropped beard and a gleaming smile. He was wearing a polo-neck and a well-meaning expression. Dr Aaron had written about 'the power of positive visualisation'.

'Every morning, look at yourself in the mirror and tell yourself, "I can do this; I CAN do this,"' Dr Aaron wrote. 'Research shows that 74 per cent of adults are more likely to achieve their life goals if they positively visualise achieving them. So what are you waiting for? Reach out to your future! Go get it!'

Looking in the mirror, she tries to believe she can do anything, but instead she just feels exhausted. The sky outside is flat and grey. The window rattles gently against the ill-fitting metal frame. She has no money for the gas meter. She needs to do something for herself, for her future. After so many years of extremes she hungers simply for predictability.

All she wants is some respect, a place in society, a sense of herself once again. A life beyond merely existing. She wants to belong to something bigger than she is. She wants to inhale without worrying where the next breath will come from.

It takes a conscious effort to gather her things – keys, phone, lip balm – and to lift her head and tilt her chin. On her way out, she blows a kiss to Susan's picture and double locks the door.

She tells herself, with a confidence she does not feel, that she is ready.

Howard

HE TELLS JOCELYN TO get the Bentley out and clean it up a bit. If he's going to face this woman, he has decided he will do it in style.

He puts on his favourite suit, tailor-made for him by a man on Jermyn Street who does not advertise but whose reputation has spread over the decades through discreet word of mouth. The tailor, whose name is Billy, has made a life for himself and his family by relying on little more than well-mannered nudges in the right direction from people of impeccable social breeding. Billy's career has, in fact, been founded on a fragile edifice of hushed conversation: a whisper behind a cupped hand at the Cartier Polo, an embossed business card slipped across the table at the Jockey Club, an address jotted down with a Mont Blanc pen on the back of a Le Caprice menu, accompanied by the necessary reassurance that 'Billy's a good chap. None of that awful flash stuff you see nowadays.'

Billy. A curiously bulbous name for a man so tall and slight. When Howard thinks of Billy, he always sees him in exactly the same setting: tape measure over one shoulder, standing in the back of the shop amidst a man-made sculpture park of moulded plastic torsos displaying expensively hemmed jackets and pocket-square handkerchiefs. Billy would stoop forward like a toothpick-limbed bird when Howard entered the shop, so that his long neck and narrow face could be spied through the shadows.

He was a fluid conglomeration of angles underneath sparse and stretched skin, arms tapering into long fingers and his forehead jutting over his eyes like an eroding cliff. Ada used to have a children's book about a Big Friendly Giant and the sketches in it looked exactly like Billy.

Howard had learned of his services through a member of the House of Lords he had sat next to at a gala evening in the Victoria and Albert Museum to raise money for a children's charity. The peer had been boring company, with appalling table manners. Howard recalled, with unfortunate exactitude, that the peer's breath had smelled as though a small woodland creature had taken up residence in his gullet and died some years previously. When he ate, the protruding nature of his buck teeth meant that it was difficult for him to close his mouth completely with the result that spittle-strewn globules of Parmesan and shaved pistachio were launched across the table in giant arcs like pieces of bait masterfully cast into a salmon river. As if to compensate for his digestive defects, the peer was incredibly well dressed. When Howard had enquired about his dining companion's suit, he was rewarded with Billy's details and a light showering of the face with bread. Howard wiped the crumbs off with a napkin and made a mental note to call Billy the next morning. Since then, he has never looked back.

The suit he chooses to wear this morning is dark blue, almost black, in colour. The tailoring is sharp and has the gratifying effect of making Howard look as though he has lost a few pounds. The hems are so beautifully turned up that the stitching reminds him of his mother's – and he can think of no greater compliment to pay than that. His John Lobb shoes have been freshly polished. His Eton shirt crackles softly as he does up the buttons. Howard's one concession to individual zaniness is a pair of Paul Smith socks, patterned with bright stripes in yellow, orange, purple and green. He believes, mistakenly, that these socks show the world that he gets the joke, that he doesn't take himself too seriously, that he retains his child-like sense of wonder and silliness, that he isn't like all those boring, stuff-shirted toffs in the Square Mile. He doesn't like the socks much but he feels it is important to keep abreast of the fashions especially when you're head of a multinational clothing conglomerate. It was the kind of thing journalists picked up on. You'd be talking to them about the banking crisis and government red tape and all they'd be focusing on was a small patch of bright material on the ankle. Looking for some ludicrously tenuous link – colourful socks, colourful character . . . that sort of thing.

Howard clicks on his Rolex and sweeps back his hair, patting the sides of it flat against his temples with pomade. In front of the bathroom mirror, he bends down to monitor his spreading bald patch. Claudia has recently been dropping hints about hair transplant surgery, talking loudly about so-and-so's 'fine head of hair' whenever they pass a virile man on the street or see a hirsute middle-aged presenter on television. The other day, she had pointedly left a copy of the *Daily Mail* on the coffee table downstairs, folded over so that an advertisement for Regaine stared out at him in black-and-white.

Still, not much he can do about it today, he thinks, sucking in his stomach and slapping it proprietorially.

He goes downstairs, following the scent of freshly ground coffee and boiling eggs all the way to the kitchen. On weekdays, he likes to eat his breakfast here, skimming through the business pages while the cook rustles up whatever it is he feels like eating. If she's not doing an early morning workout or having her eyelashes aromatherapised or whatever, Claudia will join him. They sleep in separate rooms and have done for the last two years. It happened without either of them remarking on it. Bit by bit, Claudia had simply moved her clothes into the rose-papered boudoir on the other side of their shared bathroom. She told Howard she slept better without having to put up with his snoring. He felt rejected but unable to admit this to her. He wondered, from time to time, whether she sought sexual satisfaction elsewhere. There was a Spanish personal trainer he'd had his suspicions about a while back – all ripped pectorals and olive-skinned charm and tales about how to make the perfect paella like his mama taught him – but most of the time, she seemed curiously asexual. Possibly she was too self-absorbed to give herself to anyone else.

Today, Howard's heart sinks when he sees his wife already at the table, eating tiny segments from half a grapefruit and drinking a virulent green substance from a long, tall glass. Penny used to eat a bowl of Special K with a strong cup of sweet, milky tea. He tries, as much as possible, not to compare his second wife with his first but, before he can stop it, the thought is out there and a disappointment seeps into him.

Claudia is flicking through a glossy magazine, her nails painted a bright coral colour. She makes a point of pretending not to notice him walk through the door.

'Good morning, Sir Howard,' says the cook. He can't remember her name. He thinks it begins with a B.

'Morning.'

Claudia glances up at him, decides to smile and offers her cheek for a peck. Howard dutifully obliges.

'Well this is nice,' says Claudia in a tone that suggests precisely the opposite. 'Quality time with my husband. Perhaps we can finally have a chat about the drawing-room wallpaper?'

Claudia wants to redecorate. She says the whole house is too gloomy and that the furniture is evidence of his ex-wife's lack of taste. He can't be bothered to get into the conversation. And besides, he rather likes the way the house looks. It is, after all, his home. I'm paying for it, he thinks.

'Actually, darling, I'm not stopping for breakfast today,' he says, inventing the lie as he goes. 'I've got an early meeting in the office. Board members, you know how it is.'

Claudia looks at her watch.

'It's only 7.30.'

'Time and . . . and . . . whatever it is . . . waits for no man . . .'

'Tide,' Claudia says drily, going back to her magazine.

He suppresses the urge to say something. He doesn't know

how he'd retaliate anyway. She's always been quicker than he is with words. If only their fights were played out through balance sheets, he thinks, he'd win every time.

'What's that?' he says, gesturing at the green liquid.

'Spirulina. Wheatgrass. Spinach juice.'

He rolls his eyes. Claudia, falling into the familiar role play that has become their public shtick, slaps him playfully on the hand.

'You should try it, Howie. Do you good.'

'No thanks. I'd rather drink my own piss.'

The cook giggles.

'See you later,' he says.

Claudia raises her hand in a half-hearted wave. The cook beams at him. He can already hear the soft growl of the Bentley outside.

Jocelyn drives him to Kensington, avoiding all traffic jams with the sort of sixth sense that seems to be the preserve of certain chauffeurs. Howard can see his driver glancing at him through the rear-view mirror. Jocelyn's always been astute: not much gets past him. 'Everything all right, Sir Howard?' Jocelyn says from the front seat.

'Fine, thanks.' He looks pointedly out of the window to avoid further conversation. The High Street is filling up with harried commuters trying to cross the road in the midst of perilously speeding cars and buses. A few years ago, the council had decided to remove a sizeable proportion of traffic lights in the misguided belief that pedestrians would use their common sense to cross at the safest place. Instead, Howard noticed, they just walked wherever they bloody well liked, convinced that drivers would screech to a halt in time. There is a man with a giant backpack weaving in and out of the exhaust fumes right now with a stupid grin on his face, waving apologetically at a white-van man. Tourists, thinks Howard with a mental snarl. Waste of space. He's probably Australian, come over here to clutter up Howard's local every time there was a rugby match.

He remembers Ada telling him that she had got work pulling pints in a pub in Birmingham in her first term at university. He didn't like the thought of it and had told her so.

'If you're short of cash, you only need to ask.'

Ada had looked at him critically, her head tilted to one side just like her mother.

'Dad, it's not about the money.'

'Why are you doing it then?'

She sighed, blowing out her cheeks for exaggerated effect. Her face was still too thin: the dip and curve of the bone pressing against her pale skin.

'I like it, Dad! It's nice. Meeting new people. Doing something for myself.'

She'd leaned across the table and patted his hand. Her fingers felt cold and bony. The faintest tinge of blue underneath each nail. He smiled.

'Whatever makes you happy, sweetheart,' he'd said – and he'd meant it too.

When was that, he thinks now, leaning back against the comforting indentations of the Bentley's leather upholstery. He remembers they'd been talking about the Millennium celebrations, the fireworks along the Thames, the fear of some catastrophic computer bug paralysing the country . . . it must have been early 2001, one of the last times he saw her. How long ago it seemed, and yet how immediate. It would have been before September 11. Before the world changed, he thinks, and although it causes him an instant of guilt, he cannot help but put a personal gloss on events. When the Twin Towers had been attacked, he had looked at the television screen, he had looked at that blue, blue sky, at the plane, the clouds of dust, the crumpling of steel and stone, the jumping bodies, and he had felt less than he should have. He had thought simply that at last the exterior world now reflected the anguish he felt inside. He had drawn the comparison without realising he was doing so and for a few days after it happened, he remembers feeling relief that so many other people now understood his pain, that he didn't have to explain. For a while, there was a synthesis between internal and external landscapes that had temporarily removed the necessity to carry on as normal.

Jocelyn brakes, jolting Howard out of his reverie. He scratches the back of his neck. He has to focus. He needs to think about what he is going to say to this woman, this Beatrice Kizza. In truth, he hasn't formulated a clear plan of action. He knows Rupert is anxious about the meeting, that he thinks it foolhardy for Howard to sully his hands in the matter.

'Even to be seen in the same room as her is *madness*,' his PR man had said when Howard asked him to arrange it. They were in his office at Paradiso HQ. Howard was at his desk, swivelling his chair round to look out of the floor-to-ceiling windows at a desultory stretch of West London scrubland. Rupert sat opposite, his legs crossed, his quiff gelled to one side. 'I strongly advise you . . .'

Howard held his hands up: a familiar gesture that was half conciliatory, half cautionary.

'I know what you're going to say, Rupe. I don't need you to lecture me. I've made my mind up.'

Rupert shook his head but he knew his boss. Howard would not be prised away from his ill-advised course of action. The best Rupert could do was to make the legal situation watertight and to ensure that Beatrice Kizza wasn't seen anywhere near the Paradiso offices. He had booked a suite in the Royal Garden. Howard snorted with laughter when Rupert told him.

'A fucking hotel room, Rupert? Jesus. Never let it be said you don't have a sense of humour.'

Rupert widened his eyes. 'It's the best option. I know the manager at the Royal Garden. I can rely on him.'

'OK, OK. And she's coming? You've spoken to her?'

Rupert nodded. 'I've set up that interview too, with the journo from the *Tribune*.'

'Jesus.' Howard turned back to his desk, picked up a bright

180

pink rubbery ball that was meant to help stressed-out executives and squeezed it tight in his fist, releasing it after a few seconds as if massaging a dying heart.

'No, Esme Reade,' Rupert replied, allowing himself a small smile at his own joke. 'We've discussed this, Howard. It's a good diversionary tactic. You give a warm, personal interview, announce you're setting up a foundation in Ada's memory, that Esme was the only hack you could have trusted with this sensitive piece, flatter her, give her the old twinkle. Then show her round Chateau Pink, feed her some touchy-feely stuff about living in the present but never forgetting the past, pose for a pic with the fragrant Claudia and there you have it.'

Howard knew it made sense. He had never spoken about Ada to the press before. But he is a pragmatist. He can give Esme Reade enough for her article without cheapening his most private memories. He is adept at creating a narrative. After all, he has been doing it most of his life.

The Bentley swings round into the Royal Garden Hotel driveway and slips seamlessly to a halt. Jocelyn gets out, puts on the peaked cap that Claudia insists on as part of the chauffeur's uniform, and opens the back passenger door.

'Here you are, Sir Howard,' Jocelyn smiles reassuringly. 'I hope you have a good meeting.'

He climbs out of the car, groaning lightly as he unfolds his stiffening muscles, and Howard notices that Jocelyn smells familiar. For a moment he is confused. Then he realises his chauffeur is wearing the same Aqua di Parma aftershave that Howard splashes on each morning. He grins. He's always seen imitation as the best kind of flattery, reinforcing, as it does, the notion of his own importance. He pats Jocelyn on the shoulder. I won't mention it, he thinks, don't want to embarrass the poor man.

He rolls back his shoulders, twists his neck from side to side as if limbering up for a fight and then walks through the rotating glass doors. Rupert meets him at reception and takes him up to a small suite on the ninth floor. They do not talk. Down the corridor, Rupert slides the plastic card key into the slot and pushes the door open into a room with overplumped sofas. There is an adjoining bedroom with an overplumped bed and a narrow bathroom with overplumped towels. Howard sucks in his abdomen reflexively. He feels overplumped himself, despite his lack of breakfast.

'I thought you could sit here, Sir Howard,' Rupert says, shifting one of the armchairs so that it faces the door. 'Best to be standing when she walks in though, make sure she knows who's in charge.'

'Right. And I'll teach my gran to suck eggs at the same time, shall I?' Howard snaps. He is surprised at how nervous he is.

Rupert looks stricken. 'Sorry, Rupe. Bit on edge.'

'You don't have to do this, you know . . .'

'No,' Howard says, cutting him off. 'I do.'

He thinks back to that day in the Mayfair Rotunda and wonders, with disgust, how it came to this. Did he misread the chambermaid's signals? Or had he allowed himself a moment of wilful blindness? Did he know what he was doing was wrong or had there been something more nebulous at work, an innate belief that women like her were there precisely for men like him to relieve themselves away from their wives? Does that make him a grubby little pervert? He isn't sure any more. He see-saws from feeling he has been unfairly attacked to an all-encompassing sense of self-loathing. He genuinely hadn't wanted to cause this Beatrice Kizza woman any distress. Genuinely. And he is mortified, too, that what should have been a time for sober contemplation of his daughter's disappearance has now become indelibly sullied in his mind.

He tells himself he wants to make amends for any distress he has caused but, even more pressingly, he wants to salve his own conscience. He wants to wipe the slate clean, turn over a new leaf, start a new chapter – all those irritating phrases that he has dismissed for years as New Age mumbo-jumbo. He wants to be someone better than he has become. He wants to be worthy of the fact Jocelyn has chosen to ape his style. He wants to be what he isn't. He is sure he used to be nicer, more naïve, more open to the world. Surely he can get that back?

Or is he kidding himself? Perhaps, he thinks, perhaps I've always been this brash, uncaring, selfish husk of a man. Perhaps that was why everyone he loved had left him – Ada, Penny, his father who walked out one day for bagels and never came back (at least, that's what his mother told him. Howard had never been entirely convinced. It was the bagel detail he found inauthentic).

He goes to the window and parts the chiffony curtains with a single finger. The morning sunlight bounces across the cream carpet. As Howard looks out across the green sweep of Kensington Gardens, he imagines himself sitting on the edge of a circular wall, staring into a well of self-pity. He could tip himself over the edge or he could lean back from the brink and get on with things.

He lets the curtain drop and turns round to face the room. He breathes in and exhales to the count of ten. He straightens up, checks his cuffs. He decides he is ready to confess his sins and seek absolution or whatever it is the Catholics do. He thinks of Beatrice Kizza and tries to remember her face. He can't, of course. All he can remember is a shadowy shape, a smell of cocoa butter, the release of pent-up emotion and sex and energy and grief, all of it in one sudden stream.

The way she smiled afterwards and kissed the bristle on his cheek before bending to straighten the sheets.

Or was it the way she turned and rushed out of the room, tears streaming down her face? Which version?

He can't remember. But he knows he will make it right with Beatrice (Beatrice now in his head; no need for surname or formality; in his head they have an understanding). He tells himself that this, at least, will be one entirely good thing he will do.

There have been other women, of course. A waitress at the RAC on Pall Mall who allowed him a quick fumble on the staircase. A Filipino housekeeper, working abroad to send money back for her children, who had fingered the collar on her blouse in that certain way he knew was an invitation. A secretary at Paradiso who wore tight skirts and lacquered hair piled high on her head. A few hotel rooms here and there. A few chambermaids. Give and take. He hasn't forced himself on any of them – he would never do such a thing. It's just that, with Claudia being so distant, he has had to look elsewhere for his gratification. He has found it not in the brittle society ladies of his acquaintance but with women he thinks of as being on his own level. Women he can relate to. Women he is not intimidated by. Until Beatrice Kizza, he thought everyone understood the deal.

There is a knock. The tiny vein beneath Howard's left eye begins to twitch. Rupert stands quite still, motioning to Howard not to speak. Then, after a thirty-second interlude, he walks slowly to the door and opens it.

When Beatrice enters the room, Howard's first thought is how short she is. In his mind, she has assumed enormous proportions, as if to signify the mental space she has been occupying. She is short but compact and seems to exude both strength and sensuousness, her body a combination of tightly packed muscle and smooth, shiny skin. Her face is tense – clenched jaw, tight mouth, darting eyes – and her hair is bluntly cut, tucked behind her ears. She is wearing a navy-blue jacket bobbling at the elbows, an unflattering grey skirt and a loose shirt, the white of it dulled from too many washes.

Although he is trying to keep his mind on higher things, Howard cannot help but try to make out her figure underneath all the shapeless clobber. It's an old tailor's habit, after all. She seems to have dressed both as an expression of confidence (why else choose a skirt and jacket, like a cut-price business suit?) and as a way of detracting all attention from her womanliness. He wonders if she has done this on purpose, either because she is scared of his sexual advances or because she wants to underline the fact that she's gay. Howard is not used to women like this.

Claudia always wears clothes designed to suggest her sexual availability when out of them.

'Sir Howard,' Rupert says. 'This is Ms—' He draws out the 'z' sound with unnecessary emphasis, 'Kizza.'

Beatrice steps forward and gives the slightest hint of a smile. He sees her do it and then, just as quickly, he sees her consciously remind herself there is no need to be polite and the smile disappears. She reaches out to take Howard's hand and they shake. He tries to maintain eye contact but feels ashamed and drops his head.

'Thank you for coming, Beatrice,' he says, talking to an elaborately swirled bass clef printed on the green-gold carpet, presumably an effort by the interior designer to suggest a bygone age of baronial elegance. 'I appreciate that you didn't have to do this.' There is a dry catch in his voice and he clears his throat to get rid of it. 'Rupert, could you get some water for us? Would you like anything—?' He looks at her expectantly. Beatrice shakes her head but still doesn't speak. He gestures for her to sit and she perches gingerly on the edge of the armchair facing Howard and leans forward, propping her elbows on her knees, clasping her hands. Rupert returns with the water and seems to take an age opening the bottle. It fizzes gently as the gas escapes and then Rupert pours it over a mound of ice cubes that chink loudly against the glass. The noise seems intensely brash against the silence of the room.

Once he has finished, Howard signals for him to go. Rupert nods. It has all been arranged: he will leave the room but listen in to the conversation from next door. They have set up a discreet recording device by the potted orchid. It's best, as Rupert explained, to be prepared.

'Beatrice,' Howard starts again. 'Is it all right if I call you that?'

She nods. 'It's my name,' she says and her voice, when he hears it, is low and flat.

'First of all, I want to apologise for whatever you thought

might have happened that day in the Mayfair Rotunda.' He has been told by Rupert not to admit any guilt and Howard struggles to remember the exact formulation of the words he is meant to use to ensure his back is covered. Legally speaking, that is.

'I fear there might have been some sort of misunderstanding which I am keen to put right,' he continues.

Beatrice looks at him steadily. She does not blink while she stares at him and he finds this discomfiting. He starts to stumble.

'What I mean to say is . . . I mean . . . it's just that . . .'

He crumples in his chair, mops his brow with the back of his hand and wonders what the point of it all is. He is lying to Beatrice, to himself, to everyone. He is a fraud.

'Look,' he says finally. 'Let me make this right, Beatrice. What do you want? Anything.'

He can almost sense Rupert bristling in the next room. This is a departure from the agreed script.

Beatrice leans back in her chair.

'I don't wish you harm, Sir Howard,' she says. 'I have not come to cause you trouble. I do not want your money.'

He is startled by the plain-spoken admission. Howard thought that was what all this had been about: blackmail, extortion, a healthy lump sum and a tight confidentiality agreement.

'What I would like is quite simple.' She makes a play of examining her nails. He wonders where she has picked up these gestures, like an actress in a film. He thinks, for the first time, that she must be nervous too.

'I would like a job.'

'A job?'

Howard chuckles. He can't help himself.

'Why is that funny?' she asks sharply, anxious that she is being teased, that she is missing some crucial conversational undercurrent.

'I'm not laughing at you. I'm surprised, that's all. What kind of job?'

'Nothing fancy,' she says. 'Perhaps in one of your shops. On the tills. Daytime hours, regular pay.'

Howard pauses, just to make sure he has understood her correctly. This is unbelievable. Here he was, expecting to be taken to the cleaner's, and all this woman wants is a chance to earn a decent living. Plucky, that's what his mother would have called her.

'Of course,' he says and then he waits for her to ask for something else, something more.

Beatrice gives a small smile, revealing narrow, straight white teeth slightly buckled like a fence falling in on itself. He has made her happy. It has been as simple as that. But then she starts talking again.

'Sir Howard. You are a powerful man in Britain. You have a lot of weight here. I know this. I have done my research.'

He motions for her to go on.

'I am sure you have done your research on me too. Perhaps you know why I came to the UK from Uganda?'

Howard nods. Beatrice looks down, fiddles with her necklace.

'I had to leave behind someone who is very important to me.' She shifts in her seat. 'I would like your assurance that you will protect me. From the British authorities, I mean. If they try to deport me it would be very bad. Very bad.'

Howard is surprised. A knot loosens within him. He had expected a demand for money. He had been prepared to pay. The fact that Beatrice Kizza hasn't asked for this makes him look at her differently.

'Of course,' he says again. And he thinks: This can be the start of something new and good and right. This can be repentance.

He reaches out across the low coffee table intending to pat Beatrice's knee. She flinches and moves further into the chair. He nods, accepting the rebuke.

'Leave it to me, Beatrice,' he says and when he speaks, another image rises in front of him of Ada, his daughter, running along the beach in a frilly polka-dot swimming costume. Shrieking at the coolness of the water. Giggling when he lifts her high above his head. Scratchiness of sand in his shoe. Warmth of sun on his face. Trickle of melting ice cream down his forearm. A small hand in his.

He looks at the woman sitting in front of him, the contained sadness of her, and, in her eyes, he sees himself.

'I'll see what I can do,' he says.

Beatrice Kizza allows her interlaced fingers to relax and separate.

Maybe, Howard thinks, just maybe, I can make this work.

Then he hears the click of a door and he knows, without having to look, that Rupert has walked back into the room.

Esme

*E*SME WANTS TO BELIEVE it is the winning combination of her personal charm and professional competence that has coaxed Sir Howard Pink into giving his first full-length interview about his daughter's disappearance, but she has a sneaking notion that all is not what it seems. Perhaps it's because she's become a horribly cynical tabloid hack ever since working at the *Tribune* but she can't shake the suspicion that Howard Pink has an ulterior motive. Cathy had told her once about a famous pop star who sold a story about his child's terminal illness to the red-tops in exchange for the discreet dropping of an exclusive about an extra-marital affair. That was pre-Leveson, of course, in the days when the chequebook was king and all you had to do to prove a Cabinet minister was shagging his secretary was dial in four simple digits to access a mobile phone's voicemail.

Things were tougher nowadays, Esme thought. Tougher and more boring. Last week, Dave had spiked a piece about a celebrity's honeymoon because the fame-hungry wannabe in question had got her lawyers to email claiming they'd invaded her privacy by taking photographs of her on a 'secluded' beach. What the lawyers failed to acknowledge was that the celebrity had tipped off the paparazzi in the first place. And why wouldn't she, thought Esme, when said celebrity had spent several thousand pounds on cultivating the perfect bikini body with the costly help of a pre-eminent plastic surgeon and needed some free publicity for a new range of false eyelashes she was promoting ('super-long with diamanté sparkle' according to the press release)?

Anyway, the Howard Pink thing just seems a bit too easy. Esme was used to pursuing interviews for months on end through a tireless campaign of phone calls and emails and follow-up emails and emails following up the follow-up emails, falsely claiming that there was a problem with the work internet server and could she just check that her last one had got through? But for the first time ever, a potential interviewee had come to her. Or at least to Dave.

'He asked for you by name,' Dave had said to her on the Monday that she'd rushed back to the office, leaving her mother waving goodbye from the train platform with an aggrieved expression on her face. 'Said he'd felt "a connection" with you over lunch.' Dave winked. 'A connection, eh, Es? You wanna be careful you don't end up as the third Lady Pink.'

Esme blushed and looked down at her jeans. She had thought carefully about precisely what clothes to wear for this unanticipated appointment with the object of her irrational affections. It was a tricky sartorial challenge: she wanted to look casually attractive, as though she had made no effort, and yet still manage to convey elegance and sex appeal. In the end, she had opted for skinny jeans, a t-shirt with something French written on the front and ankle boots that made her a few millimetres taller than Dave. He had turned up in awful grey trousers and a navy fleece. It was almost enough to make her stop fancying him. Almost.

'Why now though?' she asked, focusing on a point just below his right earlobe so that she didn't have to look him in the eye.

'Because he's got this charitable foundation he wants to announce in memory of his daughter. You know about Ada Pink, I presume?'

Esme nodded. She'd read the cuttings before her lunch at the Dorchester: Howard Pink's nineteen-year-old daughter. Troubled past. Anorexia. Left her posh public school under something of a cloud. Rumours of drugs, hotly denied by her family. Walked out of her university halls one day eleven years ago never to be seen again. High-profile police search. Appeals on *Crimewatch*. Blurry CCTV footage of a possible abductor's van. And then – nothing. No trails, no leads, no suspects. The case had dropped from the front pages before disappearing altogether. Howard Pink had never spoken about it publicly. Until now.

'You don't think there's any more to it than that?' Esme asked, hoping he might be impressed. Assumption, he had once told her, was the mother of all fuck-ups.

Dave glanced at her sharply.

'You don't need to be asking that,' he said. 'Just concentrate on the interview and let the newsdesk worry about the rest. We don't want to scare him off when he's more or less put a fucking great exclusive on your lap like a purring little pussycat.' Dave stretched back in his office chair, his arms forming a giant figure-of-eight behind his head. The navy fleece rode up his stomach, revealing a strip of white material underneath. She wondered idly if this denoted a T-shirt or a vest. In her fantasies, Dave has always worn crisp boxer shorts in pale blue. The thought of Dave in jockey shorts or – worse – Y-fronts makes her wince.

'You should be flattered he wants to talk to you,' he carried on. 'You need to think hard about your questions, how you want to structure them.'

He coughed. 'We could have a chat about it now if you don't have anywhere you need to be?'

She shook her head. 'No.' A heat spread over her chest. 'I'm free as a bird,' she said and then wondered why she'd used that expression. Oh get a grip, she told herself, simultaneously irritated and mortified.

'OK,' he said. 'Let's go for a drink. Get out of the office.' He stood, unhooked his coat from the door and held it open for her. Esme brushed past him. He smelled of Davidoff Cool Water. It was an unashamedly naff aftershave, redolent of oversexed adolescent schoolboys. Perhaps someone gave it to him for Christmas.

She thinks of this now, of the musty smell of him, as she walks down High Street Kensington towards Howard Pink's home. Esme has replayed the afternoon in her mind an incalculable number of times, recalling every tiny detail. They had sat in the corner of the pub, sharing a bag of roasted peanuts, so that occasionally their fingers would touch and Esme had to concentrate on not embarrassing herself by blurting out something stupid. Dave had been good company: entertaining and relaxed, teasing her gently and cracking jokes about their colleagues. It was the first time she'd had a proper conversation with him, without feeling he was about to ask her when she was going to file. She had made him laugh a couple of times too; actual belly-laughter rather than a polite titter. He had asked a bit about where she grew up, her parents, that sort of thing. When she told him about her father dying, he had stopped talking abruptly and looked so uncomfortable she wanted to reach out and touch his face and tell him it hadn't turned out that badly, not really.

'Jesus, I'm sorry,' he'd said.

'It's fine,' she said, even though it wasn't. She waved her hand, shooing the thought away. 'Honestly. Ages ago now. I don't remember him that well.'

'I can't believe I never knew that about you.'

'Why would you?' Esme watched him take a sip from his pint, the light-flecked foam forming a tidal line across the top of his mouth. Stubble, she noticed. He hadn't shaved. 'It's not something I tend to just blurt out.' She remembered, with a jolt, the lunch at Alain Ducasse and how easily she had shared this buried-down piece of her. 'Although, having said that, I did tell Howard Pink for some reason.'

Dave smirked. 'Must have been that famed "connection" he was talking about,' he said, making the quotation marks with his hands.

'Mmm,' she said, downing the last of her glass of tepid white wine.

And then there had been an odd moment where they had

looked at each other for at least ten unbroken seconds. Her eyes on his. She remembers blinking, slowly, breaking the stare in case he was embarrassed. But when she raised her eyes again, Dave was still looking at her and she was unable to do anything other than surrender herself to the examination, as if it were a test of some sort. Kids in a playground. Whoever glanced away first lost. The strength of his gaze was such that it felt more intense than if he had been touching her or kissing her or holding her head in his hands.

'Esme.' He said her name, drawing out each languid syllable. 'What am I going to do about you?'

She wasn't sure what to make of that, what he meant by it. Was he . . . no, surely not . . . he'd never shown any interest and yet . . . and yet . . . if she weren't worrying so much about the subtle inflection of his voice and what it signified, if she were in a different situation with a different man, she would be sure that he was trying to flirt with her.

Esme had wanted his attentions for so long, had pined after Dave so ineffectively for so many months, that his sudden declaration of interest took her aback. She felt panicked. She wasn't sure she actually wanting anything real to happen. Not when she thought about him as a definite prospect rather than a reassuringly familiar daydream. Not when she thought about his reputation as a shagger, or the fact of his wife, his children – the tawdriness of it all. Not when she thought about her career. There was nothing more damaging for a young female reporter than the accusation that she'd shagged her boss to get ahead. Especially when it was true. She remembers, without wanting to, the online commenter who had accused her of sleeping her way to the middle.

But at the same time, there was this sense of *wanting* him that was so deeply confusing. It wasn't logical for her to feel like this. Her brief relationships up to this point had been tame, controlled affairs. She was the one who did the dumping. She had never felt anything to excess. She had never wanted to make her happiness dependent on the vagaries of someone else's affection. Perhaps this was why she had chosen to hanker after a man she knew was unavailable, a man so unsuitable there was no danger of anything ever happening.

But now she was starkly horrified at the thought Dave might act, that he might lunge over the pub table and pounce on her in the middle of the day and then she would have the reality of his kiss to compare with all the projected fantasies. She realised, with the sickening thud of an obviously dropped penny, that it was the idea of him she loved. Esme wasn't sure she wanted the real thing.

'Dave, I—' she started.

He reached across, placed his hand over hers. He stroked the side of her thumb with his. And then, as though nothing had happened, Dave tapped her knuckles briskly, got up, put on his coat and smiled at her.

'Best be getting back,' he said. 'You'll do a great job with Howard Pink. I know you will.'

She nodded. She felt the beginning of a tear form in the corner of one eye. Not because she was upset by Dave but because she had been confronted by her own absurdity, by all the things about herself she most disliked. She felt stupid and naïve and embarrassed at the thought that her feelings must have been so clear to him when she thought she had kept them discreetly veiled from his attention in the office. She wondered who else must have known and her thoughts fixated on Cathy. Cathy was always talking disparagingly about 'the work-experience flibbertigibbets' traipsing through the office in too-short skirts and too-high heels, loitering around the photocopier with transparent flirtatious intent.

'Teens with tits,' Cathy called them in her unkinder moments. Cathy would hate it if Esme had an affair with Dave. She'd spread gossip and bile around the office. Esme knew: she'd seen it happen before.

She watched Dave walk away with a tightness inside her. He

strode towards the door, head bent down, hands in his pockets, the hairline at the nape of his neck raggedly cut as if by an amateur hand. His wife, she thought automatically. His wife would have cut it.

Esme stared at the half-empty glass of beer, willing the blurriness of her vision to recede and refusing, resolutely, to look at him as he left the pub. And for no reason that she could explain, her mind was suddenly full not of Dave but of her father. She could see her dad, with complete clarity, wearing a knitted yellow jumper, laughing and bending to put a piece of gold tinsel on the lowest branch of the Christmas tree.

The glass of beer. Let me look at that, she thought. Let me concentrate all my energies on that glass. That was all that she wanted to deal with right now.

The glass of beer.

How would she describe this pint, she thought, taking refuge in a familiar game. What words would she use? How would she express the essence of it in a way that hadn't been used before?

Liquid the colour of a varnished conker.

Droplets of white.

Cloudy fingerprints where it had been gripped.

Then, remembered: her father in corduroy trousers with a buckle at the back, laughing, helping her decorate the Christmas tree.

And the strange thing was that when she left the pub, half an hour later, Esme felt an overwhelming need to call her mother.

'Hello, darling?' Lilian's tone was inquisitive, a touch surprised.

'Hi Mum. I . . . just wanted to hear your voice.'

'Oh sweetheart. What's wrong?'

Because the thing about Lilian was that, for all the petty irritation, when it counted, she instinctively knew exactly how to be.

'I was thinking about Dad. I just remembered him decorating the Christmas tree and . . .' Esme felt a sob rising in her gullet but caught it and swallowed it back down. She could hear her mother exhale gently on the other end of the line.

'He loved Christmas,' Lilian said. 'He got so excited, like a little child!'

Esme let her continue. Listening to her mother's voice made her calmer. She somehow knew what to say.

'And there was one year that he got you a remote-control truck – do you remember?' Lilian asked gently. 'It was red and you said it was your favourite present ever. I can remember him saying to me, "Esme isn't your average girl, you know," and so he got you a boy's present. Rob was so jealous!'

'I remember.' And she did. She could visualise the truck: square-backed and shiny, zooming around the living-room carpet as she twisted the remote-control dials, careening into a side-board and chipping away a flake of paint.

'He loved you, darling,' Lilian said. 'Whatever else happened, he really did love you both. He'd be so proud of you.'

Esme tried to take in what her mother was saying, tried to store the feeling of reassurance away for the next time she needed it.

'Thanks, Mum.'

'And you know, don't you, Esme, that I love you very much too. And I'm so very proud of you even if I find it hard to show it. You mean the world to me. You and your brother.'

'I know.' Esme bit her lip. 'I love you too. I'm sorry I was a bit . . . distracted this weekend.'

'Darling, don't worry about it. I know what pressure you're under. Young women these days have a much harder time of it than we ever did. We just got married and had babies.' Lilian laughed. 'I'm so . . . admiring of what you've achieved,' she added quietly. 'Probably a bit jealous too.'

Esme felt a wash of affection for her mother. Sometimes, Lilian was capable of such clear-sightedness that Esme wondered if all the jittery tension she thought lay between them was simply a product of her own imagination. Was she projecting her own dissatisfaction onto her mother? Or maybe, she thought, it was just that she didn't allow her mother the same leniency she would anyone else. Instead, she picked over Lilian's faults like carrion.

Howard Pink lives on one of the moneyed roads off the High Street, a pocket of exclusivity denoted by automatic gates, security systems and glossy four-wheel drives with tinted windows parked nose-to-nose along the kerb. The Pink abode is set apart from the main thoroughfare behind a high wall with small purple flowers growing from the cracks between the bricks. Esme leans against the wall to change her shoes, slipping out the L.K. Bennett heels from a dirty white canvas bag filled with shorthand notepads and plastic document wallets containing thick pages of cuttings.

She pushes her feet into the patent leather, puts the trainers in the bag, and straightens up, immediately feeling the benefit of four extra inches of height. The smart shoes gleam and tip-tap along the pavement. Her BlackBerry beeps with a message from Les, the photographer, who says he'll be there in half an hour, which is good because it gives her time to warm Howard up. She suspects he'll be nervous about giving his first interview on such an emotive subject. For all his bluster and self-confidence, Esme knows from past journalistic experience that there is a deep seam of insecurity running through most famous men.

A few months ago, she'd been sent to interview a stand-up comedian who was promoting a big-budget Hollywood film in which he had a small cameo. It was the kind of film the critics called 'gross-out' – lots of jokes about breasts, a scene involving a plate of blancmange and an extended comic riff on the precise chemical formulation of excrement. The comedian had recently married a perky American singer. He was good-looking, charming and widely tipped to be the next host of a prime-time chat show. But when Esme had asked the comedian what had made him want to become famous, he replied without having to think, 'To get my own back.'

On who? she'd wondered.

'School bullies,' he'd said with a sneer. 'The fuckers.'

They'd all been bullied in one way or another, she thinks. The film stars, the pop singers, the CEOs. They all secretly felt like fraudulent outsiders, these supposed alpha males, all of them desperate to make their mark, to silence the anonymous nagging voice that told them they weren't good enough. She realised at their lunch that Howard Pink was no different.

Esme buzzes the security phone. She checks her reflection in the shiny glass panel before noticing, too late, that it shields a camera and whoever lets her in on the other side of the red-brick wall will have seen her preening and pouting.

'Shit,' she murmurs, trying to ignore her nerves. She is more panicked about this than she was for her first ever interview (it had been with a woman called Annette whose dancing Labrador had got through to the semi-finals of *Britain's Got Talent*). Dave, who hadn't even mentioned their drink last Monday, had ordered her gruffly 'to calm down and stop acting like you're sitting your A levels all over again.'

He couldn't look at her directly when he spoke. Instead, he angled his head so that she could only make out a sideways glimpse of his eyes.

Having been buzzed through the gates, Esme walks up an uneven path to a large carved oak door, shrouded by thick coils of wisteria. Standing on the front step, she unclips her hair, shakes it out over her shoulders and smiles in readiness. A pudgy-cheeked Asian woman opens the door, ushers her into the hallway and tells her to leave her coat on the hat-stand provided. The woman is wearing clothes that are presumably intended to be a uniform but look more like surgical scrubs. The blue nylon rustles as she leads Esme into the living room and shows her which chair to sit in.

'Sir Howard will be with you shortly,' the woman says. Her accent is foreign. The room smells of geranium-scented candle.

Esme takes out her notepad, her dictaphone and her sheet of questions, carefully constructed over the last couple of days and

198

scribbled down in shorthand on the back of Howard's printed-out Wikipedia entry. Esme knows proper journalists aren't supposed to use Wikipedia but she can't help herself. She clears her throat, scratches the inside of her wrist, waits.

Howard Pink's living room is, like the man himself, over-stuffed and expensive. Two enormous red velvet sofas face each other across a low coffee table on which someone has arranged a fan of auction catalogues from Sotheby's and Christie's. Behind her, there is a large fire, laid with wooden logs and dark pellets of coal despite the mildness of the day and crested by a marble mantelpiece with gold-leaf detailing. Faux Ming china bowls of potpourri jostle for space on every available surface. There are mottled paintings of elderly ancestral types on the walls, a gloomy country scene in oils with a horse and cart in the foreground and one small but exquisite watercolour of a swimming pool in high summer. To one side, a bay window overlooks a broad expanse of flower beds and the faint outline of a pale green gazebo. In front of the window is a polished sideboard, the surface of which is filled with a selection of photographs.

She is too far away to make out who is smiling from the silver frames and she wonders, briefly, whether she can risk getting up to have a look before Sir Howard arrives. Esme squints. There are a few of Howard Pink shaking hands with various luminaries. One of them looks like Mick Jagger. There is a black-and-white wedding photo. Judging from the style of the dress, she thinks it's probably his parents. She is fairly sure there is one of Ada, front and centre, her face peeking out from underneath a heavy fringe, smiling uncertainly at the lens. She makes a mental note to tell Les to take a picture of it. Just as she is about to walk over to take a closer look, the door swings open and Howard walks in.

'Esme, great to see you again,' he says, coming towards her with an arm outstretched. When she takes it to shake his hand, he leans in and kisses her on both cheeks. He has dressed relatively informally for this occasion: a pink shirt, open at the neck, blue chinos and brown suede loafers.

'Do you have any coffee?' he asks, before she can launch into her pre-interview spiel about how much she appreciates him giving up his time.

'No, but . . .'

'Well you must. Where is Theresa when you need her?' He goes to the door, leans into the hallway and bellows, 'There-saaaa!' The woman who greeted Esme appears instantly like a hologram. 'Can you get us some coffee, please? Esme, what'll it be?'

'Just a normal black coffee, thanks.'

'Black coffee for the lady. Latte for me. Skimmed milk.' Howard pats his belly. 'Claudia's got me on a health kick.' He winks, then plonks himself down on the sofa opposite Esme, the impact of his weight causing the cushions to judder and belch out a cloud of dust.

'Thanks for coming,' he says. Esme looks at him carefully. There is something not right about him today, a discordant note sounding at the edge of her thoughts. He is grinning at her but his eyes shift and flicker as he does so. He is agitated, she thinks. But why would someone be agitated if he had nothing to hide?

'Now,' he says. 'How long do you think this'll take?'

'I told your secretary it would be an hour for the interview and forty minutes for the portrait.'

He snorts. 'Forty minutes! What's he going to do? Paint me?'

'I think he just wants to get something new. We've only got old shots of you on file and they're a bit corporate. This is a more personal piece, so . . .'

'I mean, Christ!' Howard continues, talking over her. 'It'll be enough to put your readers off their breakfasts.' He guffaws loudly, throwing his head back so that a tuft of chest hair appears at the open V of his shirt then slides back underneath the buttoned fabric.

He crosses one leg over the other exposing his crotch area and looks out of the window as though some object in the garden is demanding the entirety of his attention.

She wonders how she should play this. The room feels electrified and stifling, as though Howard's nervous energy has pumped through the air-conditioning system and pushed out all the oxygen. If she is too direct, he will be angry. If she is too pliant, he will take advantage. She needs to strike a balance between deference and alertness.

'I know you're very busy, Sir Howard,' Esme begins, allowing herself to sound tentative, a bit nervous herself, 'and I really appreciate you giving up your time, so I'll get cracking if you're ready?'

Howard nods.

She places her dictaphone on the coffee table between them, presses 'record' and checks that the red light is winking at her. 'Is Rupert . . . ?'

'Rupert's not coming. I wanted to do this on my own.'

Esme gets out her notepad to jot things down as he talks, balances it on her knee and then looks across at him, trying to engage him with what she hopes is a friendly smile.

'OK, well, Sir Howard—'

'Call me Howard.'

'Howard. Perhaps you could start off by telling me what the motivation was behind setting up this foundation?'

A nice, open-ended question to get him going, she thinks. Fairly anodyne, gives him the chance to bang on about charitable giving and emphasise his social conscience.

'I wanted to do something in memory of my daughter,' Sir Howard says, picking a stray hair off the knee of his trousers, affecting a kind of boredom. He looks at her and smiles briefly, the shape of it disappearing and leaving no trace. Esme waits, expecting him to continue but when he doesn't she is thrown and stammers to try and fill the gap in conversation.

'Um, OK, yes. But, er, why now particularly, Sir – I mean, Howard?'

He sighs.

'It felt like enough time had elapsed. In the immediate after-math of her . . . her disappearance, I guess you'd say, I wasn't in a fit state to do anything much. But it's been eleven years now, and I suppose I have to face the fact that Ada isn't coming back.' There is a pause. 'I mean, she could be dead. Probably is.'

The abruptness of that statement, the baldness of it, throws her off balance. He looks out of the window again. Esme chooses not to say anything, deliberately waiting to see whether Sir Howard will carry on. Sometimes the canniest thing to do in an interview is to stay silent.

Finally, he turns to look at her and she notices his eyes are watery and there is a stubborn wrinkle above his brow. She feels a leap of surprised excitement: tears make good copy, she thinks before she can stop herself. A vision of her mother with a glum, disappointed look on her face rises in Esme's mind. Empathy, she reminds herself. Be empathetic. But be objective too. And don't get so emotional about it. Remember what Dave says: the inter-view isn't about you, it's about the person you're interviewing.

A light sweat breaks out across her brow. How on earth is anyone meant to do all of that and still give the impression of holding a casual conversation? Interviews are a bloody night-mare.

She lowers her head, scribbles a nonsensical loop of shorthand on her notepad and gathers her thoughts. She can hear Howard breath-ing: a weighted space rising and falling on the other side of the table. And instead of remembering all the things she should be doing to move the interview on, Esme remembers sitting at her father's hos-pital bed, listening to the mechanical judder of the ventilator, looking at his bruised and swollen face and his body covered with tubes. She remembers holding her brother's hand, trying not to breathe in too much of the hospital disinfectant smell because she was worried she might faint. She remembers her mother: the emptiness of her expres-sion; the hollow shock of her face.

The next question forms itself with perfect clarity.

'But no matter how much time passes,' Esme says, 'I can't imagine you get over a grief like that.'

He shakes his head.

'No, you're right. And of course, it's not a conventional grief. I mean, I've lost good friends in the past. My mum died so I know what it's like to mourn someone you love. But we, Penny and I – Penny's my first wife – we can't mourn. We don't know what happened to Ada. There's no grave to visit. So it's . . . well, an open wound. Yeah. It never heals.' He breaks off. 'Sorry. I'm just not used to, you know, talking about this . . .'

'Your mum was also called Ada, wasn't she? Did you name your daughter . . .'

'After her? Yeah. I loved my mum. Had the greatest of respect for her. She raised me single-handed after my dad walked out and I wasn't always the best behaved.'

He gives another gruff burst of laughter. Interesting, Esme thinks, that there was an absent father. She is struck by yet another unexpected similarity between them. She's noticed that a lot of successful, driven, high-powered types are from single-parent families. There's something about needing to prove yourself to the one who left, needing to get their love and approval in different ways because you feel you weren't enough to keep them there in the first place.

'She sounds like a strong woman,' Esme ventures.

He nods. 'Could be terrifying when she was angry. Terrifying. I've never met anyone who could make me as scared as she could, and I include the vast majority of CEOs in that.'

His voice dips and he looks away, rubbing the back of his neck. The carefully combed grey strands at the nape dislodge and tangle. When he removes his hand, his fingertips are greased with gel.

'But she loved me,' he says. 'I always knew she loved me deeply. And without her, I wouldn't be . . .'

The door opens and Theresa comes in rattling a tray filled with silverware.

'Ah,' says Howard, instantly switching from self-reflection to showy bonhomie. 'At bloody last. A man could die of thirst round here. Ooh biscuits,' he continues as he alights on a plate of chocolate Bourbons. 'Lovely jubbly.'

Esme writes: 'Choc Bourbons' in her notepad. She might be able to make something of that in the piece: use it as a means of conveying that Sir Howard, for all his wealth, is still a simple man at heart who doesn't like to stand on ceremony, et cetera, et cetera. No Duchy Original stem-ginger biscuits for him.

He offers the plate to her.

'No thanks.'

'Why not? You're not on a diet, are you?'

'No.'

'Good. In my day, girls had a bit of meat on them. It's terrible the pressure you young girls have to stay thin.'

Theresa scuttles out of the room.

'Of course you've got personal experience of having seen your daughter go through anorexia,' Esme says, seizing on the chance to get the interview back on track. It's a clumsy way to do it but she's running out of time.

Howard stares at her. He places the plate of biscuits back on the coffee tray without taking one. When he looks at her again, he seems to have made some kind of deal with himself, he seems to have decided to trust her.

'Yeah,' he says. 'Ada struggled with loads of stuff.'

A pause. Outside, the tinny whine of an ambulance siren. Howard shifts in his seat.

'I don't like to look back, to be honest. I try not to do it too much. Don't think it does any good, dwelling on the things you can't change. But I have asked myself recently if Ada was ever really happy.'

Esme waits.

'That's a hard thing to say about your own child, because all you want to give them is happiness and love. To make them feel secure.' He pauses, sips his latte. 'Do you have kids?'

She shakes her head.

'I just think maybe she had something missing, some chemical, some imbalance. I didn't use to believe in depression. Thought it was all a load of bollocks. Made up by psychiatrists who want to tell you it's all because your mum didn't love you or whatever. But, actually, I don't think she had the capacity for happiness. Even when she was little. She was always so . . . so uptight. Anxious. Couldn't relax. Always very aware of herself, of what other people thought of her.

'I remember, one night when I went to say goodnight to her – I always did that, you know, even when I was working crazy hours.' The lines of Howard's face soften slightly. For a second, he looks almost kind. 'Ada must have been, what? Six or seven. She was a bit down, nothing obvious, just the way you can tell with kids. I said, "What's wrong?" She goes, "Dad, I don't want you and Mum to die." It's not normal for a kid to do that, is it?' He pauses. 'Sorry. Load of sentimental rubbish.'

'No, no, not at all. This must be painful for you to talk about.'

'It's my choice to talk about it. The foundation, I mean. I wanted to do something positive.' He pronounces 'wanted' as if it is missing all the consonants. It strikes a false note. She wonders if Howard is at pains to speak like this to accentuate his humble roots. There is something about it that seems phoney, like those politicians who use glottal stops to appear of the people even though they've had a public school education and a nanny since birth.

It would be so much better if he could be honest about himself, she thinks, if he had enough confidence in his own achievements to believe he was accepted. If he could get rid of that monstrous chip on his shoulder and stop caring so much about what other people thought of him. Why else would a man as powerful, as successful, as rich as Howard be so worried about his self-image that he got his PR man to call round all the newspaper picture desks and ask them to stop using a picture he didn't think did him justice? It was absurd. And yet, beneath the absurdity, there was something real – a vulnerability, a need to be loved and admired.

'I'll never get over the loss of my daughter,' Howard is saying. 'Never. But at least this way there can be a lasting legacy, something that can benefit others.'

And all of a sudden, the intimacy is lost. Howard has moved on from his memories of Ada and sounds as though he is reciting a press release, as though someone has scripted exactly the words he should use. She knows Dave isn't all that interested in the foundation and has used it as a wafer-thin excuse to secure the interview. But she has to be seen to play ball.

'What do you want the foundation to achieve?' she asks, resting her pen. She won't need to take notes on this bit – hardly any of it will make the final edit. Sir Howard speaks fluently for the best part of ten minutes, rattling off a series of aims that seem generic and unfocused, tenuously linked together by the fact that Ada was fairly artistic and liked to paint. The foundation, he says, will raise private funding and distribute grants to after-school clubs on council estates and impoverished students who want to pursue arts degrees. It will also arrange trips to art galleries for under-privileged children. It will lobby the government for increased spending on the arts. It will provide adult education classes. It will pay for volunteers to go into hospitals, old people's homes and nurseries and teach people 'how to express themselves through the creative media'. It all sounds as right-on as it is possible to get. It also sounds ridiculously overambitious, but Esme isn't about to tell him so.

'And not just that,' Howard carries on. Esme checks her watch discreetly. Twenty minutes of her allotted time have passed. 'But I want to do some stuff with asylum seekers and refugees . . .'

'Really?' Esme asks. It doesn't seem like an obvious fit: the unapologetic capitalist and the benefit-scroungers.

'Yes. You know, I've met some people recently who have

really changed my mind on this whole issue. There are terrible things going on in the world. Do you know it's illegal to be gay in Uganda? They get stoned to death.'

Esme swallows drily. This was one direction she certainly hadn't expected the conversation to go in. She wonders momentarily if he's in the grip of a mid-life crisis, like those pinstriped bankers you sometimes read about in the Sunday supplements who give it all up to go and build bridges in Mongolian villages in an attempt to 'find themselves' in something other than the reflective surface of a gleaming Ferrari bonnet.

'Sir Howard, if we could get back to—'

'Sure, sure. But I just want to say one more thing: the way this country treats those people who are genuinely fleeing from dreadful regimes is an outrage. I'm not talking about the chancers who wanna come over here and get boob-jobs free on the NHS or whatever it is they do. I'm talking about the asylum seekers who have a genuine reason for being here.

'I'm the son of immigrants. If they hadn't been able to come to England, they'd have been marched off to the concentration camps and gassed to death. You're too young to remember—'

It's one of Esme's pet hates when an older interviewee mentions her age in an attempt to undermine her but Howard is now in full flow: 'This country's built on fuc— on immigrants! I'd like some of the foundation's funds to go towards supporting those guys who come to these shores wanting a better life for themselves and willing to work for it. I can relate to that.'

Esme waits. He seems finally to have come to a halt.

'OK, understood,' she says. 'Do you think Ada would have liked the idea of the foundation? Would she be proud of you for establishing it?'

Howard exhales, pressing the air through his teeth. His face is tight again, closed off.

'Who knows?' He squeezes his eyes shut for a moment. 'I don't know what kind of woman she'd be now. She'd be almost thirty. Maybe we'd have rows about stuff. Maybe she'd think I was a stupid old codger. Maybe I'd have a couple of grandkids – who knows?'

'Ada was beautiful . . .' He drifts off. 'But it was like she was born with a layer of skin missing, like she was too fragile for the world and she didn't have a lot of confidence in herself and I wish, wish, wish I could have changed that. I tried. We both did, me and Penny.'

He coughs, takes a gulp of his latte. The only sign of his emotion is a slight strangulation of the voice, as though he is physically having to push each word out.

'We were good parents, I'm 100 per cent sure of that. Whatever was written in the papers after she disappeared, I know we did our best. But the worst part is the not knowing. Not knowing if she's dead or alive. The cruelty of that . . . is indescribable. I don't think the words exist to explain what that's like, I really don't.'

He looks at Esme.

'She was the light of my life. This little girl with this . . . this wrinkle, I guess you'd call it . . . a frown . . . just . . . a funny frown, playing with her dollies. She used to make them sandwiches, you know? Spread the bread with honey then stick a pile of Smarties on top to make it look like a cake.'

He chuckles, then snaps out of the reverie and sweeps the emotion aside, becoming businesslike again. She has never met anyone who can switch so easily from one state to the next, as though flicking through a filing cabinet of compartmentalised feeling. What must it be like to live that way, Esme thinks. How can he remember who he truly is in the midst of trying to display so many different fronts to the world?

'There were rumours that she was on drugs,' Esme says. 'The police found evidence—'

Howard cuts her off. 'No,' he says, eyes narrowed. 'You should check your information.'

'I thought it was reported at the time . . .'

He turns on her.

'I don't give a flying fuck what was reported at the time,' he says, voice raised to the level just below a full-throttled shout, jabbing his finger at her across the coffee table. 'I'm telling you, as her father, Ada never touched the stuff.' He leans back. The triangle of skin at the open V of his shirt has turned bright red. 'Next question.'

Esme tucks a strand of hair behind her ear. Her hand is shaking. She mustn't let him see that she is cowed. But before she can ask the next question, Howard is speaking again, his voice semi-apologetic, his mood inexplicably calmer.

'Listen, I just want some good to come of it all,' he says, leaning forward, propping his elbows on his knees and seeking out her sightline. 'Chances are, I'll never know what happened to my daughter but the foundation is my way of making something positive come out of it all.'

Esme takes a sip of her coffee, the cup clattering noisily against the saucer as she replaces it. Howard flinches. She needs to give him something of her own, to make him feel as though she is sharing too.

'I don't know if you remember that lunch we had a while back—'

'Course I do.'

'I told you that I'd lost my dad when I was younger. My mum . . . I think she finds Christmas the hardest day of the year. Or even his birthday, because it reminds her, I suppose, of everything she's missing.'

Howard is nodding.

'Do you feel the same?'

'Yeah, to an extent,' he says. Silence.

'Do you mark Ada's birthday in any special way?'

His right foot starts tapping against the floor. He seems perturbed by this question. Once again, Esme wonders why he is doing this interview when he seems so against the idea of opening up.

'Yeah,' Howard says. 'I haven't ever spoken about this before so it's hard, you need to bear with me.' He coughs. His leg twitches. He sighs – a long whistle like a tyre deflating.

'Penny and I meet up at TGI Friday's in Kingston,' he says. 'It was where we took Ada every year for her birthday when she was a kid. She loved it there. The waiters always used to give her balloons and she loved the ice-cream sundae.'

He sniffs.

'We go there, just the two of us, and we order the same food every year even though neither of us ever feels like eating it. And we talk about Ada, about our memories, stuff like that. One of the hardest things for both of us has been the idea that it was always going to end up like this, you know? I mean, I'm Jewish by birth and I don't have much truck with God, not any more, but there's a bit of me that wonders if there is such a thing as fate and, if there is, was it always written that Ada would disappear off the face of the earth at the age of nineteen? What kind of a sick, perverted joke is that? What did either of us do – me or Penny – to deserve it? I don't know. I truly don't know.'

'It's good that you and Penny can still do that together though, in spite of the divorce,' Esme ventures.

'Yeah,' Howard nods. 'We've only got each other, really. We're the only ones who know what we're going through. Claudia has her . . .' He searches for the right word. 'Qualities, but she doesn't get it . . . why would she? I can't expect her to.'

The coffee has cooled. Outside, the clear skies have turned grey. Rain spits against the window. Howard looks exhausted. There are shiny pouches under his eyes and he has slumped in on himself as though his muscles have given up, as though the effort of appearing normal requires too much energy, too much honesty.

The dictaphone bleeps and stutters. Esme jumps. She feels grubby, as she often does at the end of interviews where she has exploited a briskly established closeness. It is a false conversation, this circular question and answer. A carefully scripted play masquerading as spontaneity, with neither of the main actors willing to acknowledge the fakery of it.

The art of the interviewer, Esme knows, is to coax the emotion of the interviewee to the surface, casting off with a wriggling question and letting the bait glitter and skim on the water until they have taken it and been hooked. And part of Howard has been grateful to be hooked, she knows that. Everyone wants to talk, deep down. But still she feels cheapened. She wonders what would happen if she switched the dictaphone off and threw her notes away and talked to Howard normally. Would she be able to drill down through the complex, interconnecting layers of his manufactured identity to get to the truth of who he really was? Did he even know? Could he remember what it was to be honest about himself? Or was he scared of what he might find if he did so?

'There's something I'd like you to see,' Howard says, not looking at her but picking instead at a minuscule speck of fluff on his sleeve.

She waits.

'I thought it might be helpful for you to see Ada as she was. When she was alive, I mean.'

'I don't—'

'I've got an old family video, you see. It's – it was made for my fiftieth birthday. She was fifteen . . .'

He looks up, eyes cloudy, mouth blurred.

'But, you know, it might not interest you. You might feel you have all you need. Or that it would be a bit—' He pauses, rests his hands on his knees. 'Spooky.'

'No,' Esme says, too quickly. 'No, I mean, yes. I'd be honoured to look at it. If you don't mind.'

'Good. The screening room is all set up for you. I'll get Theresa to take you down.'

'You won't be—'

Howard shakes his head. 'I can't.'

Theresa leads her down a narrow staircase to the basement. They emerge in a short corridor lined with movie stills – *Carry On* film posters emblazoned with a semi-clad Barbara Windsor in a nurse's uniform; a black-and-white James Stewart from *It's a Wonderful Life*; a screaming Tippi Hedren surrounded by silhouetted cows. The house is cooler down here, with the chill of damp in the air. The carpet is frayed at the edges and there are stacks of paper folders piled haphazardly along some metal bookshelves. It looks unfinished, as though someone had run out of energy to decorate. She doesn't believe in ghosts, but there is a sense of absence so pervasive that Esme feels she could reach out and grab it and squeeze it into a hard ball in the palm of her hand.

The posters, the shelves, the carpet – none of it seems to fit with the carefully cultivated elegance in the rest of the house. There is no surface gloss, no pretence, no show. It is, Esme thinks, the most authentic part of the entire building.

'In here,' Theresa says, motioning for Esme to follow her into the private cinema. The room is dark at first but when Theresa rotates the dimmer switch four rows of plush red-leather seats become visible. There are two oversized vases of dried flowers on either side of the screen, the plasticky petals dulled by dust. The windows, high up on one wall, are blacked out.

'Sit,' Theresa says.

Esme takes a seat in the second row, lowering herself into the deep upholstery and allowing herself to relax. For a moment, she forgets where she is and surrenders herself to the pleasurable sensation of being about to watch a film and her taste buds start to crave a bucket of sweet popcorn and a tepid Diet Coke. It is only as the screen flickers into life that she remembers what she is doing here.

And then, all at once, she is there: the lost girl, Ada Pink, projected to several times her normal size, her face filling most of the screen. She is smiling, the crinkle of it reaching up to her eyes. Her front tooth is chipped. There is a crookedness to her face that serves only to heighten her extraordinary beauty. Esme had never thought of Ada as beautiful. The newspaper images of the missing girl had always made her appear depressed, shrunken, soulless. On screen, she is vital, pinkness of flesh made real, a shine to her hair, her eyes, the ridge of her cheek-bones. And then she speaks.

'So, I wanted to make this little film for my dad to wish him a very happy birthday,' Ada is staring at the camera with those dark, serious eyes. 'You might drive me mad sometimes, but I love you to bits.'

It is a teenage voice with a North London accent and everything she says sounds light and full: a clear glass of water about to spill over.

She takes her seat at a white piano on the left-hand side of the screen. The film judders and a rash of black spots appear on the celluloid, then vanish. Ada is sitting upright on the piano stool, her posture so correct that it is obvious she cares, perhaps too much, about getting this right. Her fingers rest on the keys, palms of the hands hollowed out, knuckles lifted upwards. Her birch-branch arms are slender and pale, cross-hatched at the wrist with faded pink indentations. Looking at those thin, marked lines, Esme imagines the cut and slash of a razor blade – the pain and then the release. She has known enough teenage girls to recognise the scars.

Ada starts to play, stumbles on a chord, shakes out her long brown hair, and continues, closing her eyes, tilting her head to the light and then she sings.

'"It's a little bit funny, this feeling inside . . ."'

Her voice cracks and wobbles on the higher notes, but this only serves to underline the perfection of it, the poignancy, the heart-stopping loveliness of a fifteen-year-old girl singing a song to her father thinking she is unobserved, believing that no one apart from him will ever see this tape and certainly not a journalist she had never met, who knows of Ada Pink only as a tragic newspaper story, a story left unfinished, a question still hanging even now, so many years later, even now that she would no longer be this girl, with her brown hair and her grey trainers and her white piano and her chewed nails and her pink, blood-bloomed skin.

Esme presses the tips of her fingers to her face. This is not your story, she reminds herself firmly. Maintain objectivity. Be professional. This is not your sadness.

But somehow it was. Somehow, within her, Esme has begun to associate Ada Pink's disappearance and the acuteness of Howard's loss with the death of her own father, the truth of her own grief. And sitting here, in a millionaire's private cinema, watching his daughter sing him a song, Esme knows she has never allowed herself to feel too deeply or to acknowledge how much she loved her dad or how much she continues to love her mother. Because to do so would be to make herself vulnerable. It would mean she had to face up to certain things – things that had to do with the terrifying unpredictability of life, the fragility of each intake of breath. What guarantee was there – for any of it? She wishes she could cut the love out of her, like a cyst.

So she refuses to cry, even as Ada comes to the end of her song, stands up from the piano, takes a bow into the vastness of the world and then switches off the camera, pitching the room into shadow.

Esme sits for a minute and then walks out into the odd little corridor. Ignoring the shakiness in her legs, she finds her way up the stairs, placing the flat of one hand along the wall to steady herself. She lets herself back into the sitting room, where the fire is still laid, waiting to be lit, and the potpourri is still scenting the air and Sir Howard is sitting on the sofa exactly where she left him. He turns to look at her but doesn't get up. Their eyes meet.

'Helpful?'

Esme nods.

'It's not easy to watch,' Howard says.

'No,' Esme replies and her voice croaks. 'But I really appreciate you showing it to me. It's important – seeing Ada as she was, remembering . . .'

'That she's a real person?' Howard completes the thought. 'Yes. People forget.' He closes his eyes. 'I let her down,' he says, so softly it is nearly inaudible. And Esme is about to respond with some meaningless platitude but she stops herself because she is not sure she can form the words without everything becoming undone.

Ever since he walked through the door, she has been trying to work out what it was about Howard Pink that felt so familiar. There was an elusive quality about him that she half recognised in herself and yet she couldn't quite pin it down. It was a gap she knew the shape of, but not what it contained. But now, looking at him looking at her, it comes to her in a rush of completeness. She knows what it is they recognise in each other. It is shame.

Carol

SHE DOESN'T SCREAM. THE sound never makes it out of her. The oddness of this hits her at almost exactly the same time as she experiences the not screaming, so that she is curiously untethered from the situation, as though examining herself through the wrong end of Archie's binoculars. She is looking at the dead person's hand in her neighbour's flower bed and all she is thinking is: Well, this is strange. Why aren't I screaming? Why aren't I shocked? I seem to be taking this very calmly, don't I?

She forgets, for a moment, the presence of Archie. She feels wholly unruffled, completely in charge of every filament of her emotion. There is also a lack of surprise, an unacknowledged suspicion. She has been carrying this nebulous anxiety with her ever since that day Alan came round for tea, consciously leaving it unformed and unspoken in case it scared her, in case she had to do something about it. And now, here it was: confirmation.

Something is tugging at her sleeve. She wonders what it might be and then she looks down and sees Archie trying to get her attention.

'Grandma, what is it? What is it?' His words fall over themselves and she knows that he can sense there is something wrong. There is a density to the air, an encroaching thickness. She seems to be looking at everything through a pane of glass – a microscope slide smudged with fingerprints.

Archie's voice pierces the confusion of her thoughts. The

microscope slide slips and cracks. All at once, everything snaps into focus.

'Nothing to worry about, Archie love,' Carol says automatically. 'What I need you to do is to go back to your mother and tell her I'll be over in a minute. I've just got to finish up here.'

'But—'

'No questions, Archie. I'll explain everything in a bit. Now run along and get yourself a nice hot Ribena.'

He looks up at her, his face questioning. Then he nods, just the once, and scampers back up the garden into the kitchen. She knew the hot Ribena would do the trick. She listens for the sound of the front door slamming. When she hears the clunk of it swinging shut, Carol exhales. She hadn't realised she'd been holding her breath.

She doesn't want to look at the hand again but she forces herself to bend over, bringing her face closer to the damp, springy soil. She squints through her spectacles. It would be embarrassing to call the police when it was just a pile of old twigs, she thinks. Best be on the safe side. She regulates her breathing – in and out to the count of five – and feels the crack and twinge of her joints as she stoops.

She shudders when she examines it. Although Carol has never seen a decomposed human hand before, she has no doubt that this is what she is staring at. Slender pipe-cleaner fingers, blackened with a yellowy tinge. The bones are stripped of flesh and pointing skywards. She is reminded of lamb chops served with frilled white paper in fancy restaurants.

Thumb. Finger. Knuckle. She can see, for the first time, what clever things knuckles are, so neatly designed: the peaked cap of the socket, the perfectly shaped joint, the smoothness of the bend and flex. She wonders briefly whether the hand belongs to a man or a woman. Something tells her it is female.

Nausea rises. A dizziness comes over her, threatening to send the lawn into a whirling vortex like the fast cycle on her washing machine. She breathes in and out. Reminds herself that she needs to be calm. Imagines Derek's voice: 'Pull yourself together, love. No use crying over spilt milk.'

She has never been good in a crisis. Derek had always been the steadying hand, the person who knew exactly what to do when their car broke down on a roadside or when a pipe burst or the central heating went on the blink again. He had this male sixth sense that meant he always knew what tool to ferret out from the cupboard underneath the stairs or what telephone number to call, even when they were abroad.

'No good wishing he was here,' Carol says out loud. 'Get on with it.'

The sound of her own voice makes her feel better. Steady now, she cautions herself. Steady.

She turns away from the flower bed and, with an enormous effort of will, forces herself to walk back to the kitchen door. Her feet are heavy and unbalanced and she limps the last few steps. She feels very old. Shock, she thinks. It must be the shock. And then: What I wouldn't give for a sugary cup of tea.

Carol continues down the hallway, placing her hand flat against the wall to keep herself upright. She remembers seeing a phone by the front door and makes her way to it. It is an old-fashioned thing, moss-green in colour with a rotary dial. Before she picks up the receiver, she has a flash of fear that Alan will come back unannounced. Carol puts the safety chain on the door, just in case. Then, for only the second time in her life, she dials 999.

She is asked for her name, address and telephone number by a polite young woman on the other end of the line. When Carol tells her what she has discovered nestling in her neighbour's flower bed, the woman is perfectly relaxed, as though Carol has just been reciting the details of her weekly shopping list.

'Have you touched the hand, Mrs Hetherington?' the woman asks. Faint accent, Carol thinks. Northern.

'No, no. It's still there.'

'Who else is there?'

'No one. I mean, my grandson was here but I sent him back home. It's just me.'

'OK, that's good, Mrs Hetherington, thank you. Have you told anyone else about what you've seen?'

'Hmm? Oh, oh no. Archie – that's my grandson – he saw it too but we didn't talk about it.'

'How old is Archie?'

'Twelve last August.'

'OK, what I want you to do, Mrs Hetherington, is wait where you are. Don't touch anything. We'll send an officer out to you straight away. Just sit tight.'

'All right,' Carol says, swallowing hard. 'How long will that be?'

'Not too long at all, Mrs Hetherington. They'll be there shortly.'

Carol places the receiver back on the phone with a click. She feels sick at the thought of staying here a moment longer but she has never been good at standing up for herself. If someone has told her to stay, then that's exactly what she'll do, even if it takes several hours.

There is a pad of paper next to the telephone and a painted bowl filled with random knick-knacks: elastic bands, drawing pins, blobs of Blu-tack and a radiator key. But something at the bottom catches Carol's eyes, glinting in the fading light. She pokes a finger in the bowl, clearing aside the rubbish to get a clearer view. It is a small gold ring bearing a crest on a flat oval. She picks it up, holds it close to her face. The crest is engraved with a large bird, like a stork, and three triangular peaks. The circumference of the ring is too small to fit a man's finger. She thinks of the hand. Then of the ring. At the exact point that she makes the connection, she notices her teeth are chattering.

There is a knock on the door. Carol jumps. It is gloomy in the corridor. The sun has set and she has not yet turned on the light.

She hesitates. The doorbell rings. Another knock. She presses her eye to the spyhole and sees a blurred vision of her daughter.

'Mum, it's me,' Vanessa is saying. Carol undoes the safety catch and opens the door, feeling a great wave of reassurance as Vanessa marches into the hallway, hands on her hips, and asks her mother what on earth's going on. Carol tries to explain but for some reason the words come out in a bit of a jumble and her lips feel cold and clumsy so that she has trouble forming the syllables.

Vanessa seems to pick up on this and, without any more being said, folds her mother into a tight, expansive hug. Carol feels the back of her head being stroked and patted like a child and Vanessa is saying something in her ear, soothing, and Carol thinks how nice this is, to surrender control, to be looked after. She has never seen this side to Vanessa before.

Vanessa puts her arm around her mother's shoulders and leads her through to the kitchen where she slides out a chair and sits Carol down in it. She is about to put on the kettle when Carol stops her.

'No, love,' she says. 'The police said not to touch anything.'

'Oh, OK.'

'Thank you.'

'What for?' Vanessa says, but Carol can see she's pleased.

'Coming round. I've had a bit of a turn. Is Archie all right?'

'Oh yeah. I've left him watching *Dr Who* on Sky Plus He's happy as Larry.'

The doorbells rings.

Carol jumps. Vanessa rests her hand on her mother's shoulder.

'It's OK, Mum, I'll go.'

'They've got here quickly.'

Carol stays put, staring at the surface of the fold-out kitchen table. It has scuff-marks here and there, little pitted scars of black where the laminate has worn away. She clasps her hands together tightly in her lap. She doesn't want to leave her imprints anywhere in this house. She is irrationally worried that she will be a suspect.

'Stuff and nonsense,' she says to herself, trying to marshal her own thoughts. She can hear Vanessa talking in the corridor, her words echoed by a lower, male voice, and then the murmuring conversational sounds are coming closer and closer and then the kitchen door opens and a police officer is there, dressed smartly in navy and silver, the thick serge of his uniform so close she could reach out and graze it with the tips of her fingers. The texture of the material reminds her of a toy she'd bought Archie one Christmas, a featureless doll to which you could stick felt accessories in blue, orange and green.

The policeman introduces himself but she forgets his name instantly. His face is kind: creases at the corners of his mouth, grey eyes that droop down at the corners. For some reason, she fixes on his shoes. They are black lace-ups, positioned flatly on Alan's bluish green linoleum like a pair of ocean liners setting out to sea.

The policeman asks her the same questions as the woman on the 999 call and Carol answers as best she can.

'Now, without going into the garden, Mrs Hetherington –'

'Call me Carol.'

He smiles a nice smile. 'Carol, then. Without going into the garden, could you just point out exactly where you've seen this – this – hand?'

She pushes herself up out of the chair. Vanessa offers her arm and Carol takes it, gratefully. Normally she'd be embarrassed by these tell-tale signs of age in front of a stranger but this evening she has no strength left to care what anyone thinks. She shuffles towards the glass-panelled doors overlooking the garden and points to the flower bed with her free arm.

'It's back there, just under the jasmine, next to the hydrangea.'

'Is that the white flower?' the policeman asks, smiling. 'Not much of a gardener,' he adds apologetically.

'That's right.' There is a pause. 'Alan spent hours out there,' Carol says. 'I always thought he loved gardening but now . . .' She drifts off, leaving the thought unexpressed. But it continues to unravel in her mind. He could have been burying a body.

'Mum?' Vanessa says, concerned. 'Are you OK?'

'Mrs Hetherington?'

The room contracts around her. She makes it to the sink just in time, retching a stream of bile into the plughole.

'Oh Mum, you poor thing. It's the shock, I expect,' Vanessa is saying to the policeman.

'No need to worry at all,' he says kindly. 'It often takes people this way.'

'Can I take her back home? We're only next door and I'd like to get her comfortable.'

Carol, her head still bowed in the sink, feels a flare of irritation that they are talking about her as if she isn't there.

'I'm perfectly all right,' she protests, her voice dimmed by the slight echo of stainless steel.

The policeman carries on talking over her. 'That should be fine, miss. I'll have to come over and ask her some more questions in a bit, if it is what we think it is.'

Carol unbends herself slowly, taking care not to stand up too quickly.

'Sure,' Vanessa replies with a confident nod of the head. 'OK, Mum, let's get you home.'

The policeman sees them out of the front door.

'See you in a bit,' he says as they walk down the small path onto the street. 'You've done exactly the right thing, Mrs Hetherington, by alerting us so promptly.'

He nods at her. As soon as she is out of the house, Carol feels better, weightless with the relief of it.

Archie opens the door to them, almost as though he has been looking out for their return. He rushes towards Carol and gives her a big hug. She grips hold of him tightly and inhales the brackish smell of his hair.

'There,' she says. 'No need to fuss.'

'Did you call the police?' he asks straight away and she is

surprised that he knows instinctively this is what she would do. She thought she had hidden what was going on as best she could but Carol is always surprised by how perceptive children are. There's no point in lying. No point in trying to conceal anything from them.

'Yes, I did. And there's a very nice man in uniform over there now taking care of everything so there's nothing to worry about.'

'Archie, why don't you put the kettle on and make Grandma a nice cup of tea?'

Carol smiles at her daughter weakly. 'Just the ticket.'

'And you go and sit on the couch and wrap yourself up warmly.'

Carol does as she's told.

She settles down to watch the tail end of *Songs of Praise* and then the theme music merges into the plinkety-plonk of *Antiques Roadshow*. Milton leaps up and folds himself neatly into her lap. She strokes him, listening to the regularity of his purring, and she starts to worry that she has got it wrong, that it wasn't a hand at all and that she has wasted police time. Because, after all, how would she know? The only dead body she'd seen was Derek's. The only skeletons she knows about are the ones printed on children's trick or treat costumes. And the idea that her next-door neighbour, a man she had invited into her own home, a man she had offered a plate of biscuits to, could be involved with anything so sinister seemed increasingly ludicrous. She lives in Wandsworth, for heaven's sake! It's a respectable part of south London. It's the kind of place bankers and celebrity chefs buy their houses, the kind of place the Tory Party comes canvassing. It's not the kind of place you discover a body buried in the flower bed next door. Who did she think she was? A character in *EastEnders*?

She titters.

'What is it?' Vanessa looks at her sharply.

'Oh, I was just thinking that maybe I'd let my imagination run away with me.'

Vanessa shakes her head.

'You've never let your imagination run away with you in your life,' she says and Carol can't help but feel affronted. I'm entirely capable of making things up in my head, Carol thinks, it's just that I choose not to waste my time doing so.

Archie comes in with her tea. He hands it to her, taking great care not to spill any. She beams at him and he settles down on the carpet by her feet, snuggling close to her. It feels lovely.

As she warms her hands round the mug, a calmness descends. Carol turns back to the television screen. *Antiques Roadshow* is taking place in the grounds of a stately home that has recently been featured in a drama adaptation of a Jane Austen novel. The cameras pan back to display several long queues of sensibly dressed pensioners in kagoules and padded Barbour gilets, each of whom is waiting patiently bearing chipped pieces of Wedgwood and boxes full of paste jewellery they believe to be priceless heirlooms.

The presenter, a nice girl called Fiona who appears to be approximately half the age of the assembled crowd, is making a great show of how approachable she is and yet everything she says is somehow . . . well . . . a bit saucy.

Carol sips her tea and watches as Fiona leans over to examine more closely the saddle of a child's antique rocking horse. She is wearing jeans that are fitted far too tightly, in Carol's opinion, and when she bends, the pertness of her bottom seems almost obscene in comparison to the motley assortment of slack, greying faces in the background.

'I can't stand her,' Vanessa says.

'Really?' Carol asks mildly. 'I always think she seems quite nice.'

Vanessa snorts. It's jealousy, Carol knows. Vanessa is for ever comparing herself to other women. The irony is she doesn't realise her figure is just as good as any of those skinny Russian teenage models' you see in magazines. Carol wouldn't dream of telling her this, of course. She doesn't want her only daughter to get a big head. Heaven forbid.

The doorbell rings again and Vanessa gets up and goes to the hallway, followed by Archie. Carol shrugs herself out of the blanket, displacing Milton who scowls at her and slouches onto the carpet. She pats down her skirt and glances at her feet, embarrassed that Vanessa has made her wear her silly fluffy slippers. She likes to look her best for figures of authority. Her mother had always told her to wear matching underwear in case she was in an accident and her knickers were on show to all and sundry. The thought of this had so mortified Carol as a young girl that she had never once, in all her adult years, worn a bra and pants in different colours. Derek had made fun of her for that. Told her she was 'OCD', like David Beckham.

The policeman is shown into the lounge by Vanessa. Carol sits straighter on the couch.

'Hello again, Mrs Hether – I mean Carol,' he says, with the same kind smile on his face.

'I've had a look at the flower bed.' He stops. 'You were right to call 999. It does indeed look like a decomposed human hand.'

Vanessa gasps. Carol nods, just as she has seen Helen Mirren do in *Prime Suspect*. The confirmation of her judgement pleases her.

'Archie, go upstairs and . . .' Vanessa draws a blank. 'Play on the computer,' she adds distractedly.

'Oh but, Mum—' he starts. Something in his mother's face convinces him not to push the point and he scampers obediently upstairs.

The policeman waits until he can hear Archie treading the floorboards above his head. 'I've alerted SOCO – sorry, our Scenes of Crimes Officers – and they'll be down shortly to preserve the crime scene.'

'Crime scene?' Vanessa says faintly.

'Yes. We are treating this as a serious matter. There are necessary procedures to follow, as I'm sure you can imagine. But there's nothing for you to worry about. Your mum did absolutely the right thing.'

He turns away from Vanessa, a little reluctantly, Carol senses, and focuses his attention on her.

'What I need to do now, Carol, is to ask you a bit about your next-door neighbour, if you wouldn't mind?'

'No. Go ahead.'

The policeman takes out a notepad and pen. He flicks to a page scrawled with untidy writing.

'You told me that Alan has been living at Number 12 for over a year, is that right?'

'Yes, about fourteen months I think. He moved in sometime around Easter, I think. I remember that because we had a chat about eating too much chocolate. Silly really.'

'Good,' says the policeman. 'And his surname is—?'

'Pardon?'

'Your neighbour.'

'Oh.' A blush rises up her neck. 'Clithero.'

'How old would you say he is?'

'Oh goodness. I'd say mid-forties but I'm not sure exactly. It's so difficult to tell nowadays, isn't it?'

He jots something down in his pad.

'When was the last time you saw him?'

'The day before yesterday, when he came to drop off his keys. He wanted me to water his plants, you see, while he was away.'

'Do you have any idea where he's gone?'

She thinks back to when he came round. She shakes her head.

'I'm afraid not. He came round and was a bit . . .' She searches for the right word. 'Edgy. Uncomfortable. Normally I would have asked him where he was going but I didn't want to get into a conversation.'

The policeman cocks his head.

'Why was that then?'

'Like I said, there was something . . . off about him that day. I didn't like it. Made me feel nervous, to be honest.'

Vanessa comes to sit next to her and puts her hand on Carol's knee.

'Do you know when he's due back?' the policeman asks gently.

'He said he was going away for four days. So, tomorrow, I suppose.'

There is a fresh surge of nausea.

'I don't want him coming round here,' she says and is surprised to find tears in her eyes. 'I live on my own you see and I'm not able to . . .'

Vanessa hugs her close.

'Mum, you won't be on your own. Archie and I will stay with you for a few days.'

Carol starts to cry. It is the first time she has cried properly since Derek died, and even then, she hadn't been able to find enough tears. She grips hold of her daughter's hand, squeezing it tightly.

The policeman leans forward, resting his forearms on his knees.

'There's nothing for you to worry about, Carol. There will be police officers here twenty-four hours a day. We'll take the appropriate measures to ensure your safety. These questions are all just routine. There could be a perfectly reasonable explanation.'

Carol lifts her head and slides out a folded handkerchief from her cardigan sleeve. She wipes her nose as best she can.

'Of course, officer. I'm sorry. I don't know what came over me.'

He waves his hand. 'No need to apologise. I'll leave you in peace shortly, Mrs Hetherington. Just one last thing: do you happen to have any contact details for Mr Clithero? A mobile number, anything like that?'

'Yes, I've got his mobile. He wanted me to call if anything went . . . well, if anything went wrong.'

'I'd be very grateful if you could get it for me.'

'Yes, Vanessa, it's on the pad by the calendar in the kitchen, would you—?'

Vanessa pats her hand and gets up in one swift motion from the sofa. Carol can see the policeman look at her appreciatively as she walks to the door, then he spots Carol looking at him and drops his head.

'Would you like a cup of tea or anything?' she asks.

'That's very kind, thanks, but I'm fine.'

Vanessa comes back into the room and hands the police officer a square of pink paper with a floral print around the border. It had been part of a Christmas present from Connie last year. She thought of Connie every time she wrote something down. And now, she thinks of her friend as the policeman takes the scrap of paper in his big, meaty hand. She's not sure how she's going to tell Connie all that's been going on. She isn't even sure that she wants to.

The policeman gets up, slips his notepad back in his jacket pocket and prepares to leave with a final flurry of reassurance. He says he'll check up on them first thing tomorrow morning but that, in the meantime, the best thing is to get some rest. He hopes the work next door won't disturb them too much.

Beatrice

FOR THE FIRST DAY in her new job, Beatrice has treated herself to a new outfit from the charity shop. The dress had been staring at her for days and she saw it every time she walked past the window on the way to the bus stop. It was pinned slackly to a faceless polystyrene mannequin, the sleeves tied behind the torso like a straitjacket. Beatrice could never understand why the women in that shop took so little pride in displaying their clothes. If she worked there, she would spend hours poring over each bag of donations, feeling the cuffs, tracing the buttons with her fingers, imagining the stories they could tell.

She would cherish the sparkly sequinned skirts, discarded after some long-ago office Christmas party romance turned sour. She would carefully fold the cardigans with baggy elbows, thinking that once they kept an old lady warm through the winter. She would have hung up the wedding dresses with extra sensitivity, knowing that, beneath the off-white taffeta, the hems stained with dots of spilt champagne, there was a story, a proper human story of love and sadness and all that lay in between. Clothes were so much more than fabric, Beatrice thought. The stitching, the precision of a pleat on a trouser waistband, the sculptural curve of an armhole . . . all of it so consciously designed. All of it spoke of a person who, at some level, had made a choice, had decided that the world should look a certain way. She admired that in people. In a way, she admired Howard Pink for it too.

She is surprised at how little rancour she feels for this man now that they have spoken. Perhaps, she thinks, she has been conned by him. Perhaps what she has taken for genuine feeling on his part is little more than the well-deployed charm of a successful businessman, a man used to getting the deal he wants, no matter who he is negotiating with. And yet, in spite of herself, Beatrice was won over by Howard Pink during that forty-five-minute meeting at the Royal Garden Hotel. He had seemed genuinely moved by her plight. She had looked into his eyes and seen a film of sympathy there, she is sure of it. And he had been as good as his word. Within two weeks, she had a job at Paradiso HQ and was able to hand in her notice at the Mayfair Rotunda. Her new role came with a fancy title: correspondence secretary. She likes the sound of it, can imagine it printed in raised block capitals on an embossed business card.

The dress in the charity shop had not been styled to look its best but Beatrice could see through the superficial disappointment of a first glance. It was dark blue and dropped to just below the knee. The top half was fitted, with a low V-neck and the waist nipped in. The skirt was looser. If she wore it and spun slowly round on a dance floor, the skirt would twirl in a pleasing way. Not that she can ever picture herself doing such a girly thing in real life, but still. The possibility was always there.

The dress had long sleeves and the cuffs had tiny silver buttons. She was worried, at first, that the dress would be too small for her but when she went in to try it on (causing all sorts of consternation behind the till as the women huffed and puffed about their display being 'ruined') she found that it was a perfect fit. She had lost weight in recent weeks. Partly, it was the stress of meeting Howard Pink. But it was also because she felt a small but recognisable happiness. She wasn't used to happiness and distrusted it, instinctively. But she couldn't help it – she *was* looking forward to her new job. Which was why, when she checked the price-tag on the dress and saw that it was £12 – far more than she intended to spend – she told herself it was worth it. She needed to feel her best on her first day.

And now, here she is, Beatrice Kizza, soon-to-be correspondence secretary, dressed in her smart blue dress with the silver-buttoned cuffs, walking smartly down Praed Street, past the men smoking fragrant rose tobacco from hubble-bubble pipes, past the Lebanese bakeries with their sweet pistachio smells, past the cut-price hotels with unlit neon 'No Vacancy' signs and the minicab offices and the kindly faced young woman in a waterproof red jacket, carrying a clipboard and trying to stop passers-by to talk to them about some charity or other, past the exhaust rattle of the traffic, the flapping confusion of the urban pigeons, the ambulance with its flashing silent siren, past the leaves, the bustle, the people, the city, the cutting slice of cool, cool British air and for once, Beatrice Kizza does not feel lonely, an outsider, a mismatched button that doesn't belong. She feels part of it all, part of the gigantic sprawling nexus of the city. She feels her finger is one of the millions now plugged into a tiny hole in the vast walled dam that is London. It is a connectedness that you only perceive when you've lived here for long enough. The pattern of things continuing. Somehow it works in spite of all that is thrown in its way. Somehow, she thinks as she turns off the main thoroughfare, life keeps on going.

Paradiso HQ is reached across a pedestrianised stretch of coffee shops and mini-supermarkets and then along a wide road built under the shadow of a looming dual carriageway. The building itself is a block of grey-tinted glass, the panels of which stretch and warp horizontally in a wave formation. She stops and checks herself before entering. The dress flickers in the breeze like a loosening sail. She has worn it with her old grey jacket, buttoned in at the waist. She is too cold with just the jacket as protection against the English wind, which never seems to drop, even today when spring is meant to be melting into early summer and the supermarkets have long since exchanged chocolate Easter eggs for disposable barbecues and value-packs of sausages. But the only coat she owns is her bright red puffa and she hadn't though it smart enough for her first day at work. Her lips are chapped and dry. She takes out a stick of lip-balm and swipes it across her mouth. She has not worn make-up. It hadn't seemed right, somehow. She doesn't want anyone to get the wrong idea. In the absence of Susan, wearing lipstick feels like flirtation.

Clasping the strap of her handbag more tightly, Beatrice marches towards the reception desk with what she hopes is a convincing simulation of assertiveness. There are three ladies behind a bank of computer screens, each one with hair-sprayed black chignons and immaculately painted nails that tip-tap against the keyboards. One of them raises her head and looks at Beatrice without smiling.

'Yes?'

'Hello,' Beatrice says and her voice sounds far too low, too unfeminine in comparison to the woman's sing-song accent. 'I'm starting here today. A new job. I was told to ask for . . .' She scrabbles around in her handbag, dragging out the piece of paper with her fingertips. 'Tracy Lampton.'

The receptionist tilts her head to one side like a sparrow sizing up a bag of seed. 'Sir Howard's PA?' she says, clearly believing Beatrice must be mistaken.

'That's right,' Beatrice replies. 'She's expecting me.'

'Name?' the lady asks, wrinkling her nose.

'Beatrice Kizza.'

'All right then,' she says sceptically. The lady picks up a phone and dials a number. Her name-badge, pinned neatly to the lapel of a tailored red jacket, says 'Lauren'.

The phone seems to ring for a very long time, during which Lauren refuses to look directly at Beatrice, instead choosing to concentrate on an area of space directly above Beatrice's left shoulder. Then someone picks up at the other end and all of a sudden, her face changes. She smiles, sits up straighter in her chair.

'Oh hello, Tracy,' she says, her voice efficient. 'It's Lauren here from reception. I've got a—' There is a deliberate pause. Beatrice hears it. It is the pause of a white person, of someone who feels threatened by otherness. It is the pause of a white person who wishes to reassert control. 'Beatrice . . . Quisser here who says she has an appointment with you?' Lauren makes the last statement a question, allowing the words to wander upwards in a whiny scale. After a few seconds, Lauren hangs up and turns back to Beatrice, lips pursed.

'If you fill out a visitor's pass—' She pushes a book of perforated paper squares across the desk. 'Tracy will sort out your staff pass later today. You need one of these to get through the security barriers.'

'So she was expecting me?' Beatrice can't resist it. She shouldn't push her luck, she knows she shouldn't, but still . . .

The veins in Lauren's neck tense. She gives a brittle moue of distaste. 'She was, yes.'

Beatrice hands across the piece of paper with her name on. The receptionist tears it out of the book, folds it in half and slips it in a plastic tag.

'Wear this at all times in the building. The lifts are up there on the left. You need the fifth floor.'

Lauren bows her head and clicks on the computer mouse, thereby giving the impression of someone getting back to some extremely important administrative task that has been subjected to a rude interruption.

Beatrice walks towards the security barriers. A guard in uniform winks at her. She grins at him. He has a cheery, round face and looks Igbo and she feels warm towards him as he calls the lift, holding the doors open for her with his forearm.

By the time she gets to the fifth floor, her excitement has been replaced by nerves. What does she think she is doing? She is clearly not going to fit in here. Chambermaid. Cleaner. That's all she's good for. That's all people like her can expect. She wants to go back to her flat and lie underneath the duvet and never come out again. She wants to take this stupid dress off and crush it into a ball and throw it away. She is embarrassed. Why is she pretending to be something she's not? What if Howard Pink had lied to her and, instead of the promise of a new job, there would be a line of stony-faced immigration officials standing on the other side of the lift door, waiting to deport her? She lunges forward and tries desperately to press the button to take her back to the lobby. But no matter how many times she jabs the metal '0', the request doesn't register. The lift keeps moving inexorably upwards.

And then the doors open and neon lighting spills inside. A woman with blow-dried grey-blonde hair tucked behind her ears is smiling at her.

'Beatrice?' she says, taking a step forward, her arm out-stretched. Beatrice shakes her hand without thinking. Her chest is tight, her mouth dry.

'I'm Tracy, Sir Howard's secretary,' the woman says and she presses Beatrice's hand warmly in hers. 'Welcome to Paradiso.' She gives Beatrice a brief, concerned glance. 'I expect you're nerv-ous. First day and all that. Well there's nothing to worry about. Why don't we go and have a nice cup of tea and I'll tell you all that you need to know?'

Beatrice nods. 'Thank you.'

Tracy squeezes her arm. 'Don't mention it.' Tracy leads her through a pair of frosted-glass doors into a long corridor, lined on either side by banks of desks and floor-to-ceiling windows. All the time, she keeps up a steady stream of chatter that makes Beatrice feel calmer.

'Love your dress, by the way,' Tracy says.

'Thank you,' Beatrice replies and she tries not to show how pleased she is. She has forgotten how nice it is to get a compliment.

She follows Tracy dumbly to a small side kitchen with spot-lessly clean white surfaces, a microwave and an open cupboard stacked with mismatched mugs. Tracy makes the tea and hands it to Beatrice in a mug bearing a faded picture of Kermit the Frog.

She gestures at Beatrice to sit at the fold-out table and she is reminded of her first day at the Refugee and Asylum Seeker Support centre in London Bridge. Slowly, Beatrice feels her shoulders relax. She allows herself to lean back in her chair as Tracy explains what she will be expected to do.

'It's not too demanding,' Tracy is saying and while she speaks, she pats the back of her hair proprietorially. 'Sir Howard gets such a lot of post that he needs someone to read through it for him and sort it into piles.' She glances at Beatrice. 'You'll be such a help. I can't think why we haven't thought of it before.'

Beatrice nods. She notices the way Tracy says 'we' as though she is talking about a family.

'There are some people who write with a complaint about an item of clothing that they've bought in one of our stores,' Tracy carries on. 'These are Priority A letters which you should organise chronologically and mark for Sir Howard's personal attention.' Tracy breaks off, drops her voice and confides conspiratorially, 'He likes to answer those ones himself. He's done it as long as I've known him. Amazing really, the pride he takes . . .'

She looks at Beatrice, who realises she is expected to murmur her assent and does so.

'Then there'll be the green ink brigade.'

'Green ink?' Beatrice asks, sipping on her tea which is strong and sweet.

'The ones who've got a screw loose, who say they hear voices through the TV, that it's all part of some big government plot . . . that kind of thing. Those ones go straight in the bin.'

Beatrice nods.

'Then you've got to use your own judgement for the final two categories. Some letters will be OK with a template response: "Dear Sir, Thank you for your correspondence. Unfortunately not enough time to reply to all personally, et cetera." I'll show you where to find that on the computer. Then there'll be others who might raise something specific that isn't directly to do with the clothing and you should mark those in a file for the complaints department.'

Tracy reaches across the table and touches Beatrice lightly on her forearm. 'Do you want a biscuit? You look like you could do with a bit of sugar.' Without waiting for an answer, Tracy opens the cupboard underneath the sink, sliding out a large Quality Street tin with a white label on it. The label reads: 'Tracy's Biscuits. For Emergencies Only'.

Beatrice picks a cookie that looks expensive – full of nuts and big chunks of chocolate. She bites into it quickly, irrationally anxious in case it will be taken back – in case Tracy made a mistake in offering her the nice ones. The biscuit tastes as good as it looks. She washes it down with her tea and feels warm for the first time in days.

'There you go,' Tracy says, satisfied. 'Beatrice is a lovely name. Lovely. Does anyone call you Bea?'

Beatrice shakes her head. 'You can though,' she says, to her own surprise. She has never liked it when people shorten her name. It doesn't sound right – too insubstantial, too fly-away. But Tracy has been so nice to her, so open, that she feels like giving her something back.

Tracy blushes: a pinkness that creeps up from her clavicles to the tips of her ears.

'Thank you.' She smiles. 'I think we're going to get along just fine, don't you?'

Howard

HOWARD LIKES TOP HATS. He has always been a man who appreciates the finer points of style. He's not a poof or anything like that, although he's got nothing against them. Some of the finest tailors he knows are that way inclined and Howard has been to no fewer than three civil partnership ceremonies in the past twenty-four months. The latest one, a stylish registry-office affair in Marylebone followed by a reception at Claridge's, had required guests to stick to a '1920s *Great Gatsby*' dress code. Claudia had worn a sequinned flapper dress bought at vast expense from a vintage boutique in Portobello and soaked through with the metallic aroma of ancient mothballs. Howard had worn black tie, which he thought was concession enough. He'd never read *The Great Gatsby*. Thought novels were a waste of time, to be honest.

So the point was, he knew how to dress up. He understood it. It was about presenting the best side of yourself, being the best you could be. It was about giving an impression of yourself you wanted the world to understand. He knew how important it was to dress with precision for a business meeting – not too flash, eloquence in the details – and he knew how to dress for a day at the races. A top hat was required.

It is a shame, he believes, that the top hat has fallen out of fashion in recent years. These days, its only function is to provide a useful graphic shorthand for political caricaturists who wanted to underline the fact that the Prime Minister and half his Cabinet went to Eton.

Thank God, he thinks, for Royal Ascot. He doesn't get that excited by horse racing but he leaps at any chance to dust down the stretched black silk of his topper and this year he'd been invited as the guest of an online betting company whose chief executive had just made a substantial contribution to the Paradiso Charitable Giving Fund.

This is why he finds himself sporting a top hat, on one of the wettest days of the summer, sitting at a table laid with dainty blue gift bags and matching flowers and dishes containing iced curls of butter. To the left, sliding windows open onto the race-course, overshadowed by a leaden grey sky. When they had stood outside to watch the first race, one of the female guests had shrieked excitedly that she could see the Queen in the adjoining box, which led to a flurry of camera phones and flashes. Howard couldn't make out much beyond a blurry shadow and a twinkle of light that might or might not have been a reflection from her spectacles. He thought there was something undignified about gawping but then he'd met the Queen several times already so didn't feel the need to stare.

Her Majesty had made little impression on him beyond her extreme shortness and yet he had found himself nervous on each occasion, fumbling the bow and running out of anything to say. He wouldn't mind meeting Kate Middleton though. Or the Duchess of Cambridge as he was meant to call her these days. She was a gorgeous girl. Classy, too. A sensory flash of memory comes back to him of her slender arms, decked in intricate lace on her wedding day. He can remember the precise quality of her skin seen through the TV camera lens: a dimmed pinkish-brown, veiled by the most delicate ivory gauze. Her dress was simply one of the most perfect pieces of clothing he'd ever seen: both for the bride and the occasion. It trailed a sense of history behind it. He wishes he had seen Ada get married, soft-cheeked and smiling and sheathed in wedding white.

Although for all he knows, she would have got married dressed as a Goth just to spite him: all black eyeliner, ripped jeans and inappropriate piercings.

He has been thinking about Ada a lot since the interview with Esme Reade. He'd been more affected by the encounter than he'd expected. Esme Reade might have looked sweet-faced and innocent, but she had this way of asking a question that was both guileless and penetrating, and he had found himself saying more than he'd wanted to. Once or twice, he'd been close to tears, even though, when Rupert had suggested the interview, he'd been sure he could handle it.

The piece was due to appear this Sunday and Howard was bracing himself for its publication, hoping he wouldn't have embarrassed himself. He had a horror of showing sentimentality in public. He didn't want strangers looking at pictures of his daughter, treating her as a story, just newsprint on a page. He'd tried to talk to Claudia about it but she hadn't been particularly sympathetic.

'Why on earth did you agree to it in the first place?' she had said this morning. He had found her hunched over her iPhone in her study in the process of uploading flattering photos of herself to Facebook. 'You need to focus on the future, Howie, and not be a prisoner to your past.'

'Where'd you read that?'

'*Bedside Yoga Gems*,' Claudia said. 'It's a very helpful book. You should flick through it sometime.' A pause. 'Not many pictures though, which might put you off.'

The only thing Claudia cared about was that Les, the *Tribune* photographer, had captured her best angle. On the day of the interview, she had appeared wearing a tight, fuchsia-coloured dress and a diamond ring the size of a lychee. She had insisted on looking at each shot as it was taken, demanding he delete any of the ones that made her look 'fat', 'saggy' or 'old'. When Esme had intervened to say maybe it would be quicker if they just sent a selection at a later date for approval, Claudia had snapped at her.

'Who does she think she is?' Claudia hissed at Howard. 'The little madam.'

He sighs without meaning to, feeling the swell and drop of his stomach underneath the leather belt he has optimistically done up a notch too tightly. He takes off his top hat and a waiter appears soundlessly at his shoulder to relieve him of it. He is worried the hat has left a red band across his forehead where it sits a fraction too tightly and he tries, subtly, to rub at the mark with his fingers. Surely his head can't have got bigger along with the rest of him? You can't put on weight around your skull, can you? Isn't it just made up of interlinking plates of bone?

Across the table, Claudia is looking bored. She is wearing a turquoise fascinator with bits of netting and looped feathers, each one adorned with a miniature pom-pom. Every time she moves her head, the whole thing shivers like a peacock left out in the cold. Ironic that it's called a fascinator, Howard thinks. Claudia is being talked at by a moustached man with narrow eyes whom he vaguely recognises as the editor of a financial free-sheet and he's never seen anyone look less fascinated in his life.

At the other end of the table, there is a blousy-looking PR woman who has already had too much to drink. Amy, she said her name was when they'd been introduced: pink lipstick leaking into the small crenellations around her mouth like sewage.

The remaining places are taken up with a smattering of mid-ranking businessmen and their other halves: overfed men and overdressed women all making underwhelming conversation.

Howard makes a stab at eating his starter of poached lobster and chicken cannelloni but he has no appetite. He leans forward to get his wine glass instead, raises the rim to his lips and knocks back the contents. The acidity kicks deep into the back of his throat. Claudia looks at him blankly. She used to look at him with disapproval but now she doesn't even care enough to do that.

'So, Howard, who are you backing in the next race?' A voice cuts through. It belongs to Mike, the betting company CEO, who

240

is a nice enough fellow. He means well. Howard does his best to be cheerful.

'I was rather hoping you'd tell me that, Mike.'

Mike laughs uproariously. Howard flinches.

'Haha! Well, I don't mind telling you . . .' Mike taps the side of his nose with one finger. 'That a little bird told me Fellatio was the one to watch.'

Howard snorts. 'Fellatio?' he booms across the table so that the polite chatter is temporarily suspended. Amy, the PR woman, gasps dramatically then emits a shrill squeal of laughter. 'What kind of name's that?' Howard asks, unsure why the atmosphere has warped and buckled.

Mike hesitates.

'Haha! I think you misheard, old chap. Horatio, I said. That's the horse's name.'

The Amy woman is laughing so much she has to dab at her eyes with a paper tissue. Claudia gives an amused smile.

'Oh you mustn't mind Howie,' she says, licking her lips. 'He's got a one-track mind, haven't you, darling?'

Time was, Howard might have seen the funny side. He might even have been turned on by the salacious hint of challenge in Claudia's eyes. As it is, he feels humiliated, deliberately cut down in public. He stares at her. The blood behind his eyes pulses hot. He can see the smile shrink and shrivel from her lips and he knows she realises she has gone too far. That, at least, gives him some satisfaction.

Mike is trying to gloss things over with some hearty banter about fillies and jockeys and odds-on favourites and it's true that no one else seems to care and that perhaps Howard shouldn't take it so much to heart but he can't help it. He has always hated being made a fool of. Always. All his life he has been on guard against it, against the posh City boys who wanted to take him down a peg or two, against the public school toffs who knew he wasn't from their side of the tracks, against the politicians who sneered at him because he wouldn't kiss their arses and the

Knightsbridge billionaires who looked down on him as a glorified barrow boy. Fuck 'em, he thinks, why should I care? But he does. And he can't seem to stop himself from caring.

There is a prickle at the base of his spine. He shifts in his seat but the pins and needles spread to his buttocks. He has an urge to leave, to get back home and not have to pretend any longer that this is his milieu, that he fits in. He wants to go and watch a schmaltzy black-and-white film in his private cinema, the kind of film he used to watch with Penny, with tap-dancing men and girls with nipped-in waists and an uncomplicated sense of wonder at the world. Ada had grown up surrounded by those movies from Hollywood's Golden Age. She loved them too. She used to insist on watching *It's a Wonderful Life* the night before Christmas, even when she'd left school and he thought she'd be getting too old for sentimental nonsense like that. She was crazy about that film.

For her eighteenth birthday, a year before she'd gone missing, she'd asked half a dozen friends round for a black-tie cinema party so they could watch the film. Her eating disorder seemed to be under control at last and he'd been so relieved she wanted to mark the occasion, so delighted she had enough friends to invite, that he had allowed himself the cautious hope that perhaps she was getting better. That she was, in some small way, happy.

And on the night itself, he remembers walking in halfway through the film, anxious about how she was getting on, and as he opened the door the light from the corridor spooled into the darkened screening room.

'Dad, what are you doing?' Ada asked.

'Just checking you have everything you need, sweetheart.'

'We're fine,' she said and he couldn't see her expression to make out whether she was annoyed with him or embarrassed or – worse – sad. But then she stood up and walked over to him, teetering slightly in unfamiliar high heels, and she hugged him, kissing his bristly cheek. She had sprayed herself with Penny's bottle of Opium and the scent seemed too heavy, too grown-up for his little girl.

'Don't worry, Dad.'

She smiled as she said it but the smile didn't feel real, it felt like the wrapping paper on a disappointing gift that buckled and sagged at the edges as the sticking tape worked itself loose.

He glanced over at the group of teenagers behind her shoulder – two boys and three girls – and they all seemed fresh-faced and sensible. Too sensible, a part of him thought, like a thunderclap waiting to break. He patted Ada's back and, as she turned away from him and walked back to her chair, he felt he was losing her in some indefinable way.

She had been trying – he can see that now. She had been trying to reassure him when, by rights, it should have been the other way round.

He hasn't watched the film since she disappeared but now he is taken by the desire to do so. He has the DVD somewhere at home. He could get the housekeeper to set up the projector and settle down to watch it with a brandy. He thinks he could prob-ably remember every single word.

There is a rousing cheer from outside. On the small, wall-mounted TV screen above Mike's head, Howard can see a jockey in purple-and-yellow silks being sprayed with Champagne. The waiters have taken away the starters. A light scatter of bread-crumbs marks the place where his plate was. The tablecloth, like every tablecloth he has sat down to over the last twenty years, is starched white linen. He is sick of starched white linen. It is meant to represent freshness and yet leaves him depressed with its soulless, ironed aridity. Whatever happened to red-and-white gingham?

He needs to go home. He doesn't fit in here. Never has. The things that used to bring him joy now only seem to irritate him. He can't even take pleasure in the trappings of wealth, those triv-ial baubles he had spent a lifetime in pursuit of. He used to think, when he was starting out, that he'd know he'd truly made it when he had earned enough money to be able to waste it. Howard was at that level now, but instead of wanting to acquire more, he finds himself wanting instead to strip it all back. He craves a kind of honesty, an authenticity he has lost along the way without even noticing it was happening.

He thinks of Beatrice Kizza, of her serious face, her defiance, her plain-spoken determination and he wonders if the reason he gave her a job had something to do with the fact that he saw himself as he used to be.

He wonders how Beatrice's first week at work went. Howard must ask Tracy how his new correspondence secretary is getting on. He takes out his BlackBerry from the inside of his jacket pocket and checks it ostentatiously.

'Christ,' he says, just loud enough so that Mike can hear.

'Not bad news, I hope?'

'Sorry, Mike, I'm going to have to make a call,' Howard says, laying the ground for his exit carefully. 'Bloody nuisance.'

'Of course, of course. Please—' Mike opens the door to the box and leads Howard into the corridor before retreating. 'Take your time.'

Inside the enclosure, Howard can hear the wild screams of drunken Essex girls on a day out at the races. He peers over the barrier into the cavernous levels below and makes out a mish-mash of cerise dresses, fake tan and teetering stripper-style shoes. He spots more than a dozen race-goers in Fash Attack outfits. They'd been stocking a deep purple peplum dress in satin that was selling well and he sees it more than once on women of vary-ing size and shape which is a good sign: he doesn't like to stock fashion that's just for skinny minnies.

He lifts the BlackBerry to his ear, dials 121 and gets through to the automated voice telling him there are no new messages. Just in case anyone is still watching, he makes a show of listening intently, as though someone is imparting crucial news. After a sufficient amount of time has passed, he places the phone back into his jacket pocket, stretches out his arms wide, takes a breath and walks back inside the box. He walks straight up to Mike with what he hopes is an expression of sincere but inescapable regret on his face.

'I'm really sorry, Mike,' he starts, resting his hand lightly on the man's arm. 'I'm going to have to shoot off. Something's come up at work, you know how it is.'

Mike looks at him gravely. 'Of course, of course. No need to explain, Howard. These things happen. No rest for the wicked, eh?'

Howard laughs obligingly. 'You're right there. But I'm really sorry. I was hoping to make a few quid with your expert advice.'

'Well. Another time, perhaps?'

Howard nods. 'And listen, we must get together for dinner. You, me and the girls, yeah?' He is backing towards the exit even as he is saying this. Howard hopes Mike hasn't noticed that he can't remember the name of his wife. He leans close into Claudia's ear and tells her they need to go. She looks at him sharply, eyes glinting.

'Why?' she hisses.

He grits his teeth. 'Something's come up, sweetheart.'

Howard notices the man with the moustache glancing at him with suspicion and leans in further to block his view. He can't stand nosiness.

'I don't want to go, Howie,' Claudia says and although she uses the affectionate diminutive of his name, her face is rigid. 'You go ahead without me.'

'How will you get back?' He speaks in a low murmur. He doesn't want there to be a scene.

'You can send Jocelyn back with the car. He won't mind.' She leans away from him and snaps a tip off a cheese straw. He can smell Coco Mademoiselle and Elnett hairspray. 'Go on. Off you toddle. I'll see you later.' She pats him on the hand without making eye contact. He straightens up, grins broadly and does all he can to mask his fury. She really can be a complete bitch sometimes.

'OK, pusscat,' he says loudly. 'Try not to lose all my money on the horses.'

She throws him a dirty look, then turns towards the mous-tached man with an expression of flirtatious intent. As he walks

245

out of the box, Howard can see her propping her chin on her hand, the better to show off her impressive décolletage. The older she gets, the more she insists on wearing dresses with near-indecent necklines. The skin on her lower neck is sun-damaged and pinched, like a basted turkey. Her breasts, however, remain impressively pneumatic, owing to the judicious insertion of silicone through the years. The last time he touched them, which is going back a good few months, Howard had been put off by the preternatural sensation – they felt somewhere between springy and unyielding, like a new mattress yet to be worn in. In the past, he'd always imagined fake tits would turn him on. But that was before Claudia had got hers done and he'd realised, like so many other things, that the imagined promise did not live up to the actuality.

Anyway, the man she's talking to now doesn't seem to be unduly put off. He keeps flicking his eyes downwards then mentally reminding himself he's meant to be listening to whatever guff Claudia is spouting. Howard feels a flash of fellow recognition. Then, before he has a chance to change his mind, he leaves the box and calls Jocelyn. He'll be home within the hour, he thinks with relief.

In the back of the car, leaning against the sleekness of leather, he drops his head against the upholstery and allows his neck muscles to relax. It's only as Jocelyn is speeding up the A3 that he remembers – his top hat. The waiter took it. It must still be in some cloakroom cupboard at Ascot. Bugger, he thinks. He can't be arsed to deal with it now. He'll get Jocelyn to collect it when he gathers up the remnants of a drunken Claudia later.

His phone rings. The caller ID is withheld. He never seems to get phone calls from actual numbers these days.

'Yep,' he says in place of a greeting.

He recognises the small foreign voice immediately as that of his housekeeper.

'Sir Howard, it's Theresa here.'

'Hi Theresa. What's up?'

'There are two men here who desire to talk to you.'

He admires the way Theresa uses language like she's in a period drama. She's very correct.

'What do they want?'

'They will not tell me. But they say it is a matter of some urgency. I've told them we are not expecting you back for quite some time . . .'

'It's OK, Theresa. I'm on my way back now. Tell them to wait and I'll be there in an hour or so if the traffic stays like this.'

'Very good, Sir Howard.'

He hangs up. Immediately, he is anxious. Two men. Howard thinks straight away of bailiffs which he knows is ridiculous. He might be many things, he tells himself, but short of money is not one of them. The bad old days are long gone. The last time he opened the door to bailiffs, he'd been nine years old. He presses the button to lower the partition between him and the driver and he tells Jocelyn to get him home as quickly as possible. Whoever they are, Howard doesn't want to keep them waiting longer than he has to.

Jocelyn gets him home in just over forty-five minutes. Howard pats the driver on the back as he walks up the pathway to his front door. He washes his hands and splashes his face with cool water in one of the downstairs bathrooms before Theresa leads him through to the drawing room where the two men are waiting. As soon as he sees them, he knows why they are here. They are both wearing nondescript suits and name-badges, strung around their necks with blue-and-white lariats. He has seen enough police detectives to spot the signs.

A coiled knot of dread starts to slip loose just beneath his solar plexus. He walks into the room feeling dizzy and lost. The two policemen stand up simultaneously, one of them knocking the coffee table so that the glass of water he is drinking jingles and clatters. Before either of them has a chance to say anything, Howard speaks.

'It's Ada, isn't it? My daughter?'

One of the policemen, the taller one, holds out his hand, the palm flat as though he is trying to push a block of solidified air away from his chest. 'Sir Howard, I'm—'

Howard shakes his head. 'I don't want to know what your name is. I want to know what you've found out. Why are you here? Have you found her? Have you found Ada?' He can hear the unnatural pitch of his own voice.

'No,' the detective says but there is an uneasiness to his reply, an edginess that Howard notes immediately. In business meetings, one of his talents is being able to laser through the rubbish and get to what is really being said underneath the layers of subtext. He can smell bullshit a mile off.

'We're here because we're doing a routine review of some of our missing-persons files and we had some questions about your daughter,' the detective continues. 'About Ada. If we could just sit down . . . ?'

Howard nods and takes a seat in the armchair near the unlit fire. He feels at once both relieved and devastated. He isn't sure any more whether it would be better to know for definite what had happened to Ada and to live with the consequences of that, or whether the torture of not knowing is worth coping with simply so that he can continue believing in the possibility that she is still alive. Which one of these would make him a better parent, a better person? Which one of these is right?

The shorter man looks up at Howard.

'I know you will have been asked a lot of these questions before, Sir Howard, but if you could bear with us, we might just hit on something that could help us look at this case with fresh eyes.'

Howard nods defeatedly. Over the years, he had grown used to having his personal grief probed and trampled over, his emotions treated like interesting artefacts revealed to the light by enthusiastic archaeologists who kept returning to the same site over and over again. He had thought nothing could be worse than rehashing the same facts, coming to the same inevitably hopeless conclusion, watching the realisation dawn on the face of whichever wet-behind-the-ears policeman they'd sent to him this time around. But just when he thought they would never stop with their earnest chatter, the curiously generic attempts at informal patter (perhaps they all went on the same police training course on How to Deal with Grieving Parents), Howard discovered there was something worse than being asked endless questions. And that was being asked none. The case had slipped downwards through the police files and computer databases, spiralling from the clamour of 'urgent' into the silent limbo of 'unsolvable'. They'd stopped knocking on his door. The phone calls had ceased. The newspaper stories were stashed away in cuttings files, to be accessed every few years or so by a diligent reporter. The picture of Ada they'd used in all the media coverage – big eyes, pale face, staring out from her university ID card – became the fossilised version of her, the imprint left on the public mind, until, many years later, it was at last superimposed by the image of a blonde-haired toddler called Madeleine, the new tabloid poster girl for those missing without trace.

The picture of Ada had been reprinted so many times that, for a while, Howard found that all his own memories were overlaid by this static, haunting face. He closes his eyes tightly now, while listening to the detective's familiar spiel, and he sees it again: the disembodied Ada, her gaze accusing him of something he'd never known he'd done wrong.

'. . . so perhaps we could start by asking whether she knew anybody living in the Wandsworth area?'

Howard snaps to. 'What?'

'Wandsworth,' the taller detective says. 'Did Ada have friends there that you know of?'

Howard shakes his head. 'No.'

'You sure about that? She never mentioned anyone she went to visit there or who might have had family in that area?'

He makes an effort to think back. He can't remember.

'She used to go to a ballet class as a kid,' he starts,

desperately trying to come up with something. 'In Clapham. That's near Wandsworth, isn't it? I mean, she might have had a friend from there but it's not like it was ever a big factor in our conversations.'

Both the detectives nod. One of them makes a note of this on a pad of lined paper.

'What age would she have been then?'

Howard laughs. He can't help it. It's so ridiculous to think a ballet class from twenty-odd years ago would have had any bearing on her disappearance.

'Christ. About eight or nine. I dunno. I can't really see that this has any relevance.'

'Can you remember any of her friends' names?'

'No! Of course I sodding can't.'

'Would your ex-wife be able . . .'

'Why don't you ask her?'

'We intend to, Sir Howard. I'm sorry if this is painful for you.'

He tries to stop the irritation sweeping over him.

'It's not painful. It's a bloody nuisance. I can't understand why you're dredging all this up again . . .' The detectives lower their heads, saying nothing. He chokes back a gust of emotion.

'If this is going to take as long as I think it's going to, I need a coffee.' Howard stands up and shuffles to the door. His muscles are drained of strength. He closes the door behind him and stands in the dim, soothing hallway for a few seconds, forcing himself to breathe deeply. The intake of air helps him think more clearly. Yes, he nods to himself. That's what he'll do. He will answer their questions and then a kind of normality will resume. It is a temporary but necessary interlude, he tells himself. A transient period of aggravation, and then he will be able to get on with things. The business. The house. His marriage. All of it still exists.

He goes in search of Theresa to ask her to make the coffee. There's nothing to worry about, he tells himself, and even as he forms the thought, he knows it not to be true.

Esme

ESME IS WOKEN BY the beeping of her mobile in the middle of a frantic dream about empty swimming pools. It's a text from Cathy in the office congratulating her on the piece, which is nice of her. Most of the time, her colleagues pretend they haven't read her stuff. It's a discreet form of competitiveness, tinged with the ever-present journalists' paranoia.

She knows she won't be able to get back to sleep without first buying a copy of the paper just so she can check the subs haven't messed it up. Esme rolls out of bed, groaning and pressing the heel of her hand to her forehead. She'd had one too many glasses of Pinot Grigio last night at the pub after work. But it had been Sanjay's birthday and she'd felt pretty good about the Howard Pink piece, especially after the editor of the paper sent her an email praising her 'doggedness' in getting the interview. She didn't tell him it had basically been handed to her on a plate. It didn't do any harm to make the boss think she was a reporter in relentless pursuit of the truth.

Esme stumbles into a pair of jeans which she slides on over her pyjama bottoms. No point getting properly dressed. She'll go back to bed after she's made the dash to the corner store. She runs her tongue over fuzzy teeth, goes to the bathroom, squeezes a globule of toothpaste onto her index finger and shoves it in her mouth. She grabs her parka, hanging on the hook in the kitchen, stuffs her keys in the pocket and slams the door. Esme has found that, whenever she has a good story in the paper, she is possessed of a crazed energy, consisting of 50 per cent panic (that someone might complain about a factual inaccuracy) and 50 per cent pride (that it might be the seminal piece of journalism that would make her name for evermore).

She turns right onto St Stephen's Avenue and onto the Uxbridge Road, which is just rousing itself from whatever nefarious activities might have taken place there the night before. There is a dirt and illicitness to this part of town. It is part of what had first attracted Esme to the area – the mixture of estates and terraced houses, of burqas and business suits.

In Shepherd's Bush, there was none of that pram-pushing prissiness of Clapham or Battersea. Despite the inroads of gentrification, there was still a lazy, sideways knowingness apparent in every slow, squint-eyed nod through a haze of marijuana smoke, in each pair of trainers slung across telegraph wire, in the cars with missing hubcaps and blacked-out windows that swept along the tarmac trailed by a hip-hop number's jabbing bass lines.

But it was a manageable edginess, offset by the earnest-faced media executives who went to work each day in White City and the dreadlocked woman strung with Indian beads who ran the organic café serving gluten-free pistachio cake. Beyond it all, glinting on the far horizon, there was the newly built paean to consumerist excess: the squat, shining quadrant of the Westfield Centre. Esme had overheard a local estate agent telling someone that the construction of London's newest super-mall had added 15 per cent on to all surrounding house prices. Which would be great, obviously, if she actually owned her flat.

Fat chance, she thinks, as she rushes up to Damas Gate, the local grocery store run by bearded Arab men. They don't stock newspapers but she is overwhelmed by a craving for one of their light filo pastry rolls, stuffed with tangy cheese. Perfect hangover fodder. She'll go there first, then pop to the newsagent's.

Esme doesn't allow herself to open her copy of the *Tribune* until she gets back to her flat, puts the kettle on and places it carefully on the fold-out table. There is a photo of Sir Howard on the front page, underneath the pull quote: 'I'll never get over it.' Inside, the interview appears across three pages, complete with pictures of Ada at various stages of her childhood: in a tutu with sparkles in her hair, riding a horse on a beach, wearing a pink wig for a fancy dress party. There is one image of Ada as a teenager, clutching a diploma of some sort, arm-in-arm with her father who is beaming with pride. They look so happy together, with their matching smiles. Esme has never noticed before how similar they are.

She scans the headline, splashed across the top of the spread in 72-point: 'The Light of My Life', it says. The word 'EXCLUSIVE' is prominently displayed in capitals before the stand-first, which reads: 'Ada Pink was 19 when she disappeared without trace. Her father, multi-millionaire Sir Howard Pink, has never spoken about her loss – until now. Today, he tells the *Tribune's* Esme Reade why he'll "never get over it" and why he's set up a charitable foundation in her memory.'

Her name is picked out in bold and there is a small picture byline of her. It was a photo taken at the end of her first week in the office and, every time she looks at it, she hates it that little bit more. Her hair is scraped back off her face. Her mouth is twisted to one side which always happens when she's been fake-smiling for too long. The photographer had told her to grimace less and Esme had tried to go for a 'serious journalist' expression.

'OK. Just relax your jaw a bit,' the photographer had said.

She hadn't a clue how you were meant to relax your jaw. Wasn't it made up entirely of bone? How do you relax your bones? She had tried her best.

'Now you look like you want to kill me.'

Esme had gritted her teeth, then remembered she was meant to be relaxing her jaw. By the end of it, she was just glad she'd got through it without slapping the photographer in the face.

She was for ever being told by random strangers, to 'Cheer up, love,' as she walked down the street. Whenever it happened, she was seized by the desire to tell them something unimaginably awful had just occurred – the death of a close relative, a friend's tragic diagnosis with some terminal disease – but she could never quite find the courage. It is one of the things she most dislikes about herself: the fatal gap between her righteous anger and the means required to express it. Men didn't have this problem.

And now, because she meekly stayed silent, because she had been too worried to complain in case anyone thought she was being a diva, she's stuck with this byline picture and every time Esme sees it, she imagines all her ex-boyfriends looking at it and thinking: Well, she's let herself go, hasn't she?

The kettle boils and Esme makes herself a cup of milky tea, then retreats back into her bed with the mug and her filo pastry roll. She spreads the paper out in front of her and reads the first paragraph.

'Sir Howard Pink has never spoken publicly about his daughter before,' the introduction kicks off. She'd wanted to start with the chocolate Bourbons, but Dave had snarled at the thought of it.

'It's not poetry, Esme, for fuck's sake. Keep it simple, play it straight. This isn't about you showing what a clever writer you are. This is about Howard Pink and his missing daughter.'

Esme had gone back and bitched to a receptive Sanjay about how no one understood the subtlety of her prose style. Then she'd sat down at her computer and changed the intro. Because of course Dave was right. Howard's story told itself. It didn't need her to interpose herself into the quotes. She hated journalists who made interviews all about themselves, starting each new paragraph with a personal pronoun.

She sips her tea and reads rapidly to the end of the piece. Esme thinks it flows well and there have only been a few minor editorial changes. She's pleased that Dave put a mention of the charitable foundation in the stand-first and thinks that should mollify Howard's people, even though she hasn't mentioned it till three-quarters of the way down the page.

Her phone beeps again. Leaning over to retrieve it from the bedside table, she opens the text and feels a jolt when she sees Dave's name. 'Great job, Esme xx' it says. She smiles.

The kisses do not escape her notice.

She puts the phone back, folds the paper carefully and swipes the filo pastry crumbs off the duvet. She is aware of a tiredness slipping across her sight-line, the grey-white colour of pigeon feathers, and she lies down. She feels her head touch the reassuring heft of the memory foam pillow (an absurdly expensive purchase forced on her by a recurrence of neck and shoulder pain from too much time spent crouched over a keyboard. She'd been half-tempted to claim it back on expenses). But then, just as Esme is about to drift into a satisfied, easy sleep, her phone rings and she is awake, instantly, her heart racing. Was it work? A complaint? Some monumental fuck-up she hadn't noticed, like the accidental misspelling of Howard Pink's name? She checks the screen. 'Unknown number' flashes up sinisterly. For some reason she can't fathom, every time she sees an 'Unknown number' she is certain she is about to be told off.

'Hello,' she says croakily.

'Oh darling, you sound dreadful.' Lilian's voice pulses through the telephone wires, deep into Esme's eardrum. She keeps forgetting that her mother has somehow worked out how to disguise her caller ID. It's a fiendishly clever ploy, Esme suspects, to get her children to answer the phone to her.

'No, I'm fine. I've just—' Esme pauses, unsure whether she wants to admit she's still in bed. To do so would be to endure the usual five-minute speech on the importance of getting up and getting going and not wasting the day – or, by implication, your entire life – by submitting to the sinful temptations of sloth and indolence. Bugger it, Esme thinks. I've earned a lie-in. 'I've just got up.'

There is the unmistakable sound of an intake of breath.

'Oh, right. I'm sorry, darling. I just thought at this time of day, you'd already be up and at 'em!'

Lilian is the product of Army parents. Her father, a retired brigadier, used to insist his wife measured the exact distance between the rim of a china plate and the edge of the table every time they had a dinner party. He was the kind of man who called everything 'ship-shape', who claimed that strong tea 'put hairs on your chest' and who ended every declamatory sentence with a sharp, upwardly inflected 'what' which wasn't ever a question. He had died shortly after Robbie was born but Lilian still retained the odd conversational tick from the late brigadier. 'Up and at 'em' was definitely one of them.

Esme doesn't respond. Lilian carries on regardless.

'You know Grandma always used to get up at 5.30 on the dot, rain or shine, because she always said she got so much done in the mornings before everyone else woke up! And Margaret Thatcher—'

'Survived on four hours sleep a night, yes, Mum, I know. But I've had a busy week. I've actually got a big piece in—'

'I know! I've seen it, darling. Very impressive. Gosh, what a lot of words you write.'

Esme is caught between feeling touched that her mother has made the effort to read a paper she wouldn't normally buy and irritation that the only thing she can think to compliment her daughter on is the amount of words rather than their lyrical quality. She bites her lip.

'Thanks, Mum.'

'So depressing though. Poor man. I must say, I do feel for him. I always thought he seemed rather brash, you know. He was on that programme once, wasn't he? What's it called? The one with the politicians –'

'*Question Time.*'

'Yes! That's the one. Well, anyway, darling, I was just calling to check you'd remembered about Dominic.'

Esme flicks through all her recent conversations with her mother in a desperate attempt to fish the name out from a sea of pure blankness. She normally has a good memory but whenever she speaks to her mother, something numbs her synapses and makes Esme consistently incapable of remembering any of the salient details.

'Errrm . . . remind me . . .'

'Honestly, darling. You've got a brain like a sieve.'

'I don't actually, I've just had other things—'

'You know, Hattie's son. He's just moved to London, wants to get into media . . .'

Who doesn't, Esme thinks with silent resentment. Idiots. The only people who stood a chance in newspapers nowadays were fifteen-year-old bloggers who wore ironic spectacles and wrote ungrammatically about the postmodern semiotics of American sitcoms. They were also expected to work for free. The chances of bagging a staff job, with an actual, real-life salary, were roughly equivalent to the chances of winning the lottery without buying a ticket.

'. . . and so I told her, "But he must meet Esme. She's sure to be able to introduce him to all sorts of people who might help." And Hattie was thrilled to bits and told Dominic to call me, which he did and I must say, Esme, he's a terribly polite young man, really quite charming. He went to Oxford, you know? Read PPE like all the top-level people do these days . . .'

Esme lets her mother burble on. It's a talent, really, how Lilian manages to imbue absolutely everything she says with a sense of disappointment in her own daughter's life choices.

'. . . and of course Hattie's never got over it, not really.'

'Over what?'

'Don't you listen to *anything* I say, Esme? She's never got over her eldest marrying—' Lilian dips her voice to a low, suggestive whisper. 'A black woman.'

'*Mum!*'

'I know, I know, darling. I dare say you think I'm very fuddy-duddy. You can't say anything these days without someone accusing you of racism.'

Esme closes her eyes. She's passed the point of upbraiding her mother for her casually discriminatory comments. She used to challenge Lilian all the time when she was still living at home, believing with the naïve optimism of an idealistic teenager that these were attitudes that needed to be railed against and that it was only by getting people to change how they thought, by rebelling against their inherent ignorance, that the world would eventually spin on a more equitable axis.

She'd studied the civil rights movement for History A level and had never forgotten the picture of a bespectacled black girl, back straight, dressed in a spotlessly pressed white dress, walking to school on the first day of non-segregated education, pursued by angry-faced women shouting abuse in her wake.

When she first saw the photo, Esme had been struck by the quiet dignity of the girl at the centre. She had looked at the flat straight line of the girl's mouth and the shielded quality of her eyes and Esme had wondered if the resignation on her face reflected the fact that the girl had grown to accept the fundamental ugliness of life so that it simply didn't surprise her any more. For Esme, the fact that this girl was so stoic, walking to school in her white dress, her books held close to her chest, had somehow been more upsetting than if the camera had caught her face twisted in furious retaliation, giving back as good as she got.

She wonders, briefly, what has happened to the subjects of that photo. It might be interesting to track them down for a 'Where are they now?' type feature, she thinks, and she makes a mental note to speak to Dave about it.

On the other end of the line, her mother is still talking.

'. . . so we thought Daylesford Organic would be most convenient.'

'Daylesford?'

'Yes, darling. He's staying with his godmother near Sloane Square and I thought he might not know his way around London—'

A snaking rope of irritation wraps itself around Esme's chest. Why on earth would a grown man not be able to find his way around London? Was he mentally deficient? Why should she be the one who has to go out of her way on a Sunday morning, giving up a precious portion of her weekend to traipse across the city, to do a favour for some posh dimwit she'd never even met before? But she doesn't say anything. This is the way conversations with her mother tend to go – unspoken resentments flowing into each other until they pollute every sentiment like a pool of spreading petrol.

'Right. Yes. I remember.' Esme glances at her alarm clock. It is nearly 11 a.m. 'What time . . . ?'

'Lunchtime.' A pointed pause. '1p.m. Try not to be late. Hattie says he's terribly busy . . .'

'If he's so busy why does he want a job in media?' Esme mutters under her breath.

'Sorry, I didn't quite catch . . .'

'Don't worry. Nothing important. I'd better get going then.'

'Yes, darling, of course. I hope you have fun. Let me know how you get on.'

'OK, Mum. Bye.'

She can hear the clipped tone of her voice as she ends the call and hates herself for it. She pushes back the duvet, gets out of bed and tramples across the detritus of half-folded newsprint on the carpet. In the shower, she wonders if it is finally warm enough for her to wear a skirt without the black opaque tights that have been her faithful friend throughout winter and spring. She decides it probably is if she takes a woollen jumper along with her. It's meant to be summer, but you wouldn't know it. The magazines are constantly talking about the necessity of 'layering' and Esme has never got the knack of it without looking mismatched. The cardigans she flung over her shoulders in an attempt to embody a nonchalant Parisian style ended up looking lumpen and threadbare. The scarves she wanted to drape round her neck with casual abandon never seemed to sit in the right way and the flowery tea dresses teamed with chunky-knit leggings that were meant to be charmingly kooky were, instead, ill-fitting and old-ladyish.

She thinks she should risk the skirt. She has an entirely illogical theory that, if you dress for summer, it will eventually come. She reaches for the disposable razor in the soap dish and tries to shave her legs while standing up, doing a precarious flamingo-style balancing act to reach her ankles. The water starts to run cool before she finishes the second knee-cap. Oh well, Esme thinks as she turns the shower off, it's not as if anyone will notice.

By the time she puts on a denim skirt, looks at her pale legs sprayed with goose-bumps in the full-length mirror, scowls, decides against it and tries to cobble together an entirely different outfit where everything goes together and doesn't make it look like she's tried too hard while simultaneously trying just hard enough, Esme is running twenty minutes late.

She takes the stairs two at a time, closes the front door without double-locking – this in spite of the stringent terms of her contents insurance policy which she had gone for purely because it had been the cheapest available according to a price comparison website that advertised itself using a charmless puppet meerkat speaking in an Eastern European accent for undisclosed reasons.

It is one of those London days when the grimy ribcage of the city seems to lift and expand. The drizzle-dampened morning has given way to a spot of blue sky and the half-hearted promise of sunshine. Shallow puddles have formed in the gaps created by irregular paving stones. The smeary windows of double-decker buses reflect an unspooling of green-leaved trees. There is a sense of a collective pent-up breath being let out, of Londoners tentatively allowing themselves to believe the weather is changing for the better. Esme walks briskly, looking up at the tops of buildings, to the unexpected details found where brickwork meets cloud: carved pillars, delicate balconies, circular windows and stained glass. She is caught between enjoying the gentle beauty of the moment and guiltily wondering if she should take a picture to post on social networks, thereby upping her follower count and branding herself more effectively. When exactly had real experience been trumped by fabricated identity? When did savouring the moment become secondary to capturing it? Why did the present's natural light need to be stained by the application of computer-generated filters designed to evoke nostalgia? It all seemed so two-dimensional, so tritely self-conscious. A friend of Esme's had once compared a beautiful view to a screensaver. Now everyone was doing it.

She gets the tube from Goldhawk Road and attempts to read the paper as the train judders hesitantly along the track, stopping and starting as if it can't make up its mind whether it wants to go forwards or backwards. Eventually, it eases into Hammersmith and Esme stuffs the *Tribune* into her handbag and crosses over the giant roundabout to the District Line, ducking to avoid the pigeons who fly straight at her head, pointy beaks aimed directly at her eye-level.

She is aware of a rising level of stress – at her lateness, at the fact that she'd rather be doing almost anything else with her weekend than this, at the realisation that she should have just said no rather than allowing her mother to browbeat her into things as usual. She has to stop herself muttering under her breath at the mindless pedestrians lumbering like oxen and not seeming to realise she's in a hurry. By the time she is safely ensconced in a tube that will take her directly to Sloane Square, she is breaking out in a sweat. It is warmer than she had thought after all. She takes off her jacket, unwittingly elbowing a man with a pierced lip who grunts loudly. Esme shoots him a look, puts her handbag on her lap and then takes out the paper, feeling a wash of calm as she sees her name again in black-and-white on the page in front of her. The byline restores her equilibrium. It is confirmation that she exists. It is the reason Hattie's son – whatever his name is – wants to meet her. In his eyes, she is someone important. She has made it, in some small way. Despite her mother never believing in her, despite her father being a drunk, despite all of that, she has achieved something of her own and, secretly, this makes her proud.

At secondary school, which Esme hated, there had been a girl called Natalie Kerrins who had taken an instant and unexplained dislike to her. Natalie wore her glossy brown hair in a high pony-tail, the centre parting perfectly straight. She had pierced ears and wore small gold studs in each lobe and she would twiddle with them coquettishly during lessons, breaking off now and then to flick her ponytail round her shoulder, pinch the tip of it between her thumb and finger and lift it up to eye-level so that she could better examine her split ends. At the age of twelve, this had struck Esme as the height of sophistication. It was the kind of thing you'd imagine a cheerleader doing in those Sweet Valley High paperbacks, the ones with the sickly-sweet bubblegum-pink covers and the broken spines, which were the only books any girl ever read from the school library.

Natalie was the first girl in her class to get a perm and her lovely straight hair turned into a morass of crisp curls overnight. She thought she looked like Kylie Minogue, but no one was brave enough to tell her she didn't. Esme never spoke to her – she wouldn't dare. Esme, who was bad at games and who wore her rucksack strapped over two shoulders on the first day of school because she didn't know any better, was intuitively aware that she existed on the bottom rung of the adolescent pecking order. Natalie, with her permed hair and gold studs, was at the top.

Esme was adept at staying out of Natalie's way. As the years went by, Esme treated her with a mixture of apprehension and disdain, because it was easy to mask how much you wanted to be like someone if you pretended they were beneath your contempt. They might quite easily never have spoken, were it not for the GCSE art exhibition in which Esme's self-portrait in a Cubist style had been hung prominently on the walls in the corridor leading up to the assembly hall. The painting, executed painstak-ingly by Esme in shades of brown as a homage to Georges Braque, had been gratifyingly singled out by her art teacher for its 'tex-ture and depth'.

But when Natalie saw it hanging on the wall on her way to assembly one morning, she laughed and turned to her gaggle of friends.

'Is that meant to be Esme Reade?' she asked, loud enough for everyone going into assembly to hear, including Esme, who happened to be walking past. 'She fancies herself, doesn't she?'

And Esme, seized with an unfamiliar courage, had stopped and asked her what she meant by that. Natalie, surprised that this meek, inconsequential person had stood up to her, took a moment to respond. Then she said the words that Esme had never forgotten in all the years that followed: 'No offence, yeah? But you should take a good, hard look at yourself. You think you're so much better than everyone else. You're not.'

Natalie flicked her ponytail to one side, sending a spray of Impulse into the surrounding atmosphere. Esme watched helplessly as Natalie turned to walk towards the assembly hall, clutching her pink lever-arch file close to the pert breasts that were the envy of half the school. As she strutted away, followed by her coterie, Esme heard her parting shot: 'You're nothing.'

She hadn't gone to assembly that day. Instead, Esme had spent it in the girls' toilets, sobbing silently into a balled-up piece of tissue. She remembers it so clearly because the only way she had been able to stop crying was by telling herself that she would become so hugely successful that her very existence on the planet would show Natalie Kerrins how wrong she had been. It sounds silly now, but sometimes Esme honestly believes that the entirety of her ambition, the motivation for all her hard work and effort thus far, has stemmed from that single, pin-pricked moment in time.

Once, she had looked Natalie Kerrins up on Facebook. It turned out that she was married with two freckle-faced sons and worked as an estate agent in Basingstoke. When Esme clicked through the photographs, she took great satisfaction in realising that Natalie hadn't aged well. Her hair was no longer glossy but hung heavily down to her shoulders. She sported an ill-advised fringe that served only to emphasise the chubbiness of her features. In one picture, she was wearing a sleeveless patterned dress that Esme had seen in Monsoon and the flesh on her arms was thick and loose like a rubbery slice of squid. Her husband was tall and stocky and wore a lot of rugby shirts. At Christmas time, Natalie had posted a photo of the two of them wearing matching jumpers and reindeer antlers with a happy face emoticon and the comment: 'Happy Xmas to u and urs!!!!'

Looking at the Facebook profile of her one-time nemesis, Esme had felt a curious sense of loss. She had wasted so much time thinking Natalie Kerrins was a demonic harpy, hell-bent on the destruction of Esme's sense of self, and yet here this woman was, living a life of averages with no idea of the disproportionate havoc her thowaway comment had wreaked. She probably didn't even remember Esme Reade and her Cubist portrait. Probably didn't even read the paper to know that Esme Reade had, in fact, turned out to be something. Had, in fact, proved Natalie Kerrins wrong.

At Sloane Square, Esme glances at her watch and sees that she's now only five minutes behind schedule, which is perfectly respectable. Her phone pings. It is a text from her mother.

'Have fun with Dominic! Love, Mum xxxx'

A sinking feeling. It dawns on Esme, later than it should have done, that Lilian is obviously viewing this as a blind date. It was nauseating to have reached the age of thirty and for your mother still to be trying to set you up. And Esme knows, without having to meet Dominic, exactly what he will be like: priggish, pleased with himself, the kind of man who tucks shirts into his jeans and wears loafers. Everyone her mother had ever tried to introduce her to had been like this: what Lilian would call 'a nice boy'.

Daylesford Organic is on the Pimlico Road and rises out of the pavement like a gleaming edifice to poshness. There is a scattering of tables outside, hemmed in by neatly cut box hedges, where a handful of customers are sitting and bravely pretending not to be cold. Three women with long caramel-tinted hair, wearing Ray-Bans and navy cashmere wraps, are sipping on cappuccinos near the entrance, talking too loudly as if their conversation is a performance for a small but enraptured crowd.

'Do you ever have bad-mascara days?' asks one of them.

'Yeah.'

'Where it just doesn't go on properly?'

'Oh God yeah.'

'And you're, like, come on!'

'Totally.'

Esme pushes the door open, her hand pressing against a rough-hewn handle carved to resemble the horns of an ancient beast roaming free across the moorland. Inside, everything is clean marble, blue-veined like the organic Stilton on sale at the cheese counter. Esme, in her grey jeans and her lightly frizzing hair, feels immediately as though she is cluttering up the clean lines of the space.

'Can I help you?' asks a waitress in a beige apron, embroidered discreetly with 'Daylesford' in looping cursive.

'Actually I'm meeting someone . . .' She scans the room and can't see any obvious candidates.

'Maybe upstairs?' the waitress asks. Esme nods and makes her way up the polished white staircase, keeping one hand on the banister made from entwined birch twigs.

The second floor is filled with wooden communal tables and every available seat is taken. Esme begins to ask how long it will be to wait for a seat and whether she could put her name down when she feels a light touch on her shoulder.

'Esme, is it?'

She turns round.

'Yes.'

'Hi, I'm Dom.'

He is tall, somehow taller than she expected, with a thatch of curly brown hair. Dom proffers his hand, then angles awkwardly for a kiss on the cheek, which she doesn't notice in time so they end up doing an embarrassing half-dance of hands and kisses. His fingers are long, with square nails and tanned knuckles. His handshake is firm. She sneaks a quick glance at his clothes and notes that he is not wearing loafers or a tucked-in shirt, but dark brown boots, jeans and a grey sweater that has a hole in the cuff. She wonders if he might be gay.

He smiles at her and Esme realises that she hasn't said anything and that the silence has gone on slightly too long to be comfortable.

'I've got us a place over there—' and he gestures towards the window where there is a table laid for two people overlooking the road outside. When he speaks, he leans forwards, as though she is a little old lady struggling with her hearing.

'Great, thanks. I'm sorry I'm late.'

'You're not. I'm early. It's a terrible habit.'

'I had to come from Shepherd's Bush,' she says, and the words are out before she realises how dull she sounds.

He ruffles his hair.

'Yeah, I'm so sorry about dragging you all this way. My mother thinks I'm incapable of looking after myself.'

Esme laughs. 'Don't worry. I've got one of those myself.'

She perches on the edge of a stool and glances at the menu. She tries to concentrate on the options but is intently aware of his presence, the shape of him, the sound of his breathing, and she doesn't know why. He smells of citrus.

'I'm going to have a full English,' he says and in one fluid motion he pushes the menu to one side, takes his phone out of his pocket and switches it onto silent. He grins at her, rolls his sleeves up. The watch on his wrist has a leather strap and an old-fashioned face, round and open like the one her grandfather used to wear.

'Hungry?' She can't think of anything else to say. Internally, she is cursing herself.

He nods.

'We had a heavy one last night. I need to carb-load. What are you having?'

'Um, I thought I might go for the poached eggs.' There is a silence as they wait for their order to be taken. She hears a smattering of rapid-fire French from the table behind them, followed by a baby's piercing scream. Esme looks on as a harassed-looking man in a purple V-neck attempts to reason with a toddler.

'*Non, fais pas ça,*' he is saying. Then, more firmly: '*Qu'est-ce que je t'ai dit?*'

The toddler – a chubby girl with bows in her hair – stares at him, then continues to wail at a higher volume than before.

'Wow,' Dom says. 'I've always thought that babies' cries should be pitched at a frequency audible only to their parents. Nicer for the rest of us.'

Esme smiles. 'You mean, like those dog whistles?'

'Yeah, basically.'

He smiles, leans back in his chair and considers her. The pause draws out and he's still looking at her. Esme feels a clamminess across her collarbone, the ridge of her nose. He seems to be analysing her, weighing her up. It is not flirting, exactly, it is something else, something more serious, and it makes her feel uncomfortable, as though he knows all her secrets and is trying to work out if they match up to what he sees in front of him. She is not used to such scrutiny. She wonders, briefly, if this is what her interviewees feel like.

'So what were you up to last night?' Esme asks for the sake of having something to say.

Again, he smiles – languorously, as if playing for time.

'My girfriend's flat-mate had a birthday party. It got messy.'

He runs his hand through his hair but the curls spring up as soon as the pressure is released. He seems uncomfortable and Esme wonders whether he has already been informed by the maternal grapevine that she's a desperate spinster.

She scans the room for the waitress, wanting to get this brunch over with as soon as possible. Something about the way he looked at her made her feel she was making everything too obvious, that she was too easy to read, that he was poking fun at her.

Of course he already has a girlfriend. Stupid of her. And anyway, he wasn't even her type. Too posh. Too sure of himself.

Too . . . curly. A bitterness wells up within her. She thinks, without meaning to, of Dave. And then of Natalie Kerrins with her rugby-shirted husband. She is suddenly very tired.

Pushing the menu away, Esme decides on an Americano, no food. Let him have his fry-up if he wants – she's not going to prolong this encounter unnecessarily. Esme looks up and meets Dom's gaze with as much disinterest as she can muster and then she says, 'So, you want to get into the media?'

Carol

S HE CAN HEAR THEM talking over the fence again. This
time, it's the woman with the brown hair and the broad
shoulders, speaking with what Carol thinks is a mild Lancashire
accent and the woman is on the phone, saying something about
the need to keep the press informed and the fact that there's a
new bone fragment she wants to send to the lab and could they
please treat this as a matter of urgency because she doesn't need
to remind the person on the other end of the line that there are
now big fish involved higher up the food chain who don't want
to be kept waiting.

Mixed metaphors, Carol thinks, suppressing her tut of disapproval. Grammar is one of her things. Derek had bought her one
of those stocking-filler books for Christmas once called *I Before
E: A Pedant's Guide to Language*. She kept it on the laundry
basket in the downstairs toilet.

'Absolutely not,' the woman with the accent is saying now. 'I
don't want the press to get hold of this or they'll be all over us
like flies over shit.'

Carol flinches. There's no need for that, is there? Everyone
seems to swear nowadays, throwing out profanities as casually as
discarded apple cores. She is supposed to be watering her plants
but can't help listening in. There's only a flimsy wooden fence
between her garden and Alan's, so it's impossible to avoid hearing what's going on. The fact that she has taken to watering her

plants far more regularly than she used to in recent days is, Carol tells herself, neither here nor there. Besides, it has been sunny of late and the rhododendrons have a terrible thirst on them.

The policewoman on the other side of the fence speaks in a clipped tone and doesn't say goodbye when the conversation is over, just clicks her phone off and puts it back in her pocket. How she can find her pocket given what she's wearing, Carol has no idea. She has seen them coming and going from the upstairs bathroom window which overlooks Alan's garden, or what's left of it: a steady slow-moving stream of crinkly white figures. They are all in forensic suits like you see on the TV. Looking at them, Carol is reminded of the plastic sheeting you spread on the floor before painting a wall to keep the carpet clean. The policewomen resemble giant babies in oversized romper suits and they have masks over their faces which make her think of that picture of Princess Di visiting a hospital – the one that was printed in all the newspapers before lots of people criticised her for wearing too much eyeliner.

Carol's mind wanders. It has a tendency to do this. The watering can is still in her hand, half-poised to pour, and she finds herself thinking of Diana, shining and beautiful in waiting-room magazines. Diana, long and sleek in a blue bathing costume on the deck of a yacht; Diana in a black evening gown, eyes glittering and hair swept back from her face; Diana sitting on a marble bench in front of the Taj Mahal, her shoulders too thin for her jacket; Diana before fame swallowed her up and spat her out, standing in front of a gate, legs set slightly apart so that the sun shone through the thinness of her skirt.

Poor thing could never do anything right.

When the princess died, Carol had got on the District Line and walked to Kensington Palace to leave a bunch of flowers. Lilies, they'd been. Beautiful, sad white lilies that had stained the cuff of her blouse with pollen. Vanessa had made fun of her when she found out.

'You didn't know her, Mum,' she'd said. 'It's not like she was your friend or anything,' and Carol hadn't bothered replying because it seemed to her that Vanessa would never understand that you could still be touched by death even if you'd never met someone; you could still feel upset by the loss, by the pointlessness of it, and by the thought of those two shining young boys left without their mother.

She'd been so pleased when William got married to that lovely girl. She'd watched the whole thing on the BBC and wept when she saw Kate in her wedding dress for the first time.

'Bag it up and send it to the lab.' The woman's voice from the other side of the fence sails over and brings Carol's reminiscence to a juddering halt. She is jerked back to the present. Back to the extraordinary realisation that, for over a year, she has unwittingly been living next door to a murderer who buried a body in his flower bed.

Ever since that day when she and Archie had made their gruesome discovery, Carol has found herself swinging between two states of mind. On the one hand, there was the nauseating shock of comprehension that her neighbour was a cold-blooded killer. She went back over every single occasion she had invited Alan in for tea and biscuits, shivering at the realisation that, with each dunking of a chocolate HobNob, she could have been dicing with death. At least part of the discomfort Carol now feels stems from the fact that her ability to read people has been found to be conspicuously lacking. How could she not have known? She asks herself this again and again, the question chasing itself around like a dog snapping at butterflies. How could she not have suspected? Worse – how could she possibly have thought about setting him up with her own daughter?

And yet, there are other times when the anxiety recedes and Carol finds herself viewing the goings-on next door through a prism of disbelief, as if it really is all happening on a TV show. In these moments, a pleasant sort of detachment settles around her and she looks at proceedings with a curious tilt of the head, half-amused at the strangeness of it all, storing up the odd salacious titbit for later conversations with Vanessa, who will be satisfyingly horrified by the turn of events.

She is ashamed to admit it but Alan's newly notorious reputation has made Carol more popular than ever. She's never had so many phone calls – not even when Derek died. People she hasn't heard from for years have taken to sending her emails, idly enquiring 'how she's keeping' when she knows they secretly want her to dish the dirt. Connie has been calling every day, hungry for detail.

'Have you seen they're calling him the Southside Strangler?' Connie had said this morning. When Connie spoke about the case, it was always with an edge to her voice, like she was trying to hide her excitement.

'They're not, are they? Oh that's dreadful.'

'It's all over the front of the *Mail*,' Connie said. 'They've got a picture of him holding someone in a headlock. From his ex-wife apparently who says he was . . . wait, let me find it . . . that's it, "a bully and a liar".'

Carol fiddled with the bowl of pens by the phone then picked one out and started doodling on the notepad.

'I'm surprised they're assuming he strangled his victim,' Carol said mildly. 'As far as I know, the police haven't made any official statement on cause of death, have they?'

She knew the effect this would have on Connie, who was a terrible gossip.

'Well, Carol, you tell me.'

Carol left a deliberate pause. It was all about building up to the big reveal. She was embarrassed to be enjoying this. But Connie and Geoff had always been so superior – what with their conservatory extension, their Highgrove tins of tea and their framed photos of children in graduation caps – and it felt nice having the boot on the other foot for a change.

'Hmmm. Well—' She drops her voice. 'I did overhear the police talking about strangulation—'

'*Did* you?'

'Yes. Just yesterday this was. Perhaps the press have got hold of it.'

'I wouldn't put it past them.'

'But they're trying to keep things quiet at the moment. They don't want the newspapers interfering with the investigation.'

Carol has acquired a new vocabulary of late, picking up phrases used on the other side of the garden fence with ease. She likes the way these new-found words make her sound professional and unruffled. The police have been very good about keeping her informed. Most days, they'll pop round and check that she's all right. Her favourite is a woman called DCI Jennifer Lagan who wears plain clothes and uses Carol's name a lot when she talks. Jennifer Lagan has a calming manner and steady blue eyes. A name-badge hangs round her neck with a photo of her in dated clothes and a different haircut. She looks younger in the picture. In person, she has a tired face and there are faint lines around her lips. Carol has seen her smoking a cigarette from the lounge window. Normally, she doesn't approve of women who smoke, but Jennifer Lagan does it in a way that suggests the intake of nicotine is absolutely necessary in order to conduct police business effectively.

'Have they found him yet?' Connie asked. 'Or is he still . . . at large?'

'Still at large. They're tracing his mobile phone, things like that.'

'Oh Carol, that must be terrifying for you.'

'A bit,' she said, but in truth the police had been very reassuring and an officer was stationed at her front doorstep twenty-four hours a day in case Alan tried to make contact. Then there were all the TV crews at the end of the road. In many respects, as DCI Lagan pointed out, Lebanon Gardens was probably the safest address in the country.

'Do they know who it is yet? The body, I mean,' Connie said, lowering her voice.

Carol hesitated. She had heard a murmur of a name, when she

273

was upstairs in the bathroom and the window just happened to be open, but she wasn't sure it was right to share this with Connie just yet. She wasn't certain she'd heard it correctly. And it was the kind of name that, if she'd heard it right, would be of considerable interest to the media. Connie could be very indiscreet.

'No,' she said. There was a disappointed sigh on the other end of the line. To appease her, Carol lowered her voice and added, 'Apparently the body was *very* badly decayed.'

An intake of breath.

'Well,' Connie said, appetite temporarily sated. 'Well,' she said again.

'Anyway, Connie, I'd best be off. I've not had a chance to do any of my chores today.'

She looked down at her doodle and saw that she'd drawn a flower, growing out of a patch of soil. The whole conversation now seemed wildly inappropriate.

'Of course, Carol, of course, just . . . let me know if there are any developments.' Then, almost as an afterthought, 'Look after yourself, dear. It must be taking its toll on you as well.'

Is it taking its toll? Carol wonders as she walks slowly round to the strawberry pots with the watering can. The odd thing was that the discovery of a body underneath Alan's flower bed had made her feel curiously alive. It had brought it home to her that life could take sudden and unexpected turns. Derek's death had been cruel and unfair, but it had also been a long-drawn-out process and she had had time to accustom herself to the idea, if not the reality, of his eventual absence. It wasn't beyond the realms of possibility that a man of his age would die of cancer.

By contrast, the poor girl next door (because she'd overheard that it was a girl, a young woman in fact) shouldn't, in any natural scheme of things, have died when she did and she certainly shouldn't have lost her life in the most brutal way, at the hands of another person. Thinking of it like this, Carol feels almost lucky to have survived so long. She would never have wished to stumble across a decomposed body in her neighbour's flower bed, of course not, but given that she had, the unexpected by-product of this discovery seems to be a temporary lifting of her gloom.

Cheaper than therapy, she mutters and she asks herself, not for the first time, if some of the policewomen's defensive callousness has started to rub off on her. She's always fancied herself as a detective, to be honest. She'd never missed an episode of *Cagney & Lacey* when it was on and she'd watched *Prime Suspect*, too, although the Helen Mirren character was a bit too foul-mouthed for her to relax in front of the television – she was always bracing herself for the next f-word.

The voices on the other side of the fence have become muted. Carol thinks they have moved into the big white tent the police erected over Alan's garden to stop the media taking photographs from helicopters overhead. Carol can still make out a snatched word here and there – 'DNA swabs', 'forensics' – and the odd squall of laughter. Gallows humour, she supposes.

And in the midst of this, a clear slice of imagery rises unbidden in Carol's mind. A woman gasping, earth stuffed tightly into her mouth, great clods of it sticking in her throat so that she can't breathe. Hair wound round her neck like a noose. The woman's hands scrabbling uselessly at the soil, trying desperately to dig out a chink of light, an air-hole, anything to see the sky, and all the time someone is pushing her down, his hands pressing on her chest and her neck, until all her veins are squeezed dry. In Carol's imagination, the woman is blonde and frail and pretty, with big blue innocent eyes, and her doll-like quality makes everything worse so that Carol starts to feel light-headed and sick and also ashamed of herself, of her inability to help whoever it was, of the fact that she is capable of gossiping to Connie about what happened.

Sometimes it takes her like this: a flash of terror when she least expects it. In the garden, Carol bends gingerly, trying to stop the gentle spinning motion of her head, and she sets the watering can down by the herb planter on the patio. A mechanical sound has started up next door, like the juddering thud of a roadside digger. What could they have found now? She feels faint.

She manages to open the door back into the kitchen and then stumbles up the step, righting herself just before she falls. Her heart is beating arrhythmically. She can feel it stuttering inside her chest. She draws out a chair and sits on it at the table, regulating her breathing. Her greatest fear is of falling at home when she is on her own, breaking a bone and being unable to move for days until she is discovered, weeks later, dead of dehydration and neglect. She wonders about getting one of those red panic buttons she keeps seeing in the free catalogues pushed through her letterbox – the ones with automatic bird-feeders, embroidered draught-excluders and thermal slipper linings; all the humiliating paraphernalia invented exclusively to make money out of gullible OAPs.

She makes a mental note to ask Vanessa about the panic button. Vanessa will know what to do. Carol has been relying on her daughter more of late. It has stolen up on her, this reliance. She still isn't used to the idea that Vanessa can be a capable and responsible adult.

It is while she is sitting at the table, calming herself down and thinking about putting the kettle on, that there is a knock on the door. The knock is loud and startling, three sharp rat-a-tats and immediately, Carol senses that it is not a friend or anyone she knows. They wouldn't knock like that, she thinks. In fact, they wouldn't knock at all – there's a perfectly good doorbell right there. As if the person outside has heard her, the doorbell chimes almost instantly.

Ding-dong.

'Coming,' Carol says uselessly, her voice muffled and quiet so that whoever is on the other side of the door is bound not to hear her. She takes a while getting down the hallway and just as she has reached the end of the banister and is resting one hand on the wood to steady herself, she sees the letterbox flap open and feels the sucking-in of a gust of outside wind. She has time to notice a pair of beady eyes before it flaps shut again.

'I said I'm coming,' Carol grumbles. Honestly. No patience. It's probably another of the detectives from next door, wanting to ask the same old questions over again.

But when she undoes the safety lock and opens the door, she sees she was wrong. A small woman wearing smart grey trousers and a sleeveless blouse that shows off firmly toned biceps is standing on her doorstep. The woman's shoulder-length hair is shot through with streaks of blonde, tucked under in a way that suggests it has been professionally blow-dried. Almost as soon as Carol has taken in the impressive neatness of her appearance, she is enveloped by a cloud of heady scent: vanilla, tuberose, a musk-iness like incense. Expensive perfume, she thinks, so definitely not a police officer.

'Yes?' Carol says, keeping the door half-closed.

'Mrs Hetherington?' the woman says, her face blank.

'Yes.'

The woman smiles broadly and the entire shape of her face changes and becomes softer, warmer, more inviting.

'Hello there. I'm Cathy Dennen from the *Sunday Tribune*.'

Cathy Dennen holds out her hand, limply like a packet of wilted spinach. Carol takes it without thinking and shakes it.

'I see,' she says in clipped tones. She glances behind Cathy Dennen's shoulder to the garden gate where the police officer is meant to be. He must have gone on a tea break, she thinks.

'I've said all I want to say.'

She doesn't mean to be impolite, but really there is a limit. Ever since the forensics team moved in three days ago, there has been a steady trickle of newspaper journalists and television reporters making their way up the garden path desperate for fresh clues as to what Alan was like.

On the first day, she had been cordial but fairly non-committal to the reporters, saying simply that he had seemed a nice and fairly quiet man. Her words had been splashed across the

Wandsworth Guardian the next day: 'His neighbour, Mrs Carol Hetherington, 68, said: "He kept himself to himself. We never had any trouble from him."'

Which she was fairly certain she'd never said. At least not in those exact words. After that, she stopped giving quotes. It was true what they said about the press: you couldn't trust them.

Now, there was a police cordon at the bottom of Lebanon Gardens and, on the other side, a bank of white satellite vans bearing the logos of various TV stations. She watched them sometimes, under the guise of tidying up her small patch of lawn at the front: reporters with shiny teeth and bouffant hair jostling for space for live two-way broadcasts every hour, on the hour, attempting to talk at a slightly louder level than the person beside them.

And now – this woman. Carol looks her up and down. Cathy Dennen continues to smile. She's better dressed than the average journalist, Carol thinks, and her prejudices begin to shift imperceptibly under the surface like tectonic plates.

'I appreciate that,' Cathy says. 'And I'm so sorry to bother you at what must be a' – she nods her head ever so slightly towards Number 12 – 'tricky time. I just wondered if I could have a quick chat with you?'

'What about?' Carol asks. How on earth had Cathy Dennen made it through the police cordon? She must have been very ingenious to get past them, Carol thinks. Again, her respect for the woman on her doorstep rises infinitesimally.

'I don't have to quote you by name,' Cathy says. 'I'm really just trying to build up a bit of a picture of what's gone on for this Sunday's paper for a full-length feature.' She leans forward, confidingly. 'I'm not a news reporter, if that's what's worrying you. I know they can be a bit heavy-handed.'

Carol allows a slight smile to form on her lips. Cathy clocks this and carries on smoothly.

'If you don't want to talk to me, I completely understand and I'll go away and leave you in peace. I just thought . . . well, you might like to tell your side of the story. It can't have been easy . . .' She lowers her voice respectfully. 'Discovering the body.'

'How did you know about that?' Carol blurts out.

Cathy's eyes widen.

'Let's just say the police aren't always as discreet as they should be.'

Well, thinks Carol, if they're shooting their mouths off, why would they care what she did? And, after all, it *would* be nice to speak to someone – someone who knew a bit about the case and didn't just want to pump her for all the gory details, someone she could offload to, someone with a calm, professional manner and an inviting smile and neatly blow-dried hair. Someone like Cathy Dennen, in fact. Besides, Carol read the *Tribune*. It was a respectable paper. A tiny part of her was delighted at the thought of being featured in it. That'd be one in the eye for Connie.

'Come in,' she says, opening the door fully and inviting the journalist into the hallway.

'Thank you so much Mrs Hetherington, I really appreciate you taking the time.'

Cathy walks in, wipes her shiny brown heels conscientiously on the doormat and follows Carol into the kitchen. The journalist waits for Carol to tell her to sit, which Carol notes with silent approval, and when asked how she takes her tea, Cathy Dennen says strong, with just a dash of milk and no sugar. Carol normally has a heaped teaspoon in hers but today she pushes aside the sugar bowl, thinking of Cathy's toned arms and reminding herself that she could do with losing a few pounds. Stress always made her crave sweet things.

She chooses the only two matching mugs from the cupboard – garishly patterned purple things that never seem to be the right size for the amount of tea you want – and puts some biscuits from the tin on a dainty plate. She doesn't have a doily but she lays out two small serviettes instead. Did people use doilies any more? She isn't sure.

Once the tea is made, Carol places the mugs carefully on the table. She manoeuvres herself into the chair facing Cathy, trying to ignore the twinge in her lower back. She hopes her sciatica isn't playing up again. It's all that bending to water the plants that's doing it.

'So what do you want to know?' Carol asks, taking a sip of tea. It is hotter than she anticipated and she burns the roof of her mouth.

Cathy has laid out a plastic folder full of loose-leaf bits of paper, a spiral-bound notepad open to a blank page and a slim white rectangular object that Carol assumes is a tape recorder of some kind. Before replying, Cathy takes a bite from a chocolate Bourbon, catching the crumbs in her serviette.

'Mmm, lovely,' she says. 'Thank you so much.'

The journalist looks at her levelly, then drops her voice, ever so slightly.

'I can't imagine how draining this whole thing must have been for you.'

Carol waves her hand, as if it's just one of those things. She finds herself wanting to impress Cathy Dennen without understanding why.

'The police have been kind,' says Carol. 'The worst thing has been the coming and going, to be honest. All day and night they're traipsing in and out of that house, digging up the garden and all sorts. I don't know what Alan's going to think . . .'

She catches herself, realising how stupid this sounds.

'I mean, it's hard to get used to the idea that your next-door neighbour could be a murderer . . .'

'At least, that's what they're saying now,' Cathy prompts.

Carol nods. 'Terrible business. Terrible. That poor girl.'

'Do they have any idea who it is?'

Carol looks up sharply. 'No,' she says crisply.

'Of course not,' Cathy continues. 'Too early to know with a body in that state.' A pause. 'How did you come to make the discovery?' Cathy blows on her tea, lipsticked mouth pursing prettily. 'If you don't mind talking about it, that is. I don't want to upset you.'

'No, no, it's fine,' Carol assures her. 'I don't mind.'

And she ends up telling her the whole story: about Alan and how he sat exactly where Cathy was sitting now and drank a cup of tea and ate biscuits just as she was. About how she'd even begun to think that Alan might be a suitable partner for her daughter and thank God she hadn't pursued it because who knows what might have happened?

At this point Cathy sits back in her chair and lets out a low whistle.

'Doesn't bear thinking about,' the journalist says, scribbling a note in her pad.

'I know,' Carol says. 'I know.'

And then she tells Cathy Dennen how Alan had asked her to water his plants while he was away and, no, he hadn't told her where he was going but now she wishes she'd thought to ask.

'What was he like when he came round and asked you to look after his garden?' Cathy says and Carol can see her eyes darting towards the tape recorder, checking whether the red light was on and if it was working properly.

'Normal.' She lifts her mug to her lips but it stalls halfway. 'Although . . .' She looks out of the window above the sink. She can just about make out the flash of white from the edge of the police tent next door. She shakes her head, decides not to say anything.

'What?' Cathy puts her pen down and gives her her full attention. The journalist starts to reach out across the table and for a moment Carol wonders what on earth she thinks she's doing and then Carol realises her nose is running and tears are slipping down her cheeks.

'Sorry,' she says, reaching for the tissue she always keeps tucked into the cuff of her blouse. She dabs at her tears. 'I don't know what's come over me.'

Cathy smiles, cocks her head to one side. 'Sometimes it can

take you like that,' she says. Her hand is still there, sitting oddly on the surface of the table. Carol glances at the hand and sees clean-cut nails slicked with a coat of pale varnish. There is a single silver ring with a semi-precious stone on the middle finger. Looking at the hand, Carol thinks Cathy had probably been intending to pat her on the arm. Then she glances at Cathy, whose eyes are glassy like polished pebbles.

Cathy, sensing something has shifted, removes the hand and becomes engrossed in her notes, flicking through the pages and marking certain sections of shorthand with an asterisk. Carol sees that she has divided every page with a line down the centre, so that she writes in two columns. But the column on the margin side had barely any text in it and Carol wonders why this should be. Hasn't she said anything interesting enough?

She finds herself thinking of the one and only job interview she'd ever had, back before she was married and a friend told her they were looking for shop assistants at C&A. Carol had been so nervous that she could barely speak. Two store managers, both men in grey suits, had sat behind a desk and peppered her with questions, asking what she could bring to the organisation. She had no convincing answers, so Carol answered as truthfully as she could: that she knew very little but was willing to learn and that what she could bring to the organisation was an interest in fashion and then she stammered and realised she wasn't sure what to say next. She lapsed into a silence while the store managers mumbled amongst themselves and before they had a chance to say they weren't interested, thank you very much, she stood up, pushed the chair back into place, said a polite thank you and walked out of the office with as much dignity as she could muster. She'd never felt so humiliated.

She didn't get the job. Instead she'd got married to Derek and then became pregnant with Vanessa and a career didn't seem to matter all that much. Once Vanessa was old enough, Carol got a part-time job as a receptionist at the local GP's surgery. She'd worked there until retirement and then Derek had got ill and now she didn't have anything left with which to occupy her time, unless you counted looking after Archie and even he was getting too old to need babysitting.

'. . . so really I was just wondering: do you know?'

Carol realises she is being asked a question by Cathy Dennen and hasn't been listening for a good few minutes.

'I'm sorry, dear. What was that?'

'We've all heard rumours about the identity of the girl under the flower bed, so really I was just wondering, Mrs Hetherington, do you know?'

'Do I know who it is, you mean?'

Cathy nods.

Carol sighs. She is exhausted. Cathy Dennen of the *Tribune* no longer seems like a kindly listener and Carol is worried that she has now said too much. She has no idea what possessed her to invite a journalist in and she talks to herself sternly in her head about not being swayed by first impressions, about not trusting people, however nice or generous or lonely they seemed. Had she learned nothing from the whole Alan Clithero saga?

She is beginning to understand that she is deeply naive. Not in an appealing, young girlish way, but in the way that suggests a sheltered existence of limited experiences and a blinkered attitude to unpleasantness. For so long, all she had cared about was her family unit of three: Derek and Vanessa and then, later, Archie. She had poured her energies into looking after them, into keeping things running smoothly, remembering their favourite foods, sweeping up their crumbs, folding their laundered clothes, making their modest home as tidy and clean as possible and showing them that they were loved in countless small ways. The world beyond these four walls had been blurred. It had been a world for other people.

Now, sitting at her kitchen table exactly as she has done a million times before, it comes to her in startling clarity: she has not been open to life. It has taken Derek's death and a woman buried under a flower bed to shake her out of her self-imposed stupor. No wonder, then, that she is out of her depth.

Across the table, she meets Cathy's eye. She wants this to be over. Part of her wonders whether she should give the name she's overheard just to end the conversation. But then she thinks of the girl's poor father and what he must be feeling. She'd seen a picture of him in the paper a while back, laughing as if he didn't have a care in the world. She can't bear to think of him now, having been told the news.

'I can't tell you,' Carol says, downing the rest of her tea and hoping Cathy gets the message.

'I appreciate that.' Cathy closes her notepad, clicks the top back on her biro and picks up her large handbag from the linoleum floor. Just as she is putting her things away, she looks straight at Carol and says, without flinching, 'It's Ada Pink, isn't it?'

Carol stares at her. She can feel a flush starting on the top of her chest. She shakes her head vigorously, hair jiggling as she does so. She wants to say no, that's not it at all, you've got it all wrong and why don't you stop meddling and have a thought in your head for that girl's grieving parents, but she can't. She is a bad liar, always has been.

'I didn't say that,' Carol says and the words, when she hears them, are scratchy and unconvincing.

Cathy takes her tape recorder, slides a switch and the red button that has been winking at Carol for the best part of an hour snaps off.

'You didn't have to,' Cathy replies, so quietly that Carol isn't sure she's heard her correctly. Carol stands, snatching back Cathy's mug of tea which has hardly been touched.

'I think you'd better go,' she says, attempting to draw herself up to her full height which, after all, is only an unimpressive 5 foot 4.

Cathy gives a tight smile, 'You've been a great help, thank you, Mrs Hetherington. I can see myself out.'

And then she is gone, as quickly as she arrived, leaving behind her a trail of scent and the sound of smart heels clipping across the kitchen floor.

Carol rinses out the cups and leaves them to dry on the draining board. Then, trying not to think, she ignores the ache in her hip and limps into the lounge. She sinks gratefully into the sofa and switches on the television.

Countdown, she thinks with relief as the theme music starts up. Perfect.

Beatrice

*B*EATRICE SETTLES INTO HER new job more easily than she had expected. She has always been good at adapting to new situations, at finding the necessary camouflage to fit in. It was a necessary attribute when you lived a double life, when you had to keep secrets to survive.

She enjoys the routine. Each day, she savours the walk to the office in her smart clothes, winding through the Lebanese restaurants and clouds of rose tobacco and thinking about the impression she must be giving, about how other people look at her now and see her as a professional working woman rather than a downtrodden immigrant who is only fit for cleaning their toilets. She loves the hours, the fact that her working day now fits neatly between 9 a.m. and 5 p.m. with a lunch break and frequent coffees with Tracy, accompanied by the biscuits that Beatrice has started to bring in from the corner shop in Bermondsey.

She has grown more experimental with the biscuits of late. Today, she's bringing in American chocolate cookies she got from Poundland. Last week, she brought in a tray of sweet, nutty baklava from a bakery on the Edgware Road. Tracy had loved the baklava despite always saying she was on a diet, although in Beatrice's opinion she didn't need to be. Tracy had a lovely figure – petite but curvy – and she dressed well too, in muted colours and tailored suits that were only ever accessorised by a modest silver chain with a pearl on the end. Beatrice had asked her once where the necklace came from.

'It was a gift,' Tracy said as she spooned granules of Nescafé into their mugs. 'From a man I was in love with, if you must know.' She smiled as she handed Beatrice the coffee. 'No good ever came of it.'

'But you got the necklace,' Beatrice pointed out.

They laughed. She was getting better at laughing.

'Yes, Bea, you're right. So it wasn't all bad.'

To her surprise, Beatrice also likes the work. She has her own desk and her own computer. She has even started bringing in small objects to make her feel more at home. She now stores her pens in a pale blue mug with white polka dots and a broken handle she'd bought at the charity shop. On the partition between desks, she has Blu-tacked a postcard Tracy had sent her from her recent minibreak to Barcelona. The postcard has a picture of a cathedral on it and the entire building looks like it is melting into the ground. The information on the back says it was designed by Antonio Gaudi.

The job itself is easier than she had anticipated: a simple matter of opening letters from customers, analysing what they wanted and then replying accordingly with the correct template. After a few weeks of showing herself to be efficient and sensible, Beatrice was allowed to give out a certain number of £10 vouchers to customers who had valid complaints.

If, for instance, they had bought a faulty item of clothing with a thread unravelling from the hem or a skirt missing a button at the back and they can prove this with an accompanying photograph and a dated receipt, then Beatrice is at liberty to send out the money-off voucher and to pass the complaint on to Tracy who, in turn, passes it on to a senior manager and then Sir Howard himself.

Occasionally, Sir Howard will dictate a personal letter to a customer who is particularly outraged and will sign it in his own handwriting. Beatrice is impressed by this, by the concern it shows. She had been inclined to dismiss Sir Howard as yet another of those callous, money-grabbing fat cats and bank bosses she keeps reading about in the *Metro*. But now, grudgingly, she has to admit he seems to care about his customers, albeit in a way that continues to protect his profit margin.

He has been good to her too. Beatrice isn't stupid. She knows he didn't have to give her this job, that he was taking a risk by doing so. He could have pulled strings to have her deported, she is sure of it. Or he could have refused to meet her and, when she had gone to the press, he could simply have denied everything. Beatrice knows she probably wouldn't have stood a chance against the full might of his legal team, even though she had kept the black trousers, stained with his sperm, just in case. He thought he'd been so careful, but he'd left his mark. The trousers are folded over a hanger and hanging at the back of the wardrobe. There is a pale white smear on the back of them, just below the waistband. Insurance. You could never be too careful. You could never trust anyone. Even those you loved.

But so far, thinks Beatrice as she walks into the office building, swipes her pass through the gates and smiles at the security guard she remembers from her first day, Sir Howard has been generous. Her salary at Paradiso is twice what it had been when she was a chambermaid at the Mayfair Rotunda and she has been told she can expect a Christmas bonus, as well as discounts in all his stores.

Beatrice sees Sir Howard sometimes as he strides along the corridor, dispensing bonhomie as he goes and calling everyone by their first name. He never speaks to her directly but he sometimes glances in her direction and Beatrice always makes sure she smiles so that he knows she is grateful. She thinks, perhaps, that he is ashamed of what happened. Or maybe that's what she wants to imagine. It is a quality he has, she realises. People warm to him. They see in him what they wish to believe.

Sir Howard has a large corner office with an oak desk and leather chairs. Tracy took her in there once when he wasn't around and Beatrice had been hypnotised by the generous sweep of the view. She stood at the floor-to-ceiling windows and stared at a panorama of London that stretched all the way to the horizon. It was an overcast day and it looked as if the outline of every block of flats, every church spire and railway line and council house had been drawn by a giant hand in blunt pencil. At this distance, London displayed all its grubby glamour, all its twisted secrets and oozing promise.

Inside, Sir Howard's walls were hung with framed caricatures of himself culled from various newspapers (but only the flattering ones, Beatrice noted) and a black-and-white picture of his mother, standing outside a market stall with the words 'Pink's Garments' written in capital letters on a banner across the top.

'He's such a love,' Tracy had said once, standing at Beatrice's desk to load the printer with more paper. 'He pretends to be this big, important businessman but inside he's a total softie. You'll see.'

Beatrice didn't reply. Her silence seemed to make Tracy defensive.

'You might not believe it now, Bea, but you will. He's been through so much. He's never got over . . .' She stopped and pressed her lips firmly together.

'Got over what?' Beatrice asked.

'His daughter disappearing like that,' Tracy said in low tones. 'You must know about it. It was all over the papers.' A pause. 'I mean, in this country,' Tracy added, 'it was a big news story.'

'I know,' Beatrice said. 'Did they ever find out . . . ?'

Tracy shook her head. 'No, never.' She was on the verge of tears and Beatrice thought it was odd, this unchecked emotion for a man Tracy had only ever known as her employer. 'It destroyed him. His marriage broke up. He couldn't speak about her. I'd call round with all these documents he needed to sign and he would just sit there, tears rolling down his cheeks. You've never seen a more devoted father, Bea. He just thought the world of Ada, he really did.'

The ping of an email arriving in Beatrice's inbox made Tracy jump.

'I shouldn't be standing here nattering like this,' Tracy said, pressing a button on the printer and checking the paper was correctly aligned in the tray.

'What was she like?' Beatrice asked.

'Who, Ada?'

Beatrice nodded.

'Oh, she was . . .' Tracy got a faraway look on her face. 'She was a lovely little girl. Used to come into the office sometimes with her mum and give me home-made fairy cakes with all these sprinkles on top. But then . . .'

Beatrice waited.

'Something happened. It wasn't just a moody teenage thing, it was more than that. She never seemed happy even though she had so much. I saw her once, at the summer party, just after her GCSEs, and she had all these scars up her arms. Wearing short sleeves like she didn't care.' Tracy chewed her lip. 'She drank too much and Howard was embarrassed, I could tell.'

The printer whirred into action, as if in acquiescence.

'Then she went off to university and I never saw her again. The funny thing was—' Tracy turned away, as if considering what she was about to say.

'You don't need to tell me,' Beatrice said.

'No, no. To be honest, Bea, it's good to have someone to talk to. Most people here either don't care or don't want to be reminded. And I wouldn't dream of raising it with Sir Howard. He never even mentions her name. No, what I was going to say was that the funny thing was I wasn't surprised. When Ada went missing, I mean. It felt like it had been on the cards for a while. It felt like . . . oh, I don't know . . . like she couldn't make sense of life.' Tracy broke off and fiddled with the silver stud in her left ear. 'Does that sound mad?'

'No.' She wanted to take Tracy's hand and squeeze it but she wasn't sure if she should. In Britain, she could never tell if physical contact was appropriate. The rules were so different here.

'Not at all,' Beatrice said. 'I know what you mean.'

Tracy looked relieved. She smiled and went back to her desk. For a moment, Beatrice was reminded of that long-ago memory of the white man in Hotel Protea for whom she had brought a citronella candle to ward off mosquitoes. It was amazing to her how such small acts could be rewarded with such warmth. She had grown unaccustomed to kindness, to the simple expression of it without the expectation of a payback.

Beatrice had never had many friends. At school, she knew plenty of people to say hello to but as soon as she started to realise she was different, that she had feelings about girls that went beyond the usual crush, she began to distance herself. It was only later, at university, that she discovered the underground gay clubs in Kampala but even then she hadn't wanted to let her guard down. Too many of the people she met in these clubs were into drink and drugs and Beatrice didn't fit in. She felt vulnerable in their presence, and unable to be herself.

At home, her mother started to drop hints about marriage and Beatrice found she could no longer tell the truth. To do so would be to break her mother's heart, but it would also put her family in danger. The law said it was an offence not to report a gay person to the authorities if you knew they were homosexual. She didn't want to put her mother through that.

So the lies started to accumulate, like a pile of stones that soon became a wall and then an edifice of fabricated rooms and a maze of corridors that Beatrice could no longer see her way through.

Until she met Susan, the only person Beatrice could truly relax with was her younger brother John. As a toddler, he had been so accepting of everything, so willing to take joy and laughter as his due. She remembers lifting him high above her shoulders, then swooping him low so that his head was upside-down and he was screaming and giggling at the same time. It was the best sound ever.

Since coming to London, Beatrice had deliberately kept herself isolated. Apart from Emma at RASS and occasionally Manny and some of the girls at the Rotunda, she barely spoke to anyone. Her silence made Susan's absence more bearable, she found. It meant she didn't have to acknowledge the truth of it out loud.

But Tracy was the first person Beatrice had met in Britain who didn't judge. She had the same openness of spirit, the same child-like innocence as John. When, after a few days in the office, Tracy had asked Beatrice to tell her about where she was from, she did so with complete naturalness. It wasn't like when the loud people coming home from the pub spat at Beatrice in the street and shouted at her to go back to where she came from. There was no malice to what Tracy asked, just curiosity and an apparent desire to get to know her better.

'I come from Kampala,' Beatrice said. 'In Uganda.'

'What's it like?'

Beatrice laughed. Tracy blushed.

'I suppose that's a stupid question really.'

'No. It's a nice question.' For a second, Beatrice thought she might stop there and draw the conversation to a close. But she didn't. 'Normally people say, "Oh, is that where Idi Amin is from?" or they ask about the film *The Last King of Scotland* and they wonder if we all boil up each other's bones for soup or abduct our children to become soldiers.'

Tracy's eyes widened.

'Oh,' Tracy said.

'There's been civil war in the North for years, but Kampala is different,' Beatrice started to explain. And then she tried to tell Tracy what it was like, about the boda-boda motorbike taxis that careened through the streets, about the market stalls by the side of the road that sold everything you could possibly want – trainers, phone cards, metal suitcases, bananas, second-hand dentist's chairs – about the lushness of Entebbe and the rust-red dirt tracks that led to the edge of Lake Victoria, about the battered combi vans with mottoes on the back like 'God is not late.

Not early. Just on time', about the Kololo district with all the rich houses and wide avenues with white-painted walls topped with swirls of barbed wire, about the pristine grass of the Uganda golf course, unused by locals, and the Endiro Café where NGO workers could get Americano coffees with soya milk.

She described the house where she grew up: the pinkish-brown metal roof, the black metal gate, the brick perimeter wall, the tiled floors, the mosquito nets over each bed that swayed gently in the breeze and the single bookshelf displaying novels by Chinua Achebe and Chimamanda Ngozi Adichie and poetry collections by Jack Mapanje and Jean-Joseph Rabearivelo.

She tried to tell her about how Kampala felt, about how an electric pulse seemed to beat just beneath the ground, about how it didn't have the same silent menace as other cities.

She told her all this. But she did not tell her about Susan.

When Beatrice finished, she noticed that Tracy was leaning forward intently, propping her chin up on her hands, and that she had been talking for the best part of fifteen minutes. It was as if it had all been waiting to come out of her, all these years.

'Bea, that sounds beautiful,' Tracy said. 'Do you think you'll ever go back?'

'No,' she said, too quickly. Then, more softly 'My life is here.'

More and more, she believes this to be true. Now, when she thinks of Uganda, she feels fondness where before there was a lattice of bitterness and fear. As for Susan, she has packaged up the idea of her and put it aside. Beatrice has taken down her girl-friend's photograph and stored it in the bottom of her chest of drawers, wrapped up in a sheet of newspaper and pressed flat against the wood under a pile of T-shirts.

She is taken aback at how easy it was to do this. It is not that she is unfeeling. It is that she no longer has the energy to feel. Her love for Susan still exists, but it has been built over: a lake filled in, a river dammed, the waves halted, the flow of her affection redirected so that it no longer torments her with its current.

Instead, she has Tracy. And she has her job. For the moment, this is all she needs.

At her desk, Beatrice logs on to the computer (password: matoke) and waits for her email to download. She punches a code into the phone and takes it off voicemail. She notices her postcard of Barcelona has fallen down and sticks it up where she can see it, making sure the edges are nice and straight, bending back the dog-ears. The computer makes a whirring noise like the purr of a mechanical cat. She takes her coat off and slides it onto the back of her ergonomic seat, then crouches down to put her footrest in the right place. The cleaners always move it around at night which annoys her. Beatrice catches herself as she thinks this: has she really become a person who complains about cleaners? She used to be one of them, not so long ago.

She glances over the partition to see if Tracy has got in yet. There is no sign of her, which is odd. Tracy normally arrives half an hour before everyone else to turn on all the lights and raise the blinds. Beatrice starts to open the batch of letters the postal room has left on her in-tray. She likes it when customers send letters as opposed to emails. It appeals to an old-fashioned part of her and it makes her think they must have a proper grievance, if they've taken the trouble to put pen to paper and to buy a stamp and then to walk to the postbox and send it.

It is just as she is about to open the first envelope that she hears Tracy's rapid footsteps coming up behind her. Beatrice already knows the sound of her walk – brisk and familiar along the carpet tiles. She turns in her chair, ready to greet her with a broad smile, but then she sees Tracy's face, crumpled and tearful, and the smile drops. She stands, for want of anything better to do, and wonders what has happened.

'Oh Bea,' Tracy says, the words coming out in gulps. 'Something dreadful . . . just dreadful.'

Beatrice goes to her and puts a hand on Tracy's shoulder. She wants to hug her but at the same time draws back. She is aware, all the time, of people getting the wrong impression.

In the end, it is Tracy who rushes towards her and then Beatrice has no choice but to put her arms around her. She can feel Tracy's heart pitter-pattering through her chest. She is crying, but in a small way. There is no sobbing; no violent rush of tears. Beatrice places the flat of her hand lightly on Tracy's back.

'Tracy, what is it?' she says, trying to keep the worry out of her voice. A thousand desperate scenarios play through her mind. A terminal cancer diagnosis. A house fire in which she has lost everything. A discovery that Beatrice is not who she thinks she is. 'Tell me.'

Tracy draws back and dabs at her eyes with a balled-up piece of tissue. There is a globule of mascara on the rim of her eyelid and Beatrice wants to reach out and wipe it away. She has never seen Tracy in such disarray. She is normally so immaculate, so in control of herself.

'It's Ada,' Tracy says and when she speaks, her lips quiver at the corners. 'They've found her body.'

Howard

THEY TOLD HIM ON a Tuesday. He knows this because he was in the car with Jocelyn on his way to the office, and the radio news announcer said the time and date just before the morning headlines and Howard was listening intently to hear what the Chancellor would say in his spending review and then his mobile rang.

So much else about that morning has already blurred and warped in his mind, coalescing into a slow fog, an impenetrable opaqueness of thought, but he will always remember the radio announcer with perfect clarity. For weeks, the detail of that moment will plague him. He will have dreams about it, picturing the announcer in a black-and-white 1950s newsreel with a jaunty fedora, bending towards an old-fashioned microphone. He will replay each tiny inflection of the announcer's voice with absolute precision: the intake of breath, the sonorous, modulated tone, the incremental pause that implied a full-stop at the natural end of a sentence and then the five electronic pips that marked the turning of the hour as the minutes passed and the outside world kept on moving, wholly and complacently ignorant of the fact that some-where in central London, in the back of a chauffeur-driven car on his way to the office, the internal structure of Sir Howard Pink's world, all the beliefs, the memories, the love, the hate, the kind-ness, the nostalgia, the exhaustion, the hope, the spite, the jealousy, the grief, the rage – all the experiences he had collected through a lifetime of breathing in and out, out and in – were collapsing into a cloud of dust.

He could see it happen almost as an out-of-body experience: the entire landscape of his soul set out as a skyline of silhouetted towers, the buildings vibrating like a mirage as the lever was pulled and then imploding with the brutal force of the blast. Because none of it meant anything any more. Those teetering monuments he had built up to shelter his own self-importance: it had all been a trick, an illusion, a con. All that was left was rubble. Grey dust. The odd piece of ripped paper, snatched up by the breeze.

On the phone, they asked him to come into the police station. He wanted to refuse, to get them to come to his home instead, but then he thought there might be a reason for it – there might be a chance to see Ada. They might, after eleven years of waiting, have discovered her. He told Jocelyn to drive to the station as quickly as he could and the chauffeur, seeing Sir Howard's face, wordlessly pressed his foot down on the accelerator so that the big car seemed to float through the traffic like a boat pushing off from a riverbank.

And when they got to the police station in Wandsworth – a strange wooden building on a busy one-way system squeezed next to a carpet shop – he was still telling himself this while at the same time feeling it wasn't true. He knew that she was dead. The instinct had been there since Ada disappeared, it was just that he had never allowed himself to acknowledge it and, every time he had met his wife's gaze, he could see the same loss written there, so that, in the end, he couldn't even look at Penny's face without fear and he had pushed her away and married someone who couldn't ever begin to know.

Howard had lived with this self-imposed duality for years. It was the only way he knew how to be. Even when the police had come to his house asking questions a few days ago – even then, he had told himself one thing (that Ada would be found alive) while believing quite another (that she had been dead for years). He was frighteningly good at lying to himself.

He got out of the car, sapped of strength. Like an old man, he uncurled himself slowly onto the pavement. The light was too bright. He wished he had a stick to lean on.

'Would you like me to come in with you, Sir Howard?' Jocelyn asked.

'No,' he said automatically. 'You need to find somewhere to park.'

In the station, the first person he saw was Penny. She was sitting on a plastic chair wearing a navy skirt and a cream cardigan buttoned all the way up. Her eyes were closed, lids brushed with light brown powder that got darker at the corners. A small handbag rested on her lap. She looked as she always had done – unobtrusive, gentle.

He touched her on the shoulder and she sprang up and hugged him and she shook in his arms but she didn't cry and without saying anything, he was relieved that he knew exactly how she was feeling and that she knew too. She knew what lay inside him.

There was a detective in plain clothes who took them into a side room to tell them they believed they had found Ada. That they were still investigating and that it was a complex process, given the time-frame they were dealing with, but that all the evidence so far suggested she had been murdered. It was Penny who asked how. Strangled, the detective said.

Penny started gasping for air. Howard held her hand, told her to breathe slowly in and out. After a while, she began to moan. There were still no tears, from either of them.

Howard asked to see her.

'I'd like to see my daughter,' he said and his voice seemed to come from the other side of a cave.

The detective nodded and then spoke.

'You do understand that, at this stage, there isn't a body in the conventional sense? What we are dealing with here is' – the detective looked uncomfortable – 'remains.'

Penny flinched.

'I understand,' Howard replied. His words cracked like dry leather. 'I'd still like to see her.'

'Of course you would,' the detective said. 'We'll arrange that for you.'

Hours passed, or maybe it was only a few minutes. A lifetime, no time. The passing of the day acquired a peculiar elasticity.

At some point, they were told all the details of the case including the prime suspect's name and background. Howard wanted to know everything but as soon as he was told, he found he had forgotten and needed to ask the same questions over again. Penny stayed silent for much of it, head bowed, twisting a cotton handkerchief in her hands. He noticed the handkerchief. She was one of the only women he knew who still used fabric handkerchiefs. He felt reassured that, in the midst of all this, Penny hadn't changed. Penny was constant: a solid shape in the mist.

The police were patient. Endlessly patient. They suggested a visit to the site where she was found, if that would help. A family liaison officer was given to them. His name was Keith and he spoke quietly, with a soothing professional calm. Keith brought them sugary tea in plastic cups and then, as the morning slid into the afternoon, he gave them sandwiches that stayed untouched in their plastic containers on the table in front of them. One of the sandwiches was cheese and pickle. The other was ham and lettuce. Penny made a half-hearted attempt to open one of them, then left it there. After a while, the bread curled brown at the corners.

They went to the garden where Ada's body had been discovered. It was a next-door neighbour, Keith said, who had first raised the alarm. They walked up the road and Keith lifted the red-and-white-striped police cordon so that they could get underneath and there was a barrage of camera flashes and a low, dull sound of voices asking questions that Howard couldn't process and he could hear, dimly, Keith saying, 'Show some respect,' and a part of him still found the space to be grateful for that.

There were two uniformed officers guarding the front door of a modern terraced house and it all looked so pedestrian from the outside, so normal, as they opened the wooden gate at the bottom of the path and were ushered through by Keith's guiding arm. Howard stepped into the hallway and his limbs felt heavy, as if he were walking along a wet stretch of beach, his feet sinking into saturated puddles of seawater that threatened to suck him under. Penny was clutching on to him. He had to keep going for her sake. He had to stay strong.

In the house, there were police everywhere, wearing white suits, brushing powder on bits of furniture, taking photographs. When Howard and Penny walked in, they all stopped what they were doing and stood silently while they passed. They were wearing masks and all Howard could see were their respectful eyes.

On the wall in the hallway there was a framed picture, a bad reproduction of a painting Howard had seen once of Jesus holding a lamp. It had been knocked askew and Howard wondered if the killer had left it like that or if one of the police had let their shoulder brush against it and not realised.

They walked on, through the hallway and into the kitchen which stank of rotting food and unwashed dishes, and then out of the glass doors and onto what would once have been a patio except now all the paving slabs had been removed and some of them lay in a pile of splintered pieces to one side. He thought of the cairns you find on the top of mountains, each stone left by a passing traveller.

In the garden, there was a large white tent that smelled of sweat and chemicals. The grass had been churned up so that curls of mud lay under their feet like wood shavings. At the farthest end of the tent was a dug-out ditch, about 7 foot by 4, overlooked by two large lamps, beaming light into the blackness. At the sight of it, Penny pulled back. She was saying something, crying, and after a while he realised it was the word 'No', repeated over and over again, an incantation.

No no no no no.

He prised Penny's hand off his wrist and handed her over to Keith and he couldn't say why exactly but he kept moving towards the edge of the ditch, drawn ineluctably to it like a piece of driftwood swept into the current of a vast and bubbling waterfall. He needed to see. He needed to look. He needed the certainty of knowing.

When he got there, he stood underneath the lamp, feeling the hotness of the bulb against the back of his neck. He breathed in, holding the air in his throat as if it were a thing that might break, and then he forced himself to peer into the hole. He saw clumps of soil, pebbles, fragments of twig and leaf. He saw a worm wriggling into the dankness of the earth.

He thought about the fact that every tiny molecule, each plaited strand of genetic material, every minuscule hereditary quirk bequeathed by generations of Pinks whom Ada had never known – all of it, which had together created the infinitesimal subtlety of what his daughter was – had been shattered into a million scraps of absence. The entirety of her, the sheer beauty of that crazily complex inherited construct, had gone, had been snatched away, stolen, extinguished, murdered.

He fell to his knees and heaved with the horror of it. He imagined her struggling. He felt her terror. He despised himself for not being there to protect her. He remembered her smile and her touch and the way, as a child, that she wanted the light left on at night.

Ada.

And then, his vision blanked.

Now here he is, uncomfortably balanced on the lowest stool his housekeeper could find, watching the mourners come to pay their respects. He is sitting shiva for his daughter. The reality of it hasn't struck him yet. He is unable to grasp what has happened, unable to come to terms with the unnaturalness of a parent carrying out this act of mourning for their only child.

He has entered into a period of inward reflection and finds he cannot speak. The words don't exist. There is no way to describe the million jagged edges of his thoughts, the dislocating awareness that this is the end when for so long he has lived in a state of suspension.

There are people who don't understand, who think it must come as some kind of relief to know, at last, what happened to her. He can see the logic. One part of his thinking mind appreciates it makes sense and acknowledges that he himself once felt like this – that he would rather know, whatever the truth of it might be.

But the rest of him, the larger part that is not governed by rationality, is bewildered. He is lost, blindfolded, his hands thrashing uselessly in front of him as he tries to make his way through overgrown thickets, studded with thorns. He is a raft cut adrift at sea, buffeted by the waves that spool outwards from a listing shipwreck. He is alive and there seems no point to his continued existence.

And yet he carries on.

Now, he is sitting here, conscious of the ache in his bones, watching the silent guests push the door open and come to sit by him. His non-Jewish friends arrive bearing extravagant flower arrangements and handwritten cards. Bradley Minchin comes. So does Mike, the betting CEO whose surname he can never remember. Tracy arrives with two Tupperware boxes filled with the home-made chocolate brownies which she knows he loves. She looks at him and her face grows pale and he gets up from his stool and hugs her. She is wearing the silver chain with the single pearl he gave her once, to mark ten years of working as his PA, and he remarks on it and thanks her for being here and she tells him how she remembers Ada coming into the office with fairy cakes and how she'll never forget her, ever, and that he must take as long as he needs off work and not rush back and she will deal with his diary and inform the relevant people that he's on compassionate leave. He nods and does not resist even though he knows he will return to work as soon as he is physically able to do so because it is the only thing, apart from Penny, which makes him remember who he is. It is the only constant. A refuge.

The Jewish visitors do not speak. In the afternoon, Mark Steiner walks through the door. He is the CEO of Steiner Supermarkets and he has come to pay his respects even though, the last time he met Howard, they'd argued about whether the austerity cuts were damaging to business (Howard said no; Mark said yes) and they hadn't parted on good terms. Rebecca Spero, the eloquent and impassioned head of an organisation that lobbied to get more women on the boards of FTSE 100 companies, arrives shortly afterwards. She is always trying to persuade Paradiso to appoint more women to senior positions and Howard is always promising to do so and then never acting on it because he doesn't believe in quota systems but thinks if women are good enough, they'll make it anyway, and despite his constant prevarication, despite the fact that she knows she will never change his mind, Rebecca Spero is here. He is deeply touched that she would make the effort.

Mark and Rebecca come and take a seat next to him without a word. Mark is hunched over on a foot-stool, his gangly limbs bent out of shape like a large spider and, for a moment, Howard is amused by the vision of one of the world's most powerful businessmen attempting to cling on to his dignity as he grapples with a seat that is far too small for him. Then the moment passes and Howard is left with the same shivering ache as before. As he watches the flash of lightness recede, he wishes he could get it back. Will anything ever be funny again?

He meets Mark and Rebecca's gaze and nods to show his gratitude. There is a relief in knowing no one expects him to talk. Theresa offers them a bowl of hard-boiled eggs and cherry tomatoes which they both refuse. Rebecca has tears in her eyes. Mark reaches across and clasps Howard's hand. Howard tries to smile.

After a while, Howard is surprised to see that Mark is crying. His shoulders shake and he lets the tears fall onto his trousers, leaving irregular circles of moisture on the fabric. He has two daughters, Howard recalls. Younger than Ada. Their whole lives ahead of them.

Howard has never been observant, but he is grateful now to have a religious ritual into which he can retreat. He has been careful to do everything the way it should be done. He has asked that the front door be left on the latch so that guests can come and go at will without pressing the security buzzer. Tracy arranged for two security guards to stand at the outside gate and ensure no journalists got through. Inside the house, he has overseen the covering of every mirror with black cloth. He has not shaved or washed. He has pinned a torn ribbon to his jacket. He is wearing a yarmulke.

Claudia has kept a respectful distance. She doesn't understand why, after years of self-declared atheism, her husband has suddenly rediscovered his spiritual side but she tries hard to be sympathetic. When he first called from the police station to tell her they'd found Ada, she had immediately offered to come and be with him but Howard hadn't wanted her there. It seemed right that it was Penny instead who comforted him. It seemed right that the two of them, the ones who had brought their daughter into being, the ones who had let her down in some indefinable way, should face their failure alone.

It had been after midnight when Jocelyn had driven him home but Claudia had waited up for him. When he walked into the sitting room, the fire was on. His new wife – the one who always seemed new even when she wasn't – stood in front of the mantelpiece in a silk dressing gown. She didn't know whether to come to him or not. She was nervous, he could see that.

'I'm so sorry, Howie,' Claudia said and she started to walk towards him but he shrank back without meaning to and she started to cry, and he felt sickened by her tears which had no purpose and no reason and were only for show.

'Why are you crying?' he asked. 'You didn't even know her.'

He had turned, left the room and shut the door behind him.

The following day, as he made preparations for shiva, Claudia wanted to be helpful but he couldn't find the energy to reach out to her. In the end, he suggested she make herself busy elsewhere and she seized on this gratefully and left. Howard was relieved. It wasn't that he felt irritated by her, not any more. It was that all the emotion he had been wasting on anger or resentment had been siphoned out of him. There was no space for inconsequentiality. There was no room for any feeling other than loss.

As the guests arrive, Claudia passes round plates of food with manicured hands – mini-bagels, bowls of lentils, sweet round pastries. She has dressed dramatically for the occasion in a corseted black skirt from Alexander McQueen and high, patent-leather heels with red soles. He can see her struggling to find the right facial expression, experimenting first with a delicate frown, then a sad smile, then a familiar vacuity onto which the relevant reaction can be projected by whomever she happens to be speaking to. He feels, in spite of himself, a wave of fondness. Because he knows now it will end. He can no longer pretend.

Penny is not there. Howard had wanted her to come but she said it wouldn't seem right and she didn't want to encroach on Claudia's territory. Besides, she wasn't Jewish and he knew she'd rather wait to have a proper memorial service when the time was right. Non-denominational, she said, so that anyone could come if they wanted to. He understood, didn't he? And Howard did. It would all happen in good time, he said.

He hasn't eaten all day. He picks up a mini-bagel, filled with cream cheese and smoked salmon, but the smell of it turns his stomach and he puts it back on the platter. He hasn't cried, either. Not since that visit to the morgue to say his final goodbye to Ada. Not since then.

The police had taken him to the morgue in the evening, after they'd dropped Penny back at her flat in Fulham. He had a memory of that night he knew he would never share with anyone else. It couldn't be expressed and it couldn't be unseen and it would haunt him now until he died.

He had been determined to visit Ada for one last time; had insisted on it in spite of Keith saying that it might upset him. He hadn't known what to expect, although the police did their best to try and warn him. But when he got to the morgue, the strip lighting and the sterile chrome metal trays confused him. Howard had imagined a funeral parlour, with soft music playing and a bed with sheets and flowers. Stupid of him, really. After eleven years, there wasn't going to be anything of Ada left behind. Especially not after what the detective had told him about the murderer throwing fistfuls of maggots over her corpse. Especially not after that.

But when, in the morgue, they said it was Ada in front of him he thought at first there had been some terrible mistake. It was a collection of bones. Not even a full skeleton. Two ribs. Half an arm. A few fingers. And her skull: smaller than he'd imagined and uglier too, with none of the softness of her real face. A faint crack on the top of her head, where her parting would have been. Part of her jaw missing. No heart. No lungs. No skin.

He buried his face in the palm of his hand so that they would not see him weep. But after a while, the tears were coming so fast that it seemed pointless to disguise it.

Keith offered him a stack of tissues.

'I'm so sorry,' he said.

When they finally led him out of that cold, clinical space, Howard sensed a pure, stabbing jolt of anger. He could feel his veins pumping and throbbing, as though his bloodstream had become corrupted by a liquid cloud of rage. He could sense it thickening into black, sticky clots.

He started shouting and swearing, his limbs flailing uselessly as the police held him back. He thought of what that bastard had done to his daughter and he wanted him dead. He had never experienced such distilled hate. An electric surge of it coursed through him. Every nerve ending, every filament of muscle seemed to burst into simultaneous flame. It felt too much to bear and, at the same time, it had to be borne. This was his fate. This is what it meant. And in the midst of it all, from the depths of this riotous collision of thought, was Keith's voice: calm, clear, certain.

'We'll find him, sir,' Keith said. 'We will.'

Esme

T HE *TRIBUNE* NEWSROOM IS in overdrive. Ada Pink's identity is confirmed on Friday evening, which means the entire
section has to be redesigned in under twenty-four hours. A guilty
frisson of excitement spreads through the office. The sound of
typing becomes a frantic metronome. There are large television
screens on each wall, filtering the muted words of every major
news channel into the office. Polystyrene cups of tea are left to
cool. Ringing phones are answered with a swift, one-syllable
'Yes?'. There is no extraneous chatter and yet it feels as though
they are able to communicate and move telepathically as one.
Every word that is written seems to emerge from the depths of a
synchronised, collective consciousness. They are a multi-headed
beast, a fearsome hydra of news.

They had suspected since this morning that it was Ada Pink,
ever since Cathy had come back with her scoop: an exclusive,
sit-down interview with the woman who had made the discovery
while watering her neighbour's plants.

Dave had whooped with delight when he heard.

'It's almost too good to be true,' he said when Cathy told him.
'Tripping over the remains of one of the most famous missing
persons in the country while watering the wisteria.'

'Jasmine,' Cathy interjected.

'Whatever,' Dave said. 'Write it up at 1,500 words. Loads of
colour about the old dear, the fact she never suspected bla bla

bla, he seemed perfectly nice, et cetera, never had any trouble from him but little did she know she was living next door to a cold-blooded killer. You're a pro, you know the kind of thing.'

Cathy nodded. 'What about the Ada Pink line? I know it's her. The look she got in her eyes when I mentioned Ada's name – it was obvious.'

Dave hesitated. There was an undone button at the bottom of his shirt and when he crossed his arms, the material gaped and Esme could make out the slightest curlicue of dark hair beneath. She tried not to think about it. Ever since that pint with Dave a few weeks ago, she had felt differently about him. It was an almost imperceptible shift but she was hopeful that the ill-advised crush she had nurtured for well over a year was, at last, receding. About time, she thought gratefully.

'Tricky,' Dave said. 'But we can't go there legally. We don't have on-the-record confirmation.'

Cathy nodded.

'Perhaps Esme could work on that,' she suggested, twiddling her pen in what was intended to be a nonchalant manner, and the two of them looked over and Esme's heart sank. She didn't relish the prospect of calling up a man who had potentially just been informed his daughter had been horrifically murdered and asking if he'd like to comment on media speculation over her identity. Especially not a man who had been kind to her, professionally speaking; a man with whom she felt a kind of empathy.

She couldn't admit this to her colleagues, and especially not to Dave, but she had a connection with Howard Pink. Perhaps she flatters herself to believe that she understands him, but there is something in his manner that speaks to her.

When she looks at Sir Howard now, Esme no longer sees him as a boorish, brash millionaire whose primary concern is the bottom-line. She had viewed him like that before, when her knowledge of him was based on newspaper articles and TV appearances and disobliging profile pieces written by journalists bitter they hadn't got an interview. But now they had met, Esme saw his behaviour as a necessary carapace: a constructed defence against a world he expected to be hostile. After the disappearance of his father, the death of his mother, the loss of his daughter and the breakdown of his first marriage, Sir Howard had invented his own narrative to replace the crueller one fate had dealt him. And there was no better disguise, Esme realised, than obscene amounts of money. A personal fortune dazzles even the most curious bystander. It deflects any questions. Because how could someone be unhappy when they were so rich? What gave him the right to grieve?

'Happy to,' she said to Dave, not meaning it. She'd put in a call to Rupert and hope that it was his voicemail so she could leave a message. Cathy smiled at her.

'Thanks, Esme,' she said patronisingly. 'I'll give you an add-rep if you get anything.'

Esme pretended to smile. An add-rep was an additional reporter credit, stuck in italics at the end of a piece so that no one could see it. Cathy had said it on purpose. She knew how the older woman's mind worked, how territorial she was. Cathy defended her bylines in much the same way as sixteenth-century merchants protected their treasures by building fortified castles against pirate invasions. And if she had a chance to pull rank while doing so, then so much the better.

Cathy was going to be completely insufferable now. The editor had already sent her a herogram over email. Esme wouldn't normally have minded so much or, at least, she would have done a better job of pretending not to mind – but she felt she had ownership over the Howard Pink story and was frustrated not to have been one step ahead of her colleague. And, although she would never own up to this in the newsroom, there was a part of her that felt sad. She liked Sir Howard. She tried not to let on to the others. They would be derisive. Sir Howard wasn't the usual cuddly parent of a missing child, wheeled out to elicit sympathy every few years or so. As a reporter, she knew, you were expected only to have so much humanity but no more. If you felt too much, it would be the undoing of you.

But in the end, she never had to make the call to Sir Howard because events overtook them. The news that it is indeed Ada Pink's body under the flower bed in SW18 drops on the wires just as Esme is getting ready to go for a Friday night drink with Sanjay at the Elephant and Castle. When it happens, Dave is in his element. He thrives under pressure and treats a breaking news story as if it were a crucial military campaign.

Esme, who had been in the process of gathering up her coat and bag, sits back down again and watches as Dave comes striding out of his office in his shirtsleeves, barking out orders about word counts and drop intros and getting the fucking graphics department to pull their fucking finger out. In this kind of situation, his brain operates on a higher frequency than anyone else's.

It's not that he is callous, exactly; it's just that he sees the story in everything. He knows tragedy makes good copy. When, a couple of weeks ago, Prince Philip had been taken into hospital for a bladder infection, Dave had walked around with a flicker of a smile on his face for days and pulled up the pre-prepared obituary with what could only be described as glee. He was genuinely disappointed when the Prince pulled through.

Esme has witnessed him in full flow before. He can visualise, in his mind's eye, the way the pages should be laid out. He knows instinctively which rent-a-quotes he should call, what size a headline should be and which photo to use. He relishes the spirit of inventiveness that a tight deadline gives him. He is a human adrenalin pump, capable of injecting a surge of energy into anyone who comes within a 5 metre radius. When a big story breaks, Dave circles the office with his voice raised to just below shouting level. Occasionally he'll give a word of encouragement as he passes your desk. Sometimes, he will launch into a non-specific bollocking just to keep the pace up. Mostly, he'll give a reporter a yellow Post-it note onto which he's scribbled a single word which is intended to get them thinking along certain lines. These notes are always accompanied by a question mark, although whether interrogative or gently querying, Esme is never entirely sure.

He is walking towards Esme's desk now, bearing down on her with a furious look on his face.

'Esme,' he says and she knows that's a bad sign because he hardly ever uses her full name. 'Where did you get to with speaking to Howard Pink?'

'I put in a phone call to Rup –'

'You put in a fucking phone call? Great. Well done. Gold fucking star. And am I right in thinking that that phone call delivered precisely the square root of fuck all?'

Esme nods.

'Jesus H. Christ.'

He sweeps his hair back with his hands. Esme chews her lip. She lifts the phone, props it under her ear and says in what she hopes is a conscientious fashion, 'I'll follow up now.'

Dave looks at her. His skin is flushed and he has dry, red patches at the corners of his mouth. There is a pause and Esme can see him weighing up whether to carry on being angry or not, just to make a point. He decides to be lenient.

'Good,' he says finally and then he turns his attention to Sanjay who looks like a terrified squirrel and says yes to everything Dave asks.

She catches sight of the TV on the far wall. A blonde anchorwoman on *Sky News* is doing a two-way with a man in a raincoat at the end of Lebanon Gardens. The rolling news ticker across the bottom of the screen flashes up with 'Breaking'. Then it says that Alan Clithero, the prime suspect in the murder of Ada Pink, has been arrested in Scotland. A still photograph of Clithero comes up. It is the one all the papers have been using for days, of him wearing a green tracksuit top and smiling stupidly, a gap between his two front teeth, a sprig of tinsel hanging from a window in the background.

'Dave,' Esme says. At first he doesn't hear her so she has to stand up and tap him on the sleeve. 'Dave,' she says again.

'What?'

She points at the TV. 'They've arrested him.'

In an instant, the clatter of the newsroom dies down. Several reporters stand to watch the unfolding events on screen. Someone finds a remote control and turns up the volume so the anchorwoman's voice booms out.

'. . . that he was hiding out in a remote part of the Highlands, do you have any more detail on that, Gavin?'

There is a time delay as Gavin, his hair ruffled by a gust of wind, raises one finger to press in his earpiece and replies, 'No, not as yet, Anna. We'll get you more news on that as and when we have it. What we can tell you is that Sir Howard and his ex-wife, the former Lady Pink, have been informed and we have been told there will be a statement from them later this evening.'

The screen cuts away to show library footage from a few days earlier of Sir Howard and a petite woman with tidily bobbed hair going into a modern-build terraced house, surrounded by police. The woman has her head down and is holding a scrunched-up tissue to her nose. The police are trying to shelter them as best they can, lifting their arms so that the cameras don't get a clear shot. But then, just before he walks through the front door of Number 12 Lebanon Gardens, Sir Howard turns back and the screen freezes on a perfect still of his face. Esme keeps watching. He seems to be staring directly at her and it is a look Esme recognises.

At first, she cannot place it. But the more she stares, the more familiar it becomes. And then she remembers. A hospital corridor. Dark outside. The smell of disinfectant and boiled cabbage. Sitting on a hard chair, feeling her skirt bunched up with sweat beneath her thighs. Holding her brother's hand because Robbie was tired and starting to grizzle and she didn't want him to make a scene. Footsteps squeaking. Wheeled trolleys. A distant moan. Light snoring. The rattle of a curtain being drawn around metal rails. A nurse answering a phone call and smiling at them as she spoke. A big purple tin of Quality Street chocolates on the counter.

And at the same time, a vision of her mother walking towards them. She was walking slowly and she was covering her mouth with her hand, trying to stifle the sobs because she didn't want to scare the children and she couldn't lose control of herself, not now, not when she had to keep a grip on things for their sake.

Esme remembers her mother kneeling down on the floor in front of them and thinking how odd it was to see her do that, how she was usually so particular about the right way to behave. She didn't even wipe the floor first, Esme thought. She could be picking up all sorts of germs.

And there was that look, the same look that she sees now on Sir Howard's face. Despair greeted with numb recognition.

It is the look Esme's mother has on her face when she tells them their father is dead.

In the newsroom, the typing resumes and the television is muted again. Esme sits and tries to focus on the trail of words lengthening across her computer screen. But she feels faint and has to rest her head on her arms. Bile rises in her throat and she thinks she is going to be sick. She dashes to the toilet, letting the door slam behind her. When she kneels on the tile floor with her head over the bowl, nothing comes out and she retches drily instead.

She thinks of Ada Pink, of the single reproduced photograph of her used over and over again through the years depicting her delicate face, her sad eyes, the dip below each cheekbone and she can't help but let her mind wander to imagine Ada in the hands of that grinning psychopath, in a state of frenzied terror, being subjected to the worst kind of pain one human being can inflict on another.

She thinks of her corpse being buried, of Ada's pretty features becoming blurred and indistinct underneath scattered lumps of soil until they gradually disappear altogether and then this picture is superimposed by the memory of Sir Howard's face as he walked into that house and also by the recollection of her mother telling Esme her father had died and then, without meaning to, she thinks of her father and for the first time in years, Esme can

314

see his face, the heavy-lidded eyes, the craggy outline of his jaw, the long strip of each sideburn carefully delineated as if lit up from behind like an X-ray. She shuts her eyes tightly, unwilling to let go of this precious scrap of memory.

There is a loud knock.

'Esme, are you OK?' It's Sanjay.

She unlocks the cubicle door.

'I was worried about you.' Sanjay crouches down and hands her a cold can of Coke. 'Got you this. Thought your blood sugars might be low.'

She accepts the can gratefully and presses the metallic coolness to her neck before opening it. When she takes a sip, the synthetic sweetness hits the back of her tongue and she senses an instant release of energy. She realises she hasn't eaten since breakfast.

'Thanks, Sanj.'

He shifts into a sitting position, sliding down onto the floor, with his back resting against the paper towel bin and his legs stretched out in front of him. He appears to be magnificently unconcerned about being in the ladies' loos.

'It's awful, isn't it, when you stop and think?' he says. 'All these years . . .'

She doesn't reply. He takes off his glasses and rubs his eyes with his knuckles.

'Don't be too hard on yourself,' Sanjay continues. 'Sometimes it's good to let things get to you. It means you're human. It means you care.'

He holds out his hand. She lets him take hers and he squeezes it gently before letting it drop.

'Thanks,' she says again, her voice croaky.

'Don't mention it' Sanjay says, brushing down his trousers and pushing himself into a standing position. And then, 'Best get to it.'

They work into the night. Esme puts in another call to Rupert who – as expected – doesn't answer, so she follows up with a carefully worded email, describing how sensitively any piece would be handled and offering him quote approval (something she rarely did, but needs must). In the meantime, Dave asks her to go through her transcript from the Howard Pink interview and cull any quotes about his daughter that they hadn't already used.

'We can cobble something together,' he says, standing behind her desk as she types so that she can sense his presence, the bristle of his physicality, the barely constrained enthusiasm in his words. News is his drug, Sanjay had once told her when she first joined, before going on to explain that, for Dave, it was like smoking crack: there's a big hit at first, then you end up a glassy-eyed addict scrabbling for even bigger highs. Before you know it, you're lusting after tragedy like a rubber-necker on a motorway – more accidents, more earthquakes, more wars, anything so that you can be first, get the scoop, print it better than anyone else. And then, once Sunday comes and the paper is on the news-stands, there's the inevitable comedown. Thinking about it now, Esme wonders if that's why Dave has affairs: he needs the chaos. It is only when he is on the verge of losing control that he feels truly in his element.

'In his last interview before she was found,' Dave is saying. He is leaning forwards now, his hands on the back of her chair and she can smell him – a ferric scent like an open tin of soup. 'Then put in loads of colour about his house, the pictures of his daughter, the bedroom that's never been touched . . .'

'The bedroom has been touched.'

'I'm improvising, Es.'

They look at each other. She thinks of that pint in the pub, of how much she'd wanted him and how swiftly that intensity had dissolved. Part of her feels guilty for it and surprised at how instant the change had been. She reassures herself it wasn't that her emotions had been insincere or fraudulent. It was more that they didn't exist in a realistic space. Dave, for her, was attractive only in context – in the newsroom, like this, knowing exactly what to do, exercising power and earning respect. Outside, he was a middle-aged man with dry skin and a tendency to practice swings with an imaginary golf club. It was that simple. She can't believe it has taken her this long to come to the obvious conclusion and, now that she has, it is a relief. She isn't going to throw her life away pursuing disastrously unrequited love with a married man who shags around. She isn't going to jeopardise her career by sleeping with the boss. Her mother will not have cause to be even more disappointed with her. She can breathe again.

'OK,' Esme says. 'I'll bash this out and then I'll get started on the Clithero timeline.'

'Great. I want the whole lot: where he was born, what his parents did, the name of his fucking favourite childhood teddy.'

She grins.

'Yes, boss.'

Without thinking, Dave reaches out and rests his hand lightly on Esme's shoulder. She can see him notice what he has done and then he takes it back quickly, almost as if it never happened. But the imprint of his palm is still there.

On the other side of the desk, Sanjay is staring at her.

'You want to be careful there,' he says archly.

'Oh please,' Esme counters. 'He's old enough to be my . . .'

'Brother?' Sanjay says. They giggle and then can't stop. Sanjay starts snorting with mirth which only makes it worse. The clock on the wall says it's almost one in the morning. At this stage of the working day, a bit of light hysteria is to be expected.

In the end, she gets home just before 2 a.m. and rolls into bed in her pyjamas, forgetting to brush her teeth or turn off the kitchen light. Dave had insisted she get a taxi and expense it, even though she'd said she was perfectly fine getting the night bus. In truth, she was going to get a taxi anyway but she knew that in a climate of repeated redundancy rounds and cut-backs, it was always wise to show budgetary awareness.

Esme was up again at 6 a.m. and in the office half an hour

later. It was a Saturday and the roads were clear. There were lots of disadvantages to working Saturdays (the friends' weddings you missed, the fact you could never go away last-minute for the weekend, the knowledge that no one else with a normal life wanted to have a big night out on a Sunday) but one of the upsides, Esme always thought, was how quiet the office was.

In the early morning light, it felt curiously calm. And there was an unspoken camaraderie among the reporters that you didn't get on a daily. On a Saturday, everyone wore casual clothes which brought out their most vulnerable selves, the ones you could imagine pushing a child on a swing or going for a pub lunch with friends rather than the ones who, in suits and shirts and gelled-back hair, would doorstep a grieving mother for hours in the rain or write a hatchet job on a politician who'd cheated on his wife or make bad-taste jokes about a glamour model's disabled child. It wasn't just clothes, it was armour.

'Morning Cathy,' Esme calls out as she walks through the door, clasping a large latte in one hand and the Saturday edition of the *Tribune* in the other. Cathy and Dave are the only other people already in. Cathy, who seems not to possess casual clothes, is still in the neat sleeveless silk blouse she was wearing yesterday. She has headphones on and is transcribing, peering at the lit-up computer screen over half-moon spectacles. She doesn't look up when Esme comes in but raises a hand. Esme wonders briefly if Cathy's been here all night. She wouldn't put it past her.

Dave is in his office, leaning back with his feet on the desk, talking on the phone. He is wearing a blue fleece and bad jeans and Timberland boots. He is one of those people who has never entirely got the hang of how to dress as grown man.

Esme switches on her Anglepoise lamp, logs on and continues to stitch together the timeline of Alan Clithero's strange and disturbing life. Ever since he was found by police yesterday, hiding out in a remote bothy in a windswept part of the Scottish Highlands, details have been emerging in dribs and drabs.

He was born in Renfrewshire, the youngest of four brothers

and three sisters. Aged seven, he was sent to reform school. At fifteen, he was already in a young offenders' institution. After that, there was a series of relatively minor convictions for burglary and assault and then Alan Clithero seemed to have straightened himself out. There was nothing for a few years. He finally re-emerged, aged twenty-five, getting married to a woman called Patricia who described herself as a librarian on the certificate.

A quick Google reveals that Patricia Clithero has already been bought up by the *Sun* who have splashed on their exclusive interview. The web piece is headlined: 'The wife of the Southside Strangler speaks for the first time'. Esme scrolls through, culling each line for useful information.

'When we first met he was such a gentleman,' Patricia is quoted as saying. 'He used to open doors for me and all sorts. Lovely manners. But it wasn't long before he turned on me. He'd drink himself half to death and lash out . . . I'm not surprised he did something bad. He was a bomb waiting to go off.'

There is a photo of Patricia looking suitably grim-faced, wearing a lilac roll-neck and focusing at a point just beyond the camera, chin raised in defiance. Her skin is wrinkled and saggy. A smoker's face, Esme thinks uncharitably. She finds herself furious that Patricia Clithero didn't report her violent husband to the police when she had the chance.

Esme returns to the cuttings. Patricia and Alan lived together in Birmingham, the same city in which Ada Pink went to university. But the marriage didn't last long and many of his acquaintances from that time have told various news agencies that they don't remember him ever mentioning a wife. In fact, no one has a particularly clear recollection of what he was like.

On the Press Association wires, a man who used to play darts with Clithero in a Droitwich pub is quoted as saying, 'He didn't talk much about his past. I always thought he was nice enough but a bit slow, if you get my drift. There didn't seem to be a whole lot going on up there.'

The BBC have got hold of an elderly woman who claims

Clithero used to do odd jobs for her. 'He fixed my sink once,' she says. 'He used to talk about Jesus and knew his Bible back to front. I felt a bit uneasy around him and now I know why.'

The difficulty was that, now Clithero was one of the country's most notorious killers, everyone who had ever known him or claimed to know him would be reassessing their memories in that light. The newsroom would be inundated by phone calls from supposed former friends who 'always thought there was something a bit funny about him' and wanted payment for their startling new insight.

Esme sighs. It is a depressing business. The worst part was reading about what Clithero had done to Ada Pink. She'd been a troubled teenager. As a first-year English undergraduate at Birmingham, she'd got in with a bad crowd and started doing recreational drugs. She didn't fit in with her fellow students and kept herself apart. At nights, she would wander the streets by herself.

There is an interview with a girl called Helen from this time, taken from the *Tribune* and written by someone whose byline she doesn't recognise. Helen describes herself as Ada's best friend. A murky black-and-white picture shows Helen with neat, shiny hair held back by an Alice band. Helen recalls Ada being 'a lovely girl but a bit unstable' who never took part in university social activities.

'I was always trying to bring her out of her shell, to make her laugh,' Helen says, her words still sounding with clarity through the years. 'She said she couldn't sleep so she used to walk a lot. I used to see her through my window, walking around in all kinds of weather. I think she was lonely. I wish now I'd tried harder to reach out.'

Esme imagines Ada Pink, unable to sleep in the cramped bedroom in the halls of residence, putting on her parka and roaming the streets: a slim figure with messily tied back hair, looking for something – anything that would make her feel she belonged.

Alan Clithero had abducted her on a rainy night in February

2001. There is CCTV footage of his beaten-up white van slowing down and parking on a kerb on a dimly lit side-street just before Ada Pink walked past but he had taken the precaution of removing his number plates so the police at the time found it impossible to track him down. This single detail makes Esme's stomach lurch. The premeditation of it. The knowledge that he set out that evening intending to do what he did.

The full details of how Ada died have not yet been released, but the police have confirmed that it was by strangulation. They think she was killed the same night she was abducted which is, Esme thinks, something. At least her terror would have been short-lived. At least he didn't imprison her for months. At least any pain she experienced would have been over before the next morning.

She thinks of Sir Howard and wonders how you cope, as a parent, if these are the only crumbs of comfort afforded to you over your child's death.

She wonders if he is picturing what Ada might have been through, whether he is able to stop himself, or whether the fatal gap between the facts he has been told and all that he doesn't know will plague him for the rest of his life.

She wonders if there are others. More of Clithero's victims, buried underground, waiting to be uncovered.

Esme shuts her eyes. Presses her fingers to her temple. Tells herself to stop thinking. Tells herself to do her job. Opens her eyes. Carries on reading.

After Ada's murder, Clithero shifts around the country every few years. He lives all over the place: Colchester, Cardiff, Portsmouth, Warminster, Glasgow and then, finally, he moves to Lebanon Gardens, Wandsworth in Spring 2011. And the strange thing is that he takes Ada with him – or what remains of her. Every new town he settles in, his neighbours remember him being a keen gardener. He is good at DIY. He builds patios, decks and barbecues. He installs bird-baths and water features. He takes care of his plants. He waters them, prunes them, turns the soil when needed. He mows the lawn. Most of the time, he is a model citizen. He keeps himself to himself. He is friendly. He chats, but not too much. Sometimes he looks after things when a neighbour goes away on holiday. They entrust him with their keys. He doesn't intrude.

And always, always, there is Ada. Lying underneath the ground. The secret waiting to be found.

At lunchtime, Esme has a raging hunger. She has filed the time-line and first-person piece about the day Sir Howard Pink invited her into his home to talk about the charitable foundation set up in his daughter's name. The timing of it, she is aware, is horribly coincidental. Donations to the fund have poured in since the news of Clithero's arrest. The website has crashed under the pressure. She thinks, for possibly the one hundredth time today, that it's odd how things happen. If you invented this story, no one would believe it.

'Do you want anything, Sanj?' she asks. She gets up and feels a wash of dizziness. 'I'm going to the canteen.'

Sanjay makes a face. 'Ugh. No. Nothing from that hell-hole.'

'Not even a Twix?'

His head snaps up.

'Oh, well OK then. Twist my arm, why don't you.' He makes a big show of looking in his wallet for coins.

'Don't be silly,' Esme says as he knew she would. 'My treat.'

As she is walking downstairs to the canteen, rolling her shoulders backwards the way the lady from Occupational Health told her to, her phone beeps with a text message. It is from a number she doesn't recognise.

'Hi Esme. Thanks so much for meeting me on Sunday. Wondered if you'd let me take you out for a drink to say so in person? Dom xx.'

She feels a flash of surprise, then of pleasure. So she hadn't been inventing it. There was something between them. She thinks of him at Daylesford: his smile, his curly hair, the way he kept looking at her even after she'd finished speaking. She slips her phone back into the pocket of her jeans while she picks up a stale-looking Niçoise salad and a Twix. She hesitates at the chocolate stand and then takes a KitKat as well. It's going to be a long afternoon.

At the check-out, Esme thinks about the text. On the plus side: she likes the fact it has been written without a single abbreviation or emoticon. He had used two kisses. There is a definite undercurrent of flirtation. On the minus side: he could just be being friendly. Maybe he is buttering her up before asking for work experience. He has a girlfriend.

And perhaps it is because she's tired or because she's finally over Dave or perhaps it's because, after everything she's read today, every single gruesome detail, she doesn't have time for bullshit and knows she has nothing to lose. Whatever the reason, she texts back being more forward than she would otherwise have been.

'Don't you have a girlfriend?' she taps out with her thumbs. Then, as it looks a bit bald, she adds in a single kiss. Not two, because she's a sucker for power-play. She hits 'send' before she has second thoughts.

He texts back straight away.

'Not any more. Drink? Tonight? xx'

She says yes.

Carol

SHE ISN'T SURE HOW it becomes a regular thing. All Carol knows is that she has begun to rely on his visits and, more than that, to look forward to them. She measures out her weeks in anticipation of the doorbell ringing and seeing his now-familiar outline picked out against the frosted glass. A few times, she has rushed to the front door and found Vanessa and Archie standing there and she has been ashamed to feel a jab of disappointment, where previously there would have been straightforward happiness at the prospect of spending time with her grandson.

He never tells her when he's coming. She's told him that he doesn't need to, that he can pop in any time and just to send her a text an hour or so beforehand to check that she's in. She doesn't want him to have a wasted journey, even though he reassures her he has a chauffeur and it's really no trouble and that he likes the journey from Kensington, that he finds it relaxing, that he wouldn't mind waiting till she got back from wherever it was she might have gone.

'You can't just stand on the doorstep,' she protested.

'Why not?' he asked.

'You'd be recognised,' she said before she could stop herself, and then she saw the sadness surge into him and that shaded look he sometimes got and she was reminded, all over again, he had been to places she could never have access to. Places she wouldn't want to go, even if she could.

'You're probably right,' he said and since then, he had texted an hour or two in advance of showing up. Carol made sure she always had the kettle filled and ready to go. He wasn't one for biscuits but he had a penchant for Soreen Malt Loaf, which came in a yellow packet and was so dense it felt like a brick every time she picked it up and put it in her shopping basket. She had tried it once and thought it was chewy and bland. It stuck to her teeth like wet plaster but he loved it, especially when she sliced it and spread it with butter. Said it reminded him of his childhood.

It had all started the week after the police confirmed Ada Pink's identity. The press had gone berserk. Her phone rang so many times during the day that she disconnected it. Mercifully, they had stopped knocking at her door, ever since Cathy Dennen of the *Tribune* sneaked in and went on to print a breathlessly worded interview on the day Ada Pink's remains were officially identified. The police had stepped up security outside Carol's front gate and made sure no one went on a tea break without first getting a replacement to stand in for them. She felt trapped. She used to go for a daily walk, just to stretch her legs and get some fresh air, but these days it was impossible to venture outside without being peppered with questions everywhere she went.

Human curiosity was insatiable, she learned, to such an extent that the local residents, and Connie in particular, seemed to forget there was a human tragedy involved. Even Vanessa wanted to pump her for details about what Alan was like and she has run out of things to say. She doesn't want to talk about him any more. She wants to forget Alan ever existed.

Carol still thinks of him as Alan. The evil murderer they're talking about on the TV news exists as a separate entity in her head. It is the only way she can cope.

Out of everyone, only Milton and Archie seem to understand. She knows it's stupid to believe cats are capable of human feeling, but Milton genuinely appears to intuit when Carol needs comfort, sidling up to her and weaving between her legs, pressing his soft fur against her calf muscles before leaping up onto her lap, purring gently while she strokes him, allowing the peaceful rhythm of it to soothe her. She has started talking to the cat out loud. At times, she worries she's losing her marbles but then she reassures herself that it's probably a step forward from talking to Derek's photo on her bedside table. After everything that has happened, she finds she can handle the truth of Derek's absence a bit better. She has grown accustomed to living her life around it, even if the hole in her heart will never entirely close over.

Archie, meanwhile, is solicitous and sweet. He chatters happily about school and coming third in the 800 metres on his sports day and the new Star Trek film that he was going to see at the IMAX in 3D for a friend's birthday. He was, thought Carol, turning into a lovely young man. None of that teenage sullenness she'd braced herself for. At least not yet.

And then, of course, there was Howard.

The first time she met Howard Pink had been almost two months ago, in the midst of that mad, surreal time, when the police had asked if she'd mind talking to 'the father of the deceased'. For days, Sir Howard's tense, sunken face had been all over the news. For years before that, she had flicked past his photograph in the newspapers, not giving the multi-millionaire businessman so much as a second thought. She had seen him once on television and thought he came across as pompous and a bit flash.

But after Ada's discovery, his physical presence had shrivelled. Looking at him during the subsequent press conference, when a silky-looking spokesman had read out a pre-prepared statement on his behalf, it seemed as though Sir Howard had been deflated, as if the air had been left to leak out of him so that all that was left were baggy pouches of skin and the startlingly blue-black crescents under his eyes.

She had felt so sorry for him – a man whom she previously believed she had little in common with. She, like him, was the parent of an only child. Carol shuddered to think what she would have done if it had been Vanessa ... she left the thought unexpressed. So when the police asked, she didn't hesitate. She said that yes, of course he could come round. Carol wasn't sure she could give him anything that would be of much help but if he wanted to meet her, she told DCI Lagan, she would do her best to answer any questions he might have.

He came to her house on a Wednesday afternoon. She remembers the time because she'd just been listening to the afternoon play on Radio 4 with Milton on her lap. It was a bad play, she recalls. One of those new writing jobs where they got someone you'd never heard of to riff on one of that week's news stories and then employed a series of British actors who tried to put on American accents and make clip-clopping sounds with coconut shells to suggest horses riding into the distance.

This time, she was listening to the afternoon play to take her mind off the nerves. She'd never entertained a millionaire before, after all. Did they eat the same things as the rest of us or was it all caviar and oysters covered in gold leaf? She'd read a story a while back about a banker who'd spent his entire £250,000 bonus on champagne at a fancy nightclub. At the time, Carol had been more shocked by the size of the bonus than by the fact he'd blown it all on something called Cristal.

'Honestly, Mum,' Vanessa had said. 'That's not even a big one. Most of these guys get a million-pound bonus like that—' and she'd clicked her fingers to emphasise the point. 'It's what got us into this mess. That and sub-prime mortgages.'

Carol was fairly certain that Sir Howard Pink must have got a few bonuses in his time. She wasn't sure what he'd make of her Charles and Di biscuit tin. She had, however, managed to buy some paper doilies in Waitrose and had made a pretty arrangement of biscuits on one of her best plates. She'd covered the dining-room table with an embroidered linen cloth inherited from Derek's mother and she had put a bright vase of freesias at its centre. Looking at the display, she felt as prepared as she could be.

When the bell rang, her heart gave a little thud. She pushed herself up off the chair and Milton gave a disgruntled yelp as he leapt to the floor.

'Sorry, puss,' she muttered, drawing her cardigan tighter. She was wearing her best skirt, a pale blue blouse with pearl buttons and a smart cashmere wrap Vanessa had given her for Christmas. It was murder to wash so she only wore it on special occasions. Looking at herself in the mirror above the fireplace, she thought she scrubbed up all right.

When she opened the door, he was looking out at the street and, when he turned round, he was holding a bunch of flowers. She noticed they were freesias – exactly the same colour as the ones she had put in the dining room – but they were in a bigger, more elaborate bunch, the kind that had a bubble of water contained within the cellophane and lots of paper ribbons, like coloured straw.

'These are for you,' he said solemnly.

'Thank you,' she said, taking them from him. They weighed a ton.

He was taller than she'd imagined from television. Tall and beautifully dressed. His raincoat had a checked lining and when she took it from him, she saw that he was in an impeccably pressed suit with a lavender handkerchief poking out of the top pocket. His shoes were freshly polished. Even if she hadn't known he was rich, it would have been easy to guess.

'Please come through,' Carol said, suddenly feeling awkward and slightly ashamed of the squashed proportions of her house. She noticed for the first time the meanness of the windows, the way they hardly let in any natural light, and her gaze rested for a moment on the worn patch of her carpet, where the synthetic threads were showing through like a bald patch.

'You've got a lovely house,' Sir Howard said and he waited for her to show him where to sit. She gestured to a chair. He sat down and looked too big for it: a giant on doll's house furniture. 'Thank you for agreeing to see me.'

'Not at all, Sir Howard, I . . .'

'Please call me Howard.' His voice was rough around the edges. He almost dropped his 'H' and then stopped himself, just in time. She recognised this because she did it herself. Carol had spent so many years trying to sound just a little bit posher than she actually was that it came to her automatically. It was only when confronted with the same desire for self-improvement in others that she saw it reflected in herself. It wasn't a snobbish thing. It was simply a wish to get on in life. Not to be dismissed on first impressions. It had been important for their generation. It was different nowadays, with all those regional accents you heard on television, almost as if they were making a point.

'Howard, then,' she said, pouring the tea that had been sitting underneath a cosy, keeping warm in readiness for his arrival. 'I'm just not sure I can help you.'

He started to open his mouth but she raised a hand to stop him.

'I just want to say, before anything else, how sorry I am for your loss.' Carol had been building herself up to that all day. She had thought carefully about the right words to use. 'As a mother of a girl myself, I can only imagine what you must be going through as parents. You have my deepest condolences.'

He nodded, twice in quick succession, then slumped forward in the chair, shoulders sagging. He propped his elbows on the table. Neither of them said anything and the strange thing was that the silence didn't feel uncomfortable. It felt entirely as it should be.

'Thank you, Mrs . . .'

'Carol.'

'Thank you. That means a lot. You'd be surprised how many people don't say it. Don't say anything, really, because they don't know how. They're . . . embarrassed. They'd cross the street to avoid me.'

'I'm sure that's not true.'

He picked up his cup of tea and lifted it to his lips while holding the saucer. Lovely manners, Carol thought approvingly.

'It is.' He sighed. 'In a way, it's a relief knowing she's not alive. Isn't that a terrible thing to say?'

Carol waited. She sensed he needed her to be silent.

'And then I catch myself thinking that and I hate myself for it. Because I let her down as a dad. And I'm still letting her down by even having those thoughts. And then sometimes, at night, I have these visions . . . these horrible visions of her and what she must've been through, how she must have fought . . .'

He put the cup down.

'What was she thinking then?' he said, the words thickening in his throat. 'What went through her mind?'

Carol pushed the plate of biscuits towards him. It was her default action when things got difficult. Howard didn't notice.

'I don't need answers from you, Carol. I just need . . .' He searched for the right word. 'I need a bit of *peace*. I need to know what he was like. I need to know the worst so that I don't have to imagine it any more.'

He stared at her, baleful, the corners of his mouth slipping into deep wrinkled grooves on each side of his face. It came to her, for the first time, what it meant to be grief-stricken: literally to be struck by an outside force, slammed by the unexpected strength of it.

'Do you understand?' he asked.

'Yes,' she said. And she did.

The first few visits ran along similar lines. Howard would come in, take off his coat, sit down in his too-small chair and start, immediately, to talk. Carol listened. It became, he said, like therapy.

'But cheaper,' Carol joked.

'Yes.' Howard smiled – the first time she had seen him smile. 'Definitely cheaper.'

He had a lot of questions about Alan which she tried her best to answer. What did he tell her about his past? Did Carol ever get a bad feeling about him? Would she ever have suspected? Was he the kind of man to have been violent? Would he have tortured Ada? Would he have raped her?

This last one came up again and again and again until, in the end, Carol had to place her hand on his and say she truly didn't know and she wished she did. The police said the body had been so decomposed that there'd never be any way of telling. All she could say was that neither she nor Derek in a million years would have thought Alan capable of such a thing. Carol didn't know if that meant anything. But when she thought about it herself, in the privacy of her bedroom as she lay on her back, waiting patiently for sleep to come, she found herself believing that Ada's death was an aberration; that Alan hadn't intended it to get that far; that he didn't use her as his plaything or torture her before she died.

Carol knew she was telling herself a story in order to make the whole thing more bearable, but she wanted to believe that maybe there had been a relationship of sorts between Ada and Alan before she died. Maybe he had been in love with her. And maybe there was something fatally lacking within him that meant he couldn't cope with that feeling. He didn't recognise it or know what to do with it. Perhaps it frightened him, the vulnerability of it, the thought that he might lose it. Perhaps the only way he could hold on to the idea of it was to kill it before it was taken away from him.

She never said any of this to Howard but slowly, over the course of weeks, then months, their conversations ventured onto different territory. He told her about his childhood, growing up in Stepney and how his mother had struggled to make ends meet after his father left. He explained how he used to wear hand-me-downs and how he used to scour the streets in search of discarded shoes. He remembered the food parcels his mother got from the Jewish Board of Guardians – demerara sugar, butter beans and margarine – and the shame of going to eat in the soup kitchen. Howard had grown up poor and never wanted to go back to it.

He told her about Penny, whom he had loved, and then he

told her about Claudia, who had been a mistake and whom he was in the process of divorcing. It was fairly amicable, he said, because they'd signed a cast-iron prenup and she wasn't contesting any of it.

'What's a prenup?' Carol asked.

He was very frank with her. Beneath the bluster and the immense wealth, Carol was surprised how much they had in common. She knew that Derek would have liked him and wished they could have met. She had never imagined Howard's background would be so modest, that everything he had made was a result of his own hard work. His self-reliance impressed her. She said that to him once and he was genuinely touched.

'Not many people give me credit for that,' he replied. 'Most people just see the flash stuff and think I'm a wa—' He stopped himself. 'A bit of an idiot. Fair enough, I s'pose. I'm not a good person, deep down.'

'Why would you say that?'

He grimaced, tapped his fingers on the table edge and stared out at the garden. He took a while to respond.

'I've done things I'm ashamed of, things I can never undo,' he said finally. 'I hate myself for that. Because now, after everything that's happened, I wish I'd been a better person and then, maybe . . .'

He let the thought drift.

'Maybe Ada wouldn't have been killed?' Carol said. He nodded. 'But maybe, Howard, you did those things you're ashamed of *because* Ada went missing. Maybe you thought you didn't deserve happiness.'

She was becoming quite the psychiatrist, Carol thought. She wouldn't normally have ventured such a bold opinion to a man she'd only met a few weeks ago, but it was odd with Howard. She felt she could speak her mind. That she knew him. That she helped him. It was good to feel that again – to feel needed.

* * *

332

Today is a special day. It is the first time she is going to Howard's for tea. He had invited her, Vanessa and Archie a fortnight ago and Carol has been in a state ever since. She is nervous about how to behave in what will, she is convinced, be a vast and intimidating mansion. In her head, his house has acquired gargantuan proportions and several dozen uniformed staff so that she more or less ends up thinking of it as Downton Abbey and spends hours agonising over what to wear and how to do her hair. Underlying her anxious anticipation is a different sensation, one that she refuses to acknowledge is there. But if she were being honest with herself, Carol would have to concede that the fizzle she feels in the pit of her stomach is very close to being excitement.

Vanessa has been gently amused by the whole thing. When Carol's daughter arrives at Lebanon Gardens, she takes one look at her mother and does a wolf whistle.

'Very nice, Mum,' she says, drawing out all the vowels to make some sort of point.

Carol bats away the compliment. Archie bowls past her into the hallway and says, 'Can I go on the computer, Grandma?' and she laughs and reminds him that he hasn't even said hello so he comes up to her and gives her a nice, big hug. He is wearing a smart jumper she hasn't seen before and his grey school trousers with proper shoes. His hair is brushed.

'You look very handsome,' Carol tells him and he squirms with embarrassment.

Vanessa leans forward to kiss Carol on both cheeks. She notices that Vanessa, too, has made an effort. She has put on those three-quarter-length trousers which show off her lovely long legs and a summery red top with some sort of floral pattern around the neck, instead of her usual black.

'How are you, Mum? Do we have time for a quick cuppa?'

'Well, Howard said he'd send a car at three—'

'A car?!' Vanessa shrieks. 'Wow.'

'You don't mind, do you?' Carol asks. 'Coming with me?'

333

They walk into the hallway together. Archie sprints up the stairs and Vanessa loops an arm round her mother's waist.

'Course not. We're looking forward to it. Archie's pretty excited about meeting his first millionaire.' Carol winces. Vanessa hesitates, then says more quietly, 'It's nice that you have a new friend. I'm really pleased. We both are.'

For no reason she can understand, Carol feels sad. She busies herself at the sink so that her daughter won't notice. She looks out of the window, across to the garden fence next door, and thinks of what happened beyond it. They'd recently put Number 12 on the market. There was a red Andrews Estate Agent 'For Sale' sign outdoors. Out the back, the police had tidied up as best they could but it remained a scrappy, dank patch of earth trodden over by footprints, bearing the trace of forensic markings.

Besides, everyone had read about the case. She couldn't imagine anyone wanting to pay money to live there. Daniel, the estate agent, told her that the only viewers he'd had so far were the true-crime fans, who came armed with a thousand ghoulish questions and took photos of the home of a real-life murderer on their phones. Carol thought it was disgusting. She wished the council would raze the whole building to the ground. She knew, without having to be told, that the price of her own house would be affected but she didn't mind. Number 10 had always felt safe; it was still her little haven. Carol wouldn't want to move out of the home she made with Derek for all those years. She thinks of Derek, of all that has happened since she lost him, of all the things in her life that she will never be able to share with him and then she remembers Howard and how affectionate she feels towards him and how they are going to his house for tea and Derek won't be there and she has to bite her lip to stop herself from crying.

Vanessa comes up behind her and places a hand on her mother's shoulder.

'It's not a betrayal, Mum,' she says. 'Dad would want you to be happy.'

Carol turns away from the sink, her hands damp. Vanessa, knowing instinctively what needs to be done, wraps her arms around her without another word and holds her mother tightly to her chest.

Jocelyn, the chauffeur, comes to pick them up and rings the bell on the dot of three. Carol has got to know him a bit. When Howard visits, she always offers Jocelyn a drink because she feels bad that he has to wait outside on his own, but for some reason he never accepts and has not once crossed the threshold into her house.

Still, they've chatted, with her standing on the pavement while he leans out of the door on the driver's side. He is a shy man and speaks uncertainly, as though always expecting someone to tell him he's wrong. He's very dashing and Carol is surprised by this, even though she thinks it's wrong of her to be so. Why shouldn't a chauffeur look like Gregory Peck in *Roman Holiday*, she asks herself? But even so, Jocelyn's looks take her unawares every time she sees him. She had even wondered if she could set him up on a date with Vanessa but then she suddenly thought he might be gay and she didn't want to risk the embarrassment. Besides, her last attempt at setting her daughter up with a strange man wasn't what you'd call successful.

Archie is impressed by the car.

'Wow, Grandma, look!' he says when they are all safely ensconced in the back, breathing in the reassuringly expensive smell of leather, and he twiddles a knob that makes his seat slide backwards and a foot-rest whir up underneath his legs.

'Very nice,' Carol says, with deliberate coolness. It's important that Archie realises money isn't the be all and end all.

The journey across London is suspiciously smooth. Can it really be, thinks Carol, that when you're rich even the traffic lights go in your favour? As they sail over Battersea Bridge, Vanessa's BlackBerry beeps. Vanessa gives it a cursory look, then catches her mother's eye and groans.

'Ok, Mum, I'm switching it off right now,' and she makes a big show of pressing the power button with exaggerated emphasis. 'Happy?'

'Yes, sweetheart. Thank you.'

She reaches out to ruffle Archie's hair. Carol knows she shouldn't but she can't help herself. He shrinks away, says a half-hearted 'Gerroff' but he is grinning so she knows it's all right really.

When they get to the house, Carol is relieved to see that it is smaller than she imagined. It is set back slightly from the road, behind a security gate: an imposing, red-brick edifice with large windows and creeping branches of ivy sprayed across the façade. He'll want to cut that back, she thinks.

Jocelyn swings the car into a concealed driveway, further along from the main entrance. He has a buzzer on a key ring that he presses to open the automatic gates and when he parks up on the gravel, he comes out of the driving seat and goes straight to Vanessa's side of the car, opening the door with a flourish.

'Madam,' he says, holding out his hand. Vanessa rolls her eyes at her mother, but she takes the proffered hand anyway and Carol can tell she loves it. The front door opens before they have a chance to use the brass knocker and there is a diminutive woman standing before them in a blue uniform, taking their coats and ushering them into the hallway which is a grand, square space with flagstones and a polished oak sideboard bearing an enormous bunch of white roses arranged in a crystal-glass bowl.

There are rapid footsteps from another part of the house and suddenly Howard is rushing down the stairs, beaming at them.

'Come in, come in,' he says, rushing towards them. 'Thanks, Theresa, I'll take them through.' Carol has never seen him look so jolly. He is talking more rapidly than usual and she wonders briefly if he might be as nervous as she is.

'It's so nice of you to come,' he carries on. 'You must be Vanessa, I've heard so much about you. And this – this – well, I know who this is, don't I? You're the man of the house, I hear.

336

Apple of your grandma's eye. Archie, isn't it?' He shakes Archie's hand formally. 'Nice to meet you.' Archie, stunned into silence, doesn't speak. Vanessa jostles his shoulder and gives him one of her looks.

'Nice to meet you too,' Archie says, stuttering. Howard laughs.

'You're very polite. You'll go far with manners like those.'

Still holding on to Archie's hand, Howard locks his eyes onto Carol's and she feels a tremble of loveliness, all the way down her spine. He comes across, kisses her on the cheek and she realises that she recognises his smell. That she would know it anywhere. He leads them into the house, with a gentle hand in the small of her back, and Vanessa is smiling and Carol can tell she's relaxed, that she already likes Howard more than she thought she would.

'Do you like cake, Archie?' Howard is asking. Archie nods. 'What's your favourite kind?'

Archie thinks carefully.

'Lemon drizzle,' he answers. Howard's face drops. Archie, sensing his disappointment, continues hastily, 'Or chocolate.'

'Aha!' Howard says, pushing open the door into the sitting room. 'Now that *is* a coincidence, because look what we have here.'

There, sitting on the coffee table next to a fan of glossy magazines and in front of an unlit fire, is the largest chocolate cake any of them have ever seen.

Beatrice

THE RIVER, REFRACTING SUNLIGHT, is a sliver of crumpling tin foil. Beatrice had never imagined the Thames
would look so beautiful up close. They are standing at the edge
of Bishop's Park in Fulham, overlooking the railings and a wall
that slips straight down into the water. Tracy had suggested it
would be a nice day out.

'Make the most of the weather,' she'd said. 'We've waited
long enough for summer, haven't we?'

They had. For weeks, London had been enveloped in a blanket
of cloud. Today was the first time this year Beatrice had felt brave
enough to wear a short skirt without tights.

Standing at the railings, she feels the September breeze on the
backs of her legs. She breathes in, inhaling the scent of the river:
a rich, mineral smell like a soaked sponge.

The light is so clear Beatrice can see all the way to the opposite bank. She watches as a group of rowers climbs into a long,
slim boat that seems too fragile to carry the weight of six men.
One of them stands thigh-deep in water, steadying the boat as
the other rowers slide into their positions. From this distance,
their every movement seems elegant. They take up their oars,
push away from the bank and glide off down the river, the
unthinking fluidity of their simultaneous movement like a rip-
pling muscle under skin.

She can just about make out the drip and eddy of each stroke, the shouted orders from the cox and these sounds mingle with the other noises of a warm day in London: the cries of children on swings, the glockenspiel chords of an ice-cream-van tune, the faraway judder of a double-decker bus, the quickening pace of a weekend jogger, the thwack and thud of a football being kicked into goal.

'Beautiful day, isn't it?' says Tracy.

'Mmm.' Beatrice wipes her brow with the back of her hand, lifting her face to soak up the welcome heat on her skin. She glances sideways at Tracy, who is wearing reflective sunglasses that remind Beatrice of the security guards in Kampala, the ones who stand at the entrances of posh hotels with upturned mirrors on long metal poles to sweep under each car, checking for explosive devices. At the thought of home, she gets a tightness in her chest. But it passes just as quickly as it came. Her homesickness no longer lasts for weeks on end. She can think of Susan without the simple act of it undoing her. She is getting used to it, to her new home, to the continued absence.

'Shall we go and get some lunch then?' Tracy asks cheerfully.

'Yes. I'm starving.'

Beatrice links her arm through her friend's and they walk into the park, away from the river, past a fountain and a playground with climbing frames and a concreted-over crater that young boys are using to practise their skateboarding, and soon they come to a small café with a plastic sign outside with a picture of a red coffee cup that swings to and fro in the wind.

They sit inside and, despite the heat, they order two bowls of carrot and coriander soup and a ham and cheese baguette that Tracy divides so they each have a half. The paper plate comes with a pile of crisps on one side, an English custom that Beatrice finds ridiculous.

'Crisps are snacks!' Beatrice protests. 'Why not have something proper on there, like potatoes?'

They look at the crisps and giggle. It feels good, Beatrice thinks, to be understood by someone else again.

'This is tasty,' Tracy says, spooning the soup delicately into her mouth, dabbing at the corners of her lips with a paper towel. It is a Saturday but Tracy has still dressed for the occasion as if she's about to be called into a meeting. She is wearing a pair of freshly ironed navy-blue trousers with an off-white shirt, accessorised with her pearl necklace and a jaunty pink scarf. Even this is fairly casual for her. In Uganda, Beatrice thinks, these would be the clothes you saved till Sunday to wear to church.

Beatrice has been working at Paradiso for almost three months. For the first time since arriving in this country, she has a bank account, into which her salary is paid with reassuring regularity, and she is accumulating a healthy stash of savings that she intends to use as a deposit for a one-bedroom flat when the time is right.

Tracy says she should think about moving out of London, to Epsom, because the property prices are cheaper and the rail connections into town are so good, you'd never notice the distance. Beatrice is considering this. She likes the idea of being near her friend but, at the same time, she craves the anonymity of the city. She has grown to love the grit and bustle of London, the way it pumps through you like an exhaust fume: a dirty surge of kinetic energy pushed through the bloodstream each day. She thinks she will miss it if she moves too far away.

'Penny for them,' Tracy is saying.

'I was just thinking how long I've been working at Paradiso, how quickly the time has gone.'

'You're enjoying it, aren't you?' Tracy asks, concerned. 'You don't want to leave?'

Beatrice laughs. 'No! It's the best job I've ever had. Better than the hotel.'

Tracy tuts.

'I don't know how you put up with it there. All that mess.'

'It wasn't so bad.'

They lapse into a companionable silence, watching the café customers come and go. A tall man with a baby in a pushchair comes to the counter, trying to ignore the screams of his child as he places his order. He has sandy hair and is sporting shorts and a pair of those unappealing sandals with Velcro straps that Beatrice has noticed are the special preserve of the English middle-class male.

And then, apropos of nothing, Tracy says, 'It's Ada's memorial service next week.' When Beatrice doesn't respond, she adds, 'Poor Sir Howard.'

Beatrice looks up. She has noticed how frequently Tracy likes to get a mention of their boss into the conversation. She talks about him with such fondness and affection and respect, even though Beatrice feels he treats Tracy as little more than a reliable dogsbody. She does everything for him. It is Tracy who keeps things going. It was Tracy who, in the aftermath of the discovery of Ada Pink's body, fielded the phone calls, who typed the thank-you letters, who cleared Sir Howard's diary without anything needing to be said, who sweet-talked the buyers and the accountants and the CEOs, who dealt with the internal staff complaints and updated Excel spreadsheets without a word, as if she had been doing it all for years. Tracy had kept Paradiso afloat for weeks before Sir Howard returned to work and, when he did, he was looking thinner than before and older, too, with a greyness around his eyes that hadn't been there before.

Even after he came back, Tracy took it upon herself to shield him from the work that had piled up high in his in-tray. She was Sir Howard's gatekeeper, his protector. And it wasn't just a matter of practicality. On an emotional level, also, Tracy seemed to share the acute physicality of his grief. Beatrice had twice walked into the Ladies and found Tracy sobbing into her handkerchief, her make-up in disarray, mascara gathering in dark pools under each eye. It was almost as if Tracy thought she could lessen the burden of Sir Howard's devastation if she felt it as deeply as he did.

It was then that Beatrice realised the truth of the situation. It had been slowly dawning on her for weeks that Tracy was in love with Sir Howard and had been for years. She experienced his sadness in the deep, connected way that only an unrequited lover could. In many respects, the discovery of Ada's body was nearly as bad for Tracy as it was for her boss: Sir Howard had an outlet for his torment but Tracy had to keep it all tied up inside, packaged like a post-room parcel.

Beatrice had tried to comfort her. She would pat Tracy on the back gently as she cried, then take her out to a wine bar round the corner at the end of the day and order her a glass of her favourite Pinot Blush. They would share a bowl of pistachio nuts, flicking open the shells with their nails and leaving behind a trail of salty flakes on the scrubbed pine table when they left.

After a while, Tracy had regained her natural equilibrium and Sir Howard, too, seemed to emerge from a shadow. He still didn't speak directly to Beatrice, but he had taken to smiling at her when he walked down the corridor past her desk. And Beatrice finds that, in spite of herself, she is developing a sort of affection for her employer. The fact that he has endured personal tragedy has, in many ways, made him easier for her to identify with. She recognises pain; respects the withstanding of it. The rest of it, she finds she can almost forgive.

In the café, Beatrice takes a crisp from the side of the plate and holds it up to the light, contemplating whether to eat it or not.

'Go on,' Tracy says with a chuckle. 'It won't hurt you.'

She eats it in one mouthful. It tastes like pickled cardboard.

'When's the memorial service?' Beatrice asks.

'Tuesday morning.'

Beatrice nods.

Tracy moves the crisps back to her side of the table.

'You could come.' Tracy hesitates. 'If you wanted to, I mean.'

'I don't think so,' Beatrice says and then she sees Tracy's eyes, the pleading in them. 'I can come with you if you want company. But I don't want to go to the service. I'll wait for you outside.'

She doesn't explain why. Tracy doesn't ask.

After lunch, they take their bowls back up to the counter and throw away the paper plate so that the waitress doesn't have to clear up behind them. Tracy does this efficiently and without discussion, as though it is the most natural thing in the world. It is one of the many things Beatrice likes about her: that Tracy always thinks about other people.

Outside, the sky is a high, clear blue speckled with small clouds. Tracy proffers her arm and Beatrice links hers through it and they take a stroll through the park, into the grounds of the former Bishop's Palace, where there is a hog roast in full swing and a pretty walled garden open to the public. The two of them dawdle in and out of the neat pathways, past a flower bed filled with vivid purple blooms neither of them knows the name for. They walk underneath the sweep of a willow tree, its branches so low that they have to slouch forwards in tandem to stop their backs being scraped.

The air is heavy with honeysuckle and lavender. Beatrice breathes it in and, as she does so, something unclenches within her. She imagines all her silent anxieties, released like dandelion spores into the warm summer air. They swirl upwards with the barbecue smoke and beyond the tree-tops into the sky where an aeroplane has left a thread of white stitched into the blue so that it is almost as if Beatrice is flying above herself, looking down at the grass and the river and the rowers and there, just to one side of the frame, the two of them, arm-in-arm.

She feels the pressure of Tracy's shoulder against hers. She wonders if now is the right time to tell her, to unburden herself of all the things that she is ashamed to have kept secret. Susan. What happened with Sir Howard. How she blackmailed him into giving her a job. Will Tracy think differently of her when she knows?

'There are things I—' Beatrice starts. She stares straight ahead, focusing on an orangey pebble on the ground that has a soft grey underside like pigeon feathers. She picks the pebble up and clasps it tightly in her hand. She won't be able to carry on if she meets Tracy's eye. 'Things I need to tell you. About me. About how

I came to be working in the office. About—' She coughs. Her throat is dry. She pretends it is the pollen and presses on. 'About how I left Uganda.'

'You don't need to tell me anything,' Tracy says firmly.

'I do, I want—'

'No, Bea, you don't. I already know.'

Tracy has pushed her sunglasses up into her hair. The skin around her eyes is creased with concern. The glossy peach lipstick she always wears is smudged slightly at the corners.

'I don't . . .' Beatrice starts. 'How?'

'Who do you think got the email in the first place? I know what happened. I know what you must think of How . . . of Sir Howard for the way he behaved.'

Beatrice steps back, stumbling. Tracy leads her gently to a bench and they sit next to each other, half a foot apart, not touching.

'I know why you had to come here,' Tracy says eventually. 'I was told everything before you started and, the thing is, I was glad they told me because it meant I could look after you. Or at least, I hope I did. I haven't ever brought it up, Bea, because I thought you might not want to talk about it, that you might be trying to forget. God knows, I would. What you've been through . . . No one should have to go through that.'

Beatrice lets this new knowledge settle. She holds it, weighs it up in her mind, contemplates the size of it. And then, when she is sure of it, she puts it down and lets it go.

'It's all right,' she says. 'I'm glad you know.'

'Are you?'

Beatrice nods.

They sit there, aware that a defence has been breached, that both of them need to get used to this new thickness of the air between them.

'People you love can act in ways you don't understand, can't they?' Tracy asks. She doesn't wait for an answer. 'I'm not sure anyone ever really knows what goes on in someone else's heart.

344

I don't think it means they're bad people or that your love is wasted. It just means they're . . . well, they're trying to see their way through, I suppose. Just like the rest of us. Life's a bit of a muddle sometimes.'

They don't say anything for a while. The park starts to empty: the families with young children go first, the parents carrying their children's scooters and pink rucksacks and squidgy metallic packets of puréed fruit. It gets cooler and the early evening air warps and buckles with heat.

'Come on then,' Tracy says. 'Let's get going.'

They wind their way back towards Putney Bridge, standing aside to let past a group of cyclists. The fountain by the entrance to the park is still working, the flow of water trickling down over the stone. A boy of about nine or ten is reaching up and dipping his fingers into the shallow basin, flicking out his hand to spray his younger sister with the droplets. The little girl shrieks. The boy laughs: a pure bubbling up of joy and she thinks of her brother, of John, and she says a silent prayer for him and promises herself that one day, she will go back. One day. When she is ready. When she is no longer scared of what she will find.

'Let's go onto the bridge,' she says. 'I want to see what the view's like from there.'

They walk up the stone stairs, trailed by a group of bare-chested Australian men who are carrying a disposable barbecue and several bottles of beer. She can smell charcoal and sweat, the faint tang of charred meat. One of the men has his face painted in blue, white and red. Their conversation is friendly and boisterous and Beatrice feels warmly towards them. Perhaps it's the balminess of the day, or the relief of not having to explain all her secrets to Tracy, but she finds that she is no longer intimidated by strangers. She is no longer afraid that she will see the echo of her assailant on every street corner. She realises, at long last, that she feels safe. In this city, at least, she is free.

They walk up to the highest point of Putney Bridge and lean against the V-shaped dip in the wall. Tracy rests on the wall, her chin on her hands. Beatrice hangs back and stares at the water until her eyes begin to itch with the effort. She blinks, then keeps looking. The Thames unspools beneath her, a twisting plait of different currents studded through with a thousand shards of splintered light. A lone kayaker paddles upstream, the splash of his paddle leaving tiny indentations as he moves. The sun, lower now, is leaking into an orange-pink sky.

The pebble is still in her hand. Beatrice closes her fingers around it, feeling the coolness of the stone against her palm, pressing down to imprint its silhouette onto her skin. Then she lifts her arm, stretches it behind her and brings it forward in one swift motion, releasing her fist at the final moment and launching the pebble into the air. Beatrice watches it arc, then drop and she loses sight of it before it hits the water. She thinks of Susan, of her smile, of how she might never see it again. The thought doesn't make her as sad as it should.

She imagines the pebble falling, causing a slight spray as it lands before sinking into the silty blackness.

For a few seconds after the pebble falls, the palm of her hand has a red mark, a suggestion of a shape once held.

This too, will fade.

Howard

THE CHURCH IS FULL. He had known it would be. People want to come to pay their respects. Or they want to come and gawp. Either way, Ada Pink's Memorial Service at the Church of St Bartholomew the Great in Smithfield is extremely well attended.

It had been Penny's suggestion to hold it here, and Howard had liked the church when he'd come to look around. From the outside, it looked like a modest patchwork of brick, set against a skyline punctuated by gleaming skyscrapers in glass and metal. But inside, the church had a high, vaulting ceiling and three balconied tiers in burnished grey stone.

'And it's close to where you grew up,' Penny had said, nudging him with her shoulder.

He smiled. If he closed his eyes, he could almost hear the market traders shouting and jostling for custom. He could smell the freshly baked bagels, their dough warm and spongy in his small hand. He could listen into the stallholders plying their wares. His favourite had been the Indian-toffee man: 'Ask your mummy for a penny, and buy some Indian toffee!' he would cry. Howard used to watch the man casting the coloured sugar into a whirring silver bowl, twisting it deftly around a wooden stick before handing it over, grinning to expose a mouth crammed with gold teeth.

He could remember the old men with beards sitting outside

Whitechapel church and the kosher restaurants, still arguing about the Russian Revolution. He can see, in his mind's eye, a shoal of herrings being pulled from their barrels, sliced and filleted with rapid actions by the fishmongers.

He recalls the pride with which he used to fold each garment purchased from the family stall and the way he used to slip it into a brown paper bag with a satisfying crinkling sound.

He could see his mother at the end of a long day, bent over a needle and thread, sitting close to the window and holding up a seam to the light to check it was straight.

In the church, he squeezed Penny's hand. 'It's perfect.'

It had been fairly easy securing the booking after that. Howard had made a substantial donation towards the restoration fund and a date had been booked for six weeks' time. No one mentioned the fact that he was Jewish and he certainly wasn't going to draw attention to it. Besides, Penny was Church of England through-and-through and came with a glowing reference from her local vicar in Fulham. That seemed to swing it.

Tracy had organised most of the admin: the invitations, the RSVPs, the notice that there would be no flowers, but instead donations to the Ada Pink Foundation – and Carol and Penny had done the rest. It delights him how close the two of them have become over the last six months. They had hit it off as soon as he introduced them over tea at Eden House and he had been surprised by this, by the notion that the two women he loved could find common ground instead of wanting to compete with each other. He'd said as much to Carol that evening and she glossed over it, in that way she always did, as if it were the easiest thing in the world to love him.

'You'll always have a special bond with her,' Carol said. 'Of course you will. It's only natural.'

She snuggled up to him on the sofa and he put his arm around her, resting his cheek on the softness of her hair, and he felt, for the first time in his life, as though he didn't have to explain anything. He was understood. Howard was amazed by this, by the sheer good fortune of it.

'I couldn't have got through this without you,' he said, holding her tighter.

She looked up at him.

'You could've,' she said. 'But you didn't have to.'

The organ wheezes to a halt. The echo of the last line of the hymn catches in the air like a dust mote. There is the shifting sound of three hundred people resuming their seats. A few coughs, the shuffle of shoes, then Howard stands and walks briskly to the front of the church. The eulogy is in his jacket pocket. He pats it, reflexively, but doesn't take it out. He knows exactly what he wants to say.

His footsteps sound cleanly against the worn stone. When Howard turns to face the assembled crowd, he puts his hands on either side of the wooden lectern, clutching at its edges for support. He hadn't wanted to do this, wasn't sure, in truth, that he'd be able to keep it together, but Penny had insisted. She said it was important to say goodbye. That perhaps he'd find speaking therapeutic. Penny had been seeing a grief counsellor and kept wanting him to go along too. Howard had refused. He didn't need to talk to a stranger about his feelings. Not now that he has Carol.

He looks up and seeks her out. There she is: round cheeks, small chin and the big kind eyes he had noticed when he first met her. A lived-in face, made prettier by the faint etchings of lines, the spray of freckles. Carol smiles back at him, nods.

Next to her, Archie is sitting straight-backed in a suit that is too big for him. His mother, Vanessa, has tied her long dark hair up in a bun and looks graceful, like a ballerina. Archie's leg is jiggling and he sees Vanessa reach out and rest her hand on his thigh. Archie stills himself. It is an uncomplicated gesture, the kind only a parent could make. Witnessing it, Howard feels lost.

'I want to tell you about my daughter Ada,' he starts. His voice is weaker than he had imagined it and his words seem to get swallowed into the reverberations of the vast, echoing building. He breathes in, slowly, then out to the count of three.

'She was our only child.' That was better. His throat opens, the air flows through and he finds that each word rises before him perfectly formed, ready to be spoken. 'She wasn't meant to die before her parents. Children never are.'

He speaks and as he speaks, he can sense the curious tingle in the atmosphere, the knowledge that everyone is listening, straining forward to catch every inflection. He speaks and he forgets why he is talking or who he is saying this for and he thinks, instead, of Ada. He speaks and his mind fills with thoughts of her, beautifully crystallised memories in a threaded-together chain. He speaks and as he speaks, the sun bleeds through the stained glass, and slips across the tiled floor of the church in slivers of red, green and yellow. Apart from his voice, there is silence.

He lets his gaze wander. He sees Penny, sitting at the front, in a pale green suit and hat, dabbing at her eyes with a handkerchief. Next to her, Carol is holding Penny's hand, their fingers entwined. He wonders briefly if Carol is thinking of Derek, of her husband whom he has heard so much about. He wants Carol to move in with him. He wants to make her his. But he knows it's too soon. It's only been a few weeks since his divorce with Claudia was finalised. He doesn't want to scare Carol off. He will wait. He will learn to be patient.

Four rows from the back, he sees Tracy, shoulders hunched in tension, her face haggard. She has been working too hard and has taken Ada's death badly – worse than he expected. Howard is touched by this, by the fact that in spite of it all she still respects him enough to be here. They've been through a lot. All those years she's worked for him, never uttering a word of disapproval, never showing what she really thinks. All those Christmas presents he'd sent her to get for Claudia at the last minute – a diamond necklace, a spa voucher, a pair of Jimmy Choo heels. And then: Room 423. The Mayfair Rotunda. The whiff of scandal. A pathetic old businessman who couldn't keep it in his pants, even when he was meant to be marking his daughter's disappearance. How she must have despised him. And yet, she is still here, sitting on the edge of the pew, fidgeting her order of service, trying not to cry. What would he do without Tracy? Loyal, discreet, conscientious Tracy. He must give her a pay rise.

He thinks of Beatrice Kizza. He thought he had seen her in the street earlier as he went into the church, a flash of movement out of the corner of his eye and then a receding figure walking briskly away. But he must have been mistaken. Why would she be here? Why would she accord him the respect?

Tracy seems to like her though. Says Beatrice is an excellent worker. He's noticed her in the office, sitting at her desk, seeming more confident somehow, less apologetic. Her face has lost its sadness. She still has that dignity he'd noticed when he first met her. These days, whenever he sees her neat handwriting on Post-it notes stuck to correspondence piles, he is struck by the curved, squashed Cs, the spiky Ts, the precisely indented full-stops and commas – all of it so controlled, so careful.

He wonders if she has forgiven him. He wonders if he will ever have done enough.

But he's changed, he wants to tell her. He wants to make her understand that he was driven by shame and grief and now he isn't and that everything bad he has ever done in his life has stemmed from pretending to be what he isn't, from believing, deep down, that he would never be good enough, that the pale, spotty, knock-kneed boy from Stepney would never belong.

He feels confident enough to take his hands from the lectern.

'Ada was the one uncomplicatedly good thing I did with my life,' he says and he leans back and looks out at the crowd, the blur of expectant faces. There are friends of Ada here from school and ballet classes. There are neighbours from the past and parents of toddlers who played with her once in the sandpit. There are men and women who knew her from university whom Howard has never met before and he is taken aback by how grown-up they seem, in their suits and skirts and their smart leather handbags. Their self-confidence strikes him almost as an affront. He can't imagine Ada ever being like this. She never got the chance to grow out of her insecurities, never learned how to disguise them.

His business acquaintances are here too – Bradley Minchin, Rebecca Spero, Mark Steiner, the chairman of the Association of British Retail, whose hair is so magnificently bouffant it almost requires a seat of its own, and Mike, the betting CEO whose surname, Tracy tells him, is Foxall. There are, Howard is pleased to see, a smattering of MPs. The Prime Minister has sent his apologies.

Claudia is sitting slap bang in the middle of the church, at the end of a pew in a large black hat with elaborate feathers. She is perfectly groomed and her skin has a shrink-wrapped sheen. Her hair has grown a bit and seems less blonde than it used to. He wonders if she is finally allowing herself to go grey. Looking at her, Howard feels a surge of fondness. She'd barely raised an eyebrow when he brought up the subject of divorce all those months ago. Of course, that might have been the Botox.

In the end, it was relatively straightforward. There was the prenup, of course, and he'd been generous – more generous than his lawyers told him he had to be. Claudia had moved out, draped in perfumed cashmere and wishing him well.

He has read in the *Daily Mail* diary that she has been spotted out and about with a Russian oligarch called Oleg who made his millions in oil and is the subject of minor notoriety for his failed attempt last month to buy an apartment overlooking Hyde Park dubbed 'the most expensive flat in London'. Oleg was outbid by a Qatari sheikh who snapped it up for £21 million as a gift for his fourth wife. More money than sense, thinks Howard, so obviously perfect for Claudia.

Photographs taken of the two of them at a recent polo match have been circulating in the society pages. Oleg is short and squat, with heavy brows and small fingers. At full stretch, he barely reaches Claudia's shoulder. It doesn't take a genius to work out what she sees in him.

But there she is sitting in the pews, looking as sculpted as ever, the contours of her face maintained to ageless perfection, and unexpectedly, he feels happy for her. He hopes she gets what she wants. He hopes she knows what that is.

He will seek her out after the service, he tells himself. He wants to be kind to her. She wasn't a bad sort, not really.

'Because of the way Ada died, it has been difficult to mourn her in any conventional way,' Howard says. He feels his voice begin to wobble, each word shimmering as if caught in a cloud of intense heat. Keep it together, he tells himself. He scans the faces for reassurance and sees Keith, the family liaison officer, sitting in a group of uniformed police and plain-clothes detectives. He is so grateful to them. After eleven long years of unanswered questions and false leads and diminishing hope, they have drawn things to some sort of conclusion. Her murderer is in jail for life. Other than that, Howard tries not to think about the man who has killed his daughter. Every day, he tries anew not to give in to the rage. Carol has helped. Oddly, knowing something about Alan Clithero has had a calming effect. Why this should be, he isn't sure. Perhaps it's because, the way Carol tells it, Clithero was an incompetent misfit rather than a mastermind of evil. The police say that's often the way. Still, Howard hopes he rots in hell.

'I've tried to forgive,' Howard says. 'To be honest, I'm finding it hard.' He blinks, refocuses. 'But I think I'll get there, if only because I don't want my memories of my Ada, my sweetheart, to be poisoned by anger. He's not worth that. And she wouldn't have wanted it.'

There is a murmur of assent from the congregation. Somewhere at the back of the church, there is a clap. Howard looks up. And there, sitting by the door, is that journalist from the *Tribune*, the one who'd interviewed him, the one who'd lost her dad when she was little. He remembers now that she'd written him a note when the news about Ada broke and he'd been so surprised to receive it. It had been short and to-the-point but heartfelt in a way that many of the letters of condolence hadn't.

He'd been expecting her to ask him for another interview but she hadn't and he wonders now if she chose not to, if, in fact, she thought of him as more than the tragic self-made millionaire of popular construct. If, perhaps, she saw who he really was.

What was her name? Began with an E. Scottish-sounding. He can't remember. She is sitting next to a handsome young man with a thatch of curly hair. He looks Jewish.

She's only gone and got herself a nice Jewish boy, Howard thinks approvingly.

He is coming to the end of what he wants to say. The light filtering through the windows has acquired a buttery sheen. The sound of the traffic outside has dimmed. Howard looks out at the faces in front of him and he wonders if he has done Ada justice. He isn't sure he ever told her how much he loved her when she was alive, not in so many words. He wonders if she knew. Does anyone truly know how much they are loved?

He catches Carol's eye. She is crying, he notices, and then he feels a wetness on his own cheeks.

He doesn't wipe the tears away.

Instead, he lets them fall.

Acknowledgements

Thank you to my agents: the brilliant Nelle Andrew at PFD and Jessica Woollard, at The Marsh Agency. Thank you to Helen Garnons-Williams for her magnificent editing and her all-round loveliness and to everyone at Bloomsbury, including (but not limited to) Oliver Holden-Rea, Elizabeth Woabank, Ros Ellis and Cormac Kinsella, whose continued faith in me is a deeply cherished thing.

Thank you to Lea Beresford from Bloomsbury USA for the conversations and the kindness and the stumbling-across of restaurants in unexpected places.

Thank you to the police detective who helped me with key plot details and who, rather excitingly, didn't want me to use his name and to Rebecca Thornton, for allowing me to ask inane questions in the name of research and for being so supportive at every stage.

Thank you to Simon Oldfield and Tim Julian for giving me the chance to stay in their beautiful place in St Ives. I can't think of anywhere better to start a novel.

Thank you, as always, to Olivia Laing, one of my earliest readers and a writer of such shimmering brilliance I find it almost embarrassing she allows me to call her my friend.

To my family, especially my mother, Christine Day, who has been so strong and wise over the last year.

Thank you to a spectacular bunch of friends, without whom

nothing would be possible, least of all getting out of bed in the morning. You know who you are. But I owe a specific debt of gratitude to Jessica Bax, Melissa Boyes, Kirrily de Polnay Jacobs, Haylie Fisher, Sadie Jones, Roya Nikkhah, Alice Patten, Emma Reed Turrell, Francesca Segal and Polly Vernon. If I believed in heart-shaped emoticons, I'd be festooning you with them now.

Lastly, to Kamal Ahmed, with immeasurable love for innumerable things, but also for showing such uncompromising belief in me – and for teaching me about 36-point headlines (nowhere near big enough, apparently).

A NOTE ON THE TYPE

The text of this book is set in Linotype Sabon,
named after the type founder, Jacques Sabon. It was
designed by Jan Tschichold and jointly developed by
Linotype, Monotype and Stempel in response to a
need for a typeface to be available in identical form
for mechanical hot metal composition and hand
composition using foundry type.